X·MEN ®

CODENAME
WOLVERINE

MARVEL®

X-MEN®

CODENAME
WOLVERINE

CHRISTOPHER GOLDEN

ILLUSTRATIONS BY DARICK ROBERTSON

MARVEL®

BP BOOKS, INC.
NEW YORK

BERKLEY BOULEVARD BOOKS, NEW YORK

Special thanks to Ginjer Buchanan, Michelle LaMarca, Steven A. Roman, Howard Zimmerman, Mike Thomas, Steve Behling, and Ursula Ward.

X-MEN: CODENAME WOLVERINE

A Berkley Boulevard Book
A BP Books, Inc. Book

PRINTING HISTORY
Boulevard/Putnam hardcover edition / October 1998
Berkley Boulevard paperback edition / May 2000

The Penguin Putnam Inc. World Wide Web site address is
http://www.penguinputnam.com

Check out the Ace Science Fiction/Fantasy newsletter, and much more, at
Club PPI!

ISBN: 0-425-17111-6

BERKLEY BOULEVARD
Berkley Boulevard Books are published by The Berkley Publishing Group,
a division of Penguin Putnam Inc.,
375 Hudson Street, New York, New York 10014.
BERKLEY BOULEVARD and its logo
are trademarks belonging to Penguin Putnam Inc.

PRINTED IN THE UNITED STATES OF AMERICA
10 9 8 7 6 5 4 3 2 1

For Connie, past, present, and future

ACKNOWLEDGMENTS

I'd like to thank my agent, Lori Perkins, my editor, Keith R.A. DeCandido, and Ben Raab and the people at Marvel Creative Services for answering questions I needed answered. Thanks also to Ginjer Buchanan, Nancy Holder, Jeff Mariotte, and Tom Sniegoski.

NOW

Long shadows stretched across the arid landscape of the Arizona desert and merged with the shimmering heat to create mirages. You could drive for hours in the desert without passing another car. Go a few miles off the road, deeper into the merciless desert, and for all intents and purposes, you've left the world behind.

There are those who believe the desert isn't empty, but a vast Roman forum where ghosts and monsters erupt from interdimensional portals for the amusement of alien visitors. Reality is far more harsh and unforgiving. There is nothing amusing about the Arizona desert. Beautiful, yes, but deadly.

Except perhaps for the odd scorpion, or a lizard baking in the sun, nothing moves during the day unless it is driven by the wind. But as the long shadows stretch themselves across the sand and scrub—farther and farther until their tendril fingers interlock, merge, and become night—the desert world begins to come alive.

The predators come out to play.

When the stars came out, cold and distant in the black sky, Victor Creed emerged. Since midday, he had been hidden by the shadow from a jagged cleft in the side of a pillar of rock and earth, one of many mesas which jutted up from the barren ground as if built there by gigantic children.

Silent as the scorpions that had stung him as he lay waiting for dusk, Creed padded across the desert floor toward his objective more than two miles distant. The man called Sabretooth was savage, a primal beast for whom killing was a pleasure. He could rend human flesh with fangs and claws provided him by a genetic x-factor in his DNA that made him a mutant. Could, and did, when the mood struck him.

Six and a half feet and two hundred seventy-five pounds of slavering, stalking death, Sabretooth was still, nevertheless, human. Which made him all the more dangerous. For the human was the most cunning animal ever to walk the Earth. Animals lived on instinct, and Sabretooth had the singlemind-edness of the beast. But he also had his own agenda, long-term plans, and secrets.

Sabretooth was the perfect weapon.

Even now, he moved swiftly under the stars to fulfill a mission given to him by his captors, the United States government. Once he had been in a killing frenzy, free to do as he pleased. When he was finally stopped, any sane government would have put him to death. That was what Creed himself would have done. Instead, they put him to work.

A restraining collar around his neck would choke and shock him into unconsciousness if he disobeyed orders. Then there was the unspoken promise that if he did not play along, execution was still possible. For the time being, it suited him to coop-erate. The government made him a part of X-Factor, its own little mutant police force. Mutants hunting mutants for the good of the world.

It made him want to puke. Not to mention that, at one time or another, he'd tried to murder nearly every other member of the team.

But sometimes the government pulled Sabretooth for special jobs. Jobs that X-Factor might be a little too queasy for. Like this one.

Three and one-half miles from the nearest paved road stood the compound of the Southwestern Free Militia: one large wooden building and several ramshackle structures thrown together with canvas and odd lumber. The SFM's headquarters wasn't much to look at; that was certain. But fanaticism was dangerous, and the SFM specialized in domestic terrorism—bombs, assassinations, kidnappings.

There was a kill order on this mission, which didn't mean he had to kill, but that he was free to do whatever was necessary to bring the militia down. That could have been accomplished with an air strike, though, and would have been if it were his primary goal. But after the fall of communism, post-Soviet Russia was having a fire sale on technology and weaponry. The SFM had come into possession of a very dangerous biochemical weapon, coded S-111.

The bosses didn't want the germ destroyed. They simply wanted it. Which was where Sabretooth came in.

Barbed wire was strung from post to post in a pitiful attempt at security. Sabretooth quietly sneered as his claws sliced roughly through the wire. It sprang back and away, and he was in. Despite their distance from the rest of the world, the SFM apparently maintained a high level of paranoia. The two armed men strolling the compound bore automatic rifles and alert, darting eyes.

Creed almost laughed out loud at the comically surprised expression on the face of the first guard as he snapped the man's neck. But he controlled himself. It was wise to maintain stealth as long possible. Once he'd been discovered, it would be a massacre.

Sabretooth loved a massacre, the salty spray of arterial blood, the fear in the eyes of the prey. But the mission came first. For now.

The second guard hadn't even noticed that anything was amiss. He continued to walk the perimeter of the fence, and would do so until he came to the spot where Sabretooth had torn his entrance, if Creed waited around for him to find it. He did not. The guard was, in fact, of so little concern to him that he didn't even bother to kill the man. He loped silently across the compound to the first of the ramshackle tent buildings and sniffed at the air.

Gun oil and cordite on the slight breeze, along with sweat and beer. More than likely, they were all asleep, but they had their weapons nearby, ready for a war with invisible enemies at any time. A wry grin, malevolently punctuated by fangs, stretched across Creed's features. Their paranoia had finally borne fruit. The invisible enemy had arrived.

Sabretooth continued past the flimsy structures toward the main building. Even that, despite its wooden frame, was shabby at best. *I'll huff and I'll puff and I'll blow your house in*, he thought. Victor Creed had always rooted for the wolf, even as a child.

The wind shifted, and he caught a scent behind him. He heard a cough and the sound of a zipper sliding down. One of the terrorists emerged from the tent to relieve himself. Creed spun and spotted the man, just behind him. All the militia man had to do was look up and the alarm would be sounded.

Sabretooth sprinted at him, his speed extraordinary. Too soon, the man glanced idly up and his eyes widened in terror. Creed swung a hand, claws extended, to tear out the man's throat. But he was too late to stop the scream. Even as the terrorist's corpse hit the ground, the cries of alarm rose up from within the tents. Lanterns came on, guns clattered as their magazines were checked. The guard at the gate came running up behind him, spotted him, but held his fire for fear of shooting into the tents.

He considered simply killing the guard, and taking his weapon. But for Sabretooth, the days of bullets and blades had long since passed. A kill wasn't even worth counting if he didn't do it with his own hands or teeth.

"Intruder!" the guard screamed. "Kill him!"

Sabretooth sneered at the armed fool. Obviously, Arizona was one place where his reputation did not precede him. The first of the terrorists his presence had awoken exited through the open canvas flap that served as a door for the flimsy structure, automatic rifle in hand. Creed had disarmed him and torn open his chest in a heartbeat. He spun the man around and ran him back into the shelter. Bullets punched into the injured man almost immediately, and his feet stopped propelling him along. Sabretooth shoved him forward into his comrades, blocking their weapons for a vital moment longer.

Then he was on them, clawing and ripping, snapping and crushing. Ten of them, perhaps twelve. Creed lost count after the fourth or fifth.

Inside the wooden house, not much more than a shed, in truth, Aaron Pirkle panicked. Frantic, he slipped his pants on and picked up his treasured ArmaLite rifle. It could empty its twenty-round clip in just over a second. Aaron grabbed two more clips and shoved them in his pockets. He nearly stumbled as he scurried in a crouch across the room, taking care to avoid being seen through a window. He turned and hissed at Cindee to follow him.

"Aaron?" Cindee LaMagdeleine inquired in a frightened little girl's voice that he'd once found quite seductive. Now it merely annoyed him.

"Shut up," he hissed, "and follow me. It's like Waco all over again. Don't you get it, you little twit? The feds are here, and they're going to kill us all. Me and you've got to get out of here with the bug, hook up with one of the other militias, and start over. It can still work."

Pirkle scuttled another few steps and turned to scold her again. She startled him, she was so close, and his heart skipped a beat. He'd no idea she could move so swiftly, so quietly.

"Don't call me a twit," she whispered, but Pirkle wasn't paying any attention. Outside there were shouts of anger and alarm, screams of agony, pleas for mercy. The rapid fire of automatic weapons slowed, and after a few moments, stopped altogether. Every ten seconds or so, a renewed burst would begin, but stop almost as suddenly.

His men were being slaughtered.

"Aaron?" Cindee asked, and he hushed her again.

"Come on," he whispered, and they moved to the rear of the

building, where a hinged plank opened easily. They slipped through, and the open desert lay before them.

"Hold this," he said, handing Cindee the ArmaLite.

Pirkle knelt down behind the building and began to scoop dirt from a depression even a tracker would have been hard pressed to notice.

"It's nighttime," he said. "About four miles due west is the road. We can't afford to take a car from here, but I've got a Harley hidden by Sandcastle Butte. We'll be okay if we can just reach that."

Aaron slid a small metal case about the size of a child's lunch box from the ground and brushed it off. It was sealed tightly to avoid contamination, but he didn't have to open it to know what was in there. His ticket to the big time. His place in history.

The ArmaLite's muzzle poked painfully at the back of his head.

"Don't even breathe," Cindee said, but the plaintive, little girl tone was gone from her voice.

Sabretooth had cleared himself a path, but the SFM had more members than he'd thought. And they got smarter as more of them died. Now they were waiting for him to make a break for the main building so they could pick him off. Little did they know that he could smell each and every one of them with a little focus. Could hunt them, one by one, even if it took until morning.

But he wouldn't. *Let them shoot,* he thought. It wasn't far to the building, and his true objective was there. His passion for violence had been sated for the moment. Creed was bored with the killing.

From the shadows near a shanty, he sprang into the open area around the headquarters. Instantly, several of the terrorists appeared and began to fire on him. He moved too fast for most of them, but not all. Sabretooth didn't even wince as the bullet clipped his side.

"Not another step, Creed!" a voice shouted.

Sabretooth looked up, ready to strike. He didn't like to take orders from anyone. His lips curled back from his fangs, and he saw Aaron Pirkle, the leader of the SFM, holding an ArmaLite automatic rifle and a small metal case that he knew must contain the germ. His goal.

He almost lunged forward and slaughtered Pirkle right there. But something forced him to stop. Something . . . a scent.

"Cease fire, all of you, and come out!" Pirkle shouted. "I want you to see what kind of animal we've caught in our midst."

Slowly, and most of them doubtfully, the few surviving terrorists began to emerge. There were nine of them, including Pirkle. Each had a British SA-80 assault rifle aimed at Creed, but he paid no attention to their weapons.

Sabretooth merely stared at Pirkle and the ArmaLite he held. The muzzle of the terrorist leader's weapon swung up to aim at Creed, and the bullets tore from its gullet. He grunted twice as twin holes were punched in his chest, burning embers in his body that passed through to the other side. Sabretooth went down hard.

But Pirkle didn't stop there. With his men all staring at the downed Sabretooth, the leader of the SFM slaughtered his own soldiers in cold blood, without even a single pause for remorse.

Even as the corpses struck the ground, Creed was pulling himself to his knees. Blood flowed from his already closing wounds. Rapid healing was one of the genetic gifts of the mutant x-factor in his DNA. But bullets still hurt like hell.

As he rose to his feet, Creed stared at Pirkle.

"You shot me," he growled dangerously.

"A diversion," Pirkle replied. "And besides, you were in the way."

"Don't do it again," Sabretooth snarled.

"I'll try to remember," Pirkle said idly.

Only it wasn't Pirkle anymore. Face and body morphed fluidly, changing from Aaron Pirkle to someone else. From man to woman, human to mutant. Pale skin and fair hair to blue flesh and long auburn tresses. Her name was Raven Darkhölme, also called Mystique. Along with Sabretooth, she was a former criminal, an enemy of the federal government, now enslaved in service to that very same enemy.

Once, there had been something that bound them together. An intimacy neither was fond of recalling. Now they were merely reluctant teammates, each with bitter memories of the past.

"I should have known they'd put you on this mission, too," Creed growled. "What was I, just a threat to flush Pirkle out, make him reveal where he was hiding the germ?"

"You're not as primitive as you look," Mystique purred, shouldering the ArmaLite and holding the metal case on her outthrust hip.

"Savage, not primitive," Creed agreed.

"I replaced his little girlfriend Cindee yesterday," Mystique explained. "Then it was just a matter of waiting. I could have simply tortured him, but they wanted to play things this way."

Something unspoken passed between them. A fury, really. For like Sabretooth, Mystique wore a potentially agonizing, possibly even fatal restraining collar. That, at least, they could share.

"That's mine! Give it back! You've stolen my place in history!" a shrill voice cried.

Sabretooth glanced up to see the real Aaron Pirkle, clad only in long black pants and heavy boots, emerge from behind the main building. The man stumbled, blood dripping on his forehead. Sabretooth could smell the blood from where he stood, even with the wind relatively still.

"You didn't kill him?" Creed asked, surprised.

"He's just insane," Mystique replied. "It wasn't a specific order, and I figure I've known plenty of people I've had more reason to kill and left alive. I'd rather leave the lunatics alive and kill the sane ones."

"Suit yourself, Raven," Creed said. "I just don't—"

He paused, held up a hand.

"Choppers," he said.

"They're ours. Have to be," Mystique observed. "But I specifically said no extraction team. We didn't want an extraction team, I told them. Too conspicuous and completely unnecessary."

"Well, they're here," Creed replied, and he stared up at the running lights on the pair of approaching military helicopters.

"Didn't you hear me?" Pirkle shouted over the noise of the rotors. Sabretooth could still hear him, though he suspected Mystique wouldn't be able to. "You stole my place in history!" the terrorist leader screamed even louder. "You took my—"

There was a sharp report, and blood blossomed on Pirkle's chest and sprayed from his back. Then the choppers opened fire on Creed and Mystique.

"Son of a—" Mystique roared. "We've been set up, Victor!"

To his left, she ducked into one of the crumbling shanties. Sabretooth wanted to follow her, but three thick darts penetrated his hide with the sound of arrows finding their mark.

His vision was already wavering as he took several more steps and then went down on his knees. Creed tasted dirt, and the darkness closed in on him.

"With his healing factor, this stuff isn't going to keep him out for long," one of their attackers said.

"We'll have him properly restrained in another minute, and then even he won't be able to move," a second voice intoned.

"Animal thought he was invincible, like some kind of serial-killer superman or something," the first man said boastfully. "One thing's for sure, he never expected the past to come back to haunt him."

"Not just him, though," the second voice said. "His whole unit's gonna pay for what they did. And we're earning top dollar for it, too."

Harsh laughter was swept on the breeze to where a single

terrorist lay unwounded, merely pretending to be dead. But it wasn't a terrorist.

"Where'd Darkhölme get off to?" the first agent asked.

"No idea," the second answered. "But we'll get her eventually. She can't have gotten far."

As the choppers lifted off with Sabretooth as their prisoner, Mystique reverted to her true form and watched them go. For the moment, she could do nothing to stop them. The federal agents had talked too much. Very unprofessional, but helpful. At least she had some clues as to why they wanted Sabretooth. And before she went after him, Mystique was determined to find some answers.

Information was ammunition.

She was solo for the moment, though. Since the government was constantly monitoring X-Factor's movements, Mystique's own team would be no help in hunting down Sabretooth. She would have to find other help.

The moment she thought of it, the answer was obvious.

She had to get to Wolverine.

THEN

Angry shouts and staccato bursts of weapons fire filled the hallway behind them, but Team X didn't slow for a moment. Their pursuers had yet to realize that fire was not being returned, that the operatives who had assassinated the so-called president of El Malojo were on the run. Those few seconds were precious.

"Go, go!" Logan yelled, and nodded toward the wide palace stairwell.

Once again, he scanned the hall down which they'd run. Still no sign of pursuit. A quick glance at the stairs confirmed that the other three members of his team—Creed, North, and Silver Fox—were heading for the roof of the estate. It wasn't really a palace. He'd seen palaces. But in a tiny Central American nation whose gross national product was probably less than the average American made in a year, it was as close to a palace as even a tyrannical dictator was likely to get.

Not that it mattered. The master of the house, El Malojo's dictator and one of the primary figures in international drug trading, was dead. Creed had made absolutely certain of that before the guards had discovered them. Now they were headed for their dustoff point in high gear. None of them could be traced back to the Agency if captured, but they'd all prefer to avoid it if at all possible.

Down the hall, guards cursed in Spanish and poked their heads around the corner, finally realizing their leader's assassins were escaping. Without hesitation, they swarmed around the corner, nearly falling over one another for a chance to become a hero, to avenge the death of a man they'd all hated.

Jerks, Logan thought, then stepped out from the shadow of

the arched doorway across from the wide stairwell. In the heartbeat when the guards were too stunned by his sudden appearance to react, he hefted the iron weight in his hands and hurled a pair of Czech RG34 grenades along the hallway toward the guards.

The El Malojan troops barely had time to cry out in alarm and scramble for cover when the double explosion brought much of the hallway down around them. Several of them were thrown through windows or along the hall.

Even before the grenade detonated, Logan had reached the stairwell and taken the first two steps in one stride. He stumbled slightly as the concussive blast propelled him forward. Two more steps, and he tossed a British number seventy-seven white phosphorus grenade over his shoulder, filling the stairwell with fire and smoke in his wake.

An agonized voice shouted up from below in sneering Spanish. "You are heading for the roof, you fools!" the voice roared. "Your escape is cut off, now. It is only a matter of time before you are captured. Then you will be at our mercy, and you will suffer greatly before you are allowed to die!"

He was a soldier, true, yet Logan could not help but wince at the man's words. There was no real pleasure in war for him. But even clandestine wars had to have their soldiers. And soldiering was good for him; it meant he could let the savagery out of his heart in controlled bursts. Even better, he could do it in the service of the free world.

Logan—codename: Wolverine—was haunted by the beast within, a bloodthirsty creature that cried out for battle. Wolverine was a warrior in search of a war. His teammates each had their own story, their own background, much of which they hid from one another. David North, a.k.a. Maverick, had been a freedom fighter in East Germany before entering the world of espionage. Once, he had told Logan that he'd agreed to join Team X because he believed they could do some good. Logan had been meaning to ask him if he'd changed his mind.

The other two members of the team were more enigmatic.

Sabretooth—whose real name was Victor Creed, though he seemed at times to prefer the codename—was a vicious SOB who took great pleasure in killing, and would use any excuse to do so. It chilled Logan to watch him, at times, for Creed's butchery echoed the dreadful urges in Logan's own heart.

"Logan, move it!" North roared from above. "Dustoff's in less than thirty!"

There was a clattering of bullets far below as he turned up the last flight of stairs to the roof. Reinforcements, and those who'd survived the grenades. Logan had a MAC-11 in an armpit holster, and a Walther MPL on a leather thong slung across his shoulder, but he didn't return fire. There was no purpose. The mission was done. Escape was the only goal now.

He vaulted the last few steps and saw the shattered window just ahead. Team X had made its own door out to the roof. They waited for him there, and he had to wonder how long it would be before the El Malojans got a chopper in the air.

Glass crunched underfoot as he stepped through the broken window and onto the roof of the palace.

"Aw, and here I was hopin' we'd be able to leave the runt behind," Sabretooth said.

"Any time you think you're ready, Sabretooth," Logan said with a growl.

Creed only smiled. The man towered over Logan, who was only five foot three. Even North, at just over six feet, was a giant by comparison. But height was no match for skill, strength, speed, and savagery.

Then the fourth member of the team finally spoke up. Silver Fox was the quietest of them, and in her way the most secretive. Even Logan, who had been her lover for more than a year, knew very little about her.

"Ignore him, Logan," she said, and he was soothed by the Native American woman's words, and by the sight of her chocolate eyes and the breeze whipping her hair across her face.

"You tell 'im, squaw," Creed barked, his tone mocking. "He don't need to know about us just yet."

Logan felt his upper lip begin to curl into a snarl, and pushed the animal back down inside him.

"Leave it be," Silver Fox whispered.

"One o' these days," Logan said grimly, shaking his head.

Then Creed's head shot up. "We got company."

Logan listened, and knew that Sabretooth was right. The guards were making plenty of noise coming up the stairs. They were terrified. Logan could smell it on them.

"I don't suppose anybody's got any explosives left?" Silver Fox asked. "Maverick, what about you? Any of those thermite grenades you love so much?"

No reply. Team X uttered a collective sigh and reached for its weapons. Logan brought the Walther MPL up on its tether, holding the nine-millimeter submachine gun by its grip, and planting the folding stock against his shoulder.

"Where the hell is Wraith?" North grumbled behind him.

"Speak of the devil," an amused voice declared, "and he shall appear."

The speaker was a slender black man of medium height, wearing mirrored sunglasses and a cowboy hat, despite the fact that it was nearly midnight. John Wraith, their extraction man.

"About time," Logan said. "Why don't you get us outta here?"

"Your wish is—" Wraith began, and the air began to shimmer around them all. The sound of gunfire receded instantly.

"—my command," Wraith finished.

Logan blinked twice, stomach lurching a moment as he reoriented himself. The wind no longer blew. The stars no longer shone above. Instead, Team X was surrounded by the four blank walls of Wraith's debriefing room.

"Next time, Wraith, try to be on time," Creed whispered with menace.

Wraith ignored him, doubled over at the front of the windowless room. He was in pain, but they'd all seen it before. It would pass. The man was a mutant—as were they all with the exception of Silver Fox. Wraith was a teleporter of unparalleled skill, but even for him, transporting five people thousands of miles was a lot to ask. Yet he did it, time and again.

More so even than Maverick, John Wraith was a company man. He did whatever the Agency required of him.

When Wraith stood unsteadily, North moved away from the wall where he'd been leaning.

"Listen, I need some downtime," he said. "Can we deal with the debrief in the morning?"

"No," Wraith replied curtly. "We don't even have time for a debrief. You're on your way to East Germany in ninety minutes."

Logan and Creed said nothing. They had nowhere else to go.

"You promised us three days' leave," Silver Fox reminded Wraith.

"Not this time, boys and girls," Wraith declared.

North grumbled, stared at Logan, who shrugged almost imperceptibly in response.

"It better be good, John," North snapped.

Logan smiled thinly. *Poor kid actually thinks he can do the kind of work Team X does and still have some kind of normal life. He really is a dreamer.*

"I think you'll enjoy this one, Sergeant North," Wraith said archly. "You get to go home."

North raised an eyebrow.

"East Berlin?" Logan asked.

"Hooray, a vacation behind the Iron Curtain," Creed growled. "Let's kill us some commies."

"What's the mission?" Silver Fox asked.

"Save the free world," Wraith replied.

"I could be sleeping right now," North complained.

"I'm not kidding," Wraith protested, and the tone of his voice made Logan take notice. He really wasn't kidding. The idea was profoundly disturbing: the fate of the world could rest on the actions of a group of borderline—or in the case of Creed, complete—psychotics like Team X.

"A pair of KGB agents have come into possession of some very sensitive information," Wraith explained. "They stole a data disk that contains the locations and codes of America's entire nuclear arsenal. In the wrong hands, it could mean the nuclear devastation of the United States."

"Folks shouldn't ought to leave that kind o' thing layin' around," Logan grunted.

"So we snatch the disk back," North said, obviously trying to hurry the proceedings along.

"And terminate the KGB agents?" Creed asked, a broad smile on his face.

"If necessary," Wraith replied.

Sabretooth grinned even wider.

NOW

On the southern end of Manhattan Island, Greenwich Village is a neighborhood filled with contradictions. Despite the approaching twenty-first century and the homogenization that seems to be sweeping over America, the bohemian lifestyle survives in small pockets. The tourists and yuppies cannot completely erase the taste of danger, the scent of daring that exists here. In truth, there seems almost a line drawn between the neighborhood's past and future.

To Wolverine, the difference was most pronounced inside the White Horse Tavern, a venerable establishment that had been one of his favorite watering holes for decades. Within the White Horse, the line was drawn between bar and restaurant. For the most part, the tourists sat in the restaurant and ate hamburgers. Locals favored the bar.

"Here you go, Logan," said Erika, an attractive waitress he'd come to know and appreciate over the years she'd been working at the White Horse. Far fewer, to be sure, than the years he'd been going there. She slipped his dinner onto the bar: Delmonico steak with portobello mushrooms and mashed potatoes with gravy.

"Thanks, darlin'," Wolverine replied and offered a haggard smile.

"You should smile more often, handsome," Erika said, and his smile broke into a grin. Wolverine wasn't a handsome man. He knew that. But he'd never had to complain about his love life. Some women just took to him. An animal attraction, his old friend Yukio had once said.

"Flirt," he grunted, and looked down to his steak as Erika gave a sexy, husky laugh and moved back toward the restaurant.

The steak was delicious, prepared just the way he liked it. They weren't supposed to cook it that rare anymore, but any establishment that wants to stay in business knows how to treat its regulars. The one thing they couldn't let him do was smoke one of his favorite cheroots. Not in Manhattan. Still, Wolverine couldn't complain much. After all, his healing factor would take care of any damage the smoke might do him, but he couldn't stop whatever harm secondhand smoke might do to others around him. That's why he stopped smoking around Cannonball, the newest, youngest member of the X-Men. Bad example, and bad for him.

Buddy Guy sang scratchy blues on the tavern's jukebox, his sweet guitar a counterpoint to his voice. But anything would have been better than listening to the audio on the national newscast unfolding on the television over the bar. The nation's fear and hatred of mutants had multiplied a thousandfold since the assassination of Graydon Creed. Creed had been a presidential candidate, considered a shoo-in for the job until someone stopped him dead. He became a martyr to his cause. In this case, the cause was rabid antimutant hysteria.

With Creed dead, the furor only increased. There was an ongoing struggle to fill the spotlighted void left behind. The current frontrunner for picking up Creed's cause and, consequently, his supporters, was a senator named Peter Zenak. Zenak's views had even gotten him appointed to some hotshot watchdog oversight committee after another senator, Terence Hill, died in a plane crash.

Pretty morbid, but the man was making a career out of capitalizing on the misfortune of others. Then again, Wolverine had always thought that was what politics was primarily about.

"Hey, Ronnie, change the channel, will ya?" a burly black man called from a stool down the bar. "I'm sick of hearing from this bigot."

There was some whispering, some exchanged glances, but Ronnie did change the channel. Wolverine was surprised the man's comments hadn't elicited an argument from anyone. Surely a lot of them agreed with Zenak's views. But nobody spoke up. Maybe nobody wanted to be called a bigot. It had been Wolverine's experience that ignorance usually thrived only in its own company.

"Here you go, Logan," Ronnie the bartender said amiably as he sat a sweating pint glass down next to the nearly empty one Wolverine had been working on.

"You tryin' to take advantage o' me, Ronnie?" Wolverine asked. "What's your hurry?"

"Not me, buddy," Ronnie replied. "It's from your secret admirer over there."

Wolverine turned to look where Ronnie was pointing. Across the room, at a small table by the window, a stunning red-head sat with her legs elegantly crossed and smiled seductively at him. Logan smiled back, nodded slightly in appreciation of the glass, and took a sip, regarding her over the rim of the glass.

The redhead raised her own glass, and an eyebrow, as if in salute, and took a sip. Erika the waitress was passing by, and the redhead beckoned her to the small table. She said something so softly that, even concentrating and with his acute hearing, Wolverine could not pick it up. Erika glanced up at him as the woman was talking, and then moved swiftly across the room toward Wolverine. All business.

"You know the lady, Logan?" Erika asked.

"Jealous?" he asked, then shook his head. "Nope, never seen her before."

"She knows you," Erika answered, and the two of them looked over at the redheaded woman together this time. The woman caught Wolverine's eye again, and her smile turned wistful.

"Some kind of message for me?" Wolverine prodded, and lifted the pint glass to his lips once more.

"Yeah," Erika nodded. "She said, 'Tell Logan Victor's in trouble.' "

He paused imperceptibly, glass to lips, then slowly lowered the condensation-slicked pint to click down on the mahogany bar.

"Thanks," he mumbled, and immediately stood.

Wolverine slipped two twenties out of his wallet and threw them on the bar. He grabbed his battered leather jacket by the collar in one hand, and his beer in the other, and started toward the redhead, on guard. When he was going into battle, he preferred his working clothes, the blue and gold uniform he'd had since his days with Canadian intelligence—Department H. But the clothes didn't make the man. In faded Levi's and rattlesnake-skin cowboy boots, Wolverine was no less dangerous, no less talented in his field of expertise.

He had no reason to think there was going to be a throwdown, but when anybody mentioned Victor—whom he knew better as Sabretooth—he figured he ought to be prepared for anything. And he didn't know this girl from Eve.

Halfway across the bar, he realized he was wrong. He did know her. The scent had been blocked by hops and barley and broiling meat, but he had it now. Which didn't mean he was about to drop his guard.

"Logan," she said, by way of greeting, as he slid into the chair opposite hers. "Nice boots, by the way."

Wolverine took a long sip from his pint.

"What do you want, Mystique?" he asked.

"You didn't get my message?"

"I got it," he said softly. "So Creed's in trouble. What's that to do with me?"

"It's got a lot to do with you, since I believe you're on the hit list," she sneered. "Maybe you don't want to hear about it. I'll find Victor myself."

Mystique, in the guise of the gorgeous redhead, began to rise on shapely legs. She had no trouble at all with the spiked heels, though they were hardly her style. Wolverine calmly drank, and Mystique turned to leave.

"Sorry about your boy," he said grimly.

She stopped, turned slightly, then all the way, and sat back down with him. Ironically, the fiercely antimutant lobbyist Graydon Creed was the offspring of two mutants: Mystique and Sabretooth. There was no love lost, though, either between the two parents, or between them and their son. For a moment, Mystique chewed her lip and didn't look at him. When finally she did look up, she narrowed her eyes.

"No, you're not," she said with nonchalance—perhaps feigned, Wolverine thought. "If you are sorry, it's only because of the fallout from his murder. But you're not any sorrier than any of the rest of us. Victor and I haven't even discussed it, but I know he feels the same sense of . . . of relief that I do. It's a horrible thing, to have wanted your child dead," Mystique whispered.

Wolverine only stared at her, surprised that she'd revealed so much of herself. Or apparently revealed, for Mystique had so many faces, so many disguises, it was impossible to know what was real with her. The two had known one another for a long time, sometimes as allies but more often as enemies. But for a man like Logan, such definitions were often situational.

He glanced away from her, across the restaurant. Tourists laughed together at wooden tables. Two women who seemed very much a couple whispered together in a far corner of the dining area.

" 'And death shall have no dominion,' " Wolverine whispered to himself.

"What the hell are you talking about?" Mystique asked. "Aren't you even listening?"

Wolverine met her questioning gaze with a wan smile.

"Old friends are a royal pain in the behind, darlin'," he growled, shook his head, and looked back toward the restaurant. "They never stay who they were when the friendship began, and a lotta times, you end up nostalgic for a person even though they're still around."

"You're talking about Victor?" Mystique asked, her surprise obvious. "He was always a savage. I'm surprised you can work up any nostalgia for him at all."

"You forget," Wolverine replied without even glancing at her, "I was a savage once, too. We were friends once, though barely. More important, though, is that we were brothers in arms. I guess I was talkin' about Sabretooth, but I was thinkin' about another old friend. Used to sit right at that table over there and drink himself blind. One night he lined up so many shots that it killed him. He wasn't even himself anymore at the end. The whiskey'd taken his nobility.

"I was here the night Dylan died, and when it happened, it didn't feel like much of a loss. I'd been grievin' for him for years," Wolverine said quietly.

"You're talking about the poet, Dylan Thomas," Mystique said as the realization struck her. "But that was in the early fifties, you couldn't have been more than . . ."

"Nineteen fifty-three, actually," Logan drawled. "I'm older than I look. So's Creed, and all the rest of the old team. Those that are still alive, that is. What I'm trying to tell you, Mystique, is that Victor Creed's been dead to me for decades. I don't much care what happens to him now. Someone kills the murderin' psycho, I'll be sad all right, but only 'cause it wasn't me who did it."

Wolverine downed the remains of his drink. When he stood, the heels of his snakeskin boots slapped the wooden floor in punctuation. He slid into his jacket and zipped it partway.

"Nice to see you, Raven," he lied. "Don't be a stranger."

"Suit yourself, Logan," she sighed. "But you'll be seeing Victor, and me, again real soon. These guys don't kid around. They've got federal connections and federal funding, enough firepower to blast one arrogant mutant, one little Canadian runt, into cinder and ash. Me, I'd like to find them before they find me."

Wolverine studied her, then sat back down and put his boots up on the table.

"You've got about three minutes. Tell me what happened," Wolverine suggested, then listened carefully as Mystique complied.

When she had finished, he merely watched her through slitted eyes for several moments. He'd have been a fool to take Raven Darkhölme at her word, and she knew it. Wolverine had been many things in his long life, but never a fool.

"Let me see if I have this straight," he began. "You just hung out while Creed was being hauled off, even though you were close enough to hear these morons talkin' about you, and about me and the rest o' Team X?"

"If I'd attacked them, you wouldn't ever have known anyone was after you, and then we'd both be where Sabretooth is. Wherever he is—dead is only one possibility, and I can think of some worse ones," she said ominously.

"So you warned me, but why not bring your team in on it?" he asked. "My guess is X-Factor's got a lot more interest in savin' Creed's hide than I'll ever have."

"You know why," Mystique insisted. "Why are you wasting my time? X-Factor would have to report its actions, meaning whoever snagged Victor would almost certainly be made aware of my plans and location. I might as well send up a flare announcing my position."

Wolverine didn't like any of it. Mystique would do nearly anything for her own benefit, and rarely did anything that was not. But try as he might, Logan could not figure out what she might have to gain by lying about Creed's abduction. If she wanted to be free of X-Factor, he had no doubt she could find better ways. And despite their enmity, he knew of no special grudge she might hold for him.

If it wasn't a setup, he reasoned, it had to be true.

"We need to get to Maverick," he said, and saw the surprise in Mystique's eyes when she realized he had believed her.

"What about Silver Fox?" she asked.

Wolverine sucked in a shallow breath, and his lip curled back, a tiny rage growing in his gut, blossoming into something larger. He might have hurt Mystique then, if not for the sincere curiosity he saw in her eyes. She truly didn't know.

"How could you not know?" he asked. "How could you be with X-Factor, and be around the X-Men so much, and not know?"

"What?" Mystique asked. "I'm lost here, Logan. Help me out."

"Fox was murdered years ago," he said, his voice a low rasp. "Creed killed her with his bare hands."

Mystique put a hand to her forehead and closed her eyes a moment. For a heartbeat, Wolverine thought there might be some humanity in the shapeshifter after all.

"I'm sorry," she said. "I didn't know. If I had, I never would have come to you."

"It was a long time ago," he said, as if the pain had receded with the passing of the years. Which was untrue. The void her death had left within him had not even begun to heal, despite the loves that came after.

"For now, we gotta find out who snatched up Creed, and what it has to do with the rest of us. First, though, we really gotta let Maverick know somebody may be gunnin' for him," Wolverine explained. "And I think I know just where to find him."

It had been nearly a decade since Wolverine had been inside Maverick's safehouse in Manhattan. But his memory of the place was still sharp. It was perfectly camouflaged in a stately brownstone apartment building on the Upper West Side, a haven for upwardly mobile twenty- and thirtysomethings.

Last he knew, Maverick had pretty much gone to ground and dropped out of the life. There were any number of such properties around the world where David North might be staying. But if he was in New York, the safehouse on Seventy-third Street was a sure bet.

Wolverine guided his rebuilt classic Norton motorcycle north on Amsterdam Avenue, navigating through early evening traffic. Mystique, still wearing the shape of the gorgeous, long-legged redhead, sat behind him on the Norton, her slender hands wrapped around his abdomen, laquered nails digging into his leather jacket.

Raven Darkhölme was a dangerous woman for many reasons, but her ability to become anyone was a devastatingly powerful tool. It made her the perfect covert operative. If not for his own enhanced senses, Wolverine would never be able to pick Mystique out of a crowd. For the moment, though, keeping an eye on her was not going to be a problem.

He left the Norton on Amsterdam and walked down Seventy-third toward Columbus Avenue. Halfway down the block, a small iron gate about three and a half feet high stood open in front of the apartment building. Maverick owned the building, which made it simple for him to install everything he needed to turn the top floor into a safehouse.

"North has always seemed like such a cipher to me," Mystique said, without a trace of irony in her voice. "I never could get much of a handle on him. Quite a warrior, but very insulated from the rest of your team—at least from an outsider's point of view."

"He always kept to himself," Wolverine agreed. "Maverick's a good man, but very private. Still, I don't know too many people I'd rather have at my back in a firefight. Even now, with his health failin' him."

Despite the questioning look Mystique shot him, Wolverine did not elaborate. *None of her business that he's got the Legacy Virus,* he figured. North had come down with the fatal disease that primarily targeted mutants. Finding a cure had been slow work, especially since the mainstream medical community wasn't terribly motivated to cure such an illness.

The foyer of the apartment building was dark beyond the locked glass and steel door. There were buttons with which they might buzz any one of the brownstone's residents. Wolverine pressed the top one, the one that would tell Maverick they had arrived.

No response.

The darkness bothered him. He narrowed his eyes and peered through the door window into the shadowy interior. Like his other senses, his vision was extraordinary. Yet he saw nothing amiss other than the lack of lighting. He buzzed for Maverick again, and again there was no response. Once more, he studied the foyer, the stairwell, and the apartment doors in the first floor corridor, all visible through the glass.

The door to apartment 1C was open six or seven inches. The tips of a woman's fingers were barely visible past the doorframe. Whoever she was, lying there on the threshold of the apartment, she wasn't just napping.

"We're too late," he said matter-of-factly.

Snikt!

With a quick flex of muscles humans didn't even have, Wolverine bared his claws—a trio of foot-long blades which erupted from the calloused flesh between the knuckles of his right hand. They were pure adamantium, the strongest metal alloy in the world, and totally unbreakable. He had a set housed between the ulna and radius in each arm, sharp enough to cut through anything. His entire skeleton was laced with adamantium as well, which, when combined with his healing factor, made him almost impossible to kill.

The locking mechanism on the apartment door sliced like overripe fruit. There might have been easier ways to break in, but using the claws was instinctive for Wolverine. When they retracted back inside his arm, there were a few drops of blood from between each knuckle, and then the holes healed and disappeared.

In practiced silence, Wolverine and Mystique rushed to the open apartment door. The woman lay inert just inside, but there were no obvious wounds and no blood.

"Dead?" Mystique asked, and Wolverine realized she had reverted to her true face: the dark blue skin, yellow eyes, and auburn hair of Raven Darkhölme.

"No," he replied after checking and finding a strong pulse on the woman. "Just tranked, looks like. More than likely, so are the rest o' the people livin' here. Except Maverick, o' course."

They didn't bother trying to keep quiet on the stairs to the fourth floor, where Maverick's apartment and safehouse was. Whatever had gone down there had been done and the perpetrators had moved on. Sure enough, on the top floor, the vibranium-reinforced door to North's supposedly secure quarters stood open. The door and the corridor walls were blackened with scars left behind by the firing of energy weapons.

The inside of the safehouse was completely trashed. It looked as if a small fire had begun to burn in one corner, and been hastily doused by Maverick's abductors before they left with him in their custody. All of it was in keeping with Mystique's recounting of Sabretooth's abduction. Seeing it now though stoked the flame of rage that always burned deep within Wolverine. Most of the time, he ignored it. This time, he let it come on, welcomed it.

"We've got to find these guys, Mystique," he growled. "And soon. Maverick put up a good fight, but he's in no shape to be anybody's captive. If he dies because o' them, the feds are goin' to need a battalion o' reinforcements."

Their eyes met, and Wolverine could see clearly that Mystique was with him. Despite their differences, this mystery threatened both of them, as well as people they had both cared about once. But there was more to it where Maverick was concerned. And Mystique knew that now.

"He's got it, doesn't he?" she asked softly.

Wolverine nodded. "He came to me a couple o' months ago, wanted me to punch his ticket for him. Since then, I've only seen him once, but he seemed better to me. Like he'd learned how to live with the Legacy Virus. Maybe it'll kill him, but he's not goin' down without a fight. On the other hand, we don't know who's snatched him and Creed up. Whatever they've got in mind, I don't know that Maverick's in any condition to deal with it."

"He's a warrior, Logan," Mystique said. "He'll hold on until we can get to him."

Mystique said a few other encouraging things, but Wolverine had stopped paying attention. He was listening, instead, for the sounds of danger. Something had distracted him, a sound, a shift in the air. Then it came again.

"Company," he said in a gruff whisper.

He crouched a bit and took several silent steps toward the open door. There he waited, prepared to spring on any attacker. Another sound intruded: the near-silent *whoosh* of a stealth helicopter. A scuffle from above told him that their enemies— agents from some federal agency or another, but not necessarily on any government-sanctioned mission—were dropping from the chopper to the roof of the brownstone.

"They're risking a lot coming at us so openly," Mystique whispered.

"It's dark, and they're very quiet," Wolverine replied. "Just not quiet enough."

Then the first gunman appeared in the doorway and opened fire.

NOW

I n front of a high arched window that overlooked the grounds of Xavier's School for Gifted Youngsters, Sean Cassidy lit his pipe. He knew it'd probably kill him eventually, and he smoked rarely. But when he truly wanted to relax, he still returned to his pipe now and again. It was a bad habit, but Sean believed in that old saying about teaching old dogs new tricks.

And he was getting to be an old dog, wasn't he?

Well, perhaps not all that old, he thought. But still, it amazed him the way life changed, and the world moved on. Sean was a man of action, not prone to frequent contemplation. But with Emma Frost, his fellow headmaster at Xavier's School, having taken their young mutant students into town for the afternoon . . . well, it had been a long while since Sean had any real time to himself. And it was good to be back on the grounds of the school after the recent cross-country jaunt Sean, Emma, and the students had taken in a pair of recreational vehicles.

He enjoyed the view of the pretty patch of Massachusetts ground outside his window. If he tried very hard, it was possible for him to pretend the landscape was an Irish one, that he was back in his homeland. Make-believe. He was still capable of make-believe, so perhaps he wasn't that old after all.

Maybe it just seemed like a long time ago, those days in Ireland. He'd lived in Cassidy Keep, his family's Irish estate, with his cousin Tom until the love they both felt for the rebellious beauty Maeve Rourke had created a rift between them that had grown ever wider over the years. In the end, Sean had won Maeve's heart; it had been the greatest gift he had ever received. Later, Sean had followed his life's dream, become an agent of Interpol. It hadn't been a simple task, but it was a fulfilling life.

There was a brief, glorious moment where he had everything he had ever wanted out of life. Then it all ended in a single blast, an explosion that took the life of his Maeve, and took his heart and soul for far too long. He had been injured on an Interpol operation, was laid up in a hospital thousands of miles away when it happened, and it tore his heart out.

Yet it would be long years before he would discover the second half of that tragedy—that Maeve had borne him a daughter, a daughter who had been spirited away from her home when her father did not return to Cassidy Keep. A daughter who was raised by his cousin, Tom—the only decent thing Tom Cassidy had done since the day Sean and Maeve took their vows.

Sean Cassidy's heart had grown cold. His new, darker attitude was not appreciated by his Interpol superiors, and though he continued as an agent for a brief period, it was clear he was not going to last—not with the bitterness that haunted his every step.

Eventually, there was nothing more for him in Ireland. America beckoned, and he spent time there on both sides of the law. And in all that time, he'd never really thought about what it meant to be a mutant. Until Charles Xavier had asked him to become one of the X-Men, showed him how divided the world had become over the question of genetic identity.

Sean Cassidy, or Banshee, as he was christened for his ear-shattering sonic scream, had always been a loner, and never more so than after his wife's death. In truth, he liked the name partially because of what it represented: a banshee was a fairy spirit whose shrill, wailing cry was meant to mark the death of a member of the old Irish families. After her death, his cry had always been for Maeve.

A loner, without question. That was part of what drove him out of Interpol. They didn't need any gunslingers in their tidy little agency. But with the X-Men, he'd found both family and purpose. Years later, though he'd spent time with and away from the team, he found himself in a position he never would have imagined: Teacher. Instructor. Mentor.

What Charles Xavier had been to dozens of mutants over the years, Sean Cassidy and Emma Frost had become to a small group of young men and women whose only desire was to learn to cope with a world that hated them for an accident of their birth. In a way, he'd become a father again. And to his great fortune, when he had finally been reunited with his daughter Theresa, she had forgiven him.

Not at first. And not easily. But forgive him she had, and Sean thanked the good Lord for that. He didn't deserve it. Theresa was all grown up now, and out on her own with a team of mutant youngsters called X-Force. A warrior in her own right. He ached to find time to spend with her, quiet time between father and daughter. To learn what she believed in, what she thought of the world. So far, there had been precious little such time; they both had responsibilities.

But soon, he vowed. Very soon.

For now—well, he had papers to grade that night, but for now, for the two or three hours that Emma and the students would be gone, Sean wanted to stop. Stop working, stop fighting, stop teaching, stop worrying.

In a ragged gray Boston Celtics T-shirt, faded jeans, and thick gray socks with holes in their heels, the man sometimes called Banshee settled into his favorite chair. He picked up *Lonesome Dove,* a book he'd started to read weeks earlier, and hadn't so much as glanced at since.

For just a moment, a glorious moment, all was right with the world.

Robert Crain sat high in a tree on the grounds of Xavier's School. He was wrapped in dark Kevlar, but wore no mask to hide his identity. The men and women of Team Alpha didn't have to worry about witnesses. They never left any.

Crain peered down the scope of his sniper rifle. Satisfied with what he saw, he pulled the cell phone from his belt and pressed the star key.

"Colburn," a voice answered gruffly.

"He's ours, Steve," Crain said quietly. "He read for about ten minutes, but he's out cold now. Taking a little nap. This'll be a cakewalk."

"You think?" Colburn replied, his voice crackling slightly over the phone. "You read this guy's dossier?"

"He's an old man," Crain sneered. "For God's sake, he's sleeping!"

"All right, we're coming in," Colburn said. "Give us ninety seconds to get in position, then take him down."

Crain slipped the phone back onto his belt and settled into the tree branches again. He sighted along the rifle again, peered into the scope. The target was still there, off in dreamland. The book had slipped off his lap and he hadn't even woken up.

Wistfully, Crain regretted that the rounds in his weapon were only tranquilizers. He didn't often get such an easy shot on target when it came to live kills. Still, orders were orders.

Ninety seconds had ticked by. He squeezed the trigger. With a nearly silent pop, the trank fired from the rifle. The arched window shattered, and the target fell over in his chair, slumped to the floor, out of sight.

As Crain watched, Colburn led the rest of Team Alpha out of the trees and up to the main school building. The doors were opened by force, and several windows shattered, as the team poured into the house. Crain didn't understand what their hurry was.

Cassidy was bagged and tagged.

Sean had always been a light sleeper. He'd honed his reflexes when he first joined Interpol nearly twenty years earlier, and he'd kept them sharp. The window shattered, he rolled, felt something tug at the short cotton sleeve of his Celtics T-shirt, just under his left arm. As he lay on the floor, heart racing with adrenaline, he reached carefully under his arm and plucked the trank dart from the cloth.

He stared at it for a single heartbeat, curled his fingers around it, and began to crawl across the floor, avoiding broken glass as best he could. Banshee had learned a valuable piece of information from that dart.

They wanted to take him alive.

That was all he needed to know.

On the first floor, the doors crashed open and several windows shattered. Sean moved fast, rising to his feet out of sight of the windows and slipping quickly into the hallway. Already, he heard pounding on the steps. Somebody's private little army, it sounded like. Acting rashly, running to collect a target before anyone's confirmed the target is down.

Scratch that, he thought. They'd taken out the school's security system before the trank dart was even fired. That was a professional job. So if there were armed grunts running up the stairs, they wouldn't be the only members of the team. Just the obvious ones.

Sean faded back into Paige Guthrie's room—perfectly kept as always—and left the door slightly ajar. The first of his attackers jogged past a moment later, male and female, which meant they weren't in any kind of regular American military unit. Women didn't get that much play in any conspicuous way in the armed forces. Not yet.

But they acted like soldiers, covering one another and moving in a sweep down the hall. Still, they only vaguely glanced into the other rooms. Either they weren't as good as he'd guessed, or they were better. He thought the latter. They knew he was the only one in the house. Still, they ought to have played it safe, just in case he hadn't been tagged by that sniper.

Which meant the sniper was cocky. Commanding officer probably was, too. Two other pieces of information Sean could use.

Shouting began from his own bedroom. They'd realized he

wasn't as unconscious as they'd planned. Feet pounded the hardwood once more, and bedroom doors began to open and shut. He'd left Paige's door open just for that purpose. Logic would suggest he ought to have closed it. The room would be searched, certainly, but whoever came into the room wouldn't be expecting him to be inside a room whose door was open.

He stood just behind the door. When the Kevlar-clad gunman slid into the room, Sean knew his first move would be to check behind the door. Only a rank amateur wouldn't do just that. Which was fine.

One hand on his gun, one hand on the door, the gunman began to shut the door to Paige's room. His eyes lit up when he saw Sean, but Banshee was already on him. Swiftly and silently, he ratcheted the gunman's weapon arm up behind him, gun falling to the throw rug Paige's mother had made for her. He slammed his left forearm up into the soldier's throat, cutting off his air and his voice, and held the man's right arm close to the breaking point.

The gunman didn't make a sound.

"Ye're a smart lad, then, aye?" Sean whispered. "Your employer and your mission, now. Y'interrupted my nap, boyo. T'weren't very neighborly of ye. So speak up, 'fore I get truly angry."

"You're a dead man, Cassidy," the gunman croaked.

"Aye, perhaps," Banshee replied. "But ye'll not be around to see it."

He choked the man, then, but Sean Cassidy was no killer. As soon as the gunman lost consciousness, Sean lowered him slowly to the floor and picked up the weapon he'd dropped. Assault taser, he realized. Meant to zap him good, knock him unconscious. Not meant to kill.

If these guys were as professional as he thought, they'd have come prepared for his sonic scream. Some kind of ear filters, he assumed. So unless he had to give himself away, it was best to keep his location to himself for as long as possible.

With a quick glance into the hallway, he moved to the back of the room, keeping to the shadows. There was a door that connected Paige and Jubilee's rooms, and he opened that door now as quietly as he could. There was a short wall to his right, built to accomodate the long closets that all the girls had begged for in this old house. Sean was grateful now for their lust for wardrobe. Undoubtedly, there was someone searching Jubilee's room, and that three feet of blank wall kept him hidden for the moment.

He took a step into the room. Sharp pain lanced into his foot, and he looked down to see that he'd stepped on some kind of barrette or other girl's hair accoutrement. Banshee rolled his eyes. Fighting without shoes lacked a certain dignity.

But it helped him keep quiet.

Banshee stepped out into Jubilee's room and fired the taser at the woman in black who stood at the center of the room. Her mouth opened in a surprised "o," then her eyes rolled up as her muscles spasmed and she fell to the floor.

"Shipman?" a hushed voice asked from the hallway.

The door opened several inches, and Sean had a moment to decide. Duck back behind the wall and hope the new arrival would be green enough to rush to the fallen woman's aid, or make the presumption of professionalism—that the soldier would know better—and just attack.

Better, he thought, to be on the offensive.

He stood his ground as the door opened. A dark face appeared, and Banshee caught him in the side of the head with the taser. He could only guess how badly such an attack would hurt, but he didn't flinch. This fight wasn't his idea.

The man crumpled to the floor, but Sean was already striding past him into the hallway. He could see the top of the stairs—a woman stood there staring at him in astonishment. He wasn't behaving according to their expectations, and it bought him half a second. Half a second to reach up to his ear, where the trank dart that had been meant for him was lodged like a carpenter's pencil. He threw it unerringly, and it lodged in her chest even as she shouted for backup.

Should have used the taser, he thought.

Then doors opened and feet pounded the stairs and weapons ratcheted, and he saw that not all of them carried tasers. Some had projectile weapons, maybe with live rounds. So maybe keeping him alive was only Plan A. If there was a Plan B, he didn't intend to stick around and find out about it.

"Drop the weapon, Cassidy, you don't stand a chance," a tall, black woman said grimly.

Sean took her down with the taser.

Then he opened his mouth, and he screamed.

His sonic scream ought to have thrown them all backwards, clutching their ears in pain. It should have, but it didn't. He didn't have time to think about the tech involved, as the sound was somehow turned back on him. *Sonic refractor, or something like that,* he thought. He'd have to ask Hank McCoy how it was done, if he lived long enough.

His own power threw him back into Jubilee's room where he crashed painfully to the hardwood amidst dozens of plastic CD jewel boxes. He rolled, ignoring the pain of what he thought might be a dislocated shoulder—gritting his teeth, roaring through it, his sonic scream tearing from him to shatter the tall pair of windows in Jubilee's room.

They were coming in after him. Silently. No cries of "mutie" or curses about his genetic heritage. This wasn't that kind of attack, obviously.

Banshee opened his mouth and began to wail again, this time using his control over his powers to warp the air around behind him, propelling him forward on waves of sound. A framed poster of Sheryl Crow shuddered off its nail and fell to shatter on the floor of Jubilee's room.

Then he was out. From the ground, weapons fire started to erupt, and he looked down to see the backup he'd expected. He could fly off, he thought. Just take off and come back later, try and figure out what these guys wanted in the first place. But that wasn't his style. Especially when the answers were right here, in the minds and mouths of his attackers.

He dove, riding the air and the sonic waves that swirled

around his body at his mental command. Banshee flew quickly around the house, downing with his fists the soldiers who were shooting at him, bucking and weaving to avoid being hit. One by one, they fell.

The last one didn't even raise his weapon. But he didn't look alarmed in any way. *The commander,* Banshee thought. He dropped to the ground just in front of the man, and the commander swung the butt of his weapon at Banshee's head. Sean ducked inside the attack and clipped the commander hard on the jaw. He went down.

"Ye've made a horrible mistake, boyo," he rasped, his voice a bit hoarse as it often was after using his powers. "Ye'll not find me an easy mark."

"I never expected to," the commander said, rubbing his chin. "But nobody can remember everything. And it's been a long time since you had to do any of the cloak-and-dagger stuff. That's what I was counting on."

Banshee frowned, confused.

Then the dart hit him in the back of the neck. He clapped a hand to it as if to swat a mosquito, but already his legs were growing weak. He crumpled to the lawn; the commander walked over to look down at him.

Idiot! Sean chided himself. *Forgot the sniper!*

"You're good, Cassidy," the commander said. "But Team Alpha is better."

As he lost consciousness, Sean realized that the other man was right. His squad, whoever they were, had been better. But they wanted him alive, and so he knew he would get another chance.

Next time, he'd make it count.

THEN

t was a rare day in London. The sky was as blue as ice, with thin clouds trailing like cracks through the firmament. The temperature was warm, near eighty, with a cool breeze that was just enough to stop any complaints about the heat. Which was a good thing, since a perfect day like this didn't come around very often. It wouldn't do to curse it.

Wouldn't do at all, Piers thought.

Piers Locke sat on the steps in front of the fountain in the middle of Piccadilly Circus and enjoyed the weather along with his coffee. The coffee paled by comparison. It was dreadful really, but Piers wasn't about to give it up. His friends and co-workers, his wife and children, they all thought it beastly that he'd eschewed the pleasures of tea for the less refined beverage. But he'd always hated tea.

It was a bit too warm outside for coffee, but Piers sipped from his cup just the same. People passed by on foot and bicycle, and went round the circus in their autos, and none of them paid him any notice at all. Piers Locke was a very nondescript man. For more than thirty years, he'd been paid to be nondescript. For the last six, he'd been bureau chief at Interpol's London branch. But the stout, balding man rinsing his china cup in the fountain drew not the slightest attention, despite the oddity of his behavior.

It was an art, really.

Oh, Piers was no spy. He was a detective, really. But if he'd ever wanted to become a spy, Interpol would have prepared him quite well indeed for that career choice. You didn't rise in the ranks of the organization without knowing how to conduct a discreet investigation.

Piers watched the front of the building across the fountain

carefully, but not because he was on a case. The bureau chief didn't handle cases directly anymore. He stared at the white-washed building's front steps and rounded edges, the tiny second-story balcony and the alabaster lady crowning the rounded corner of the roof above, and wondered what he would do with his time come the following Monday.

Piers Locke was about to retire.

Meanwhile, he had Cassidy to deal with.

The bureau chief had only just sat down in his leather chair when a ruckus began in the hallway outside his office. The opaque glass set into his office door seemed to bulge inward, but it was mainly illusion. There was shouting, cursing, and then a heavy knock on the door.

"Come," he said.

The door swung in, and the red, nervous face of Andrew Chapman, his deputy chief, popped around the edge of the door.

"Sorry, sir," Chapman said anxiously. "But it's Cassidy. Insists on seeing you, he does."

Piers took a deep breath, sat back in his chair without shame for his expansive belly, and nodded sagely, as if resolved to the burdens of his position. At least for another week.

"Send him in, then, Andrew," Piers said.

"Very good, sir," Chapman replied, then stammered out an affronted, "See here!" as Cassidy shoved past him into the bureau chief's office.

Agent Cassidy looked wild. His reddish-blond hair was wild, face unshaven even beyond the ragged sideburns he'd always worn. He was a young man, far younger than most senior agents within Interpol. But Cassidy had always been very devoted to his work, to becoming the best the agency had to offer.

Up until last month.

"Ye'll forgive me, sir, but I had to see you," Agent Cassidy said. "Brigadier McBride's me section chief, as ye probably know, but I can't get any answers out of him, nor from Mr. Lipton."

"Despite your relationship with Patrick Lipton, Agent Cassidy, and despite the deep respect we all have for the man, he isn't bureau chief here anymore. Hasn't been for over two years, as you know," Locke replied.

"I've tried to call ye time and again, so I have, but ye've not returned my calls, sir. I'm through with me leave now, and it's a return to active duty I'll be wanting now. If it's all the same to you."

He was polite enough, was Cassidy. But Piers could see the wildness in the lad's eyes and it set off an array of alarms within him. He'd always favored Sean Cassidy. But now Piers pitied him, and feared for him as well. The boy had grown up in a good family, with money and title, though nothing of any real political value. He'd earned his degree from Trinity in Dublin with the highest honors, and joined the agency right out of college.

He'd had a passion for the game, had Sean Cassidy.

But that had died along with his lovely wife, Maeve. The fire in Cassidy's eyes on this day was far different, far darker than the one it had replaced.

"Please sit down, Sean," Piers began, and saw the cloud of suspicion pass over Cassidy's face at his use of the man's Christian name.

But Cassidy didn't argue. He sat in silence on the edge of one of the pair of leather chairs facing the bureau chief's desk.

"So, you feel you're ready for active duty again, then?" Piers asked, trying to find a way to the real subject of this meeting.

"Aye," Cassidy replied. "I cannot grieve forever, sir."

Piers saw the lie on Cassidy's face. As far as the man was concerned, he *would* be grieving forever.

"There is a concern, I must tell you, Sean, that you might use active duty status to further your own ends," Piers told him bluntly. "In effect, that you will pursue some vendetta against those you believe responsible for Maeve's death."

Cassidy's eyes narrowed. He was breathing through his

nose, Piers noticed. He realized, for the first time, just how dangerous a man Sean Cassidy could be. Once, it might have been a comforting thought. Now, with the man as volatile and unpredictable as an animal, Piers found Cassidy's wildness disconcerting, to say the least.

"Agent Cassidy?" Piers ventured, returning to less personal, more familiar territory.

"Sir?"

"What do you have to say to address such concerns?" Piers asked.

"I'll be honest, Chief Locke, as ye've always been straight with me," Cassidy said. "I don't believe that my Maeve's passing was anything other than a horrible tragedy, an' nobody's fault. But what haunts me, sir, is only that I wasn't here. 'Twas her birthday, y'know, only days before she . . . before the explosion. I promised her I'd be home, but I missed it, sir. Again.

"I missed it because that witch from the KGB led me a merry chase across half of France," he said grimly.

Cassidy would say no more, and Piers knew better than to ask. The KGB agent was little more than a slip of a girl. Cassidy had been embarrassed when she had snatched the defector, Dr. Smitrovich, who had chosen to leave his country with the aid of Interpol—a service they vehemently denied, of course. But worse, during that operation, in which he was to capture the girl, she had hurt him, and Cassidy had ended up in hospital in Nice.

He was there, healing, when Maeve had died. Cassidy blamed the girl, Romanova, for the fact that he hadn't been at home when Maeve died, that he wasn't there to stop it or at least to be with her when it happened.

"Sean," Piers began, but Cassidy cut him off.

"I'll never forgive her that, sir. If that makes me a vigilante or some such thing, I suppose that's what I'll be."

Piers stared at Cassidy, astonished as much by his forthrightness as by his obsession.

"You understand, Agent Cassidy," he said, "that you might

just as well blame Interpol for your absence. It was on our behalf that you were attempting to capture this girl to begin with."

Cassidy's eyes narrowed again.

"Yes, sir," he replied. "But we are the law. It's our duty to bring people like Natasha Romanova to justice, to shed light on the atrocities of killers and spies and thieves, and this girl is all three."

Piers sat back, stared intently at Agent Cassidy, and tried desperately to think of an alternative to what he was about to do. Short of dismissing Cassidy altogether, he couldn't think of anything. And even if he did that, Piers suspected it wouldn't prevent Sean from pursuing the Romanova girl on his own.

"What is it, sir?" Cassidy asked. "If ye have something else to add, please share it. Otherwise, please give me your decision: can I return to active duty, or not?"

Piers nodded quickly, resolved. "Indeed you may, Agent Cassidy," he replied. "But there is one condition."

"I suspect I know what ye're going to ask, sir, and ye know I cannot vow—"

"Let me finish, Sean, please."

Cassidy nodded.

"It isn't what you think. Actually, I rather think you'll be pleased with this assignment. But even within the assignment itself, there are conditions."

The wild-eyed Irish man was silent.

"More defectors," Piers explained.

That got Cassidy's attention.

"A man and woman, according to our sources," he went on. "They've stolen some kind of computer disk. The information stored on that disk will tip the balance of power in the Cold War toward whichever side gets to it first.

"A covert unit codenamed Team X is being sent into East Berlin to retrieve the disk. The disk, Agent Cassidy. Not the defectors. But the Zhevakovs have asked for Interpol's help.

Officially, of course, we can do nothing of the sort. It would undermine our position as a law-enforcement agency. But that doesn't mean we won't help. That disk, and the agents themselves, could be invaluable to the Western effort in the Cold War. That's where you come in. Papers are being prepared which should get the Zhevakovs past the Berlin Wall. Your job is to make certain of it, and make sure that disk is retrieved as well."

Cassidy's eyes narrowed. "The KGB will send a team of their own, of course."

"No team," Piers replied, and looked away. "Just one agent."

"The Black Widow," Cassidy whispered, almost to himself.

"You realize I should not do this, Sean," Piers said. "I should assign someone else. But you're still the best I've got. Just remember that we want the Widow alive."

"If possible," Cassidy replied.

But Piers could see the hatred, the fury burning in Cassidy's eyes, and he knew that Interpol had already lost one of its best agents.

Piers Locke turned to glance out his window and saw that the London sky had begun to cloud over. *What a surprise,* he thought bitterly. And he prayed that his last week as bureau chief would pass without incident.

NOW

uess we're gonna find out what this is all about," Wolverine snarled. "Move it!"

He grabbed Mystique by the hand and got her moving toward the kitchen. They had a few seconds before the hallway outside would be filled with troops. If he wasn't certain Maverick had reinforced the apartment's outer walls, he'd be concerned about small-arms fire just blowing the wall in.

"Windows?" Mystique asked.

"They'd have come in that way if they could have," Logan said, shaking his head. "No, they'll be coming right through that front door."

Mystique kept glancing over her shoulder as Wolverine led her into the kitchen. He went immediately to the white refrigerator, its face as blank as the life of the soldier who owned it, and put his shoulder into sliding it back. The fridge rolled easily—testament to the fact that something was hidden beneath it. The average refrigerator would have torn up the ancient linoleum. This one was made not to.

Beneath it was a large, black metal square on the floor. The strongbox had no obvious seams, handles or locking mechanisms. Logan didn't have time to figure out the trick. Adamantium claws descended, carving through metal in one smooth stroke. With his other hand, he reached down into the tear in the metal and pulled. The top of the strongbox came away as the few strands that still held it to the rest of the box snapped.

"Tell me that's what I think it is," Mystique said.

In the main room of the apartment, automatic-weapons fire popped and Logan could hear the crack of wood and the shattering of ceramic as the place's furnishings were obliterated.

"This building has been sealed by order of the Department of Defense," a voice shouted. "Come out with your hands up, and you will not be hurt."

"Yeah," Logan snarled quietly. "If you'd said that before you started shootin', I mighta believed ya."

He slammed an AR-18 ArmaLite assault rifle into Mystique's waiting hands, and watched her face light up with a smile that made her exotic blue skin and yellow eyes seem more savage than ever. He then handed her a MAC-11 submachine gun with the stock removed, and she slipped it into her waistband.

"Just like old times, huh?" she said.

"Try not to kill anyone," Wolverine replied gruffly.

"Maybe not so much like old times at that," she muttered, then turned and went to the kitchen door.

Logan reached into the strongbox and pulled out a pair of nine-millimeter Heckler & Koch semiautomatics and several grenades he had determined to be concussion rather than fragmentation.

"I'm going to count to three," the loudmouth in the other room was shouting.

"Three?" Mystique muttered. "What happened to ten? Even five?"

"We ain't gonna let him get to three," Wolverine said.

They looked at each other, a pair of warrior-spies who'd come to grudgingly respect one another over the years. Respect, true, but they didn't like each other, then or now.

"One!" the loudmouth cried.

"Go," Wolverine said.

Logan went high—he could survive getting shot—and Mystique went low. The nines barked in his hands even as he surveyed their opposition: half a dozen hard-looking, professional soldiers in Kevlar jumpsuits. Just what he'd expected. Anyone with the guts and the smarts to nab Sabretooth and Maverick had to be very good.

But very good wasn't enough. When it came right down to it, Wolverine was the best there was at what he did. Bar none.

He loved the Kevlar. It meant he could shoot at the soldiers without worrying about killing them. All he needed to do, for the moment at least, was hurt them.

Wolverine took two bullets in his lower abdomen and one in the shoulder, which bounced off his adamantium-laced clavicle. He advanced into the room, and the pair of nines grew hot in his hands as he focused on a trio of soldiers in the front. They stumbled backward under his barrage. Two of them fell. The other, a mountainous human being, was forced back into the hallway.

Mystique had dived through the door, landed on her belly, and opened up at the legs of the three soldiers on her side. Part of him wanted to think she was doing as he'd asked, trying not to kill anyone. But as he heard the shouts of pain and saw the three men's legs shattered and torn up by bullets, he wondered if he was being naïve. Mystique was probably just shooting for whatever wasn't protected.

Of course, she could have gone for head shots.

"Logan, drop it and back off!" the man-mountain in the hallway roared, and Wolverine realized it had been him speaking to them before. "You and Darkhölme don't have a chance of getting out of here. The place is surrounded. You're both coming with us."

As if to punctuate the soldier's words, Logan heard shouting and running on the stairs outside the door. He looked around the room quickly. The three men Mystique had shot were either out cold or writhing in pain. The two Logan had knocked down were winded, trying to get up. Neither was stupid enough to go for his gun at the moment.

"We should get out of here," Mystique said quietly, her eyes and weapon trained on the shattered apartment doorway.

"Not without some answers," he replied, and took a step toward one of the soldiers he'd knocked down.

The man recoiled in fear, began to slide himself back toward the wall, wincing with the pain of the many bruises that

Logan's shots would leave him with, Kevlar or no. Logan himself winced slightly at the pain in his gut where the flesh was knitting back together. It was a pain that would have crippled anyone else. But Wolverine lived with it every day.

"Tell me, bub," he snarled. "You don't want me to make you."

The soldier's eyes were wide, his mouth opened slightly.

A pair of grenades popped through the shattered doorway and rolled across the floor. Frag bombs, too—not nice, gentle concussive explosives.

"Mystique!" he thundered.

Without waiting for a response, he took three strides toward the window, used both arms to slash a huge hole in the wall, and turned just in time to catch Mystique as she slammed into him. They tumbled out the window into the darkness together, an eyeblink before the grenades exploded, blowing the hole in the wall much wider, and killing everyone in the room.

They fell, then. As they plummeted toward the ground, Wolverine did everything he could to keep Mystique above him. Finally, he pulled her to him in an embrace, and was about to close his eyes when they slammed into the roof of a white cable van, crumpling the metal.

Mystique was off him in an instant, but Wolverine was completely disoriented at first. His bones wouldn't break, but the flesh of his back and legs would be bruised and broken, lacerated and torn. At least for several minutes.

But he didn't have several minutes. His brain was a bit scrambled as well, but that too would pass shortly. The moon wasn't bright, but he closed his eyes a moment against the meager light nevertheless. He smelled the acrid odors of the explosion, and a strong whiff of Chinese food from the restaurant across the street.

"You saved my life," Mystique sneered as he dropped to his feet from the van's roof. "Don't do it again."

"Not much to worry about there, darlin'," he replied. "Special circumstances and all."

"What was that all about?" Mystique said. "I thought they wanted you alive."

"They do," Wolverine replied. "They just don't want any of their own boys giving anything away."

"You mean they expected you to live through that?"

In answer, three soldiers, a man and two women, rounded the corner of the building, led by man-mountain himself, spotlit by a streetlamp. They'd gotten downstairs quickly, but Wolverine saw that the explosion had already garnered attention, particularly from several people who had come out of the Chinese restaurant, and now huddled near the front door of the place.

The soldiers opened fire.

Wolverine reached for the concussive grenades he'd hooked to his costume, but only one remained. He pulled the pin and lobbed it toward them. The seven-foot soldier took the brunt of the blast. It threw him back nearly ten feet and when he hit the pavement, he hit hard, and didn't move.

The others were coming on, but Mystique opened up with her ArmaLite, strafing across their bodies. One took a bullet in the cheek, but didn't go down, and Mystique glanced at Logan as if in apology.

A dark sedan screeched to a stop in the middle of the street and the three soldiers ran for it, laying down suppressing fire which forced Logan and Mystique to take cover behind the cable van until the sedan had already pulled away.

Wolverine growled, low and dangerous. "Not what I had planned," he said angrily. "We needed someone to—"

They looked at one another, glanced around the van again. Man-mountain was lying in the street, completely unconscious.

"I'll cover you," Mystique told him.

Logan wanted to turn, to search her eyes, to see if he could trust her in a way he never had before. He didn't dare; he knew what he would find. But he went anyway.

Ignoring the onlookers in front of the Chinese restaurant,

and the others he assumed were staring out some of the windows above, Wolverine loped across the moonlit pavement. He knelt by the side of the fallen man and felt for his pulse. It was strong, despite the bloody wound on the forehead where the man's head had smacked the tar.

In the distance, police sirens began to wail. Time to move out.

He tested the soldier's weight. Logan was short, but stronger than he looked. However, this guy was going to be way too much for him. And now he was becoming increasingly aware of the attention of witnesses all around. But if he couldn't carry the big goon out of there, maybe Mystique . . .

Even as he turned to look for Raven Darkhölme, he heard the near-silent thump of stealth chopper rotors against the air. It was dropping down on them from way up, and fast. Logan moved for cover instantly, but he knew he wasn't going to make it. Automatic-weapons fire exploded from the chopper, and Logan tensed to take the bullets, heard them biting chunks out of the pavement.

Then he was diving behind the cable van, rolling, staring up at Mystique as he realized he hadn't been shot at all.

"What . . . " he began.

"They want to make sure we stay in the dark," she said grimly.

Wolverine knew before he looked that the man-mountain would be dead. But he wasn't prepared for the way the big man's body had been torn up by the attack. Hollow-point rounds, he figured. Or even exploding rounds. The guy was a mess. Nothing he hadn't seen before, but it really ticked him off.

The police sirens had grown closer, and he heard tires screeching not far off. Suddenly, an NYPD prowl car skidded around a corner, lights blazing, siren blaring.

"Meet me back at the White Horse," Logan drawled.

He watched as Mystique shapeshifted into a disgusting-looking old homeless woman, dressed in rags and smelling of sickness and waste. Raven Darkhölme was a very clever woman. In this guise, the police wouldn't even detain her long enough to give an eyewitness statement.

Wolverine melted into the shadows, even as Mystique walked straight across the street toward the gathering crowd of people who would claim to have "seen it all," even though most of them had probably been hiding during the entire firefight.

As he made his way through a darkened alley, Logan dwelled on something that had occurred to him when they were first attacked. It wasn't just him they were after. They wanted Mystique, too. They already had Sabretooth and Maverick, and they wanted Wolverine. But Mystique had never been a member of Team X.

He had no idea what the motive for these attacks and abductions was, but now at least he had the first clue. Now, at least, he knew where to trace it all back to.

"East Berlin," Logan said, sipping at a foamy pint. "You remember?"

"Of course I do," Mystique replied.

She looked even better than before. Copper skin and eyes the color of milk chocolate. Logan had known a woman once with similar features; Lettie, her name was. But Mystique was even more beautiful. Perfect. When she shapeshifted into someone like a homeless person, her disguise was impenetrable. But when she took on personas like this, there was the one thing that gave her away to someone whose eyes were trained to look for her: she was too perfect.

"That was a long time ago, Logan," she said.

"Not to whoever has this vendetta against us, darlin'," he replied. "I've had my fill o' mysteries, Mystique. It's a game I quit playin' a long time ago. Let's see if we can't get to the bottom o' this quick."

"Well," Mystique said, cocking her head to one side and tapping long red fingernails against her satin cheek, "who else was involved with that fiasco?"

Logan was up and moving toward the pay phone in the back

of the White Horse even before Mystique finished the thought. She followed, sipping at her scotch.

The phone rang half a dozen times before the machine picked up.

"You have reached Xavier's School for Gifted Youngsters," Emma Frost's regal voice declared. "At the tone, you may speak."

Bleeeep!

"This is Logan. I need to speak to . . ."

There was a click as someone picked up the phone on the other end.

"Wolvie!" Jubilee said excitedly. "Where are you, can you come—"

He was about to interrupt when he heard Jubilee complain as the phone was taken from her.

"Logan."

"Emma," Wolverine replied, with as much courtesy as he could muster.

Which wasn't a lot, when it came to Emma Frost. He trusted her even less than he did Mystique. But these were strange times, and that made for strange alliances.

"I need to talk to Irish," Logan drawled. "It's important."

There was a brief silence on the other line, then a dry chuckle.

"Yes, well, we'd all like to talk to Sean right now," Emma replied. "Sadly, he isn't here at present."

Wolverine felt a cold fire blaze up in his gut.

"He's been taken?"

Logan could hear Frost's surprise over the phone.

"What . . . how did you . . . what's this all about, Wolverine?" she demanded. "That wasn't just a lucky guess. What are we talking about, here?"

"Don't bother yourself, Emma. I'll see to it Irish gets home safely," he said coldly, and hung up the phone on her angry shouts.

He let out a long breath and turned to face Mystique. Their

eyes met briefly, and he wondered what was going on in her head. Wondered if she knew more than she was letting on. But he'd never know until she wanted him to—of that he was certain.

Mystique knocked back what was left of her scotch.

"So how do we find the Russian?" she asked. "She's no longer with the Avengers."

"You want to find the spider, you go to the web."

They waited outside the Upper West Side high-rise until they saw an obese woman in a garish yellow dress approach the doorman inside and reprimand him for something. After which she strutted from the building and hailed a cab. Obviously a tenant.

Sixty seconds after the cab pulled away, they walked across the street to the front of the building. Mystique had changed again—rolls of fat in yellow polyester, hardly the perfection she favored—and for the first time in the many years since he had first met her, Wolverine wondered if it tired her at all.

The doorman plastered a ridiculously false smile across his face and opened the door for them.

"Mrs. Hastings?" the doorman inquired, feigning concern. "Anything the matter?"

"Should something *else* be the matter?" Mystique sneered. "Or haven't I suffered enough?"

The doorman's jaw dropped. Apparently Mystique had been even harsher with him than the real Mrs. Hastings. Logan had to smile. Mrs. Hastings would have a very chilly reception when she actually did return.

They walked to the elevator without the doorman so much as glancing at Logan. After the doors closed, and the elevator began to glide up the metal gullet of the high-rise, Mystique changed once more. Not to her true form, but a more human appearance, in case someone else should board the elevator on its way up.

Wolverine thought she seemed greatly relieved to leave the body of Mrs. Hastings behind.

They reached the top floor of apartments and left the elevator. They would have needed a key to unlock the elevator's security and get it to bring them to the penthouse, which had been their destination all along. Instead, Logan padded down the hallway in silence, Mystique following his lead. Though he wore street clothes, he suspected that his leather and denim might be out of place in this corridor of wealth.

At the end of the hall they came to the emergency stairs. No alarms here, he noted, and pushed on through. As he suspected, there were stairs leading up as well as down. The fire marshal wouldn't be happy if the penthouse didn't have stairwell access. They went up quickly and found a door at the top that had three separate barrel locks, and was more than likely wired with a complex security system.

"Maybe we should have called first?" Mystique asked.

Logan sniffed at the air.

"What is it?" she asked.

"Somethin' don't smell right," he growled.

He reached out and touched lightly at the edge of the door. It opened an eighth of an inch. Wolverine pulled at the edge of the door, and it came open with the smallest of squeaks.

Mystique looked at him. He knew what she was thinking, and shared her observation. The soldiers after Natasha Romanova were quiet going in. That meant they might still be inside; Wolverine and Mystique would have to be quiet as shadows going in after them.

But they'd both spent years mastering the art of silence.

The apartment was elegantly decorated, but understated, almost Spartan. Logan didn't know who paid for the digs— could have been the Avengers, S.H.I.E.L.D., even the Widow's own money—but it hadn't come cheap.

They emerged into a long hallway down which they could see where the elevator doors would open right into the penthouse. There were several rooms off the hall, but Wolverine didn't catch any scent except the Widow's and the intruders'. They moved along toward the wide arch across from the elevator doors. It opened into a vast foyer that might as well have been the interior of a mansion in Gramercy Park. Despite the dim light, they could see Persian carpets and huge green plants, paintings that had to be original, and carved hardwood columns.

Nothing broken. Nothing even obviously amiss.

Unless you looked at the stairs. Up the stairs, to the second floor of the massive penthouse. Unless you saw the burn marks on the carpet and the way the wall was shattered in several places in the stairwell, the way the banister had been cracked in two halfway up.

Without a word, they moved up those stairs. Three steps from the top, Wolverine got a good idea just how much damage the second floor had sustained. The Black Widow had not been taken without a fight, and it had been a good one. But, he was now certain, she had been taken. Otherwise, there was no way to account for the quiet. It had happened recently, though. It was near one in the morning now, and Logan figured no more than two hours since the Widow was snatched.

He was about to tell Mystique exactly that when he heard the sound of a new clip being loaded into an assault rifle. It was a sound he was familiar with, but one he'd never really enjoyed.

Snikt. Logan popped his claws.

"Haven't you done enough?" a voice growled from the shadows below.

Even as he turned and dove over the broken banister, falling down upon the man with the weapon with his claws ready to slash through gunmetal and flesh, Wolverine realized that he and the gunman had both made a mistake.

He retracted his claws even as the man fired. Two bullets tore into Wolverine before he could knock the assault rifle aside, even as the gunman crumpled beneath his falling body. The two of them sprawled on the floor together, the assault rifle still firing, tearing chunks of meticulously carved wood from the walls, punching holes in priceless tapestries and shattering windows thirty stories above Manhattan.

"Bastards, where is she?" the gunman roared as he gripped Logan's jacket. "What have you—"

"Ivan, no!" Wolverine shouted.

Recognition lit the big man's face, and he relaxed his grip. It was as though all the strength went out of him, and he let his head fall back to the Persian rug.

"Logan," he said gruffly. "They took her." Ivan Petrovitch closed his eyes. "Ah, Natalia Romanova, my prima ballerina, what am I going to do?"

Wolverine stood, stretched, heard the calcium pop in his neck and spine, then reached a hand down to help the old man up.

"Do?" he answered. "We're gonna find her, Ivan. You can bet on it."

They sat in the kitchen, sipping Earl Grey tea as Ivan recounted the events leading up to the abduction of the woman called the Black Widow. There was a massive bruise swelling to golf-ball proportions on the back of his head, where his salt and pepper hair was thinning.

"I did all I could," Ivan said mournfully.

Wolverine only nodded. Ivan didn't need to defend himself. The old man—and Logan couldn't stop thinking of him that way despite the fact that, appearances aside, he was certainly older than Ivan—had taken care of Natasha for years. He'd been her father figure, her chauffeur, bodyguard, and source of wisdom since she lost her parents as a child. He loved her as much as any parent had ever loved a child.

Natasha Romanova had begun her life as a privileged little girl in Stalingrad, and grown up to become one of her nation's treasured ballerinas. Between those lives, she had suffered tragedy, and Ivan had been a soldier whose own heart was empty of light. They had become family more than many families ever do.

To please the state, Natasha had married very young, still just a girl. Her husband, famed cosmonaut Alexi Shostakov, died soon after, and once more she wept in Ivan's arms. In her grief, she was easy prey for the KGB, whose lies honed her into the perfect tool against the West. Her participation was against Ivan's better judgement, but it was what she wanted, and he had never been able to deny her anything.

Only when the truth of Alexi's death came out, and she began to see the web of lies and deceit that had been spun around her, did the Black Widow defect to the United States. Over the years, she'd been both spy and super hero, working as the former both for S.H.I.E.L.D. and on a freelance basis, as the latter on her own and with such teams as the Avengers and the Champions, even serving as field leader for both teams.

But none of those things concerned them now. If Wolverine was right, and he was as certain as he'd ever been, the Widow's abduction went back to a time when she was still the KGB's tool. She couldn't have been more than nineteen, at the time. Maybe younger.

But Ivan was there, as always.

Logan and Mystique just let him talk for a while, at first. Wolverine was surprised that Mystique was so patient, almost sympathetic. She watched Ivan closely, an odd look on her face. Logan wondered if it was envy, if she longed for the kind of unwavering dedication and love that Ivan so readily gave to Natasha. It was a strange thought. He'd never even considered that Mystique had feelings about anything before. Logan pushed away from that thought process. She might be working for the government now, but it wasn't by choice. She was a criminal, a murderer, a terrorist.

That was all Wolverine needed to know. Or, at least, all he wanted to know.

"I don't understand," Ivan said, his usually very American,

unaccented English now tinged with the memory of his homeland. "The Soviet Union is gone. The Iron Curtain is gone. The KGB is having enough trouble policing itself without worrying about one minor skirmish out of thousands at the end of the Cold War."

Mystique interrupted. "Well, the soldiers who came after us seemed American enough, but they could be mercenaries working for a larger organization like A.I.M. or Hydra. But those groups don't have any connection to this mission. It could be anyone behind this."

"Even the KGB," Logan observed.

"There are two major holes in that theory," Mystique countered. "First, as far as I know, nobody but the Mossad and the members of Team X, and of course, Cassidy and the Widow, knew that I was involved in that mission. Second, the Widow was on the KGB's side back then."

"That was then," Logan replied. "Natasha ain't exactly on the KGB's party list these days."

Ivan nodded slowly, the lines around his eyes betraying his age far more than the white flecks in his hair and bushy mustache. He must be over sixty, Logan guessed. And yet the tall, stocky man was in extraordinary condition. It was rare for the average human being to have such discipline. But then, Ivan wasn't really average. And he had Natasha depending on him, after all.

"They hate her now," Ivan said. "Call her a traitor. But I just don't see the sense in abduction versus murder. If it was revenge, they would just kill you all."

"They want something," Logan agreed. "Maybe it's me. Maybe it's Mystique. Maybe it's just information. But none of those things really point to the KGB."

He glanced at Mystique. "Mossad?" he asked.

"I'll make a few phone calls," she replied. "But as far as the Mossad were concerned, that was a failed mission. My report was filled with lies anyway. They wouldn't have had any real idea what happened."

"What a surprise," Logan drawled. "Still, you'd best make those calls, just to see if anything comes outta shakin' the trees."

Mystique rose to go to the phone, and Logan watched her go. He couldn't help but wonder if she knew more than she was telling. Eventually, he'd find out, one way or another. Problem was, they'd both have to get a lot closer to the fire to find out who set it, and to see how badly they were going to get burned.

NOW

Maverick felt like throwing up.

For the first few months, the Legacy Virus hadn't been that difficult to live with. But recently, it had begun to show itself on his body and face, ravaging his skin in almost leprous fashion. And inside? God, all his insides felt like shattered glass. He'd always been a serious person, didn't really have much of a sense of humor. Now he was grim simply because of the pain.

Living hurt.

But he was pretty sure he'd like dying even less, and so he fought the disease as best he could. There'd been a time when he wanted to die, even asked Wolverine to do it for him. Tried to force his old comrade-in-arms to take his life. That was panic for you, made you do crazy things. Suicide was a coward's death, and David North had been many things in his life, but a coward was not one of them.

He grunted against the pain, lip curled back in a passable imitation of the savage whose arms and legs were clamped to the wall right next to him.

"You mockin' me, boy?" Sabretooth snarled.

"You're not worth the energy, Creed," Maverick replied.

Then silence descended upon them again. There were four of them, all mounted to the wall like hunting trophies. Maverick raised his eyebrows as he realized that might be exactly what they were. Whoever had captured them all had gone to a lot of trouble and expense, and they'd yet to see this mysterious "benefactor."

"Any of you seen restraints like this before?" he grumbled, and weakly tested his bonds, long metal sheaths that completely encompassed his legs from the knees down and his hands from midforearm to fingertips.

When he didn't receive an answer, Maverick looked up to see that all three of his fellow captives were testing their own restraints, though all but one of them wore a metal suppression collar around the neck with a tiny red light at the front. The only one without it was Natasha Romanova.

The Black Widow strained against her bonds, muscles rippling across her arms and legs, perfectly visible through the skintight black costume she wore. North didn't remember her being as beautiful as she was now. But she'd been a girl then, so maybe that was the difference. She was a woman now, a real heartbreaker.

It occurred to him that he was probably done with romance. It wasn't a pleasant thought.

Sabretooth roared and threw himself hard against his own bonds. Maverick heard something crack in the murderous savage's left arm, and Creed winced. Maverick felt sick. The maniac had probably just broken his arm trying to escape—and with the collar suppressing his mutant powers, including his healing factor, the arm would stay broken for the forseeable future. Sabretooth was even more insane than he had been when they worked together on Team X.

On the wall to his right, next to the Widow, Sean Cassidy let out a wild scream, but it was nothing more than that. Maverick closed his eyes, and his stomach lurched once again. He thought of the hero in Poe's "The Pit and the Pendulum," about the slashing of the razor pendulum and the gnawing of the rats on the man's belly. Maverick figured he knew just what the poor sucker had gone through.

"Enough, Cassidy!" he grunted.

"Apologies, lad," Cassidy replied. "I was tryin' to see if me sonic scream was workin', but it seems these restraints aren't just for show. I've got a little power stored up but not enough to make a difference. This collar is sappin' me mutant gifts, all right. I've seen such technology before. Magneto had such."

"And the government," Creed added.

Maverick stared at him.

"What're you starin' at, North?" Sabretooth snarled. "I been captured before. All I'm sayin' is, I been held in a setup just like this once or twice. Was the government done it, too."

"What part of the government are we discussing here, Creed?" the Widow asked, and Maverick admired her tone. She had her own brand of snarl, did the Black Widow.

"Who knows? CIA? The Shop? DOD? The Agency? SAFE? Doesn't really matter, does it?"

Nobody had an answer to that.

"Well, I for one don't have any desire to sit around and wait to find out who our captors are or why we've been taken," the Widow said. "We've got to figure a way to get out of here, and quickly."

Sabretooth snorted. "You come up with somethin', cupcake, you let me know. 'Til then, I'm just gonna sit back and wait for Mystique to come and get me."

"Why in the name o' God would she want to do that?" Cassidy asked, incredulous.

"Creed and Darkhölme go back a ways, don't you, Sabretooth?" Maverick taunted.

"We're teammates now, and that's what matters," Creed said. "She was there when I got snatched up. She'll come after me."

"If they don't get her first," the Widow added grimly. "The four of us only have one thing that connects us all, and Mystique was a part of that as well."

"Hell, she might be the one behind our being here," Maverick noted with sudden realization.

"Seems to me if we're all here because of that Zhevakov mess, there are a few players from that game still not accounted for," Cassidy observed.

"Silver Fox is dead," Maverick told them, and glared at Sabretooth.

"It happens," he grunted, a sly smile on his face, fangs showing.

"Other than Mystique, that leaves Wolverine and Kestrel," Maverick continued. "Chances are, these guys have already gone after them. As long as they're still out there, we can figure they're trying to find us."

"Yeah, maybe, but I'm not bankin' on gettin' help from either of those two," Creed snarled. "At least I know what to expect from Mystique."

"True," Maverick agreed. "She's an animal, just like you."

In a dark room, a man with hatred in his heart stared at three monitors showing the inside of the cell where the objects of that hatred were being kept. Behind him stood Colburn and Crain from Team Alpha.

"What of the others?" the man inquired. "I want them all before we begin. I'll never know the truth unless I have them all."

"Don't worry, sir," Colburn replied. "It'll go just as we agreed—I promise you that. Teams Alpha and Omega deal with these kinds of operations every day. We've spent our lives training to handle every imaginable crisis. The dinosaurs who used to be a part of Team X don't really stand a chance."

"You said that before, Mr. Colburn," the man said, voice tinged with venom. "But Wolverine still eludes you."

"We'll have him, sir. No more than forty-eight hours, guaranteed."

"You'd better, Mr. Colburn. If you expect me to follow through on my end of the bargain, you'd best perform on your end."

As the old teammates began to argue and threaten one another, the Black Widow silently worked her fingers and wrists inside the metal sheaths that bound her hands. Their captors had removed the hardware she usually wore around her wrists. It looked a lot like slightly gaudy jewelry, but actually contained a taserlike weapon she called her "widow's bite," which held more than thirty thousand volts of electricity. They'd known about that, of course. But she'd find a way to escape, no matter what.

After several minutes of intense concentration, she rested, determined to try again, to keep trying until they were out. As she rested, she became uncomfortably aware of the presence of Sean Cassidy, clamped to the wall nearby. Their relationship had always been awkward at best, and often even outright hostile, even after she defected from the KGB.

"Strange, isn't it, lass?" he asked, as though he could read her mind.

"Very," she agreed, but didn't look up to meet his gaze.

"To think that, whoever our unseen enemy is, we're apparently being punished for a confrontation that we stood on opposite sides of those long years ago," Banshee said aloud. "It's a horrible irony, don't you think, that we're trapped here together?"

Finally, she looked up and met the Irishman's eyes. He had the kindest eyes she'd ever seen. She hadn't remembered that about him, and it struck her as profoundly sad. Natasha Romanova had known a great many men in her lifetime. Most of them were cold-eyed warriors or snake-eyed spies. A select few were wise, and even fewer were warm and kind. She wondered if Sean Cassidy's heart had been so filled with hate those long years ago that his kind eyes had grown cold for a time.

If so, she was pleased to see that he had changed. It happened to everyone, she knew, but not always for the best.

"Ironic, yes," the Black Widow said, "but horrible? No. Whoever it is that put us here, they're the enemy. As long as I know I'm on the side of the angels, I'll take whatever comes my way."

A cloud passed over Cassidy's face, and for a moment, Natasha remembered what it had been like to be his enemy, those years ago. Maybe, in some small way, he still held her responsible for not being there when his wife was killed?

But there was more to that look than just memory. There was doubt and hate, even disgust.

Cassidy's eyes narrowed, then turned away from Natasha and focused on the other side of the room, where Victor Creed still strained against his bonds.

"Aye, Widow?" Cassidy said slowly. "And what makes ye so sure ye're on the side of the angels?"

Natasha stared at Sabretooth for a long time. She never did come up with an answer.

THEN

Agent Sean Cassidy stared at the forbidding gray expanse of concrete looming just ahead. It was unique in all the world, a symbol of humanity's greatest weakness as a species: hatred. Sean remembered one of his professors at Trinity College commenting that the difference between humans and other animals was the ability to love. He'd been a romantic fool himself then, and had heartily agreed.

It had been another student, someone Sean didn't know, but who had surely become a cynic at far too young an age, who'd pointed out the other half of that equation. Humans could love, but they could also hate.

After World War II, the Allies quickly began to look at one another with suspicion. The British and Americans, and later the French, had joined their occupied zones in Berlin together into one. The Soviets weren't even invited. West versus East. It was the beginning of a conflict that would blossom into the Cold War and lead to the creation of America's Central Intelligence Agency, among many other things. It also was the starting point for an invisible barrier between the ever-growing Soviet Union and the rest of the world: a barrier called the Iron Curtain.

A decade and a half after the war had ended, that invisible barrier was a reality. But it wasn't enough in Berlin, where the line between enemies literally split a city, and a nation, in two. In 1961, the East German government, puppets of the Soviets, built a physical barrier of concrete and barbed wire.

The true irony of the Berlin Wall, however, was that it was built not to keep Westerners out, but to keep East German citizens in. They weren't afraid of invasion or immigration—the conditions were such that nobody would choose to emigrate to East Germany. No, they just wanted to make certain that their people could not leave. East Germany, then, and East Berlin in particular, became a sort of enormous prison, most of the inmates of which weren't even aware of their captivity.

What many people seemed to forget, however, was that Berlin was one hundred and ten miles inside East Germany. West Berlin was the lone refuge of democracy behind the Iron Curtain, a pimple on the face of communism.

The wall itself was a jagged scar across the city, twenty-eight miles in length, but even that fifteen-foot-high chunk of concrete was only the last of the obstacles separating the two halves of the city. Or the first, if you were East German and yearned for freedom. Which, Cassidy figured, was pretty much a given. Otherwise, why have the wall at all?

Another misconception was that the wall merely split the city. No, that was merely the most intense section of the conflict represented by that barrier. In truth, the wall ran the entire circumference of West Berlin, just shy of one hundred miles. It was a fortress city, and yet the walls around it had been built by the enemy.

In his days as a student, Sean Cassidy had considered that one of the great ironies of the twentieth century.

The rest of the wall was not as immediately forbidding in appearance as that which divided the city. Yet in some ways, it was more treacherous ground. The no-man's-land between the concrete wall and the barbed wire fence was as wide in some places as three hundred yards. Three hundred yards of dog runs, tank traps, hidden flares, mines, alarms, infrared cameras, and machine gun towers occupied by *Grepos*, the East German guards whose main occupation was to kill anyone who tried to cross without authorization.

Yet several times a year, according to the prep research Cassidy had done, someone still managed to escape. And each escape was analyzed and responded to, which made it that much harder for the next person. But it was possible. Which was good to know.

And this was the place where Agent Cassidy had to search for the Black Widow. It didn't matter. He would go to Moscow itself—to hell, in fact, if it meant bringing down Natasha Romanova.

On the other hand, Cassidy could fly. So, theoretically, he could leave whenever he wanted. But then his sonic scream would bring him unwanted attention and make him an immediate target. No, better to do it this way.

"Halt!"

Cassidy looked down from the expanse of the wall, barren but for the barbed wire. He stood on Friedrichstrasse, right in front of what was still called Checkpoint Charlie—the only place where non-Germans could enter East Berlin. Cassidy could see through the checkpoint to the far side of the passage, the East German side, where the *Polizei* guarding the gate were arguing with a man who was attempting to pass through into West Berlin. The man was obviously German, but East or West was impossible for Cassidy to determine by simple observation. However, when he overheard the man arguing that he was American, that his passport was genuine, even Sean had to doubt him.

At the risk of aggravating the border guards even further, he pressed on, hoping to take advantage of the momentary confusion. Perhaps in their frustration, the guards would not give him as much of a hard time as he had expected.

Now the guards had begun to argue with their West German counterparts. But it was clear where this thing was heading. Cassidy walked up to the guardhouse on the Western side even as more East German guards appeared on the other side of the gate and escorted the shouting man away.

A sign to his right read: YOU ARE NOW LEAVING THE AMERICAN SECTOR.

"Halt," said a West German guard to his right.

The man had close-cropped blond hair and ice-blue eyes. He wasn't unpleasant, but neither did he smile as he examined the papers that Cassidy held out for him. It gave Sean pause to wonder exactly how different this man was from the one who performed the same function on the other side. It was the same city, after all, or it had been back in 1961, when the wall was built.

The two could be brothers. The thought disturbed him and all too sadly reminded him of home. While there was no city split in as dramatic a way as Berlin had been, Ireland was also torn in two by hatred and ignorance.

"*Schon gut, danke,*" the guard said, and gestured for him to move on.

"*Guten Tag,*" Cassidy replied, wishing the man good afternoon in his own language, and nodded his head slightly.

Halfway through to the other side of the world, halfway through the Iron Curtain, he looked up again at the East German guards, then up to the machine-gun–wielding *Grepos* on the wall, and he froze. Cassidy couldn't help but feel the tension roiling in the air around him, stirring the acid in his gut and speeding his heart. He watched the way the afternoon sunlight glinted off weapons held by the East German guards, and he started to question the wisdom of his mission.

But only for a moment. Of course they'd never believe he was who he said he was—he'd known that going in. More than likely, they'd have a tail on him from the moment he entered the country. But, he reminded himself, the Widow was in East Berlin.

As if just thinking of her were some kind of beacon, he stared out at what little of East Berlin he could see through the gate, and felt a chill run through him. She was there, somewhere. She might be close by, for all he knew.

The guard stared at him as he approached the east-side checkpoint. The man's hard eyes flicked down to Cassidy's blue jeans, scanned his leather jacket, then lingered on his thick reddish-blond hair and sideburns. Sean had known he wouldn't be able to hide who he was. He was an Interpol agent, an investigator, not a spy. He spoke German, and rather well in spite of his brogue.

But he was as Irish a man as God had ever made.

The guard gestured for him to follow, then directed him to a building just beyond the watchtower that loomed above the wall. Already, there was a line of people waiting to pass through, and Sean was relieved. It wasn't just him. Most of them seemed to be Turkish migrant workers, and from the flowers and other gifts they carried, he suspected they were waiting to visit girlfriends in East Berlin.

While Cassidy waited, he filled out a customs declaration. Fifteen minutes later, a stone-faced functionary looked at him sternly through a window—the setup reminded Sean of a train station.

"Papiere, bitte," the humorless man said.

Cassidy sensed the burning eyes of the guards in the room on the back of his head, but he kept his attention on the man in front of him. He offered his passport, his international driver's license, identification that claimed him to be a reporter for the London *Times*, and a falsified invitation from one of the many bureaucratic agencies within the East German government to come and take a tour of East Berlin in order to disprove the horrible things the capitalist West had said about the city.

The man stared at the documents for a very long time.

Cassidy shifted his weight and didn't bother to try to hide his nervousness. If he'd actually been Seamus McArdle, as his papers identified him, he would have had every reason to be nervous.

The armed guards inside the building hadn't raised their weapons, nor had they seemed to pay any attention to Cassidy at all. Nevertheless, the barrels of their rifles seemed conveniently angled toward where Sean now stood.

Someone coughed behind him, and Cassidy twitched slightly. The door was open behind him, and Sean could smell someone cooking not far away. Something fried, which was no real surprise in Berlin. A small chill had crept into the air, and he felt it very keenly. He felt everything very keenly in those few moments. His heart beat loud enough to be a distraction.

"Sprechen Sie Deutsch?" the man with his papers asked, watching his face.

"Ja," he replied. *"Das ist nötig, nicht wahr?"*

The man nodded sagely. He'd merely told the man it was necessary for him to speak German in order to do his job. But it seemed to be enough, combined with the finely crafted false documents, to free him from their scrutiny, at least for now. He'd be shadowed at all times, and the *Polizei* would most certainly be looking into his "invitation." He had a few days, at best, before the *Stasi,* the DDR's answer to World War II's Gestapo, would start paying him extra-special attention. Then East Berlin would become a very inhospitable place for a certain Irishman. Even more so than usual.

Cassidy stood by calmly as his one small bag was searched meticulously. The guards didn't do the best of jobs because they didn't really expect to find anything. If he was a spy, he wasn't going to be stupid enough to carry weapons or any incriminating documentation in his bag.

Six minutes later, he had his back to the Berlin Wall, and was moving deeper into East Berlin. The Iron Curtain had been swept aside. It was disturbing to realize that none of the rules of existence familiar to him were of any use here. But, Cassidy thought, as he took note of the raggedly dressed woman who had already begun to tail him, it was also liberating.

The rules didn't apply anymore.

That could be very dangerous for him. But it could be dangerous for his quarry as well. And for anyone who got in his way.

Cassidy sat at a sticky table in the corner of a *Bierstube.* The raggedy woman who had been following him had waited outside the tavern until a stern-faced, bearded man had entered. Her departure was enough to identify her replacement, and

Cassidy studiously avoided looking at the stern man who drank beer and read the local newspaper by himself at the center of the room. It looked like the *Stasi* had taken an interest in him earlier than he'd expected.

When the barmaid arrived to ask if he wanted anything, he ordered a bowl of *Königinsuppe,* an odd stew of beef, sour cream, and almonds. Then he simply waited.

It wasn't until the barmaid was leaning over to clear the empty bowl that she whispered his name.

"*Herr* Cassidy."

Sean started to look up, but turned the movement into a long reach for his stein. The woman knew his real name. She might be his contact, or an East German agent trying to bait him into revealing his true intentions. If she was the latter, and she knew his real name, it wasn't likely he'd get out of East Berlin alive.

"*Gibt es ein FKK Strandbad in dieser Gegend?*" he asked suddenly, as if he'd just thought of it.

The waitress looked affronted, glared at him with an expression of disgust. "*Sind Sie von einem Rettungsdienst?*" she asked archly.

Cassidy smiled at the response. He couldn't help it. She had given the appropriate code phrase, confirming herself as his contact. Despite his smile, she scowled in disgust and grabbed his nearly empty stein, marched away to get him another.

When she returned, she didn't lean over nearly as far, keeping a look of annoyance on her face. Still, she managed to whisper to him quietly enough that even the couple at the next table could not have heard her.

"I've lost track of your packages. But your friend left Moscow yesterday," she said, in perfect English. "She favors fine hotels."

And that was all. The barmaid fled to the back of the bar as though Cassidy had insulted her yet again, and this time she did not return. He left his money on the table and rose from his chair. The stern-faced man who'd been put on his tail was good. He didn't even look up as Cassidy left.

When Sean exited the tavern, he saw the raggedy woman again out of the corner of his eye, across the street half a block away. He ignored her, and walked on. Time to find a hotel for himself, and begin tracing his target.

The stern-faced *Stasi* officer was called *Haifisch* by those he worked with. The shark. And Haifisch was no fool. He followed the barmaid into the back room of the tavern and saw her slip into the ladies' room. Several moments later, an absolutely putrid-smelling old woman came out, brushed past Haifisch without even glancing at him. The old woman muttered something nasty in German.

He waited nearly three minutes before going into the bathroom. There were no windows. No means of egress whatsoever, save for the door he'd just walked in, and yet the filthy little restroom was empty. His rage was matched only by his confusion as he burst from the bathroom, ignoring the stares of the tavern's patrons.

On the street in front of the tavern, he searched for the barmaid without any luck. The old, malodorous woman was also nowhere in sight. Haifisch snarled and returned to the tavern for another mug of beer. *Fräulein* Feuer would keep an eye on the spy for the moment. The barmaid, however, would have been a greater coup. Haifisch hated traitors above all else, and he would have liked to make the woman suffer before she confessed her treason, and the name of her co-conspirators.

Haifisch smiled at the thought, and hoped he'd get another chance.

Outside the tavern, an old man in rural peasant's clothes walked slowly away. But he was not German. He was not, actually, even a man. He had been both the barmaid and the smelly old woman only minutes earlier. He was Mystique. And Mystique was also searching for the Black Widow. If her own contacts couldn't find the KGB's dangerous little girl, Mystique hoped that Sean Cassidy could. She was determined to complete her mission, no matter what it took.

The marketplace in Karl Marx Allee roared with the voice of a thousand transactions. Bartering and theft were equally common. Items considered common in the West were often luxuries here, and so everything was sold at market. Some things, however, were sold out of sight of the general public, in the shadows of alleyways or behind stalls hung with woven cotton and wool.

Natasha Romanova was clad in simple, drab clothing common among locals. She moved through the marketplace gracefully, silently avoiding human contact despite the crush of people around her. A large man with white hair and a bulbous red nose spotted her, averted his gaze, and brushed hard against her anyway, obviously enjoying the feeling of her lithe body against his own.

As he apologized, he smiled at her, and put a firm hand on her shoulder. She was five feet, seven inches tall. Not a small girl, but thin and almost dainty-looking. At nineteen years old, she was far too young to be a widow already, but so she was. Her face looked even younger, she knew, and she might have been mistaken for as young as sixteen. Even fifteen, depending on the way she smiled or the cut of her hair. Such self-knowledge was important in the game of espionage.

The red-nosed man with his hand clamped on her shoulder saw only a delectable little treat he hoped to manhandle. His smile said as much, as did the way his tongue hung, like a panting dog's, between his slightly open teeth.

But he was looking at her body. At the alabaster flesh of her face. When his gaze locked on her eyes, the big man's smile vanished as if it had been burned from his face. She knew what he saw there: a frozen, barren landscape more deadly than

Siberia. It was her soul. Once, there had been love and life there. Now it was a hard place, cold and dead as her heart, ever since her Alexi had been taken from her. It was his death that led her to work with the KGB, to become the Black Widow.

The red-nosed man apologized again, and stumbled backward, unwilling to turn his back on the woman with death in her eyes. He nearly fell as he collided with a merchant's cart loaded with rough, multicolored linens.

As quickly as he disappeared, he was forgotten. The Widow made her way through the marketplace, then walked along Karl Marx Allee until she came to Alexanderplatz, a square filled with hotels, shops, and flats that had been built up in the past decades as East Berlin's trade and tourist center. Not far from Alexanderplatz, she found the mouth of a dark, cobblestoned alleyway. She counted the windows on the top floor of each building to her left. At seventeen, she went to the opposite side of the alley and dropped down into a stairwell, huddled down like some poor wretch who made a home of garbage.

She sat and waited for her target to emerge. Several hours passed before a middle-aged man in a tattered gray jacket and cap came out of the building. He glanced from side to side, missing Natasha entirely, and then began to walk down the alley in the opposite direction from the marketplace.

The Widow followed.

"His name is Grigorii Zhevakov," her KGB controller had told her. *"He was never a very good agent. But his wife, Katrina . . . she was one of our best. She would do anything to fulfill a mission. It's Katrina you must be careful of. Doubtless she will have the disk."*

Scientists. That was the cover the Zhevakovs had used in their real life. But it had been a thin cover at best. They were spies, just as she was. Now they were hoping to defect to the United States, and they had stolen a data disk vital to the security of the Soviet Union to present to the Americans as proof of their good intentions. Natasha had no idea what was on that disk, but it wasn't her business to know. She had a job to do, that was all that mattered.

The Black Widow was going to make certain the Zhevakovs never set foot on American soil.

She set off after Grigorii, knowing full well that his love and loyalty would be the things that destroyed his marriage. Grigorii would lead the Widow to Katrina, or eventually Katrina would meet up with her husband back here in this alley. Natasha would retrieve the disk, and then, if the traitorous couple did not force her to take their lives, she would see that they were returned to the Soviet Union, where they would most surely be made to pay for their duplicity.

Defection. It was something she found hard to understand. It would be like turning away from one's own family, from one's own mother. Certainly, there was an allure to the capitalist West, the glitter and glamour, the forbidden fruit of selfishness and depravity. But with all that Mother Russia, and her KGB superiors, had done for the Black Widow, she could feel only a righteous fury toward those weak-willed souls who would fall to the temptations of capitalism.

Fury, and a bit of pity as well.

But pity would not keep her from punishing the betrayers.

The Widow followed Grigorii Zhevakov, ignoring the appreciative glances of men she passed. After Alexi's death, she had no more interest in love or passion, except where it served her KGB masters.

It was a commercial flight, following a preordained path southeast across East German airspace on its way to Vienna. Or at least, that's what the East Germans would think it was. In truth, it was flying unusually low for a commercial flight, something that would have been attributed to instrumentation malfunction if they were questioned. They weren't.

But there were only five passengers on this flight, and four of them weren't going to be staying onboard all the way to Vienna.

Wolverine stood in the open hatch and watched the world pass by miles below. He turned to make certain Team X was ready for the drop. Silver Fox was right behind him, her face unreadable as always. Well, almost always. You knew what was on Fox's mind when she was ticked off. Other than that, she kept her own counsel.

Maverick's face didn't give much away, but it didn't have to. He was more than happy to supply his teammates with his opinion. He was a great soldier, and Logan was always happy to have North at his back, but Maverick was a bit too holy for his tastes. The boy was trying too hard to get into heaven. When you worked the spy game, pulled black ops in countries where nobody'd seen God in years, Logan figured it was a bit of a handicap to have a conscience.

North would bear watching, then, as always. He'd never fouled up an op before, but Wolverine could sense it coming.

Then there was Sabretooth. Creed couldn't hide a thing. He loved this gig, Logan knew. Plenty of opportunity to kill people. Wolverine was no innocent. Killing came with the job. But he didn't take lives unless it was absolutely necessary, and Creed had a habit of purposely putting the team into a position where killing became the only answer.

They had to pull together if this mission was going to come off smoothly. They'd done it before, of course, but it was getting more and more difficult, the divisions among them too broad.

Silver Fox leaned forward, and Logan moved aside to let her look out the hatch. But it wasn't the view she wanted. He was surprised when he felt her lips touch his own, dry from the air rushing into the plane. Wolverine smiled, but Silver Fox didn't bother. It was odd, he thought. He did believe she loved him, and yet she never seemed all that impressed with love in general. Or maybe she just didn't trust love.

Hell, why trust at all—in anything, or anyone? They were in a business that made you realize trust was nothing but foolishness, or fear of the truth, or both.

"What do you think about this op?" Fox asked him.

Logan blinked, stared at her through his goggles. He couldn't make out the deep brown of her eyes past the plastic in front of his face, and the goggles she also wore. He longed for it, that earthy brown that just sucked him up and brought him home to the mountain woods he loved so dearly.

How could he love someone who kept so much of herself inside? But then, he knew he wasn't much different. Still, like a lot of things, like Team X itself, he figured time would take its toll.

"What're you askin', Fox?" he replied. "Seems on the up-and-up. Pretty simple, actually, if you skip the whole part about it bein' nearly suicide. In and out, do the job, it's Miller time. What's confusin' you?"

"Nothing's ever simple, Logan," she explained. "I always wonder who we're really working for, you know?"

Logan smiled. "They don't call it black ops for nothin', darlin'," he said.

"I don't mind the dirty work," Fox said in a low voice. "I live for it. And I'll take orders like a good little soldier because that's the only thing I can believe in. It'd just be nice to know for sure if we really are the good guys."

"Can't say for certain there are any more good guys, Fox," Logan replied. "Just us and them."

"I won't believe that," she argued.

"Then you're in the wrong business, babe," Wolverine growled.

Silver Fox seemed as though she was about to say something else, but the cockpit door opened and John Wraith emerged. He'd been up in front talking with the pilot. His appearance meant they were over their target area. Wraith was a teleporter, and a powerful one, but there were limits to what he could do. Sure, he'd jumped half a dozen people thousands of miles in one 'port before. But it put him in a world of hurt to do it. So teleportation, when possible, was left for extraction.

Incursion was up to Team X.

"Ten seconds!" Wraith called over the roar from the open hatch. "Everybody set?"

Team X signaled thumbs-up to their controller. The plans for dropoff and pickup had long since been worked out. It was time to jump. No pep talks from Wraith. It wasn't his style. He did the job. As long as he kept on doing it, that was good enough for Wolverine. But Logan didn't have any real faith in John Wraith, codename: Kestrel. Nope. Codename: Wolverine had faith only in himself.

Falling.
  What a rush.

The ground barreled up at them and the wind tore the breath from Logan's lungs. He had a supply pack on his back, weapons and disguises. The black jumpsuits Team X usually wore were good enough for jumping out of planes, but once on the ground, they'd need to start doing the spy thing.

He adjusted his goggles, watched the ground rising up toward him as if the whole world were on the attack. It was a HALO—high altitude, low open—drop over land, which was never a good idea. They wouldn't open their chutes until they were dangerously close to the ground. No room for foul-ups.

Wolverine pulled the ripcord. Instantly, the chute hauled him up short and hard, and he held his breath a moment. Then he was sailing down with the dark chute wide open, scanning the ground, and praying nobody had seen them. Nobody who would take notice.

He glanced around and made certain the others had their chutes open. He couldn't hear anything but the air ripping past him. A forest range opened up just ahead of them, and Wolverine angled his chute as close to the tree line as he dared.

The ground came up fast. He hit, buckled, and rolled. Immediately, he was up, gathering his chute, and dragging it toward the woods. The others did the same and they buried the chutes quickly in a shallow hole.

"No turning back now, kiddies," Creed said gleefully, his savage grin enough to give away his mood.

"Stick to the mission agenda, Sabretooth," Wolverine said.

"Whatever ya say, runt," Creed replied.

It wasn't long before they had covered their jumpsuits with the rough linen clothing common to the East German countryside. For Creed and Logan, who spoke a little German, and for North, who had grown up in East Germany and spoke the language fluently, it was enough. Silver Fox needed something more. But with the appropriate attire and a little strategic makeup, it wasn't difficult to disguise her as a gypsy woman. The disguise wouldn't hold up under intense scrutiny, but it would serve their purposes.

If not, there'd be trouble.

But then, Logan thought, there was bound to be trouble on this op anyway. Just the way Creed was acting, and Silver Fox starting to show some kind of twisted morality, the mission had been off from the start.

They'd been walking for more than an hour, the countryside quickly giving way to the spillover from East Berlin, the homes of those who would not deign to live within the city limits, including the higher-ups in the SED—East Germany's communist ruling party. They were men and women of power who were, themselves, little more than puppet soldiers to a puppet government whose true master was the Soviet Union.

With East Berlin still at least ten miles ahead, they passed a vast, secluded estate whose gates were more cosmetic than secure.

"This'll do," Logan said. "Creed. Fox. Go in and get us a car. Quietly. And make sure it don't have any identifiable markings. Maverick and me'll make sure you don't get any surprise visitors."

Creed showed his fangs in a nasty little smile and disappeared over the fence. Silver Fox followed in silence. Logan went to the edge of the fence and hunkered down so that he wouldn't be conspicuously visible from the road.

Maverick stood in the center of the dusty road, staring at him.

"North," Logan growled. "You got head trauma, kid? Get some cover."

"Have you lost your mind?" Maverick asked, too loud, and stalked across the road to drop down into the brush by the gate with Wolverine.

"You lost yours?" Logan drawled. "You want to blow this op?"

They stared at one another. Their peasant clothing did not hide the fact that they were dangerous men anywhere near as well as it did the weapons they each had hidden amongst their clothes.

"You have a problem, Maverick?" Wolverine asked.

"We could have gone for that car," North replied bitterly. "You didn't have to send those two."

It was what Logan had expected. Maverick was angry, and it wasn't because he was jealous, that he actually wanted to go for the car. No, Logan knew just what was bothering David North.

"In case you didn't notice, kid, we're in the middle of a covert operation, here," Wolverine said. "For this op, at least, I'm field command. Let's just get in and out of communist country as fast as we can."

But Maverick wasn't about to give up.

"Logan, you know what's happening up there right now!" he snapped, gesturing toward the mansion. "You don't think Creed and Fox are going to just go up and ask to borrow a car, right? You and I, we might have taken any witnesses down, bound and gagged them and put them in the wine cellar or something. That isn't what Creed's going to do."

Wolverine didn't reply at first. Maverick's words were echoed by the complaints of his own conscience. But the op was the most important thing. He hoped Creed wouldn't waste time killing anyone he didn't have to kill, but part of him knew that sending Creed and Fox would be more expedient simply because of what they would do to witnesses. They didn't have time to play nice.

Maverick stared at Logan, waiting for answer. He didn't have one. Two minutes later, a Mercedes rolled silently down the estate's drive, motor off. Wolverine felt relief wash over him. If they hadn't turned the engine on, that meant they had left somebody alive inside the house. Maybe they hadn't killed anyone at all.

It was a nice thought. And just to make sure he kept it, Wolverine chose not to ask.

Once they had driven into the pollution-blanketed, industrialized core of East Berlin, they turned onto a side street and abandoned the car—it was a little too nice a ride to be driven by a bunch of folks dressed like common laborers.

With the heightened senses that were part of his genetic mutation, Logan could not escape the horrible chemical smog that clogged the air. Pavement and cobblestone and cement alike were all coated with a layer of grime that might never come off. Certainly not unless East Berlin underwent radical changes.

They had been fortunate on the road. While they had passed plenty of *Volksarmee* units, none paid much attention to them. But Logan suspected things would be a little more intense in the city proper. And he'd been right. *Volksarmee* soldiers goose-stepped along Unter der Linden and in Alexanderplatz. *Kampfgruppen*—citizens who played soldier part-time— marched in formation dressed in their gray, featureless drone uniforms. But Team X was already on foot, and beneath the notice of soldiers with a job to do, as long as they stayed inconspicuous, and as long as no *Stasi* officers got a good look at them.

The facet of East Berlin that Wolverine found most disturbing was the almost surreal emptiness of the place. Other than the marketplace and the squares where the military displayed their marching prowess, East Berlin seemed nearly a ghost town. In a sense, he knew, that was true. The city was severely underpopulated. Team X tried to stick as much as possible to areas where civilians did congregate.

The sky was overcast, and it seemed to threaten rain, something Logan prayed would not happen. It was enough that the smog was damp and heavy, but for it to fall in poison rain from the sky would disgust him even more. In the gray streets of East Berlin, he longed for the freedom of the Canadian wild more than ever.

"Tavern ahead," Creed grunted in German. "That our goal?"

"No. We still have a few blocks to go," Logan replied in the same language. "It's a nice restaurant called the Bucharest. Gonna be hard not to draw attention to ourselves, but we'll work it out."

Silver Fox slipped up beside him and grabbed his hand, gave it a lover's squeeze. But he knew there was nothing romantic in her touch. It was unlike her, and she used that to draw his attention to the interior of the tavern's entrance, where two *Stasi* officers were shouting at a man, presumably the proprietor. Wolverine strained to listen.

There had been a murder, apparently. A barmaid. Nobody knew what had happened, but that wasn't good enough for the *Stasi*.

For a moment, one of the officers glanced their way. Wolverine didn't know if it was paranoia, but the man's gaze seemed to linger on Silver Fox. He hoped it was only lechery and not suspicion.

"We should just kill them," Creed whispered in German. "If they've spotted us, they might just sit tight until they can call out some help from their buddies."

"Shut up, Victor," North snapped. "Just keep walking."

Logan strained to hear more of the officers' shouted words, the tavern keeper's plaintive excuses. He wanted to know why the *Stasi* were here and not the police. But they didn't dare slow down to pay more attention. In moments, they had passed the tavern and the officers hadn't given them a second glance, despite the one's lingering look at Fox.

Logan breathed easier.

Now if they could just find the restaurant where they were supposed to meet their contact, they could get on with the mission and get home.

Home. With the exception of the Canadian wilderness, Logan knew he didn't really have a home. Truth be told, the Agency was all the home he could lay claim to—Team X the only family. Which meant that no matter what his misgivings about this op, he would do whatever it took to complete their mission and get everybody back alive.

Even Creed.

Wolverine would protect Sabretooth with his life if it came down to that. As far as he was concerned, if Creed ever needed killing, it'd be Logan himself who would do the job.

NOW

I still don't get it, Logan," Mystique said angrily.

For once, it seemed like the ice queen had had her feathers ruffled. Wolverine was glad. It made her seem more human. She wasn't scared, exactly. He wouldn't have expected that of her. But she was anxious and annoyed. Raven Darkhölme clearly didn't like being on the receiving end of a covert operation—didn't like being a target.

Logan tipped his coffee mug up, took a long drink, and completely ignored her. They were barely allies, as far as he was concerned. He didn't like what was happening any more than she did, but he did enjoy seeing her sweat.

"Wolverine!" Mystique snapped in frustration.

"Good coffee, Ivan," Logan drawled, forcing himself not to smile.

A lot of people could be dead, including a few that Logan thought of as friends. All but Creed, actually. And if he had a choice, he'd prefer to kill Creed himself, if it came to that. Probably should have done it a long time ago, he thought. If he was the same man who'd run with Team X those years ago, he surely would have.

But the X-Men had a little problem with indiscriminate killing. Killing of any kind, actually, unless it came down to saving your own life. It had kind of rubbed off on Wolverine. Sometimes he wished he hadn't changed; sometimes he felt it would be easier.

Thing was, nobody ever said life was supposed to be easy. Killing and dying and lying and hiding . . . those were the easiest things in the world. Being out in the world and trying to do the right thing, that was hard. He would have liked to explain it to Mystique, but he didn't think she'd ever understand.

Besides, he was no preacher. He'd leave that to the X-Men's founder and mentor, Professor Charles Xavier.

"Thank you," Ivan said, but his response was half-hearted. He was being eaten up inside by the idea that something might have happened to Natasha. "What are we going to do, Logan? You know the connection behind all of these . . . abductions, but you have no idea who would have any interest in such a huge effort at vengeance. In fact, we don't even know that's what it's about. Wasn't there anyone else involved in that mission?"

Wolverine's eyes lit up.

Mystique looked surprised, stared at him.

"What?" she asked finally.

Logan shook his head. "John Wraith," he said. "He was our extraction man, and he still works for the government, far as I know."

"Do you think he'll have answers for us?" Mystique asked.

"Let's find out," Logan snarled. "First, we gotta find him. We need access to top-secret government files. The kind o' things that can't be hacked into from your average PC."

"S.H.I.E.L.D.," Mystique said.

"Huh?"

"There's a S.H.I.E.L.D. base in midtown, under the Viacom building," she explained. "Even if they don't have direct access to the files, we'll be able to hack them easily from there. The priority security system is already bypassed by S.H.I.E.L.D.'s computers. If we can get in there, I can find your pal Wraith for you."

Wolverine had logged a lot of time in New York City over the years. Granted, his memory had been played with so often, and so drastically, that a lot of things were lost to him forever. And some of what he remembered, he couldn't really trust. But he knew Manhattan Island almost as well as he knew the wilds of Canada.

Both were home. They were just different kinds of wilderness.

Times Square had once seemed so majestic to him. The center of the world, you'd think, at least for the minutes you spent there. One moment in Times Square he would never forget was the euphoric celebration, the wave of relief and good feeling and pure, undiluted joy that swept through the city when it was announced that the war in Europe was over.

In moments, the streets were filled with people weeping and laughing. Men who would have crossed the street to avoid him clapped him on the back and called him brother. Women who would have tittered nervously if he caught their eye kissed him full on the mouth in the middle of a crowd, in a day when such things were just not done.

He'd never forget it. No matter what had been done to his mind.

But Times Square didn't seem like the center of the world anymore. Nor was it the majestic symbol of America it had once been. It had gone through extraordinary changes over the years. Most of them for the worse. For a long spell, Times Square had been a place to be avoided if you valued your wallet and your safety.

They finally cleaned it up, of course. It would never be what it once was. It was still purely New York, and he was fond of it for that alone. But now it was garish and cold, the ultimate outdoor mall.

In spite of the situation, Logan smiled at the thought. He wondered if Jubilee had been down in Times Square at all since the big renovation. She would have loved it. Maybe, if the world ever allowed them a day off, he'd drag her down from Massachusetts and get her reacquainted with the Big Apple.

Listen to me, he thought. Planning an excursion into the city like some kind of suburban uncle didn't exactly match the covert operative who went into East Berlin all those years ago. Neither did his relationship with Jubilee, which he'd always thought of as mentor-student. Father-daughter, though, wouldn't have been too far off the mark.

"This one," Mystique said.

She had changed again, back into the chocolate-eyed woman she'd been in the White Horse earlier. Wolverine wasn't complaining. The look was striking. His only problem was that it might be too striking. The last thing they needed right now was to draw attention to themselves.

They stood on the east side of Times Square, looking west at 1515 Broadway: an enormous office building that comprised the entire block between Forty-fourth and Forty-fifth Streets. It housed a number of major corporations, including Viacom. If they only knew what was beneath their feet.

"You sure?" Logan asked.

"Very," Mystique said, and that was all.

"How do you want to play this? I don't want any S.H.I.E.L.D. agents gettin' hurt," Logan cautioned her. "Nick Fury would never let me beat him at cards again."

"Nobody's going to question you, Wolverine," she said sweetly. "You'll be with me."

"What, you gonna tell me you're a S.H.I.E.L.D. agent now?"

"Not exactly," Mystique said.

She turned and walked away from him, turned the corner, and started east on Forty-fourth. The second storefront down was a deli, and Mystique ducked into it. A few seconds later, a tall, burly man emerged. He had stubble on his chin and a newly unwrapped cigar in his mouth. There was white in the hair at his temples, and a patch over his left eye.

Not exactly, Mystique had said. Wolverine understood now. Why take the chance of shapeshifting into some kind of low-ranking S.H.I.E.L.D. agent when you can take the appearance of the agency's director? Nobody was going to question Logan showing up with Nick Fury. It sure wouldn't be the first time Wolverine worked with S.H.I.E.L.D. In fact, it made him feel a little guilty to use his association with Fury to pull one over on his people.

But only a little.

"Too bad we couldn't just go to Fury directly," Mystique/Fury said, not bothering to actually light the cigar. Her gravelly voice was a perfect reproduction of Fury's own. "You don't think he'd tell you what you want to know?"

Logan considered the question carefully. A cabbie leaned on the horn as they crossed toward 1515 Broadway, but rather than slowing, the driver sped up and swerved around them. Wolverine and Mystique kept walking. Didn't much matter if they drew attention to themselves now.

"Nick's a friend," Logan finally replied. "But he's also director of a UN-sanctioned espionage and antiterrorist operation. We could go to Fury directly, and maybe we'd get what we want."

"But?" Mystique asked as they passed through the revolving doors at the southern entrance to the building.

"I got two reservations," Wolverine explained.

They stepped on the escalator and let it pull them up toward the building's lobby.

"First, who knows if he'd have easy clearance for the information?" Logan said. "Nick isn't going to break into federal computer systems he doesn't have clearance for. Not on somethin' like this. Second, there's no guarantee Nick'd tell me what I want to know. Instead, he's likely to tell me what he thinks I need to know. The difference could get us killed."

Mystique only nodded, and Wolverine was glad he didn't have to explain any more. He didn't really know why he had bothered to explain to her at all. Perhaps it was only because she would understand the delicate nature of relationships in their business. She had gone from spy to criminal and sometime terrorist, but she had to have feelings of her own. She had to know that most of the time, it would be easier not to have them. No friends. No lovers. Just the job.

Once upon a time, Wolverine had actually bought into that belief, in spite of his love for Silver Fox. But the X-Men had changed his mind, had taught him to expect more from life—taught him that nobody was beyond redemption.

With that thought, he stared at the back of Nick Fury's head—not Fury's head, but Mystique's—and wondered what it would take to redeem a woman so gloriously amoral.

Together they crossed the lobby, walked down the narrow passage between elevator banks, and turned a corner to the alcove where the service elevators were. Nobody looked at them oddly as "Fury" pressed the elevator call button.

When the elevator arrived, they stepped inside. The doors slid shut and Mystique reached out with Nick Fury's hand and pressed "B" for basement. She allowed her finger to linger on the button for several seconds as the elevator started to move. The button erupted with light, scanning the print from her finger, taking DNA samples, maybe, from the oils on the skin.

"Voiceprint analysis beginning. Identify," crackled electronically over a small speaker in the ceiling.

"Fury, Nicholas J.," Mystique said. "And Logan, no other initial. My guest."

The elevator slowed to a crawl. On the row of numbers above the elevator doors, the "B" lit up. But the doors didn't open at the basement level. Several seconds ticked by, during which Wolverine hoped it wasn't going to turn ugly. He didn't want it to play out that way, didn't want to hurt any of Fury's agents.

There were several loud thumps and the sound of gears grinding, and then the elevator seemed to simply let go, dropping into a nauseating free fall. It lasted only a few seconds, during which they must have descended at least fifty feet, perhaps twice that distance.

The doors slid open. Wolverine tensed for a confrontation. But their only greeting party seemed to be an officious, twenty-something college girl, fresh out of S.H.I.E.L.D. training, who must have been an extraordinary student if she was an officer already. The woman's hair was cropped in an attractive yet severe cut, and her eyeglasses added to the stern quality of her face. But she positively beamed at their arrival.

"Colonel Fury!" she said happily, and saluted. "I'm Lieutenant Clancy, sir. Lisa Clancy. You're a little ahead of schedule, but we're almost ready for you. Let me just say how pleased we all are to have you working out of our location this week. If there's anything I can do . . ."

Wolverine's eyes widened. This kid hadn't even noticed him, just as he'd suspected. He was with Fury, that was enough. But from what she'd said, Fury was supposed to be coming here anyway. Which would not be good. Not at all.

"There is somethin' you can do, Lieutenant," Mystique snapped. "You can quit your yammerin' for a minute, and let me get down to business."

The smile seemed to tumble from the woman's face.

"Yes, sir. I'm sorry, Colonel, I was only . . ."

"Yeah, I'm early," Mystique replied gruffly, playing up the role of Fury to the hilt. "How early am I, Clancy?"

"Um, nearly an hour, sir," she replied uncertainly. "But we are ready for you, Colonel. As you requested, we've got the X-317 flight suit ready for testing, and plenty of space available for you to try it out on the premises. We're—"

"Clancy."

"Yes, Colonel?"

"Enough."

"Yes, Colonel."

"Now, listen carefully. I've got a crisis on my hands, top priority and eyes-only clearance. I need a secure room with computer access and I need it right now."

"Yes sir!" Clancy snapped in military style. "Right away, sir!"

She led them silently down a long hallway. "Fury's" presence was electrifying to every agent they passed. Heads popped out of offices and up from cubicles. Many saluted; others just stared.

"This is the office we've set up for you, Colonel," Lieutenant Clancy said. "If there's anything else you'll need, of course . . ."

"Thank you, Lieutenant, that will be all," the false Fury said, not even bothering to face Clancy while dismissing her.

"Yes, sir," Clancy replied immediately.

But Wolverine couldn't help noticing the combination of hurt surprise and annoyance on her face. Like most every new agent coming into S.H.I.E.L.D., the young woman probably thought of Nick Fury as a hero, a legend of sorts. Maybe even her idol, if this was really what she wanted to do. Mystique had squashed that image but good.

Clancy turned and strutted away, and with his enhanced hearing, Logan could not miss the word she muttered under her breath.

"Jerk."

Wolverine frowned. He hoped this little stunt wouldn't burn any bridges with Fury, though the two of them had gone through worse. At best, though, he was going to have a lot of explaining to do the next time he ran into his old comrade. For now, they just had to concentrate on getting out of there before the colonel arrived. They had less than an hour.

Mystique dropped her guise as soon as the door was closed. She seemed relieved to slip back into the red-haired, blue-skinned appearance that Wolverine had always thought of as her natural form. And, given the fact that his old buddy Nightcrawler, who also had blue skin, was Mystique's son . . . well, it only made sense that this would be her true face. But, then, there was really no way to know.

The office was sizable, and decorated to please Fury. Instead of the cold white box of plastic and metal that was sort of par for the course at the close of the millennium, the room had been outfitted to appeal to an older sensibility. Nick Fury had fought in World War II. Something called the Infinity Formula had slowed his aging process, so he was really an old man with a much younger man's body. Wolverine could relate.

He was pretty comfortable in the office himself.

The walls were painted an off-white, but there was real carved woodwork at their tops and bottoms, and around the doorframe. There were bookshelves built into one side, a huge cherrywood desk, and a high-backed, burgundy leather chair that must have come from an antique store.

The computer looked out of place. Wolverine remembered when entire banks of computer equipment, enough to fill the entire room, would have been needed to perform the same functions, if that, of the little unit on Fury's desk in his little home away from home.

"Nice office," he said.

Mystique didn't bother with a response. She slid into Fury's chair and turned the computer on. In seconds, she had the fibre-optic dataline running, searching S.H.I.E.L.D.'s own database until she gained access to the Department of Defense computer systems.

"Easy enough," Wolverine observed.

He reached for a wooden chest on Fury's desk and was pleased to discover it was exactly what he'd hoped: a cigar box. He pulled an expensive Cuban from the box, popped a claw to slice off its end, then used a bronze lighter to set it aflame. Mystique pulled her eyes away from the screen for a moment to stare at him.

"That's a disgusting habit," she said. She had already tossed the cheap cigar purchased in the deli into Fury's wastebasket.

"So's terrorism, but I ain't said a word to you since we started on this little mission, now have I?"

Mystique's eyes narrowed, but she turned silently back to the computer. On the screen, the DOD system was demanding a password. Mystique sat and stared at it for several minutes, and Wolverine began to grow anxious. Nick Fury was never late. Early, on the other hand, was entirely possible.

"Raven, we ain't got the time to . . ."

"If I enter the wrong password, not only will the system shut us out, but it will trace us back here immediately. I don't care if they think Fury's hacking their files, but we need that information," she explained.

"I thought you were hot stuff with this kinda thing," Logan grumbled. "Ain't there some way you can just bypass this stuff entirely?"

She nodded. "But it might take a while."

"Just do it."

Mystique bent her head slightly and focused completely on the computer. So completely, Wolverine thought, that she had dropped her guard in his presence for the first time. Ever. Probably the last, too. She knew as well as he did that just because they were working together, it didn't put them on the same side. In fact, right about now they were walking the fence together. That was all.

"It's odd, isn't it?" Mystique asked suddenly.

Wolverine puffed on his cigar. "What is?"

"Or at least, ironic," she added. "I know we're really not doing this for him, but I never thought I'd see the day that you went out of your way to save Victor Creed's life."

"You're right," Logan grunted. "We ain't doin' it for Creed. Sabretooth ain't on my list o' people I owe favors to. Neither are you, come to think of it."

"But he used to be your partner," Mystique reminded him.

"Yeah," Wolverine admitted. "An' he used to be your boyfriend, or whatever it was you two were to each other. But that was a long time ago, for all of us."

Mystique smiled. "Oh, I don't know. It wasn't so long ago I don't remember that you weren't always as righteous and upstanding as you are now. Your friends in the X-Men wouldn't have even recognized you back then, Logan."

"Sure they would. At least, those that knew me when I first joined the team. It's only since then that I started actin' like a grown-up. You might try it sometime, Mystique."

"We've all changed, Logan. You're not the only one," she said, turning back to the computer screen. "I know what you think of me. For the most part, you're right. But in the years since we first met, I've come to know what it's like to care about people and then lose them. There are a lot of things I regret, a lot of things I've done that I wouldn't do today."

Wolverine was quiet for a moment, watching her, her blue skin and yellow eyes lit by the glow of the computer.

"Maybe you have changed at that, Mystique," Wolverine said. "But I'm not gonna take any bets about how much. No offense."

"None taken," she said, and smiled again, this time without looking up. "In fact, we've all changed. All of us involved in this thing, anyway. Maverick's nowhere near as naïve as he was back then. Cassidy's becoming a responsible old man, a role model, which is pretty funny actually. The Widow smartened up, too. Got a life and a philosophy of her own."

"We haven't all changed," Wolverine replied grimly. "Silver Fox is dead. Creed is more bloodthirsty than ever, no matter what his government keepers want anyone else to think. Then there's Wraith."

"I guess we'll see about Wraith," Mystique said.

"Yeah," Logan agreed. "We'll see. I'll tell you this much, though. Wraith was our only direct contact with the Agency. Plausible deniability, they called it. They gave Wraith orders to make somethin' happen, didn't tell him how to go about it. They knew about Team X, o' course, but Wraith never talked about us with the Agency—they couldn't be held responsible for what they didn't know.

"I didn't much trust Wraith back then, and I don't even know him now. But he was always good at one thing in particular."

"What was that?"

"Following orders," Logan told her. "John Wraith was a good little soldier. Kinda like Lieutenant Calley's men."

Mystique grimaced. She got the message. Even the hardest-hearted of human beings would be appalled at the reference. A U.S. Army officer had ordered his men to line up more than four hundred Vietnamese in the village of My Lai—mostly old people, women and children—and to execute them all. And they'd followed his orders to the letter.

Good soldiers.

Wolverine trusted Wraith to do exactly what his superiors told him. Anything beyond that . . . well, who knew, maybe the man had changed like the rest of them. Maybe not.

Logan glanced at the clock often over the next fifteen minutes. Every so often, Mystique would curse under her breath. The cigar smoke got pretty thick with the door closed, and Logan wanted Mystique to be able to concentrate, so he put it out. But not before he grabbed two more and put them in the inside pocket of his battered leather jacket.

Mystique grunted, leaned back, slapped the desk on either side of the computer.

"In," she announced.

Wolverine crouched next to her. "Run the search for John Wraith."

She typed the name in and clicked on the search icon. The computer started running, but seemed slow to Logan.

"If anyone can help us figure out who's behind this whole thing, it'll be him," he said idly. "He would have known a lot more about the mission than anyone on the team."

"Yeah," Mystique replied. "You were just following orders."

Wolverine glared at her, a little bit of rage igniting within him. But it was directed at himself just as much as it was at Mystique. Maybe more.

"Nothing," she announced.

"Try codename: Kestrel," he said quickly.

She typed it in. The answer came up in seconds.

"Got him," Mystique said. "Address is in D.C."

That was when the alarms went off. Wolverine glanced at Mystique, but she was already changing, morphing back into

Nick Fury. The alarm could have been anything: a real emergency, a drill, the Department of Defense calling to complain about S.H.I.E.L.D. hacking their computers.

It could have been anything. But it was the worst thing.

Logan pulled open the door and heard the ratcheting sound of more than a dozen S.H.I.E.L.D.-issue sidearms being cocked. There were a pair of plasma rifles as well, one of which was being held by Lieutenant Clancy, who stood just in front of the door and held the barrel of her weapon inches from Wolverine's forehead. Behind him, Mystique froze.

"Not another move, little man," Clancy growled.

Wolverine didn't move, but not because of Clancy. She had spunk, and he had to respect that. But that wasn't the reason he had a hard time deciding what his next move would be.

No, that reason wore an eyepatch and smoked a cigar, and stood at the center of the line of S.H.I.E.L.D. agents now holding weapons trained on Wolverine and Mystique. Fury didn't even bother drawing a weapon of his own.

"Hello, Nick," Wolverine said.

"Logan," Fury replied, by way of greeting, then his eyes flicked over Wolverine's shoulders to glance at his doppelgänger—Mystique—before returning to stare at Logan. "Take it that ain't a Life Model Decoy back there?"

"Nope."

"Guess you had some business you didn't think I'd want to help out with?" Fury asked.

"Yep," Wolverine agreed.

"Care to tell me what it was all about?"

"Nope."

"You know I've got to hold you until you explain yourselves, you and Ms. Darkhölme, that is?" Fury noted.

Behind Wolverine, Mystique shapeshifted back into her own body. Why not? Fury had already guessed it was her.

"Can't let you do that, Nick," Logan said, truly sorry. "I got some business to take care of that won't wait. Now, you wanna sit tight for a few days, you know I'll be back, and then we'll work it out over a game o' blackjack. Seems to me you still owe me about five hundred from our last game."

"Four seventy-five," Fury corrected. "And you know I can't do that, Logan. It'd be an invitation to my other card-playin' pals to pop in for a visit any time they like. I take it you stole some of my cigars, too. I'll just deduct those from my debt, if you don't mind."

"Not at all," Logan agreed.

There was a pause before Fury said, "Take them into custody."

Snikt. Wolverine moved fast, claws slashing the barrel of Clancy's gun to ribbons.

Then he was falling, throwing himself back through the door as bullets whipped past above him. Mystique forced the door closed behind him, and Wolverine drove the desk against it with all his strength. Bullets slammed harmlessly into the outer wall—impenetrable, of course.

But a couple of blasts from a plasma rifle and it would all be over with.

"What now?" she asked.

Logan didn't even answer. He moved to the back wall of Fury's office and started slashing with his claws. Three seconds later, they had a ragged back door that hadn't been there before. They emerged into a hallway juncture, at the cross of a T, and on either side, they could hear the pounding of feet as the agents came running. Straight ahead was their only option.

They ran. Unarmed, it was their only choice. Plus, Logan had no interest in hurting any of Fury's troops, and Mystique wasn't about to do it with Logan standing by. Maybe she had changed, he thought. At least a little.

Just before the pack of agents on their trail would have rounded the corner behind them and opened fire, they passed a pair of huge white double doors with LAB: AUTHORIZED PERSON-NEL ONLY stenciled on the outside. He grabbed Mystique by the arm and kicked the door open.

"You're Fury," he told her.

A pair of scientists, undisturbed by the alarms, were working diligently on what looked like a back brace—or would have, if it weren't for the twin cones jutting from the back of the thing. There was a heavy jumpsuit stretched out on a table, with a pair of gloves and boots on top.

"C-C-Colonel Fury!" one of them stammered. And then, as if finally noticing the alarms: "What's happening, sir? Are we under attack?"

"It's a drill, Doc," Mystique replied. "Is that what I think it is?"

"Yes, sir!" the other scientist snapped. "The X-317 is ready for you, sir. We've just finished calibrations. It isn't just a pack, you know, sir. The suit itself will protect you from the elements, and from any engine flare that . . ."

Wolverine grabbed the thing that looked like a brace and snapped it together around his chest and shoulders. The rockets on his back weighed almost nothing.

"Sir? What's . . ."

"How do you operate it?" Mystique/Fury asked.

"The gloves, sir. If you'll give us a moment to explain . . ."

But Wolverine was already putting on the gloves.

"And the exit?" the false Fury demanded.

One of the scientists walked to the wall and pressed a button. A portion of the ceiling in the far corner slid aside immediately.

"It will take you up to the subway tunnels, Colonel. But this is most irregular. The X-317 isn't safe without the flight suit, and . . ."

They ran for the opening in the ceiling, Logan glancing down at the straps across his chest for some clue how to turn the thing on. Behind them, the doors slammed open and the scientists shrieked like children.

Mystique was herself again as Wolverine slid his arms around her and held on tight. He felt something inside the right glove, and he squeezed it. Bullets ripped the air around them even as the rockets erupted into life on his back, and they blasted off the ground at dizzying speed.

The entire way up through the exit tube, Wolverine was roaring in pain as the rockets burned the flesh right off his back. The moment they burst up into the subway tunnel, he dropped Mystique and squeezed his fist together again.

The engines cut out, and he fell to the tracks.

A subway train screamed toward them, spotlighting them in the tunnel.

"Logan!" Mystique shouted. "Move it!"

Biting back the pain, Wolverine rose to his feet and they dove from the train's path. They hustled, jogging a few hundred feet to the Times Square station. It was the N train, heading downtown, and they pulled themselves up onto the train platform and boarded the train that had almost killed them.

"Won't they be able to trace us?" Mystique asked. "To follow the train?"

Wolverine grimaced and tried not to lean his already healing back against the seat.

"I know every back alley in this city," he grumbled through gritted teeth. "Even Fury won't be able to find me if I don't want to be found. We gotta set some priorities, though. I gotta get me a new shirt."

THEN

I t wasn't a heavy rain that came out of the gray German sky, not the type that might have sent anyone on the street running for cover, but a light, chilly drizzle that only served to make the day that much more miserable.

Like many wild animals, Logan didn't really like to be wet. It put him in a foul temper—as if he needed anything else to give this op a nasty little sense of foreboding.

North was at point and Silver Fox batting cleanup. Logan and Creed strode side by side, talking in low voices in German, just enough to create a semblance of normalcy among men trying very hard to look like common laborers. Fox kept back a bit—her gypsy clothing drew a little attention, but none of it the suspicious kind.

"You an' the squaw gettin' on pretty good, eh?" Creed whispered.

Logan frowned. *"Auf Deutsch, Viktor,"* he snarled.

With a cruel smile—the only kind at his command—Sabretooth repeated himself in German. Or, at least, he tried. There was no direct German translation for "squaw," and Creed couldn't manage the same tone of lecherous disdain in another language.

Wolverine told him it was none of his business, but Creed wasn't about to let it go.

"Let me know if things don't work out," he said in German. "I wouldn't mind a taste of that."

His guts burned with anger, but Wolverine laughed heartily, bent over slightly, and clapped a hand to Creed's back as if they were the best of friends.

"One of these days," Logan said in German, menace informing his tone despite the smile on his face, "you're going to go too far."

Sabretooth smiled back, stopped walking to stare down into Logan's eyes. He snarled. "You have no idea."

The moment lasted longer than it ought to have, considering they were trying to stay inconspicuous. It ended only when Maverick backtracked to step between them.

"I don't know about you two," he said, "but I would dearly love a beer."

Logan looked up, keeping the forced plastic smile on his face, and was about to tear into Maverick when he realized what his teammate had meant. They had reached their initial destination. Just ahead on the left side of the street was a glass- and wood-fronted building with BUEHAREST RESTAURANT engraved in German on a sign in front. It was a nicer establishment than they ought to be going into dressed like this, but there was nothing to be done for it now.

Across the street from the restaurant was a big, ugly, ancient Wartburg truck—a model manufactured in East Germany—whose broad-shouldered driver wore a shiny leather apron and was busily unloading beer kegs from the back.

"Creed," Logan said, "hang back, keep an eye on the door. If we're in trouble, you'll know it. We don't want any rude surprises while we're inside."

Sabretooth nodded, eyes narrowed and filled with danger. But he didn't argue. He did exactly what Logan told him to do. Logan was field command on this op, after all. And, for the moment at least, Creed was willing to be the good soldier. As long as that involved bloody murder.

Logan and North moved to the front door of the restaurant and looked inside. They went in and each of them stepped to one side to allow Silver Fox in after them. Fox walked straight ahead, finding a table near the back. While anyone interested in watching them followed Fox's progress across the room, Logan and North scanned the interior. It was almost a full house, which surprised Logan because he'd figured East Germans didn't have the time or the money to be sitting around inside a restaurant/tavern in the middle of the day. On the other hand, he figured, those that did have some spare time didn't have a whole lot else to occupy it.

They went to join Silver Fox at the table, sat down noisily, as if they were laborers who'd finished their work for the day. Logan's German was passable if he didn't draw too much attention to himself. But North was German, so he did most of the talking in public. Fortunately, they didn't have to wait long.

Logan was halfway through a drink when they were joined by a thin, plain woman whose dour features were reflected in the severity of her short, black hair. It had been recently shorn, and was all practicality. In the picture they'd been shown of their German contact, the woman had been younger, more attractive, with long and flowing hair. But it was a hard world, and it wore some people down all too quickly.

"Nice to see you again, *Fräulein* Haupt," Maverick said in German, as though the two were old friends, though none of them had ever met the woman before.

"And you, *Herr* Nord," the woman replied, and Logan raised his eyebrows.

She'd used Maverick's real name, which wasn't a good idea, not at all. Of course, Nord had to be a relatively common surname, but still . . . it wasn't professional.

Fräulein Haupt ordered herself a *Märzenbier* and then turned to smile at Silver Fox and Wolverine.

"Wie geht es Ihnen?" she asked, an inquiry as to their well-being.

But her eyes were on Logan, then. Greeting him. Noticing him. Admiring him. Had she been more beautiful, he might have wondered about that. He'd been in love with some extraordinary women in his long life, and incredibly enough, some of them had loved him in return. But Logan knew that at first glance he was only barely handsome. His face was too hard, chiseled, and his hair was wild. And, truth be told, he was damn short.

But here was *Fräulein* Haupt, checking him out. It made him decidedly uncomfortable for several reasons, not the least of which was the proximity of Silver Fox, whom he loved with the same passion he felt for the wilderness of his homeland. He and Fox belonged together, as far as Logan was concerned.

Still, there was something about that look in *Fräulein* Haupt's eyes. A mischief that danced there as she looked at him, a playful seductiveness which belied her severe exterior.

"Gut, danke," Maverick said.

Logan realized that he'd never returned *Fräulein* Haupt's greeting. He felt more than a little foolish. It wasn't like him at all to be so distracted. Not at all. He frowned slightly and looked at their contact more closely. There was something not quite right about her, and he wondered what it could be.

Before they had drained their steins, *Fräulein* Haupt had suggested they move to her rooms nearby where they could speak more freely. A moment later, they were following her out of the tavern. On the street, Logan didn't see Creed anywhere, which was good. Creed wasn't supposed to be seen right about then. He was supposed to watch. Still, Wolverine knew he hadn't gone far. Sabretooth had a scent he would never forget, and never miss even in a crowd. No, Victor Creed was nearby. Despite his misgivings about the man, if there was trouble, having Sabretooth around was always a good idea.

Logan almost smiled at the thought. Even if he wasn't good for anything else, Creed was a pretty big target. Soldiers were likely to shoot at him before they did anyone else. Which would be a crying shame, if you had any affection for homicidal lunatics.

Fräulein Haupt led the way, arm in arm with North as if they were lovers. Logan and Silver Fox walked side by side as well, but they did not link arms. Even if they were out on the town in Paris together, it just wasn't the kind of gesture they would have shared. That sort of innocence was lost to them, and not easy to feign, even for those in the business of espionage. North still retained some of it, and perhaps that was why it seemed to come to him so naturally. But *Fräulein* Haupt? Wolverine had to wonder.

Even as he considered this, she glanced over her shoulder at him and began to make excuses for the mess they would find in her rooms. Her bedroom, particularly, was a disaster. When she said this, she winked at Logan very purposefully. He ignored her, but felt Silver Fox stiffen at his side.

He couldn't help feeling a bit of pleasure at Fox's reaction. When they were on an op, she was so coldly professional that he was frequently forced to wonder what she really felt. But here it was. And it made him painfully aware of how dangerous their lives were. It was a danger they had lived with from the beginning; a cruel, harsh thing that would never truly allow them to love without reservation.

Enough of that romantic crap, Logan thought. They had a job to do.

They followed *Fräulein* Haupt into the rathole where she had rented rooms. The fat old man at the front desk raised his eyes as they walked in, but averted them just as quickly when Haupt slid a pile of deutschemarks across the desk. Cash. It wasn't a guaranteed insurance policy, but it was fairly reliable.

As she held the door for them, *Fräulein* Haupt smiled knowingly at Logan. He'd had enough. He let his upper lip rise in a kind of silent snarl, and the woman reacted instantly, her face registering, first surprise, then anger. The hell with her. "Just do the job," he wanted to say. But he didn't. He'd done enough.

"Where are they?" he asked her in English, but quietly.

Logan didn't think there were unseen listeners. He didn't hear or smell anyone within the rooms or outside the door. Well, except for Creed—and he had to wonder how Sabretooth had gotten past the fat old desk jockey downstairs—and he was part of the team.

"They split up yesterday," *Fräulein* Haupt answered. "I

don't know when they'll be back together, but you should wait. I don't know which of them has the disk."

A soft knock at the door caught her attention. It was the cadence of "Shave and a haircut," without the "two bits" at the end.

It was Creed.

But not an emergency, or he wouldn't have bothered to knock. So what was he doing?

Fräulein Haupt pulled a Walther *Polizei Pistole Kriminal* semiauto from under her skirt, but Logan held up his hand.

"A friend of ours," he said, and the irony of the word *friend* wasn't lost on him. "Let's see what news he's got."

North opened the door to admit Creed, who met Logan's questioning gaze with a hard stare. He looked at each of them, then walked slowly across the room to *Fräulein* Haupt. He sniffed at her, the way a dog might sniff a stranger. The woman's eyes were wide, but Logan sensed that she was more anxious than afraid, an odd reaction to Sabretooth's even odder behavior.

"Creed?" Logan asked.

"What are you doing, Victor?" Silver Fox wondered aloud. "Have you lost your . . ."

Then Creed started to laugh. Almost genuine laughter—a kind of tainted amusement. He reached behind *Fräulein* Haupt and gave her a pinch, to which she reacted not at all. Again, Logan was surprised. At her lack of reaction. At this entire weird scene.

"Good to see you again, darlin'," Creed said, and offered a final chuckle before the mask of the killer once again fell across his face.

"Sabretooth, what's goin' on here?" Logan demanded. "This mission's got enough bad omens without you freakin' out."

Creed looked at him. "Ah, Logan. She pulled one over on you, runt. She try to pick you up? Girl can twist a man a hundred ways just with a glance, can't you, Raven?"

He looked at *Fräulein* Haupt, who only stared at Wolverine.

"Aw, come on," Creed said, growing frustrated now. "This ain't *Fräulein* Haupt!"

Logan stared at him, then at their contact. She looked exactly like the pictures they'd seen of her, with the exception of her hair. So, unless she had a twin . . .

"The Haupt babe is probably dead in an alley or a dumpster by now," Creed claimed. "I knew this one was wrong when I followed you all into the building. Might not even have noticed if I wasn't lookin' for somethin' out o' place. But only one woman I ever met smells like this lady here. And her name ain't Haupt.

"It's Mystique."

Logan was about to speak again. Then the woman just changed. One moment, *Fräulein* Haupt was standing in front of them. Then her entire body seemed to just . . . shift, slightly. Her skin flowed and became something else, someone else entirely.

Her skin was blue, her hair a flaming red. Her eyes were yellow, but that mischievous quality never left them. She was a mutant—that much was obvious. Nobody in the room questioned it either. With the exception of Silver Fox, they were all mutants.

Mystique glared at Creed. "So nice to see you again, Victor," she said, voice dripping with venom.

"Yeah, babe, it's a thrill for me, too," Creed replied with just as much enthusiasm.

"So now we know your name," Silver Fox said, moving in closer to Mystique, taking control of the room.

But Logan wanted to caution her, tell her not to be so sure of herself. There was a danger that radiated from the blue-skinned shapechanger. A quality not unlike the waves of cruelty that came off Creed every time he stepped in a room.

"Before you all get crazy," Mystique said, "I'll answer the questions I know you have."

"You're right," Maverick said grimly. "You will."

"Ooooh, North gets tough," Creed taunted. "Raven, I think he likes you."

Both Mystique and North glared at Creed, but he only chuckled to himself.

"I killed your contact," she said, so bluntly that Logan was taken aback.

"You . . ." North began, but Mystique cut him off.

"She was a double," the woman said quickly. "You should thank me. If I hadn't killed her, you'd all be dead by now.

"I wasn't lying about the Zhevakovs," she continued. "I know where the husband, Grigorii, is staying. But I don't think he has the disk. And we're not the only ones looking for them. Until the wife, Katrina, shows up again, there's nothing we can do."

"What is this 'we'?" Silver Fox sneered.

Mystique smiled. "Jealous, honey?"

Fox said nothing.

"You need my help," Mystique said. "Haupt is dead, and would have turned you in anyway. You want to know where Grigorii Zhevakov is? I can show you. We get the disk, I'll take a copy, that's all I ask."

"Who are you workin' for?" Logan asked, and watched her face carefully.

"Not the KGB," Mystique replied. "That's all you really need to know."

Logan felt them all staring at him, waiting for a decision. He was field commander on this op. It was up to him. He could throw it out to a vote, but that wasn't the way covert ops were played.

"All right," he said at last, and ignored the looks of astonishment on the faces of his teammates.

Even Creed looked stunned.

"Well, let's go, then," Mystique said easily, and turned to leave the room.

The others were still staring at him. Creed started to open his mouth, to say something, to ask him what he thought he was doing.

"Stay with her, no matter what," he told Creed.

Sabretooth grinned, and followed Mystique out.

"You don't mean to let her have a copy of that disk?" North asked, obviously disgusted at the thought.

With good reason. It didn't matter who Mystique was working for. The Agency wouldn't want anyone having the information on that disk. Anyone. It was the kind of information people killed for on a regular basis. The kind of information they might all have to kill for before this op was over.

"No," Wolverine said, once he was sure Mystique and Creed were out of earshot. "No, I don't."

THEN

Long after midnight, the only sounds that could be heard on the streets of East Berlin were the thunder of marching soldiers, the drone of distant car engines, and the churning of factory machines that ran through the night. Amidst these mechanical harmonies, barely perceptible, were the sounds of suffering, of hungry children crying and frustrated parents shouting.

A horrid-smelling man in filthy rags huddled down into a stairwell's depression in a narrow alley where some of the city's poorest laborers made their homes. The chemical smells wafting through the city to compete had made it a challenge for the man to get his clothing to smell as noticeably bad as it did.

But that was all part of Haifisch's job.

It astounded him that agents of the KGB and Interpol, among others he was certain, could sweep *en masse* into East Berlin and not expect the local espionage community to take notice. Using his contacts, it had been simple enough to find out what they were all after. Or, rather, who: renegade KGB agents who traveled with secrets worth killing for.

Huddled as if cold and sick in the narrow stairwell, the shark smiled and waited for his prey. He would move in quickly and silently, and strike before they even knew he was there. The *Stasi* would promote him and the KGB would praise him, once they got those agents and their stolen information back. Then the chase would be on, as the foreign agents tried to get out of the city without being captured. It ought to be very exciting. Perhaps, if things worked out in his favor, he would be able to kill some of them—even torture them for information he didn't really need.

Haifisch smiled even wider, and watched the doorway across the street where he expected to see one of the KGB defectors appear at any moment.

What he didn't expect was the sudden thrust of cold metal against the back of his head, and the low, feminine whisper that instructed him, in Russian-accented German, not to move at all.

Frozen in place, Haifisch remained silent, waiting for the woman to make the next move.

"If you wish to see the dawn, find another place to spend the night," she whispered.

A slow smile crept across Haifisch's face. The woman didn't know who he was, nor why he was there. She believed his disguise—and who wouldn't with that stench? She merely wanted privacy.

He would be more than happy to give it to her.

Feigning terror, he whimpered and begged to be allowed to stand so that he could do as she instructed. He would leave, he promised, and not come back until morning.

"Go, then," she ordered.

He rose and moved toward the open end of the alley, beyond which the marketplace stood empty for the long night. He jogged lightly, not wanting to appear too healthy to her.

Whatever was going to happen, it would be tonight. Soon. And Haifisch was going to be a part of it. But he had the advantage of territory. There were half a dozen *Stasi* officers, dozens of *Polizei,* and hundreds of *Volksarmee* soldiers at his disposal.

As he stripped away the outer layer of malodorous clothing, Haifisch stood a little taller, held his chin a bit straighter. It was as if the promotion he had been hoping for had already been granted to him.

After the disgusting old man was out of sight, Katrina Zhevakov looked carefully around the alley, and at the doors and windows of the buildings on either side. Nothing.

She crossed to the door of the hovel where she and Grigorii

had been waiting for Interpol to come through with the papers they had been promised. They would have to move on, now, and quickly. Their defection, it seemed, was going to be much more difficult than it had originally seemed. But they would find a way, somehow.

Katrina didn't even have to deliver their signal knock. Grigorii opened the door before her knuckles could touch the wood.

"You should have killed him," her husband said in Russian, nodding toward the end of the alley where the filthy creature had fled.

"He's got enough troubles," she replied.

"It would have been merciful, and more secure for us," Grigorii said.

Katrina agreed, but she wasn't about to tell Grigorii that. Especially when they had far more important things to concern themselves with—like escaping East Germany before the KGB found and executed them.

"Martina is dead," Katrina told her husband.

Grigorii's face reflected his despair.

"Murdered?" he asked, though she was sure he knew the answer.

"Of course," Katrina replied.

"No sign of her comrade, the one who was to come for us?" he asked.

"If she had been able to tell our escort where we were, I suspect we'd have seen him by now," Katrina said sadly. "We'll have to think of another way to get out, Grigorii."

The couple embraced with a desperation Katrina had never imagined she would feel. They were both capable. The KGB had trained them well. Even without help, they ought to be able to get themselves into West Berlin somehow. It would take some thought, some deception, possibly some killing.

They had both been trained to kill, but neither of the Zhevakovs had ever actually had to do it until several days earlier, when they fled the Soviet Union. There had been a lot of killing since then. And it looked as though it wasn't over yet.

"Come," Grigorii said, still speaking in Russian. "Let's go inside. We've got a lot to think about."

Grigorii stepped aside to let her pass. Just for a moment, Katrina felt her years. She knew that she was still attractive, and not only because Grigorii told her so. Forty-four years old, and men still looked at her when she passed on the street. Despite the lines around her eyes and the bit of gray creeping into her hair, she looked good. Most of the time, that alone was enough to make her feel good as well.

But she felt her age now, weighing on her as she stepped past her husband—a man who was only days away from turning fifty. This was something they ought to have done years ago, when they still had the strength for it. But now . . .

No! She wouldn't allow herself to think such thoughts. They would make it, she vowed to herself. No matter the cost. Freedom waited for them, not so far away at all. Freedom, and a life they had dreamed of for more than twenty years.

The inside of the building was absolutely disgusting. The rats were everywhere, and they left nothing undamaged. The construction had been shoddy to begin with, but there was far worse than that. Water damage had stained the walls and floor. The ceiling bowed in many places. What had once been curtains were filthy, stained rags. Nobody with a choice would ever have lived there. Even so, they'd had to drive a pair of filthy squatters out the first day. They might have been laborers, but Katrina didn't think so. Not these men.

In the dark, she started up the stairs. They had sealed one room up rather well. The rats had grown braver of late, but they were still able to keep away from them for the most part.

Suddenly, Katrina was distracted by a slight, whispering sound at the top of the stairs. An image formed in her mind of a fat rat with its distended belly sliding along the grimy floorboards as it moved across the room. The image was nauseating, but it wasn't anything she hadn't seen before within these walls.

There was a low rumble, almost a growl, from above. That was when Katrina knew it was not a rat.

The landing at the top of the stairs was in almost complete darkness. It was nearly two in the morning, and what little light filtered in from the street outside was merely reflected down the alley from the main street beyond.

So she had to wonder if the red eyes glowing at the top of the stars had picked up the ambient light or if they glowed on their own. Either way, it was all Katrina could do not to scream. They were animal's eyes, and Katrina realized she had never felt more vulnerable, more exposed, in her life.

"What is it, darling?" Grigorii asked from below.

"It is death, my love," she whispered in Russian, barely able to hear her own words, never mind communicate her terror to her husband.

"Welcome home, darlin'," a voice growled in English.

Katrina went for the Glock that she had stashed in the rear waistband of her pants. She was fast.

The thing on the stairs was much, much faster.

Huge hands like talons gripped her by the shoulders, then the gun was ripped from her grasp. She was turned around, away from her attacker, so that she faced Grigorii. But she had gotten a shadowy glimpse of him before he forced her around. Huge and savage, the blond man was dressed in peasant clothes. He didn't seem to have any weapons but his hands—at least that she could see—but they seemed deadly enough.

"Kat? Katrina?" Grigorii said, almost stammering, as he saw what had happened.

She wanted to curse him, to blame him, somehow. But the beast had moved so fast; what could Grigorii have done? And, after all, she had been trained just as well as he had. No, whatever this man was, she was no match for him.

"Darlin'," her attacker whispered, "you ain't so bad for an

old broad. You an' me could have some real fun . . . if we had the time."

"Bring her down, Creed," a woman's voice said from the dark, rat-infested room below.

Then she was being manipulated, physically moved as if she were a marionette and the beast who held her throat the puppeteer. He moved her down the stairs effortlessly.

Something flared brightly in the darkness. A match. As Katrina was forced to the bottom of the steps and into the room beyond, she saw that Grigorii had also been captured. A handsome young man held a gun to her husband's back, but he didn't say a single word.

The woman who had spoken looked like a gypsy, but on second glance, even in the dark, it was easy to see that she was not. Or perhaps Katrina only concluded that because of her voice, which was certainly American.

"Americans," she said in a low voice, her English passable. "But why do you come at us like this? We want to defect, yes? Are you from Interpol?"

The end of a fat cigar burned in the darkness, flared brightly as the smoker inhaled deeply. He stepped forward, and she could see him a little better. A small man, but clearly powerful. His hair was as wild as his eyes. At his side was a dark-skinned woman who nearly blended into the shadows. There were at least five of them, then.

"What does Interpol have to do with any o' this?" the little man asked, and his English had an accent she didn't recognize.

Katrina knew better than to answer. She'd made a mistake by mentioning Interpol at all. She had just been so hopeful, and now she had made a significant error.

"You are not here to help us, are you?" Grigorii asked.

"What was your first clue?" the large man holding Katrina growled.

But she kept her eyes on the short man. He seemed to be the leader.

"You want to live?" the wild-haired man asked. "You want to make it to America? Maybe we can work something out. But before we talk about any of that . . . where's the disk?"

Katrina stared at him. She could feel Grigorii looking at her, silently pleading with her to cooperate. But she could sense what was happening in the room. These Americans might not kill her and Grigorii, but they would not help them to defect. They had come for the disk. Nothing more.

The short man repeated his question, in Russian this time.

Katrina blinked but still did not respond.

"Wolverine. We could just kill them, and then search their corpses, and this hellhole, for the disk," the dark-skinned woman suggested.

Grigorii stared at Katrina, his eyes reflecting his panic.

"We don't have time to search the place," their leader said gruffly. "I get the feeling we ain't the only ones who know about these two, and their little package."

The man called Wolverine dropped his eyes, shook his head sadly, then looked up at Katrina. No, not at Katrina. At the huge human animal who held her too tightly, whose hot breath felt insidious against the back of her neck.

"Sabretooth," Wolverine said. "Fox is gonna count to ten. At ten, you can kill her."

"You don't want me shootin' her here, Wolverine," Sabretooth replied. "Too loud. Draw too much attention."

The short man inhaled deeply, chewing on the end of his cigar.

"It comes to that, you can kill her any way you like," Wolverine said.

The false gypsy began to count. Katrina closed her eyes so she wouldn't have to look at Grigorii. At *five* her husband said her name.

"Grigorii, no," she said simply, and opened her eyes to stare at him, to command him.

At *eight* Katrina closed her eyes again, steeled herself for the pain. Working with the KGB, she had seen death many times. She had imagined her own death dozens, perhaps hundreds of times. She didn't want to die, but she also didn't think that these Americans would kill her without knowing how to find the disk. What if Grigorii didn't know, after all? They couldn't risk . . .

"No!" Grigorii shouted. "Stop. I will tell you what you wish to know."

"Too bad," the monster gripping her throat said softly, then kissed the back of her head. "I was really lookin' forward to that."

Katrina stared at Grigorii. "You will not," she said simply, in Russian.

The one called Wolverine understood Russian. He stepped forward, still smoking his cigar.

"You will agree to take us out of here, and we will bring the disk with us," Katrina insisted.

The end of the cigar flared, the little man exhaled smoke.

"All right," he said.

"How do we know we can trust you?" Grigorii demanded.

"You don't," Wolverine replied.

There was silence then. After several moments passed, Katrina moved forward slightly, and the animal called Sabretooth relaxed his grip on her throat. He still held her weapon, but she was free to move around on her own.

Katrina reached inside her waistband, undid the hook that held her skirt up, and let it drop six or seven inches. Beneath her belly button, on the gentle slope of her lower abdomen, silver tape ran around her body several times. She tapped the tape on her belly and they could all hear the hollow plastic sound it made.

"See, we should have killed them," Sabretooth said. "Woulda had that disk and been gone by now."

Katrina tried to pull her skirt back up, but Sabretooth grabbed her from behind. The skirt fell around her ankles as he slammed her against the filthy wall and pinned her there. With his other hand, the animal caressed her belly. His fingers ended in claws that were inhuman, like nothing she had ever seen. With his index finger, Sabretooth traced across the tape to where the disk was. Then he pushed.

A little yelp escaped Katrina's mouth as the claw penetrated the tape and just punctured her skin.

"Sabretooth," a voice warned.

Somewhere in Katrina's mind, she realized that the voice belonged to the silent young man she had thought handsome. But he was with them; he didn't seem handsome anymore.

"Not a word, Maverick," Sabretooth said, and she could hear the danger in his voice. "Not a word."

The claw sliced through tape and skin, and the disk was torn from her belly. Katrina bled, but not very much. The cut was very superficial. But the damage was far beyond any flesh wound.

Sabretooth tossed the disk to the false gypsy, who caught it and slid it inside her own clothes. Katrina saw something heavy and dark inside those clothes. A weapon, obviously. So she had more than one. They were all very well armed.

Despair washed over Katrina. It was over. She knew that, even before Sabretooth said, very bluntly: "We ought to just kill 'em all now, Wolverine. Can't be bothered with an extra pair o' warm bodies on our way home."

Logan stiffened at Creed's words. He had no intention of bringing the Zhevakovs with them when they took off to meet Wraith at the extraction point. But just killing them outright seemed a little unnecessary.

Apparently, Maverick thought it was a little more than that. "Sabretooth, these people are defectors," Maverick said, and glanced over at Logan, staring over Grigorii Zhevakov's shoulder. "They're looking to us for help, for asylum. We've got what we came for. There's no reason we can't take them with us. Kestrel can handle two more on evac without breaking a sweat."

Wolverine met Maverick's gaze without flinching. His mind

raced. He looked over at Creed, saw the perverse smile on the big man's face, and almost agreed with Maverick.

Almost.

"Mav, our orders have nothing to do with the Zhevakovs," he said. "Except to say that they're expendable. You don't want to kill them, that's aces in my book. But we ain't bringin' 'em home with us."

"Orders don't say we can't," Silver Fox said from the shadows.

That brought Logan up short. Fox was changing a lot, it seemed. Or maybe she was just a little soft this op, for whatever reason. But she was siding with Maverick on this one, and Logan couldn't think of a reason why. Except that maybe they were both right.

"They're stranded now," Fox went on. "Mystique killed their contact. She's admitted as much. Interpol won't know how to find them, and Mystique's been using the agent sent to get the Zhevakovs out to hunt for this 'Black Widow' that she's supposed to kill. I think we ought to take them with us."

"You're a bunch of bleeding hearts," Mystique said suddenly. "But if you could make up your minds, I'd appreciate it. I get a little anxious just standing around."

Mystique's right, Wolverine thought. They were asking for trouble, wasting their time. And the last thing they needed on an evac was a bunch of dead weight.

"We leave 'em," he announced.

"Wimp," Creed grunted, and shoved Katrina Zhevakov sprawling to the floor.

"Wolverine?" North said, obviously about to protest.

Logan shot Maverick a hard look that shut him up quick. North wasn't stupid. He knew that look. It told him that the Zhevakovs were lucky to still be breathing. Wolverine was glad North didn't push it.

"Let's go, then," Silver Fox said grimly.

She didn't want to leave the defectors behind either. But it was the only practical choice. Fox was the first to the door. Maverick and Mystique followed her out, and then it was just Logan and Creed inside the rat-infested apartment with the Zhevakovs. And Logan wasn't about to leave them alone with Sabretooth. He was neither that cruel nor that foolish.

"Go," he said.

"Wolverine . . ." Creed began to argue.

"Go."

Creed glared at him, but only for a moment. Then Sabretooth just shook his head, smiled, and went out the door. But Wolverine knew it could have gone the other way. That was the thing with Creed—you just never knew.

Wolverine looked at the Zhevakovs. Relief had already released some of the tension in them; they weren't going to die—that was the good news. The bad news was they were still stuck behind the Iron Curtain and very much wanted. They looked at Logan as if they expected some kind of apology, as though he was on their side.

"Good luck," he said, and turned to follow Creed out the door.

But Creed hadn't gotten very far.

"What is . . . ?" Logan started to ask.

Creed didn't even turn around. "Company," he said.

Logan sniffed the air, realized Creed was right. They had a lot of company.

When the lights came on, it was like a night game at Yankee Stadium. Only in this stadium, the fans were much better armed. To the right, the alley ended in a high wooden fence. To the left, it opened into what, by day, was a marketplace.

There were trucks there, now, blocking the mouth of the alley. Lights were mounted on the trucks, but there was no missing the dozens of *Volksarmee* soldier silhouettes that cast long shadows. A dozen or so soldiers stood in front of the fence at the other end of the alley. Their weapons were aimed directly at Team X.

The foremost silhouette began to shout at them in German, telling them to throw down their weapons, to put their hands over the heads, and to surrender. They wanted the Zhevakovs, of course.

Only a heartbeat passed before the defectors came out of the house into the street, with their hands held above their heads. Smart, actually. They didn't really have any way to get out of that house, and if they stayed inside, they were almost certain to be killed by the East German soldiers.

Team X was silent, awaiting Logan's instructions. They didn't wait long.

"Maverick, take out the lights," Wolverine growled, almost inaudibly. "Sabretooth, you and me'll hit the fence. Shouldn't be too much trouble. Fox, cover Maverick and follow our lead."

Silence followed. They were waiting for him to count.

"One."

The East German officer shouted at them again.

"Two," Logan whispered.

The Zhevakovs were cursing them from behind. But getting captured was not part of the game plan. Not at all.

"Go!" Logan roared.

Maverick spun, pulling a modified Uzi from inside his baggy shirt. He fired at the precise moment that the Germans did. Their huge spotlights exploded with his gunfire, and David North went down, hit by a dozen bullets, at the very least.

In the new darkness, Wolverine and Sabretooth ran at the soldiers in front of the fenced-in end of the alleyway. Logan only got a few shots off before he took a bullet in the shoulder and dropped his weapon. Creed took several bullets as well, but he and Wolverine both kept moving.

Both men were already healing as Sabretooth shot the last of the guards.

Silver Fox blinked as her eyes adjusted, but she picked up Maverick's Uzi without even glancing down at it. Her own semiauto pistol wasn't much good in this kind of firefight. And Maverick didn't need the Uzi anymore. He had other weapons.

David North rolled across the filthy cobblestones of the alley and rose quickly. He was virtually humming with energy, absorbed from the impact of the bullets that had hit him. They hadn't penetrated his skin, of course. Maverick was a mutant, and he had the ability to absorb the kinetic energy of any such attack, and turn it back on his attackers.

Maverick lifted his hands, and energy erupted from them, streaking across the alley and slamming the East German troops back into their trucks with the force of a tornado.

He and Fox turned to keep pace with Logan and Creed, but Maverick glimpsed something from the corner of his eye that brought him up short. In a widening pool of blood and gore lay Grigorii and Katrina Zhevakov. It seemed they'd caught a bullet or two. North was saddened, but he'd seen senseless death hundreds of times before. The defectors knew the chances they were taking. Traitors often ended up taking a bullet.

"Maverick, move!" Silver Fox shouted.

Some of the soldiers behind them had recovered, and bullets were flying again. Fox started after Creed and Logan, toward a massive hole in the fence that clearly marked the trail of Sabretooth. But even as he moved away, something else registered in Maverick's mind. Something not quite right about the bodies of Grigorii and Katrina Zhevakov.

Their throats were bloody. Even torn? There were bullet wounds as well, but bullets hadn't done that.

Maverick was furious, but there was nothing to be done for it now. That was war. He wished he could believe that he wasn't getting used to it, to the death and deceit. But he knew he'd be lying if he did. Where once David North's stock-in-trade had been freedom, it had now become death.

They ran past dead East German soldiers, and Maverick pushed it all from his mind. If he had to be numb to do the job, then numb was how he'd live. He and Silver Fox ran through the hole in the fence, weapons at the ready. Wolverine was waiting on the other side.

"Where's Creed?" Fox hissed, as they fell into step with Logan.

"He took point," Wolverine replied. "Fox, you'd better give me the disk."

Maverick frowned. They kept moving, but Fox reached inside her blouse to retrieve the silver disk. She hesitated a moment, and Maverick didn't blame her. Now wasn't the time or the place for . . .

A whistle.

Team X whistle, coming from straight ahead. From the open street where two men, one huge and one short and broad, stood silhouetted in the light from the street. Wolverine and Sabretooth.

"Fox, don't!" Maverick snapped.

But Silver Fox had figured it out as well, and Mystique knew she'd blown her shot. She laughed, even as her body morphed into the stern-faced and short-haired *Fräulein* Haupt, whose face she had used when she first met them. Yet another person she had killed.

"Can't blame a girl for trying," she said.

Logan and Creed were twenty yards ahead when the voice came down from above.

"No," it said. "You can't."

She'd leapt from a second story window, and the tiny, lithe young woman's kick dropped Mystique to the cobblestones. Maverick knew fast. He was fast. But this newcomer . . . dressed in a black jumpsuit, her red hair cropped in a pageboy cut, she looked like a high-school kid, even as she blocked Silver Fox's punch, and then took Fox down with a kick to the gut.

Somehow, the girl had the disk in her hand, and it glinted in the light from the street. Wolverine was shouting, running toward them. Any second, the East German soldiers would be coming through the hole in the wall. Sirens wailed not far off.

Maverick had his H&K semiauto in his hand, aimed at the girl's heart.

There wasn't anything she could do to him. She hit him, it would just give him more energy, power up his mutant battery. He hesitated.

Electricity arced from her wrist, and David North screamed as thirty thousand volts surged through his body. It only lasted a second, but that was enough to drop him where he stood. Electricity wasn't kinetic energy. At least he was still conscious. Any normal man would have been out cold.

When he managed to look up, Mystique and Fox were already on their feet, drawing an aim at something moving high up on the wall to the left. It was the girl, of course. But how?

Of course, *how* didn't matter. They had the girl in their sights.

"Move it!" Wolverine shouted behind them.

Gunfire erupted from the shattered fence they'd left behind, and Creed and Logan returned fire, trying to keep the *Volksarmee* from coming through the fence. But the distraction had been enough. Both Mystique and Fox had been thrown off. The girl was gone.

So was the disk.

Team X was up and moving.

"Meet back at the pickup," Wolverine snarled. "I don't care how you get there, just get there!"

"What about me?" Mystique asked.

Wolverine glared at her. "What *about* you? Go!" he shouted.

All hell broke loose, but they didn't need to fight anymore. Running was easy. Fox would have it the hardest, Maverick knew. But she'd find a way. She always did.

As she fled across the rooftops, the Black Widow slowed for only a moment: just long enough to grab her long coat and the peasant scarf she used to cover her hair. Only half a block from where soldiers were still trying to make sense of what had happened—not to mention trying desperately to find any of the spies they thought for certain they had cornered—Natasha Romanova crawled carefully down the side of a building to the street.

She hadn't believed her KGB controller when he'd first explained how the gloves and boots would work. That the synthetic stretch-fabric could possibly stick to anything—especially since the science used to create the microsuction technology was top secret—seemed too much like science fiction for Natasha.

But it worked after all. It had saved her life, in fact.

The Widow moved along the fronts of buildings, trying to keep out of sight as much as possible. Dawn was only a few hours away, and any lone woman walking the streets at this time of night was likely to be stopped and questioned—particularly if she didn't look like a prostitute.

Soon enough, however, she was moving into the newer section of East Berlin, where shining metal and concrete towers had sprung up in what was once the center of Berlin. Natasha considered the newer architecture, side by side with venerable old structures, a scar on the city's face. But that was one of the many costs of progress. It disturbed her deeply.

She glanced up at the TV tower, nearly twelve hundred feet high, and saw that even with the moon only a sliver, the tower's stainless steel sphere reflected its light. There was something about it that gave her hope, like a beacon, of sorts. Natasha turned left and was comforted to know that her warm bed in the Berolina Hotel was only a few blocks away.

In the distance, sirens still wailed. But as she walked, one siren singled itself out. It grew louder, as if it were heading this way. She thought to hide out in a recessed doorway, try to get off the street.

Then she realized it was not a siren at all. It was a voice. Screaming. Wailing.

Not him, she thought. *Not now!*

The Black Widow ran. Not because she feared her pursuer, but because she was angry. She'd been so close. But then, she realized, Cassidy could not have found her by chance. He had to have been following her.

She tapped unconsciously at the belt pocket on her jumpsuit, inside which she had hidden the disk. He would not have it. The last time they had met, he had forced her hand. The Widow was a spy, not an assassin. She would not kill unless she were endangered, or specifically ordered to do so. But Cassidy had forced her to hurt him.

She'd do it again if she must. Kill him, if it came to that. But she wouldn't let him have the disk.

Plate-glass shop windows reflected only the night off to her left. The wailing grew louder and lower. He was almost upon her. The Widow ran to the shop's door, used all her strength to kick at the wood next to the lock. The frame shattered, and then she was inside.

Even as she ducked her head into the shop, the plate glass shattered from the power of Cassidy's voice. Natasha shielded her face from the glass. She crouched in the dark and listened. If she could get the jump on Cassidy, get him with her "widow's bite," the electrical charge she could fire from her gloves, she would get away clean.

But if he saw her first, that sonic scream of his would take her down instantly. Then all would be lost.

Footsteps crunched in glass. In the distance, there was shouting and the sound of approaching vehicles. *Polizei,* or *Volksarmee.* Either way, Cassidy wouldn't want them finding him. Whereas if they found Natasha, it might be uncomfortable at first, but she would get to go home alive. If she had some way to signal them . . . if she was conscious long enough to signal them.

One grating foostep. Then another. Then . . . nothing.

"Well, well," a gravelly voice said from outside the shop. "If it ain't Sean Cassidy. Fancy meetin' you here, Inspector."

The Widow recognized that voice. It belonged to the agent named Wolverine. But how?

"Aye," Cassidy agreed. "An' I'd say the same to you, Logan, if I didn't have a little rabbit down a hole, and not a great deal of time to complete the hunt."

Shouting, even closer now. A gunshot or two.

"Yeah, the Widow," Wolverine agreed. "I got her scent."

Scent! Natasha's mind reeled. Had he actually somehow followed her trail based upon her scent? What kind of man could do such a thing?

"Ye're after her too, then?" Cassidy asked, his voice tightening.

"She's got somethin' I want," Wolverine explained. "What happens to her after that, I don't much care."

"Good," Cassidy said. " 'Cause I mean to kill her."

In the darkness, the Black Widow's eyes grew wide. For the first time in a very long time, she felt like the teenager she was. Espionage was a dangerous game, but it was a cold, unfeeling one as well. Yet there was something in Agent Cassidy's voice that told her this was very, very personal.

And that he meant what he said.

NOW

Washington, D.C., was a contradiction unto itself: a glorious testament to the history of the United States to some, a hellhole to others.

Not every neighborhood was home to congresspeople and corporate lobbyists. The real people, the working people, of Washington did not live next to centuries-old, gleaming marble-and-granite monuments to an era of righteousness long since passed. Not even close. Instead, they lived in an intensely paced metropolitan environment in which they were trapped between wealthy suburbanites and a massive population of the working poor and the unemployed.

There were some very nasty areas of D.C., areas the average citizen knew enough to avoid. Mystique and Wolverine had found their way into one of them.

"You sure this is the address?" Logan asked.

"This is it," Mystique replied. "Why, it's not up to your old friend Wraith's usual standards?"

Wolverine didn't respond to that. Instead, he stared at the building in front of them. It was old and without character, unless you considered decay to have a personality. Half a dozen air conditioners jutted from random windows on the three upper floors. Some of the windows were boarded up, others just broken and left unattended. Yet a peek at the many personal items left on the fire escape—children's toys, hanging clothes, plants and bicycles—made it clear that the building was occupied.

The second through fourth floors, then, were made up of apartments. The first floor, however, was given over to an establishment called Danny's Dojo, according to the home-made sign in the window. Another sign, inside the glass door, announced that Danny's Dojo was open.

Logan studied the building for several seconds longer, then turned full circle, scanning the neighborhood. The next building to the left had a deli on the bottom and some kind of church group's offices on its second floor. A ways down from that was a storefront police station or, at least, some kind of annex to the local precinct house, which they'd passed on their way over.

Some empty storefronts, a couple of really ragged-looking older homes converted into apartments, and a pizza joint that apparently had no name at all filled out the block behind them, across from Wraith's building.

"Apartment number?" Wolverine asked.

"Two-C," Mystique told him.

"Hang on." Logan stepped away from her, up on to the curb and to the door of Danny's Dojo. He opened the door—which set a bell ringing—and stepped inside. The place was warm and bright but empty, for the moment. No classes this morning, apparently.

The man who responded to the bell was white, probably in his early forties, and balding on top. He didn't look like much—until you got to his eyes. His eyes told the whole story.

Danny was a warrior. Logan liked him right off.

"You Danny?" he asked.

"I am," the man replied, sizing Logan up with a look. "But I'd guess you're not looking for a teacher."

"No," Wolverine agreed. "No, I'm not. I'm looking for a neighbor o' yours. Up in 2C. Name'a John Wraith."

Danny didn't blink. Just stared at Logan again, more intently this time.

"He's a little taller than me. Skinny guy. Black. Got a few years on you, I guess, but not too many," Wolverine continued.

"Ray Johnson," Danny said.

"Huh?"

"That's the name I know," Danny explained. "Ray Johnson. From the sound of it, that's the guy you're looking for. He shows up every few weeks, stays a few days, then he's gone again. Says he's got a lady friend on the other side of town."

"He around now?" Logan asked.

"Haven't seen him in weeks."

"He friendly with any of the neighbors, anybody else around here?"

"He's not friendly," Danny answered. "But if you're asking me does anyone else know where to find him, I can't answer that."

Wolverine's eyes narrowed at the phrasing.

"Can't?"

"I mean I don't know," Danny corrected.

"I hope that's what you mean," Logan said, glaring at the man.

"Look, I don't want any trouble, buddy. This is my business, y'know? You have a beef with Ray, you take it up with him. I barely even know the man," Danny said.

Logan considered, then nodded. "All right. Thanks for your help. Now I'd like to ask a favor."

Danny's face responded, lips twisting up, perhaps preparing a sarcastic comment, or just to tell Logan that he had a lot of nerve. He took another look at Wolverine, and obviously thought better of it.

"Let me guess," Danny replied. "You want me to keep quiet about you looking for Ray?"

"That ain't it at all. If he's not up there, I want you to spread the word. Make some noise. Tell anyone you like that someone's lookin' for Ray Johnson, claims his name is John Wraith, and he's got a lot of skeletons in the closet he might not want his neighbors knowin' about."

Danny smiled, amused by it all.

"Sure," he said. "I can do that."

Wolverine nodded his thanks, turned, and went back to the

door. When he opened it, bells chimed again. Before he stepped out, he glanced back at Danny.

"One more thing, bub. I'd take it real personal if anything happened to my motor while I'm looking around upstairs," Logan said.

For a moment, Danny said nothing.

"This is a good neighborhood, man," Danny replied. "Nothing's gonna happen to your bike."

Logan let the door shut behind him, glad to be rid of the ringing bells. Mystique stood half-leaning on his antique, rebuilt Norton motorcycle. Beautiful as always, she had morphed into a Latina again. This time, she looked a lot like Selena, the dead singer. She wore jeans and sneakers and a green cotton blouse that looked especially good on her.

Wolverine had changed as well. His back had nearly healed, but he wanted something soft on the raw skin, so he had donned a worn flannel shirt to go with his jeans, and changed into hiking boots. It wasn't that he never wore sneakers. They just weren't his style. Besides, cowboy boots or big steel-toed workboots were more durable.

They went up the stairs together. The walls had water stains here and there, and the plaster was cracked in several places. All in all, though, it wasn't as bad as the outside had led them to believe.

Outside the door to 2C, they paused.

Logan knocked, waited half a minute, then knocked again. After the second knock, the door to 2B opened, and a shrill, nervous old woman stuck as much of her face into the door as she could fit in the gap allowed by her security chain.

"He ain't home," she said. "Ain't never home, that man."

"You know Ray Johnson, ma'am?" Wolverine asked, his gravelly voice pitched as reasonably as he could make it.

The door slammed. The old woman was silent.

Mystique had a grin on her face when she looked back at Wolverine. Logan chuckled as well. He drew back his leg, prepared to kick the door open.

"What if it's rigged?" Mystique asked.

But Wolverine had considered that already. If Wraith used this place as a flop, maybe a safehouse, it was possible he'd have a security system installed, black-ops style. Meaning, the whole place could blow up if somebody tried to break in. On the other hand, in a not-so-nice neighborhood like this, a man gets a rep for not being at home is more than likely to be subject to burglary eventually. So if a few kicks would be enough to open the door, then the building probably wasn't going to go up in a thunderous C4 explosion.

However, if he couldn't kick it open, if the place was significantly reinforced like Maverick's had been . . . that might be another story.

The third kick shattered the frame and the door swung in. Inside the room, directly across from the door, a red light was blinking.

"Trap?" Mystique asked.

"Naw," Logan replied. "But I'll bet wherever he is, Wraith knows he's got company."

"So we just sit and wait?"

"I didn't say he'd care," Wolverine explained. "If there isn't much in this place he cares about, he might not come back at all now that he knows the place has been compromised."

They searched the apartment and came up dry. A mattress and blankets lay on the floor of the one, large room. The tiny pantry kitchen had a half-size refrigerator that was empty but for a jar of mayonnaise. They began checking the walls and floorboards, searching for a secret cache where Wraith could hide weapons or documents.

Nothing.

Nothing under the mattress. Nothing in the empty closets. Nothing floating in the toilet tank. Nothing in the medicine cabinet but a half a package of antihistamines.

Wolverine closed the medicine cabinet door, stared for a moment at its mirrored front. He was a bit surprised that they'd come up empty, that Wraith wouldn't, at the very least, have some weapons hidden somewhere in a place like this. Otherwise, why bother to keep it up at all? Frustrated, he ran water from the sink and splashed some on his face. When he opened his eyes, Wolverine noticed a fine white dust on the porcelain top of the sink, behind the faucets.

A tiny detail, but one he wouldn't have missed. It hadn't been there a moment ago. What had he . . . ah, the medicine cabinet. He bent over and looked at the bottom of the cabinet, saw that the entire thing was not actually hung against the wall so much as resting inside it. The white dust was plaster.

"Mystique, in here," he said in a low voice.

She popped her head in as he was pulling the medicine cabinet out of the wall. The cabinet itself was a false front to a large metal case. It had three separate keyholes. It would have required an extraordinary lockpick, or a locksmith. Either one would be a waste of time. More than likely, the police would arrive eventually, if Wraith's neighbors even cared that the man's apartment had been broken into.

Snikt. Wolverine popped a single claw and carved the metal box like a can opener.

"What have we here?" Mystique muttered as she reached into the box.

Inside, there was an old Walther pistol and two yellowed journals, the kind schoolchildren might keep for notebooks, Wolverine thought. He flipped them open, glanced at the gibberish inside.

"Code," he grumbled.

"Anything you recognize?" Mystique asked.

He shook his head. "But they could be something Wraith values, so we'll just hang on to them for a bit."

"You don't trust him at all, do you?" Mystique asked suddenly.

"That ain't it," Logan answered. "I trust Wraith to be completely loyal. Just not to me."

Two minutes later, they were on the street again. Logan waved to Danny as he and Mystique straddled the old snortin'

Norton, as he called it. He stashed the journals in a saddlebag he had on the side of the motorcycle and kick started the metal beast.

Mystique tapped his shoulder.

Wolverine looked up.

The chopper was still a ways off, and couldn't be heard at all over the roar of the Norton's engine.

Wraith might not be coming for them, Logan thought, but they'd sure gotten somebody's attention.

THEN

Logan sniffed the air, stared through the shattered window into the darkness of the shop, and nodded.

"She's in there, all right, Irish," he told Cassidy.

His boots crunched broken glass as he moved a bit closer to the shop window, narrowed his eyes, and peered inside. Wolverine had excellent vision. Even in the darkness, the Widow had hidden herself well.

"I can hear you breathin', Widow," he said. "An' I got your scent, too. I didn't come here to kill you, girl. I just want that disk. If you toss it out here, well, then whatever mad-on Irish has got for you is just between the two o' you. But if you make me come in after that disk . . . well, let's just say it'll throw your odds into the crapper."

Nothing stirred in the darkness of the shop's interior. But he knew she was in there. What he'd said about hearing her breathing was not exactly true. His aural senses weren't *that* acute. But he did have her scent. Kind of nice, actually.

The wail of a *Polizei* siren had begun to grow distant. Which was a good sign, considering how much attention Cassidy's screaming had probably pointed in this direction. Wolverine suspected that one of the others had drawn the Germans' attention for the moment, and a selfish part of him hoped it wasn't Silver Fox.

"I think we may've a wee problem," Cassidy told him.

There was shouting a few blocks up. Gunfire erupted not far off, perhaps the next street over. Too close. Like the rumble of thunder, Logan could hear the familiar East Berlin sound of dozens of boots slapping pavement in syncopated rhythm. The sound was growing closer, but there didn't seem to be any hurry in its approach.

"What's that?" Logan asked, eyes narrowed.

The idea that Cassidy might give him a problem didn't sit too well with him. They'd met in a snowbound Canadian tavern and drank beer by the fire, found a lot in common, strangely enough. Logan genuinely liked the man, so he hoped that "a wee problem" didn't mean he'd have to hurt Cassidy.

At least not too badly.

"The man in charge asked that I bring him back that very same disk," Cassidy explained.

Wolverine sighed. It looked as though it was going to be a problem after all. But not for long. He felt the weight of the two fighting knives he wore sheathed against his lower back. An apology for what he was about to do came to his lips, but remained unspoken.

Something more important had come up.

"I think we have an even bigger problem, Irish," Logan snarled.

Which was when the shouting started, and the bullets began to fly. In the years he'd been in the game, Logan had been shot too many times. *Hell,* he thought, *I been shot too many times today.* He healed up fast, but that didn't stop the pain of taking a bullet in the first place.

He was about to fade into the shadows, leave Cassidy and the Widow where they were to face the music. But as he turned, he caught a glimpse of the tank that was rumbling around a distant corner several blocks away. And the goose-stepping soldiers marching alongside it. Some of them began to run in his general direction, unslinging their weapons.

Logan sighed. "Cassidy, can you get us outta here?"

The Irishman blinked, stared a moment into the darkness where the Black Widow huddled, then scowled angrily. He grabbed Wolverine under the arms and let out a scream that nearly burst Logan's sensitive eardrums.

Then they were flying. Bullets roared past, seeming to bend around Cassidy. One caught Logan in the left calf, and he cursed silently. Soon, they were far away from their attackers, but they wouldn't be hard to follow. Not with Cassidy wailing like that. Logan motioned that the Irishman should bring them both to the ground. He knew the Interpol agent would be angry at having to leave the Widow behind, and Logan was none too happy about it himself.

But there'd be another shot at her. He'd make certain of it.

In the chaos that ensued upon Cassidy and Logan's escape, the Black Widow emerged from the shattered storefront where she had taken refuge. Unwittingly, they had provided the perfect diversion for her to slip away without the delay that a meeting with the East German authorities would entail. It wasn't long before she met with her contact, and began the long journey that would take her home.

Commercial air travel had been sufficient to get her to East Berlin, but a more circuitous route would be required for the return trip. The airport and train station would be buried in foreign agents after this evening's events. A slow, scenic ride back to Moscow would help her unwind, and would throw her followers off her scent, as Wolverine had put it.

Wolverine.

A dangerous man, that. She would have to be careful of him in the future.

"What do you mean he never showed?" Logan snarled at nobody in particular. "Wraith was supposed to be here for evac, and it is definitely time to go. Every fascist moron in this city is after us. This ain't the time for the Agency to flake."

They all stared at him.

"Be that as it may, Logan," Maverick said—almost patronizing but not quite enough to deserve a punch in the mouth—"Wraith isn't here."

Wolverine shook his head in disgust and took in their surroundings one more time. It was not the ideal place to be stuck without their extraction man. The *Französischer Dom* had been a beautiful church, before World War II. It faced another, the *Deutscher Dom,* across the *Platz der Akademie,* which had sustained nearly as much damage. Both churches had been built in the eighteenth century, but air raids had scarred them forever. Or, at least, until the DDR got around to fulfilling its promises to reconstruct the churches. For the moment, Team X had to be grateful that they hadn't done so as yet.

The night sky was open above them, and Logan was surprised to see the stars in this city so well known for its pollution. He was also surprised, and somewhat comforted, by the green vegetation that grew wild all around, an odd counterpoint to the extraordinary friezes in each false doorway and window on the blackened walls.

In a melancholy way, it was an amazing, wonderful spot, despite, or perhaps because of, the ravaged echoes of a long-ago war. Another time, he might have liked to linger while contemplating the spirit and beauty of the place.

But they were still stuck. Things had gone very wrong. The defectors were dead, which wasn't a great loss and certainly not outside the parameters of the mission, but Logan thought that if they'd been alive, they might have been helpful in recovering the Widow. And, of course, the disk. That kind of help would have been worth whatever hassle came with forcing Wraith to extract the Zhevakovs along with Team X.

That wasn't going to happen, of course. No Zhevakovs. No Wraith.

It didn't help that they suddenly found themselves with uninvited and unanticipated company. Mystique was a spy, a stone-cold mercenary, and a natural killer to boot. But she was at least predictable in a way; they could count on her to betray them whenever it was convenient for her.

"I don't know what yer all gripin' about," Sabretooth grumbled. "All we'd have been able to do was tell Wraith to go home. No way can we evac without that disk. And at this point,

I don't think we should go home without that little Widow girly's head on a stick."

They were all silent. Wolverine studied Maverick's face. Anger and frustration burned behind David North's eyes, but he kept quiet, waited for Wolverine to make the call. Silver Fox looked much the same, but he thought she looked tired in a way. Tired of the game, maybe. Or just tired of having to put up with Creed. One of these days, if Creed didn't shape up, Logan wouldn't be surprised if Fox cut him open and left him for the vultures. He figured it wouldn't bother him much, either.

So long as it didn't happen during a mission.

"You tried the safe line?" Wolverine asked Maverick for the second time.

Maverick only looked at him with hooded eyes. If Logan asked a third time, he knew he'd probably have to dodge a punch.

"We're cut off," Silver Fox said suddenly. "We can't get home right now, can't even report that we botched this mission. I don't suppose anyone wants to go over the Wall into West Berlin?"

Wolverine stared at her a moment. When he was certain she had not been serious about abandoning the mission, he took a deep breath and scanned all their faces again. Mystique hung back from the team, and he was glad. It wasn't her place to participate in this discussion. But she was listening, that was certain.

"Sabretooth is right," he said at length. "We gotta go after that disk."

"Too bad you didn't bring your Interpol buddy back here with you," Maverick said. "If he's as crazy for the Widow's blood as you say, he's probably got a few excellent ideas as to how to track her down. Sounds like he was better prepared for all of this than we were. The Agency sends us in with less information than they could have gotten just by asking Interpol, then

Wraith doesn't show up for evac. If he was here, I'd have to beat some explanation out of him."

Creed had been crouching like an animal in a corner filled with crumbled stone and green foliage that swayed slightly in the breeze that blew through the shattered church walls. Now he sprang up violently, faced Maverick, and stared down into the other man's eyes. Creed was a full head taller than North, at least, but Maverick didn't back off at all.

"I'm gonna tell you this one time, boy, and I ain't gonna repeat myself. I'm tired o' your whinin'. You fight real good, and you can take a lot of punishment. That's the only reason I haven't killed you myself already.

"Now listen up, all o' you. Maverick may sound like a damsel in distress half the time, but he does make one decent point," Creed said, and turned his cruel smile on Logan. "Wolverine, you should have brought Cassidy along just so we could kill him. Procedure, *field commander,* or have you forgotten Team X is a covert operation? Agency's gonna be none too happy to know we're compromised."

Wolverine only stared at him. Returned the cruel smile. Let a low, dangerous laugh roll up from his gut and through his gritted, too-sharp teeth.

"You got a lot o' gall, Creed," Logan said through his laughter. "But I'm glad you do. And I'm glad you spoke up. I guess I'm a little too angry about this whole snafu to think straight. Leastways I was, until you got all uppity on us.

"You're right," Logan continued. "I'm field commander on this op. That means we're gonna put all this democratic bull behind us. No more questions. No more answers. Just orders. You all clear on that?"

"Clear," Fox agreed, and Logan could feel the energy burning off her as she readied herself to back him up if Creed should make a move.

"Clear," Maverick said. "Just so long as we're moving. We're just targets if we keep sitting here."

The smile on Creed's face had not disappeared. If anything, it had grown wider—a little more dangerous, a little more insane. But Victor Creed wasn't insane. Not really. At least, not yet. He was just the meanest human being Logan had ever come across. And he'd run into some nasty individuals over the years.

"We clear, Sabretooth?" Wolverine asked, glaring at him intently.

"Oh, yeah," Creed said after a moment. "We are very clear."

"Good," Logan said.

He pulled one of the knives from its sheath at his lower back and flipped it toward Creed. The big man's speed was nearly as great as his own, and it was no problem for Sabretooth to snatch the knife from the air. The blade cut his palm a bit, and Logan couldn't escape the sudden thought that he'd allowed it to happen. Just for the blood.

"You want to kill someone, Creed?" Wolverine growled low. "You can kill your girlfriend over there."

He heard the intake of breath from Mystique, but that was her only reaction. She could have run, then. Logan had kind of hoped she would, but not really expected it. The blue-skinned woman wanted something from them, wanted the disk and probably the Widow, too. And she obviously meant to stick with them if she could, let them do the real work and then grab the glory when it was over. Maybe even take Team X down along with the Widow. What she did was covert ops, too. Her superiors wouldn't want live witnesses any more than the Agency that employed Team X did.

Creed turned to look at Mystique. He was still smiling, but the smile had changed somehow.

"Victor," Mystique said, and Logan heard the warning in those words.

"Oh, so it's Victor, is it?" Maverick said. "Isn't that nice. Just one happy little family."

Sabretooth's eyes flicked over to Maverick, just for a second, but Wolverine saw the death those eyes held for North, and wondered what was between Creed and the shapeshifter that could leave such a deep wound.

"I agree," Silver Fox said.

Logan was surprised, but said nothing.

"Mission security is compromised every moment she is with us," Fox concluded. "She should be terminated."

" 'She' is right here," Mystique said archly. "If you're planning to kill me, at least don't pretend I can't hear you."

"She's all right," Creed said suddenly.

They all stared at him, even Mystique. In fact, Logan would have had to say that none of them looked as stunned as Mystique herself.

"What?" Logan asked, unable to stop himself.

Sabretooth glared at him, as if Logan had just pointed out a horrible weakness in him. It occurred to Logan that that might not be far from the truth.

"I've worked with her before," Sabretooth said. "She's all right."

"That'll do," Mystique said suddenly.

She walked forward until she stood at roughly the center-point of the gathering of Team X. One by one, she changed her appearance, becoming each of them in turn. Just to show them that she could.

"You could try to kill me, I suppose," she said, stopping to stare into Wolverine's eyes. "Or we could work together. I was well aware of the Black Widow's presence and her plan. I know the way the KGB works, far better than you or your Agency. Apparently, they couldn't even be bothered to give you information they undoubtedly already had."

Logan frowned. Not because her claim was preposterous, but because it had a ring of truth.

"Who are you working for?" he demanded.

"The Israelis."

"Mossad?"

"Of course," Mystique admitted.

"So if you're such an expert, where will the Widow go next?" Silver Fox asked.

"Well, my guess would be that your own Agency, as well as the Mossad, MI6, and a handful of others will have people covering the airport and train stations. I mean, they all have double agents within the East German government, so they're certain to know if the Widow were to work with the East Germans.

"Logic says that if she wants to get out without anyone knowing about it, she'll go by car. And if she is going by car, the nearest KGB rathole after East Berlin is Warsaw," she concluded.

"Which brings us deeper behind the Iron Curtain," Maverick observed.

"You didn't honestly think she'd head for London, did you?" Mystique asked. "She's going back to Moscow. We've got to stop her, and get back that disk."

"We?" Silver Fox asked.

"Makes sense," Creed said, though he didn't smile anymore. Nor did he even look at Logan.

"All right," Wolverine agreed.

The rough linen clothes they wore over the black jumpsuits of Team X would have to last them for the duration. Or until they could steal something else. They checked their weapons and small stash of supplies, and then they were ready. All they needed was to steal another car.

Wolverine approached Creed, who stood by Mystique. The two were arguing, their voices low, and there was a hatred in the eyes of both killers that crackled like an electric current between them.

". . . nothing I'd like better than to gut you, Raven," Creed snarled.

"Why didn't you?" Mystique challenged.

"You know why," Sabretooth said. "You owe me, now, lady. But don't think the day won't come when I will rip your throat out."

Wolverine was interested to hear Mystique's response to this threat, but she had noticed him. Creed spun on him, raging, but only narrowed his eyes and waited for Wolverine to speak.

"My knife?" he asked.

Creed handed it back to him.

"You change your mind about wanting to kill her, you can have it back," Logan told him.

"That might be for the best," Creed admitted.

"Another time," Wolverine corrected. "You'll have to make other plans to see her, though."

"What's that mean?" Mystique demanded.

"It means you're staying here," Logan told her pointedly.

Mystique laughed. "You don't honestly think I'll . . ."

Wolverine's eyes flicked to Creed's face, and Sabretooth caught his meaning immediately. The big man's fist slammed hard into the side of the blue-skinned woman's face, and Mystique went down in the rubble hard, striking her head on a chunk of granite.

Logan crouched to check her pulse. She was fine. Or as fine as one could be after being knocked out by Victor Creed. Wolverine glanced up at Creed, silhouetted against the void of dark, star-filled sky through the shattered ceiling far above.

For the first time in Logan's memory, he thought Sabretooth looked happy.

He shivered at the thought, and was glad to know that his knife was back where it belonged.

NOW

H old on!" Wolverine yelled, and opened up the throttle on his ancient Norton.

The motorcycle threatened to flip them backward, but Wolverine kept the front wheel on the ground as the tires found purchase and smoke rose from the burning rubber. All they left behind were black smears on the pavement as the bike shot away from the place Wraith had used as a bolt-hole. Though the road ahead rose up into a small hill, Wolverine did not turn away. He'd rebuilt the Norton himself and knew what it could handle. They'd make the top of the hill.

It was the other side that he was worried about.

Bullets chewed pavement on either side of the bike. Logan kept her as steady as he could, even as he cursed the bike to go faster. Mystique was a slender woman, but even her extra weight might make all the difference in this race. Not that it was much of a race. No way would the Norton, or any other bike, for that matter, be able to outrun a helicopter.

But they didn't need to outrun it. They just needed to stay ahead of it for a little while longer. At least, if Logan's short-term memory wasn't lying to him. He thought he recalled a subway station a ways back along this road. Helicopters couldn't fly underground.

"They're not trying to hit us!" Mystique yelled.

"No, but they ain't bein' too careful about missin' us, either," Wolverine growled in response. "Seems to me if they wanted to bring us down, they'd use somethin' that wasn't lethal."

"At this speed, anything is lethal," Mystique said.

Which was when the ground ahead of them was pounded by blasts of crackling light that refracted harmlessly off the gray pavement. Wolverine cursed loudly and swerved the bike from left to right, hoping to make them a more difficult target. A bullet shattered the rearview mirror on the Norton's left handlebar, and Logan began to snarl through his gritted teeth.

The bullets had created a corridor, forcing them to stay their course. If Wolverine deviated, he and Mystique would be cut down by their pursuers' traditional weapons. But if they didn't swerve, they could not possibly avoid the plasma bursts from above.

"What is it?" Mystique asked, her frustration evident in her tone.

"Some kind of stunner," he guessed. "Hang on!"

Logan gunned the Norton up the hill. They crested it and took flight. Hang time was no more than two and a half, maybe three seconds, then the tires bit into the pavement again. They were heading downhill now. The streets were closer together, and Wolverine could see the subway station ahead on the left.

A stun bolt hit the Norton's front tire and was harmlessly absorbed by the rubber. A second hit the bike itself, and Wolverine felt the shock of it pass through him like a bolt of electricity. Mystique twitched behind him and the starter shorted. The Norton was taking a beating, and completely apart from any concern for his and Mystique's safety, Logan felt an almost absurd fury begin to burn in his gut over the motorcycle. He'd begun to realize that he was going to have to ditch the bike.

"Those idiots should probably think real hard about whether they really want to take us alive," he said angrily. "If I end up wreckin' this ride, they're gonna wish they had killed us."

Mystique grunted. For the space of a heartbeat, Logan thought she was merely agreeing with him. Then he sensed an increase in her weight against his back, the loosening of her grip around his waist, and the way her body had begun to slide to the left on the Norton's seat.

"Aw, hell!" he snarled. "Not now!"

His left arm whipped around behind him, clamped tight on Mystique, and held her against his back. It was a terribly awkward position, and despite his strength, he wouldn't be able to hold her there for long—not and still steer a motorcycle at an insane speed downhill.

Wolverine threw his weight to one side, turned the front wheel, and applied the brake. The bike slewed to one side, rubber burning, staining the pavement black. But he'd been going too fast. The bike couldn't take the momentum. It kept going, flipped forward, and Wolverine and Mystique were thrown into the air along the same path.

Logan spun, held on to Mystique, and twisted his body to try to keep from getting tangled up in the Norton as it cartwheeled off the pavement and then slid.

When they hit the ground, Wolverine was under Mystique. The pavement tore through his jacket, and then they were rolling. He kept her away from the road as much as possible until they came to a stop. He was momentarily disoriented, but then his mind focused and he saw that Mystique had only some surface scrapes and cuts. Those would heal the next time she changed, he knew.

Problem was she must have hit her head. Mystique was unconscious.

Anger continued to grow in Logan's gut as he ran toward the subway entrance. He carried Mystique over one shoulder. It wasn't an even distribution of weight, but it freed the rest of his body for the business of running.

"Tell ya, Raven," he grumbled to the unconscious terrorist. "Never thought the day would come when I risked my own tail to get you to safety. Must be gettin' soft in my old age. Workin' to find Creed, and now pullin' your fat out of the fire."

Not that she had much fat. He left that notion unvoiced. There was no mistaking the mystery and beauty of Raven Darkhölme. But it was almost suicidal folly to do more than notice.

And he had not forgotten for whom he was really doing all this. For Maverick. For Cassidy and Natasha. And for himself.

Those guys in the chopper wanted a piece of Wolverine.

He meant to give them more than they bargained for.

As Logan hurried down the steps into the subway station—careful of his footing so as not to send Mystique tumbling down ahead of him—a powerful wind slammed him from behind, and pushed past him as air was forced into the station. The chopper had landed. The goons who'd been after them before were still on the trail. Team Alpha, whoever they were, weren't giving up easily. Wolverine figured it was time to show them the error of their ways.

At the bottom of the stairs, he turned to the left and let Mystique slump from his arms to the filthy floor of the station. In midmorning, there were only a handful of other people in the station, including a man selling flowers and a college-age girl with unwashed hair accompanying her own singing on a battered acoustic guitar.

Or she had been, before Wolverine and Mystique appeared amongst them. Raven was blue again, of course. That had happened as she passed out, and Logan had barely noticed until now. Until he heard the first civilian shout: "Muties!"

They scattered in fear, and he didn't even have time to be disgusted by their bigotry. He heard the rumbling of Team Alpha's boots as the soldiers ran down into the station after them. Logan thought about his bike again, realized it was probably lost for good.

He barely noticed as his claws popped out. He felt them, a part of him just as much as his fingers or his eyes, and just as important in their way. The savage beast who still surged within his heart wanted nothing more than to rip those claws through flesh and bone. Even the calmer, human part of him was tempted by the idea.

But killing wasn't a way of life for him anymore. It was just a way of staying alive. Other than that, he didn't have much use for stone-cold murder. On the other hand, some well-chosen bloodshed always seemed to generate a useful reaction.

The first soldier rounded the corner at a run, expecting to catch Wolverine and Mystique fleeing. What the man didn't expect was to find Wolverine just off to the side, waiting for him. The plasma stun rifle in the soldier's hands began to turn ever so slightly in Logan's direction, but the man didn't have time to do any more than that before the rifle was sliced to useless scrap by adamantium claws.

Adamantium. For all its curses, the metal had become part of what Wolverine was. In addition to the claws, the integration of adamantium into his physiology had made him almost unkillable. Which didn't stop people from trying. And in times like this, Wolverine wouldn't have it any other way.

The soldier reached for another weapon. Logan lashed out and with a flick of his wrist the guy's Kevlar bodysuit and the shoulder underneath were hacked to ribbons. He screamed and went down, just as the rest of his squad realized what was going on.

Wolverine couldn't run, not with Mystique at his feet unconscious. That was fine with him. With blood on his claws, and the animal inside him rising dangerously close to the surface, he crouched to spring at the four black-suited soldiers who'd already turned the corner to aid their fallen comrade.

A voice came out of nowhere.

"Another time," it said, and a hand gripped Logan's bicep from behind.

Even as reality warped around him, and his stomach lurched slightly, unused to teleportation, Wolverine recognized the voice. A moment later, they were inside a cheap motel room with water stains on the ceiling and peeling wallpaper. The television was bolted to the bureau and the curtains were saturated with the smell of cigarettes. All of that was in Logan's first observation of the room. It barely registered.

His attention was on Wraith.

John Wraith, who'd been codenamed Kestrel in their days as

Team X, crouched over Mystique and checked her pulse and respiration. He said nothing as he lifted her to the bed, but already, Raven was beginning to come around.

He was a lanky black man who'd apparently abandoned, at least temporarily, his fondness for cowboy hats and dark sunglasses. The Wraith who turned to face Wolverine was a different man. Hard and angry, absent the charming smile that so often hid his true feelings. His eyes flashed with an almost hysterical amusement that didn't reach his lips, and he tilted his head back as he regarded Wolverine across the bed where Mystique finally opened her eyes.

"I hope you're happy, Logan," Wraith snapped, punctuating his angry words with his bobbing chin. "You can bet I'm not. I don't know what the hell you thought you were pulling, trying to smoke me out or whatever, but you've caused me a lot of trouble today. Cost me one of my hidey-holes, too, and I'm not likely to forget that any time soon. I don't know how you found me, and I don't want to know. I saved your tail for old times' sake, and now that I've done it, you and the shapeshifter here can hit the road. Whatever you're in, leave me out of it. Just clear out. We were on the same team once upon a time, but that doesn't make us friends."

Wraith looked as though he might happily have continued this rant for several more minutes if something wasn't done to stop him. Wolverine didn't want to hear him anymore. With the sharp sound of metal on metal and the click of joints locking in place, his claws popped out. Logan stepped up on the bed, over Mystique, and back down again in front of John Wraith. The other man glanced down at the claws, gleaming in the diffuse sunlight streaming through the filthy hotel room windows, and the words stopped erupting from his mouth.

"You're right," Wolverine said. "We ain't friends. Thanks for pointin' that out. Now we both know where we stand. You can see where you stand, can't you, Wraith?"

"What do you want?" the skinny man asked bluntly.

"You don't know?" Logan asked skeptically.

Wraith didn't bother answering.

"Right," Logan replied. "Those jumpsuit boys, looked like they were wearing the old Team X overalls? They call themselves Team Alpha. I don't know who they're working for, but they're not the amateurs they seem to be. Somehow, they've managed to snatch Sabretooth, Maverick, Banshee, and the Black Widow without too much trouble."

"Wolverine and I gave them a bit of a hard time," Mystique said, rubbing her forehead and squinting painfully. "We had the advantage of knowing they were coming. Thanks for the save, by the way. Sorry to say the journal we grabbed up from your flop got trashed with Logan's ride."

"It wasn't anything important," Wraith said, but Wolverine didn't think he sounded very sincere.

Then, as if an idea had just struck him, Wraith looked at Mystique as though she were under a microscope.

"What?" she asked.

"Those morons weren't after you because you were kicking up dust looking for me?" Wraith asked.

"You been listenin' at all?" Logan said with a snarl.

"So they've come after you as well?" Mystique asked Wraith.

"Hard and fast," Wraith replied. "But escaping is sort of my specialty. I've been hiding out for days."

Wolverine stared at him, trying to decide if he could trust Wraith or not. What worried him was that he found he didn't have much of a choice.

"I don't see the connections," Wraith said suddenly. "Cassidy. The Widow. What do—?"

Logan cut him off. "You remember that time you left us high and dry in East Berlin, Kestrel?" he sneered. "That's the connection. That op is what we're looking at here. Near as I can tell, nobody should be able to put all the parties involved in East Berlin at that time except your employers, Interpol, and possibly the Mossad."

"Not the Mossad," Mystique said. "They never knew Team X was involved. It wasn't in my reports."

This was the moment where he figured Wraith would end the conversation. He was a loyal soldier. If he was also being hunted, he would never figure his bosses were involved. He'd be more likely to just go in and ask them than to be sneaky about it. For a spy, he was too damn predictable, as far as his loyalty went.

But there was a first time for everything.

"You're right," Wraith said. "So what do we do about it?"

"We were hopin' you could help us with that," Wolverine admitted. "We need to find the others before somebody decides they don't need 'em alive anymore. We need to find out who's behind this whole thing, and why."

"We need access to the Agency's files on Team X, " Mystique said. "Everything. Do you have access to that kind of thing?"

Wraith looked thoughtful for a moment, stroked his chin. The smile that Wolverine had become so familiar with over the years he spent with Team X blossomed on the man's face. It was radiant and almost always a mask for something else.

"You're going to love this, Logan," Wraith said. "I know how we can get to those files."

Logan said nothing, only stared at Wraith awaiting an answer.

"We've got to break into Langley."

Wolverine stared at him. Mystique's mouth was open.

"You're talking about CIA headquarters, I assume," she asked, and blinked several times as the absolute insanity of the idea became clear to all of them.

"You broke into a S.H.I.E.L.D. base yesterday," Logan said. "What's the difference?"

THEN

Once out of East Berlin, Warsaw was a straight shot across several hundred miles of Eastern Europe, mostly made up of farmland, small towns, and several rivers. They had been fortunate enough to find a Wartburg truck sitting overnight behind a clothing store in Alexanderplatz, particularly since motor vehicles of any kind were increasingly rare the deeper behind the Iron Curtain one might delve. But Team X did not feel fortunate as the truck bounced and rattled along the road that would take them to Poznań, Poland, which lay sleepily along the Warta River.

They had lit out of East Berlin as dawn approached. Though they had undergone a certain amount of scrutiny, that was completely normal for a nation as paranoid as East Germany. Still, Logan had been stunned that they didn't have more trouble.

"They're looking for Western spies," Silver Fox commented as they bounced along in the back of the truck. "Western spies would be insane to get in a jam in East Berlin and then go *further* into communist territory."

Wolverine had smiled. But Fox was right. The border guards had looked them over carefully, but not with the air of soldiers looking for spies. North was German by birth, and he knew the language and customs well enough that the guards didn't seem suspicious at all. At least, no more so than their job demanded.

One of them had even given Maverick a cigarette.

The Polish countryside was completely different from East Germany. Though at first it had looked the same, it quickly became obvious that the atmosphere in Poland made it nearly another world. The pressure and the paranoia seemed to lift the further they got into the farmland. Early risers tilling their fields or making their way along the road by foot or horseback waved as they passed.

Logan had always admired the Poles for the way they had held their heads high under the yoke of communism. But he had never felt any benefit from their fortitude until now. The peasants in Poland had resisted the Soviet-style collective farms, and most of the nation's land remained in private hands. The sense of the value of the individual was not dead here.

He suspected that these people would neither be on the watch for spies, nor would they be likely to care much if they actually found some. Warsaw might be another story, more than likely overrun by Soviet agents. But the Polish countryside offered no threat to Team X save for the chance that they might pass communist authorities on the road.

For now, they concentrated on making sure their transportation didn't break down before they reached Poznań, where they hoped to find enough fuel to make it to Warsaw. At the rate they were traveling, however, it would likely be midafternoon at the earliest before they reached the Polish capital.

Creed, Logan, and Fox had been quiet for some time in the back of the truck. In the front, North drove in silence, sometimes humming to himself. He was comfortable here, Logan realized. And in an odd way, he understood. This was familiar territory for Maverick, the same way mountain forests and snowy valleys felt, to Wolverine, like home.

But they weren't silent out of their appreciation for the beauty of nature, or the less stressful atmosphere of the Polish countryside. The weight of unfinished business lay upon them heavily, and the conflicts that had already arisen, the questions that had been raised, brewed slowly into a maelstrom among them. Logan sensed it, and didn't know what to do to stop it. In truth, he wasn't at all sure that he wanted to stop it.

In the end, to no one's surprise, it was Creed who broke the silence.

"So, we're gonna kill the girl, right?" Sabretooth snarled suddenly.

Silver Fox jumped a bit, startled by his voice. Amazingly, Creed did not call her on it. He must have felt it, too, Logan thought. The storm brewing, there among them. A small window separated Maverick from the back of the truck, and it was open so that they could speak to one another.

But North didn't respond.

In the back with the others, Logan frowned. "The Widow?"

"Who else would I mean?" Creed grunted. "This op has gotten pretty sloppy. Mission specs would seem to indicate that you oughtta let me rip her throat out. Never mind the simple fact that she's a commie spy.

"Come to think of it, I'll say it again. We come across him, we ought to kill the Irishman, too. I doubt if the Agency is going to want the choirboys in Interpol to have any information about us in particular, or the Agency in general. We'll have to shut him down, and it won't break my heart any if we have to do it messy."

Wolverine didn't answer. Hard as it was to admit, there was logic in what Sabretooth said, particularly regarding the Black Widow.

Through the window that looked in on the cab, he saw a sprawling farm. A pair of horses drew a wagon across the property and a man walked beside them. A burst of bitter envy swept through him, but Logan pushed it away. His life had never been that simple, and he strongly doubted that it ever would be.

It had turned out to be a beautiful, green and blue day. But not here. Not in the sterile darkness in the back of the truck, where murder was discussed without any more gravity than farming. It was part of the job, sometimes.

"You're not going to agree with him, are you?" Fox said.

Logan only looked at her.

"I can see the Widow," Fox elaborated. "I've no objection to taking her down. She's KGB, and wouldn't think twice about doing the same to us. But Cassidy's on our side. He's one of the white hats."

Creed bellowed deep, thunderous laughter.

"You got brain damage, squaw," he said cruelly. "What makes you think we're the white hats?"

Silence again. It was a question that Silver Fox definitely did not have an answer for.

But after a moment, she did. "Fine. You want to take out everyone who knows too much? What about Mystique? Long before you consider murdering an agent of Interpol, you should think about the shapeshifter. She's an assassin and a liar. And I think we can all agree that she is most definitely not with us on this."

Creed nodded. "If that's what it takes, I'll kill Mystique myself."

"Of course you will," Fox replied grimly. "You'll kill anyone if you get the opportunity."

"Darlin'," Creed replied, "I'll make the opportunity."

"That's enough," Logan said.

The subject was hard enought to dissect without having to listen to the team bicker.

"We do the job," he said simply. "The Widow makes it hard on us, we'll make it hard on her. Anyone, and that means anyone, gets in our way, tries to keep us from completin' this op, we take them down. If that means they don't get back up again, then that's the way it's gonna be. Any questions?"

Creed smiled.

Fox glanced away.

Only North spoke up. "Yeah, I have a question," he said through the open window between cab and truck. "Do you really think that's warranted? Under any circumstances at all, I mean? You're willing to kill an Interpol agent just to fulfill this mission?"

"If we don't get that disk—" Wolverine began.

"The hell with the disk!" Maverick snapped, glancing over his shoulder. "If Interpol gets it, what's the great loss? The West is safe for another few weeks, until some other moron with a big mouth and even bigger weapons comes along. Okay, you want to keep it out of Mossad hands, but are we prepared to cut Mystique down in cold blood to do it?"

He'd grown even angrier now, and kept glancing back to emphasize his points.

"Why can't we just grab the disk up, use only what force is necessary, and get it home before anyone knows we were even here?" he demanded.

"You knew what kind of game you were getting yourself into, junior," Wolverine said.

"You're right," North admitted. "I did. And if I'm put into a position where I have to kill to save myself or one of you, or to secure my mission objective when there is no other alternative, I'll do exactly that. But if killing isn't absolutely necessary, that's another story. How far do we go before it stops being soldiering and starts being just plain murder?"

"Little late for a conscience now, Maverick," Logan said. "I know you started out as a freedom fighter, but what we do ain't that black-and-white. They don't call it black ops for nothin', North. You knew that when you signed on."

"So we just follow orders, do what we're told, kill anyone who gets in the way, and then we're supposed to sleep at night?" Maverick asked, turning so sharply to glare through the small window that he jerked the steering wheel and the old truck bounced onto the soft, crumbling shoulder of the road.

"I sleep like a baby," Creed said happily, obviously enjoying the conflict.

"A bloodthirsty baby," Fox added, and Sabretooth glared at her.

Maverick had righted the truck, brought it back onto the road, and now he sat, brooding darkly, eyes forward. He stared out the windshield in silence, until Logan gave his response.

"Op parameters are established for the purpose of secrecy, security, and the safety of the team," Logan explained. "You know all this. We follow our orders."

"But sometimes we improvise, don't we, Logan?" North

said softly. "You do it all the time. Now Creed wants to use his own interpretation of those op parameters you seem so proud of. Well, I choose to interpret them differently. I think we need to improvise."

His hands carefully holding the wheel steady, Maverick turned to meet Wolverine's gaze, staring through the tiny window with a look of cold iron.

"Can you honestly tell me," he began calmly, "do you truly expect me to believe you're nothing more than a shorter version of Creed? Stone-cold psycho? Is that it?"

Maverick looked back at the road. Wolverine couldn't see his mouth move, or his eyes, and his words had a kind of bodiless, ghostly quality as they floated to the back of the truck.

"I know you've got that beast inside you," Maverick said. "That there are times in a battle when pain drives you over the edge and you have that berserker zone you go into. I've seen it."

"That's the only thing the runt's got goin' for him," Creed snarled.

Maverick turned to look at Wolverine again, continuing as though Sabretooth had never spoken.

"I've never seen you kill without reason. I can't believe you'd just murder somebody who isn't a target . . . someone who's on the side of the angels, for God's sake!" North snapped. "I don't even know Cassidy, but if we're willing to kill him . . . hell, who's next?"

"That ain't up to you, Maverick," Logan said angrily. "You do the job and you take your pay and you go home. And if you need somethin' to help you sleep, well, you can sure afford it with what we're paid."

Before Maverick could answer, Silver Fox spoke up.

"You're wrong, Logan," she said simply, and he stared at her. Her features were jagged. Bitter.

"I don't know about you, but there isn't anyone in the world that can make me do something I don't want to do. I make my own choices. Whatever we choose to do here, each of us, that's up to us. We follow orders, we don't follow orders, that's a choice. I'm not saying I agree with everything Maverick's said, but I'll tell you this: if I kill a man, his blood is on my hands, not the Agency's.

"I'm with Creed on the Widow, and frankly I think we ought to kill Mystique as well. But Cassidy? I can't believe you'd even think about killing him," she said, glaring at Wolverine.

"Hell, nobody else wants the job, I'd be more than happy to hack up the big leprechaun," Creed growled. "You bunch of bleedin' hearts are startin' to make me sick."

Wolverine leaned back against the wall of the truck. His skull banged lightly against the wall in time with the vehicle's bouncing in and out of the ruts in the road. He was deeply disturbed by the conversation, not because of the subject, but because of the team's seeming eagerness to attack one another. There had always been conflict within Team X. But it was growing worse with every operation. And this one was tailor-made to split them apart once and for all.

"Listen up, folks, and listen good," he drawled. "I never said I was gonna kill Sean Cassidy. Never said I'd be willin' to kill anyone in cold blood. Cassidy's a good man. I'd like to have a drink with him when all o' this is done. What I said was Team X ain't got the luxury o' lettin' anyone get in the way of us doin' our jobs. Cassidy's smart, he'll know that. If he's not as smart as I think he is, he might end up wearin' a toe tag. That's the way this game is played.

"Any o' you have a problem with that, or a problem with the fact that I've got command o' this op, hop out and walk home right now. Otherwise, shut up and do the job."

Maverick's knuckles were white on the steering wheel, but he didn't speak for more than an hour after that. Silver Fox glared at Wolverine from time to time, and also kept silent. Sabretooth leaned back against the wall of the truck with his arms crossed behind his head and his eyes closed and a small smile on his face that showed the sharpness of his teeth.

Wolverine had called what they did a game. There had never been a time when he was more aware that it was exactly that, and yet it was a game with no winners.

Poland made the Black Widow nervous. She had only been involved in the espionage trade for a little more than a year, and already she had an international reputation, but at heart, she always felt like a nineteen-year-old girl who still grieved for the loving husband she had lost. She drew her strength from anger and bitterness and the memory of Alexi. But she could never put her fear behind her, not completely. Instead, she faced her fear, analyzed it, and in so doing, transformed it into caution. It had served her well.

In the case of Poland, the Widow's caution led her to travel as inconspicuously as possible. She had been met in East Berlin by her contact, a tall, white-haired, bearded man named Mikhail. In a car that looked nearly decrepit on the outside but was finely tuned within, they had set off for Warsaw at an almost plodding pace. At least, Natasha felt as though they were plodding along. She only wanted to be home. The hatred that she had felt coming from Sean Cassidy had disturbed her deeply. She didn't understand it, but now she only wanted to forget about it.

She and Mikhail shared the front seat of the car. Anyone seeing them pass might think them father and daughter. Absurdly, she felt safe in his presence, though she could likely have killed him in seconds. But it was the fatherly qualities in the man that allowed her to relax even a little in Poland. He would leave her at the Soviet border, but once there, the Widow would feel at home, and confident. Until then, it was just something else she would try not to think about.

Natasha Romanova had traveled in several Western countries already. She had been cautious, of course, but neither truly afraid nor anxious. She knew where she—where any Soviet, particularly a member of the KGB—stood when she worked a mission in the West. They were the enemy. Crass, simple, materialistic people without honor or compassion or loyalty.

At home in the Soviet Union, or in most of its satellites, from East Germany to Czechoslovakia to Romania, the Widow also knew where she stood. Soviet power was unquestioned. Without the power of the U.S.S.R. to protect them, these satellite nations would be prey to the whims of the West. As an agent of the KGB, she would be not only respected, but feared throughout these lands.

Then there was Poland. The KGB was feared, yes. But respected? Not necessarily. The Polish people had never truly accepted communism. Had, in fact, spurned it whenever possible. While the Poles were certainly thankful when the Nazis were defeated at the end of World War II, they did not see the Soviet Union as liberators, but rather as nothing more than a new oppressor. Though she would never have voiced such an opinion, Natasha had wondered if the Polish view might not have been partly justified, particularly since the Soviets had redrawn the Polish borderline, forcing millions of Poles to migrate west in order to remain within their country's borders.

Though Polish authorities cooperated with their Soviet counterparts, Natasha remained dubious about the population at large. So much so, in fact, that when she traveled through Poland, she made it a point to remain as inconspicuous as possible.

Lost in thought, she stared out the passenger's window of the car. Despite her anxiety, despite the spring that threatened at any moment to puncture the skin of her lower back even through a coat and two layers beneath it, Natasha felt herself drifting off to sleep. As her eyes fluttered closed, she saw a woman hanging laundry behind a farmhouse in the distance. And as she surrendered to the world of her dreaming mind, she felt, curiously, a pang of sadness she didn't understand. When she woke, she would not remember it, which was just as well.

• • •

"Wake now, Natalia Romanova," a deep, warm voice called to her from somewhere beyond the wall of sleep.

The Widow's eyes fluttered open. The sun still shone but it had moved across the sky quite a distance. She was surprised at how long she had slept, and a little embarrassed. She steeled herself for Mikhail's disapproval, but when she looked at him, he smiled kindly at her.

"You feel better now, I trust," he said in Russian. "I did not want to wake you, but we are almost to Warsaw."

"Much better, thank you," she found herself admitting, and blinked in surprise.

She was not usually so open with people she did not know well. And, if she were truthful with herself, since Alexi's death, she had kept all others at such a distance that she did not really know anyone well.

Natasha let her head fall against the seat and her eyes lingered on the smoking factories that loomed on either side of the road ahead. The farmland remained all around them, but perhaps half a mile ahead it became overgrown scrub brush and then there were only the factories jutting from the earth like mechanoid volcanoes.

That was Warsaw.

Or at least, the factories were the outer edges of Warsaw. It had been the capital of Poland since the tail end of the sixteenth century, but during World War II, like so many other European cities, it had been reduced to ashes. After the war, the Poles had used old paintings and photographs and rebuilt the capital from the ground up. Around that new old city, modern Warsaw had been built, and around modern Warsaw, the factories had gone up. Passing through, toward the center of the city, was not unlike traveling back in time.

"We'll go to our checkpoint right away," Mikhail told her. "You can sleep some more if you like. Otherwise we'll get fuel, enjoy a quiet meal—you will have access to a shower if you wish—and then we'll be on our way."

"Yes," she agreed. "A shower and something to eat. But unless you want to sleep, and don't want me to drive, I'd like to continue on."

Mikhail said nothing, only nodded his understanding. The Widow wondered if he did, in fact, understand. She would not be able to truly relax until she was home again. Or, at least, back inside the borders of Mother Russia.

They had passed the factories and were in the thick of the offices, government buildings, and apartment complexes that made up modern Warsaw. The Widow idly gazed out her window at the people on the street and the buildings they passed. For all its complaints, Warsaw was a far healthier city than many others she had seen within the Soviet sphere of influence.

She studied the faces of a pair of old women who walked along in front of the façade of a some kind of office structure. Wrinkled lines and silver hair beneath the scarves they wore tied over their heads. They passed a small shop that sold violins and other musical instruments, all made by hand, if the window sign could be believed.

At the end of the block, a man gazed back at her from a street corner. A man with red hair.

The Widow opened her mouth to scream in perfect synchronicity with Sean Cassidy. Mikhail didn't have time to react to her warning, even if he had heard it. Every window in the car shattered and it rocked up on two wheels before rolling over onto its roof with a crunch of glass and the hideous, eerie scream of metal scraping pavement.

Her eyes flicked open, and Natasha realized that she had been unconscious. But for how long? Where was Cassidy?

Something hot and sticky on her face; it had to be blood. She licked her lips, tasted it, and wondered idly, barely interested, how badly she was hurt. She glanced over at Mikhail, saw the huge shard of glass jutting from his chest and the way the older man's blood had soaked into his clothes and spattered the dashboard. His white hair and beard were splashed as well, as though he'd been painting and gotten sloppy. But this wasn't paint.

For several seconds, her mind went numb. Then she saw that Mikhail was breathing, though lightly. The knowledge that he yet lived was compounded by her realization that he wouldn't be alive for long if he didn't get medical attention right away.

Dark rage burned inside the Widow. Sirens whooped in the distance, and she hoped that at least one of them was an ambulance. People shouted on the street not far from the car. She almost didn't hear Cassidy's approach. But even if she hadn't heard those footsteps, she would have known he was coming.

The fool announced himself.

"Your time is up, Romanova," Cassidy said, in English, not even attempting to hide himself.

His attack had shocked her. The Widow had never imagined that an agent of Interpol—albeit a mutant—would stage a daylight, very public assault on anyone, KGB agent or not, anywhere. But especially not deep inside the sphere of Soviet influence. Yes, this was Poland. But no matter what misgivings the Poles had toward the Soviets, they wouldn't support what appeared to be a Western mutant terrorist attack on unarmed Soviet citizens.

Despite a pain in her back that she didn't want to think about, and the blood on her face from cuts she received from the shattered windshield's fragments, the Widow felt strong, confident, and very angry.

She closed her eyes, measured her breathing, and waited.

Several times more, Cassidy called out to her. But she knew that his anger and impatience would get the best of him. As the sirens grew closer, he crouched down beside her broken window. She lay upside down, only her seat belt holding her up. Cassidy reached inside the car, began to search her clothing for the disk she had retrieved from the Zhevakovs.

Natasha lashed out, her right hand gripping Cassidy's neck. He shouted in surprise, tried to pull back, but even weakened, she held on long enough to fire the electric charge from the glove on her hand. Tens of thousands of volts slammed right into Cassidy's throat.

He stumbled backward, mouth open in a silent scream, and fell to the pavement. The Widow cursed him in Russian, glanced over at Mikhail to make certain he was still breathing, then fumbled at her seat belt, trying to extricate herself from the car. She'd felt weak, at first, but now adrenaline was pumping through her system.

The seat belt released, and she brought her legs down first and managed to scramble out through the shattered passenger window without scraping herself too badly. The Widow stood, stretched, glanced at the small crowd of laborers who had gathered to stare in shock at the totaled car, then she looked at Cassidy.

And he was moving.

He shouldn't have been moving. She'd hit him up close with a full dose of what her KGB controller had called "the widow's bite." He should be completely unconscious by now.

But Cassidy was obviously made of sterner stuff than most. Perhaps, Natasha thought, his mutant constitution made him more resilient than the average human. It didn't matter. She'd just shock him again.

First, though, she wanted some answers.

Sean's head felt as though it was going to explode. Pain lanced through his skull and his mouth felt dry. But he had to get up. Had to get at the Widow. If he just killed her and went back to London without the disk, Interpol would probably bring him up on some kind of charges. He needed the disk to justify whatever else happened today.

"Get up, Cassidy," he grumbled to himself.

Or he tried. The words came out a halting croak. The electroshock that the Widow had hit him with had done something to his voice. Suddenly, Cassidy panicked. If his vocal cords were damaged, he was in big trouble. He wouldn't be able to fly out of here when the job was done, and it was a long way back to West Germany if you were a redhead and the Russkies already knew you were a spy.

He shook off the shock, rolled over, and got to his knees, looked up . . . and saw the Widow.

There was blood on her face in several places, and glass in her hair. But what stopped him cold was the hatred in her eyes. It hadn't been there before, and for just a moment, he wondered if his own eyes looked the same.

"You cold-hearted son of a . . ." she began, in English.

Cassidy railed at her. "Ye dare much, Widow," he croaked weakly. "Ye may be a wee slip of a girl, but ye're the most evil little wench I've ever set eyes on."

She kicked him then, not quite stable on her feet. That was probably the only thing that saved him, as Cassidy turned his head slightly to the side and the Widow's boot caught him just under his right ear. He sprawled to the pavement again, but the kick seemed almost to have cleared his head rather than muddled it further.

Cassidy rolled to his feet, tried his sonic scream . . . and only got a hoarse little roar for his trouble.

"What've ye done to me, witch?" he whispered. "As if it weren't enough to ambush me the last time we met?"

The Widow danced closer to him, moving with more confidence now, and spun into another kick. Cassidy was ready for her, and blocked it with his forearm. He hit her then, a weak, backhanded blow across the face, filled with disdain and hatred.

But Romanova ignored his hate. She spun away from the blow and turned into a fighting stance. Her eyes and her body told him that one-on-one, he could never beat her. She was a far superior hand-to-hand fighter. But neither of them was up to much of a fight at the moment, and Cassidy planned to take advantage of that.

She tried to kick again. Cassidy dodged. But he'd played right into a feint on her part, and the Widow brought her elbow down on the back of his neck. Sean went to his knees, and she had him.

"There's a good man dying in that car and his blood is on your hands," she said in heavily accented English.

Cassidy wanted to say something about the man being KGB and deserving what he got. But he couldn't. He could barely think beyond the idea that he might have killed a man he didn't know, a man who'd done nothing to him. A man who might have had a family, a wife and children of his own.

It wasn't him. He knew that. He was an inspector for Interpol, a lawman. He hoped that the man would live, but after a moment, the echo of the Widow's bitter words came back to him.

"Ye've got a lot of nerve, I'll give ye that, lass," Cassidy croaked. "When last we met, ye put a man's life in danger because ye knew I'd try to save him. And when I did, ye caught me down defenseless and tossed me from a rooftop. By God's grace alone, I'm still alive today. But I was in hospital for near a month, girl. When I got home, me wife was gone. Dead, Widow . . . and what an appropriate name for a creature such as yourself. I wasn't home, nor can I ever go back there without thinkin' of what might have been if I'd been home."

"But . . ." the Widow began, and Cassidy saw that she was startled by his words. "But this is what we do. How can you blame me for . . ."

He took advantage of her confusion. Swiftly, Cassidy lunged at her, grabbed the girl's jacket at the collar, and brought his fist down hard on her. Hard enough that he lost his grip and she stumbled back, away from him, and went down on the pavement. And now their positions were reversed.

"It's not what *I* do, ye stupid git!" he roared. "I'm a policeman, is all. Maybe it's more complicated than that, but I'm not a spy. Not some terrorist!"

The Widow frowned, gingerly touched the place where he had struck her. Cassidy stalked toward her again.

"Give me that disk, girl," he demanded.

"I'm not a terrorist," she snarled.

"By God, Widow, if ye don't give me that disk now I'll pry it from your dead—"

A voice shattered the intimacy of their conflict. A barked order. Not from the civilian bystanders, that was for certain. No, though the voice shouted in Polish, it came from behind Cassidy. He turned, slowly, to the sound of a dozen pistols being cocked, and saw the uniformed Polish police officers who aimed their weapons at him. He knew what they saw. A Westerner beating a young girl who'd barely survived a car accident.

In a sense, they were right.

Cassidy opened his mouth to let loose with his sonic scream, to clear himself a path and fly off to a place where he could think about all of this. He desperately needed a place to think.

Nothing came from his throat but a strangled squeak.

Cassidy stared at the weapons. At the anger on the faces of the men who held them. After a moment, he held his hands in the air, and realized he was going to have plenty of time to reflect on his battle with the Black Widow.

If he lived past the next thirty seconds or so.

THEN

The afternoon was almost gone and dinnertime was fast approaching when the stolen truck carrying Team X rolled past the factories that lay on the outer edges of Warsaw. They needed gas and food and rest, but Wolverine figured they'd be fortunate enough to find the first two. Rest wasn't on the agenda, not until the op was concluded.

Gray buildings belched black smoke on either side of the road, and the truck was running on fumes. Logan was at the wheel now. They'd stopped a while back for him to switch places with North. Maverick spoke perfect German, but Wolverine spoke fluent Russian, with a good enough accent that most Poles, at least, would believe him to be exactly that.

Logan peered through the grimy windshield, trying hard not to think about how close to empty the gas tank was. This was familiar territory—he'd first been to Warsaw more than fifteen years earlier—but there were a number of new factories, newly developed areas, and enough time had passed that he found it hard to navigate the streets.

The "new" section of the city, built around the reconstructed old center, was just ahead. If they passed more than a few blocks into that, they would have gone too far.

Then, suddenly, a whitewashed, two-story building with three wide garage doors came into view on the right, straddling the line between the industrial section of the city and the broad expanse of offices and apartment buildings just ahead. Logan forced the gear shift down with a horrible grinding noise, and pulled the truck over to the side of the road. A much larger truck, belching its own noxious fumes, trumpeted its driver's disapproval just before it thundered by.

"What's goin' on up there, runt?" Creed asked.

Sabretooth was getting antsy. He'd been riding in the back with Silver Fox and Maverick for more than two hours, and Wolverine had been surprised at how little argument there'd been among them. But now Creed wanted out, no question. And Logan couldn't blame him.

He made sure the brake was set, then turned to look through the narrow window at the rest of his team.

"We can't exactly ask the local authorities if they've seen a Russian teenager who just happens to be a KGB agent," Wolverine explained, bristling at having to state the obvious. "There's a mechanic's shop right across the street. I used to know the guy who ran it. If he's still there, he might be able to help us find out what we need to know."

"Able, okay," Maverick said grimly. "But willing?"

"That's a funny thing about me askin' people for information, North," Logan replied. "Even if they ain't willin' to share at first, they always come around in the end. Now you just get up here, and if anybody comes by to make you move the truck, or ask what you're doin' here, don't even try speakin' Polish. Use your German. That's authentic and they'll be able to tell. Then, even if they think there's somethin' fishy, they won't know which side of the Iron Curtain you're employed by. I think that's the best we can hope for, right about now."

Wolverine hopped out, and North came around and took his place at the wheel.

"Gimme ten minutes," Logan replied. "You don't see me or get some kind of signal from me, come and fish me out."

"You got it," North confirmed. "But what if this old friend of yours doesn't pan out?"

"I got a contingency plan," Wolverine said dismissively.

But North wasn't about to let it go. "I'd like to hear it," he said. "I think we should know what you've got in mind."

Wolverine stared at him a moment. He thought about smiling, trying to offer some kind of reassurance that they weren't on a suicide mission, but found he didn't have it in him.

"My old buddy doesn't have any answers for me, then we start makin' noise," Logan explained. "We'll draw attention to ourselves, bring the KGB down on our heads, then turn the tables, kick their behinds, and find out what happened to the Widow."

Maverick stared at him, expressionless.

"That's not much of a plan," he said at last.

"No, it ain't," Wolverine agreed.

"Well, I for one think it's a hell of a plan," Creed called from the back of the truck, his voice floating through the narrow window. "Probably get us killed, but I like a challenge."

Maverick's grim countenance actually crumpled into a smile. He hung his head, chuckling. Logan was surprised and pleased to see him relaxed, even for a moment.

"Well," Maverick said, "I'm sure that gives you a lot of confidence in your plan."

"Yeah," Logan agreed. "That kinda endorsement always gives me a sorta warm, fuzzy feelin' inside."

North smiled again, then shook his head with a look of bemused disbelief. "All right," he said. "I'm going to try to take a little nap. Try not to get yourself killed or, even worse, do something that would require our help. That'd be bad."

"I'll keep it in mind," Logan replied, then turned and walked across the street toward the pale face of the auto mechanic's garage.

It occurred to him that it didn't look much different from a lot of auto body shops he'd seen back home. The place was good sized, with the interior of the triple-doored garage rising up through the second story. But above the office area, there were several rooms given over to the residence of the shop's owner, Janek Sniegowski. He only hoped the man was still alive.

At the office door, Logan rapped on the glass several times. It was late, and he'd reasoned that any mechanics who might work there during normal hours had probably already left for home. The dying sunlight created a glare on the office windows, and it was difficult to see inside, but Logan was certain he saw someone move within.

When a face appeared beyond the glass, eyes narrowed at his intrusion, he realized that his disguise was not likely to inspire a stranger to open their door to him now that this area of the city was relatively deserted. The man at the door was young, perhaps twenty, and his face and hands were smeared with black grease and oil stains.

"What do you want?" the young man asked in Polish, his tone bordering on the belligerent.

"I want to see Janek Sniegowski," Wolverine told him, but he spoke in Russian, in the clipped, almost imperial accent of Moscovites.

The mechanic's eyes widened slightly. The belligerence didn't disappear, but along with the man's hostility there bloomed a respect tinged with fear. Oddly dressed and speaking the way he did, the young man had to assume he was either KGB or something very like it. The hard look he gave the mechanic didn't do anything to dissuade that impression.

Less than two minutes later, a white-haired man just a bit shorter than Wolverine, and with a solid paunch at his belly, came to the glass. He stared in silence at Wolverine for nearly half a minute before he shook his head in disbelief and unlocked the door.

"Come in, old friend," the man said. "I did not recognize you at first . . . or, perhaps it is that I recognized you too well. How can this be Logan, I wondered, unless he has not aged a single day since last we met?"

"Good genes," Wolverine replied, and the two men exchanged a glance that told him that Janek knew better, but was willing to accept that the subject was closed.

If only he knew how close that was to the truth, Logan thought.

"This is my son, Wladek," Janek said. "He is an excellent mechanic, but it is all he knows. Wladek, leave us, please. Finish what you were doing in the garage."

The young man, Janek's son, stared at his father in surprise. He had seemed prepared to defend the old man against Logan, or at least to try. Even now he seemed certain that Logan would harm the old man in some way, but after a moment's hesitation, he obeyed. The door from the office to the garage swung shut behind him, and Logan could hear the kid growling with disgust just before the door closed fully.

"What'll you tell him later?" Logan asked.

"That it is none of his business," Janek said, and his tone told Logan that the old man's family affairs were none of *his* business.

"Why did you not just shatter the glass?" Janek Sniegowski asked, nodding toward the front of the office. "You are known for your less than gentle entrances, my old friend."

Logan smiled. "Didn't want to give you any headaches," he said. "Just coming here is asking too much as it is. I owe you, Janek. Now my debt will be even greater."

"You saved my life, once, Logan. You owe me nothing," Sniegowski replied, the wrinkled skin at the corners of his eyes bunching even more as he narrowed them. "Now, you need something from me. What can I do for you?"

"Looking for a girl," Logan replied.

Janek raised his eyebrows but said nothing.

"KGB. Name o' Romanova. Also called the Black Widow. She's traveling by car from East Berlin to Moscow, and I've been told this would be her first stop. I was hopin' that you could tap your old KGB contacts and find out if she's passed through, and if not, where she would meet her own contact," he explained.

Janek stood, stared thoughtfully out through the glare. He walked over to a corner table and picked up a pack of cigarettes. Logan remained silent as the old man knocked a butt from the pack and lit up. The cough that ensued was awful, and Wolverine knew immediately that Janek Sniegowski was dying. He might not even know it yet, but the cigarettes had taken his life. Had killed him just as surely as the KGB would have if they'd ever found out that one of their Polish informers was working both sides of the street.

That was a long time ago, but from the way the old man's

brow furrowed, Logan knew Janek had remained in the information loop. Once a spy, always a spy. To the death, all too often.

Janek took a long drag on his unfiltered cigarette, then looked up at Logan.

"She's been through already," he said.

Logan cursed silently.

"Her next stop will be Minsk, but if you want to stop her, you'd better try to do it before she reaches the border," Janek said. "Once inside the Soviet Union, she will be much better protected. She was traveling with another agent, but the man is in the hospital here in Warsaw, so the Widow now travels alone."

"What?" Logan snapped. "What happened to the other agent? Why is he in the hospital?"

"They were attacked on the road," Janek replied. "Right in the middle of Warsaw. The man was arrested, of course."

"Tell me about this man," Logan growled.

"He has red hair," Janek said. "From England, I think."

"Ireland," Logan corrected, then cursed under his breath. "You know him?"

Logan admitted that he did, and Janek spent the next fifteen minutes telling him everything he knew about the jail where Sean Cassidy was being kept. It would take a lot of guts and firepower to break the man out, but once they got out of Warsaw, they would probably not be pursued.

Unless they killed somebody.

But if they could break Cassidy out without managing to kill any of the guards, they'd be all right.

Wolverine thanked him, and turned to the office door. He reached for the knob, but something stopped him. A scent. Logan had noticed it before, of course. It had been there all along, the whole while that Janek had been speaking. But he'd paid no attention to it because it belonged there. What he'd failed to notice was that the scent had lingered, not as a trace odor in the air, but as a real, tangible presence.

He turned back to look at Janek, then glanced at the door that led into the garage where the mechanics worked. Janek couldn't have missed Logan's hesitation, nor the sudden diversion of his attention. The old man frowned, a thundercloud passing across his face as he took a step toward the door to the garage.

But Janek never got there.

Logan smelled the gun oil too late.

The door banged open. "Traitor!" Wladek Sniegowski shouted in Polish.

Then he shot his father twice in the chest. The old man was dead before his body hit the floor; his heart had stopped instantly, and Logan would later wonder if it was the heartbreak of his son's betrayal that had killed him.

"You . . . animal!" Wolverine roared, completely unaware of the irony, and went after the killer, unsheathing the pair of large knives that had remained hidden at his back.

"Die, you dog!" Wladek screamed in terror, and swiveled to aim the pistol at Logan's chest.

Wolverine planted one foot on the office chair and sprang off it, vaulting across the room. His blood raced, adrenaline surged, and the horror of seeing a man he'd cared for gunned down by his own son threatened to drive out any semblance of reason.

A bullet slammed into his lower left abdomen, kept from penetrating by the Kevlar woven into the black Team X jumpsuit he wore underneath his peasant clothes.

The mechanic had known his father worked with the KGB, had perhaps been approached by them as well. He executed his father as a traitor, and now intended to kill Logan.

A second bullet hit between Wolverine's clavicle and shoulder.

Wladek Sniegowski would blow the whistle on Team X and the KGB would be all over them. The mission would be over if the young man with the grease-smeared face was allowed to live.

Logan landed on him, the gun fired again and missed, and then the knives fell and struck home. When Wladek Sniegowski stopped moving, Logan wiped the blades of his knives on the man's already greasy shirt and stared down at him with a nause-ating mix of emotions roiling within his gut.

"He was your father," Wolverine whispered.

Then he walked out into the swiftly falling night and across the street to where his team waited for him. It was warmer here than it had been in East Berlin, but Logan didn't notice. There was a coldness in his heart that he felt certain would be with him for some time to come.

"Tell me again why we're doin' this," Creed whispered.

It was full dark now, after nine P.M., and the night sky was overcast and threatening rain. They'd gotten lucky with that. No stars, no moon, no lights but what Warsaw's own energy would provide. On the main roads, that meant intermittent street lamps. But on side streets and alleys, it could just as well mean absolute darkness, black as pitch.

Garbage cans—mostly overfilled—lined the narrow street on either side. There was a restaurant on one side, and whatever aromas might have come from within were tainted irrevocably by the smell of rotting leftovers, particularly vegetables that had long since ceased to be edible. The smell was horrid, and distracting.

"Tomorrow had to be trash day?" Silver Fox asked aloud, but Logan knew she didn't expect an answer. It was an obser-vation, nothing more.

The four members of Team X stood in the darkness close to the brick wall, dotted with barred windows, that made up the rear wall of the Warsaw police headquarters. Inside, Sean Cas-sidy sat in a cell, more than likely being questioned by KGB agents, or awaiting their arrival. Why Cassidy hadn't used that shriek of his to escape was a question Logan looked forward to having answered. But it didn't change what they needed to do.

"I told you why we're doin' this," Wolverine growled, nar-rowed his eyes, and stared at Creed. "Cassidy's a good man. He's on our side, if we even have a side, and he pulled me out of a one-on-one with the East German cops back in Berlin. I owe him one."

"We could be endangering our mission," Silver Fox whispered.

"Yeah," Logan nodded. "You said that already."

"I also said I'm with you," she reminded him. "I just don't want anyone to forget what we're here for. In and out, nobody to recognize us. Hopefully they'll think we're Interpol or something, or just here for Cassidy."

"Doubtful," Maverick said. "But it doesn't change the fact that we've got to get Cassidy out of there. They'll kill him if we don't. Interpol asks around, Cassidy was never supposed to be here in the first place. We're the only chance he's got." Maverick turned to glare at Creed. "What I don't understand," he whispered, "is what *you're* doing here."

Creed smiled, his mouth a jagged wound in the darkness, and his eyes glinted with mischief. When he spoke, his tone was patronizing.

"I'm here for the team," Sabretooth said, almost a sneer. "All for one, one for all, all that crap. Doesn't matter anyway. We break Cassidy out, I'll still hold Wolverine to his word. The Irishman gets in our way, he's just as dead as any of the others. Right, Logan?"

Wolverine felt six eyes on him, but he ignored them all. He was thinking about the pair of dead-eyed, dark-suited goons he'd seen on the front steps of the police station. KGB guards, no question. Your average Warsaw police officer probably didn't own a suit other than his uniform.

"We ain't gonna get past the KGB watchdogs," he said. "And we can't take 'em out in public without riskin' the rest o' the city knowin' our business too soon, includin' the cops inside the building."

He looked at Silver Fox. Her gypsy disguise wasn't going to work so well up close. But if she covered her head until she was past them and they didn't stop her . . . that was a lot of ifs, but it could work. And if it didn't, well, there was going to be a lot of shooting.

"It's on you, Fox," he said. "There's plenty of women spies, but they ain't gonna be as suspicious o' you as they would o' one of us. Creed especially, with that blond hair o' his. Here's the idea . . ."

Seconds later, Silver Fox rounded the corner in front of police headquarters. The granite steps in front were wide but they led up to a single heavy double door, probably oak. On either side of that door, several steps down, stood KGB agents.

Wolverine counted Fox's footsteps and after she'd taken twenty paces, he followed her. The KGB goons noticed her a moment later, a nice-figured woman with a scarf over her head coming their way. She started up the steps and the two men smiled at one another. One raised his arm and opened his mouth, about to say something to Fox.

The other had noticed Wolverine.

Though he wore Kevlar that would likely stop a direct shot to the heart or lungs—and though he was as hard a man to kill as God had ever made—he still felt vulnerable. They were deep behind enemy lines in the most frigid days yet of the Cold War. He was about to break *into* a jail in the middle of the Soviet sphere of influence, and the place was crawling with KGB.

He was certain he'd done more foolish things in his life; he just couldn't think of any at the moment.

As Logan started up the steps, Silver Fox walked right between the KGB agents and up to the front door of the police station. Several more steps, and the two goons started down toward him. Wolverine saw that Fox was inside the station, and he smiled at the agents and greeted them in Russian.

"Hello, my friends!" he said in their own language. "I have just heard that you captured the man I have been hunting for days."

His accent was not perfect. The implications of this claim were almost preposterous. But this was the KGB. How were individual agents to know what the agency as a whole had been up to? Wolverine's words were just confusing enough to distract them from a direct confrontation for several precious seconds.

A tiny, choked scream issued from the foyer of police headquarters. The KGB agents turned, saw the door was open slightly, and saw a limp hand lying across the threshold.

"Don't move!" one of them barked at Logan in Russian.

They ran up the steps, and Wolverine was right behind them. Inside the foyer, Silver Fox waited. Logan stepped inside and closed the door. Swiftly, silently, the two agents were rendered unconscious in the space between the massive double doors and the more humble interior doors. A moment later, Wolverine opened the outside doors to the signal knock that told him Creed and North had arrived. Then they all stepped over the inert bodies of the KGB agents, and Fox opened the inner door that led into the station proper.

Maverick tossed a pair of concussion grenades into the room. They skittered across wide wooden floorboards, and Fox slammed the door again.

The explosion cracked the door down the middle and blew the hinges nearly off the frame. Creed kicked at the cracked center of the door, and it split in two. He and Logan went in first, ready to take whatever bullets might be coming at them. But most of the cops were still hiding behind their desks, hoping there were no more grenades coming.

"Maverick, Fox, check the cells," Logan barked. "Me an' Creed got your backs."

The police started to rise then, at the sound of Logan's voice, but they'd relieved the KGB agents of their AK-47s, and now brought those weapons into use. It wasn't quiet, that was for certain. But if they could find Cassidy fast, they didn't have to worry about quiet very long.

"Stay down!" Logan shouted in Russian, hoping they all knew the language.

He and Creed sprayed the desks and walls and windows with bullets. He was surprised that Sabretooth didn't just start blowing away the cops, and wondered if Creed had a little bit more logic in his head than they gave him credit for. Kill a few policemen, and their comrades were more likely to try fighting back. They were also likely to get a taste for vengeance when it was all over.

No, if they could just get in and out without . . .

A door off to the left slammed open with a crack. The men's room! The gunman who emerged wore a suit and tie—another KGB man—and he had the barrel trained on Logan's face. Logan dove for the floor, and a bullet whizzed past his head as he went down.

Creed's AK-47 coughed for three seconds, then silence reigned as the steaming, bullet-ridden body of the KGB man slid down the wall, leaving streaks of gore behind.

"Sabretooth, I told you . . . " Logan was shouting as he leapt to his feet.

The cops had started to go for their guns.

"Keep your heads down or all your wives are widows!" Creed snarled in German.

His tone said he meant it. So had his actions. Most of the men in the Warsaw police station apparently understood enough German to get the gist of it, or they could take his meaning just from the tone of his voice. In any case, they stayed down, and Logan was glad.

"Maverick, we don't have much time!" he roared down the hall. "We're gonna have company soon!"

"I don't see him!" Maverick shouted back. "He's not in a cell!"

Logan cursed under his breath. He walked to the nearest police officer, put the muzzle of his AK-47 up against the man's forehead and poked him with it hard enough to make blood well up in a little circle.

"Where is the man with red hair?" he demanded in Russian. "Now!"

The man sputtered, closed his eyes and prayed, and finally told them that Cassidy was being kept upstairs in an interrogation room.

"Maverick, get back in here!" he shouted.

As soon as he saw Maverick at the end of the hall, Wolverine sprinted for the stairwell over to the right. Silver Fox followed and after a few strides she was right behind him. At the top of the stairs were three doors, two of glass and one of thick oak with a barred window in it. This, he guessed, was the interrogation room. Probably soundproof, he thought. When the KGB interrogator arrived, they would want to put Cassidy somewhere where it didn't matter how loud he screamed—not knowing how loud the Irishman could scream when he put his mind to it.

"Check the offices," he told Fox.

She slid with her back against the wall, gun in the air, and kicked open one office door. As she moved to the next, Logan peered into the narrow bathroom across the hall. Then he looked in through the barred window of the interrogation room door.

It was dark, but he could see Cassidy. The hair was unmistakable, as was the blood on his jacket and on his face. He stood in a far corner of the room, warily staring at the door, probably wondering if he was about to be rescued or executed. *Best to be ready for anything,* Logan thought. Cassidy was no fool.

Wolverine backed down the hall a ways, put his weight forward, and ran at the door, head down. He wasn't a tall man, but he was broad and muscular, not to mention durable. If he'd had a concussion grenade, or if he hadn't given his AK-47 to Maverick, he might have tried another mode of entry. But they didn't have time for any but the most extreme actions.

With a final thrust, he threw all his weight against the door as though he were a human battering ram. With the shotgun crack of splintering wood, its hinges and lock tore through shattered frame to crash to the floor of the interrogation room with Logan stumbling in behind it.

His shoulder spiked shards of agony along the bones of his arm and up to his neck, but already they were subsiding. Blood dripped from a gash on his forehead. Wolverine saw the astonishment on Cassidy's badly beaten face, and he grinned through the blood that stained his teeth and made him look like a wild animal.

"Hello, Irish," Logan said. "I'd like to stand around and trade spy stories with you, but we don't really have that kinda time."

"Aye," Cassidy agreed, his voice a mangled croak. "I don't suppose we do at that."

Sean bolted from the room, past Silver Fox—to whom he nodded his greeting and thanks—and started down the stairs with Fox and Wolverine close behind.

"KGB gave you a good workin' over, eh?" Logan asked.

"They did," the Interpol agent replied. "And the Widow give me twenty thousand volts or so to my throat."

"I was wonderin' why you were still sittin' in that cell," Logan admitted.

"Well, now you know," Fox said sharply. "Can we get out of here, please?"

They reached the bottom of the stairs. The cops' weapons were in a pile in the middle of the room, and they still had their heads down. Creed and North were near the interior doors, AK-47s still aimed into the room, but Logan's concerns all had to do with what they'd find outside now.

"You boys all right?" Logan asked.

"Right as rain, runt," Creed snarled. "Now you got your girl-friend, can we go?"

"Sabretooth managed not to kill anyone for all of the minute and a half or so that you were upstairs," Maverick said, his voice clipped, angry.

"It's a record," Silver Fox taunted.

"Managed not to kill Maverick through this whole op," Creed growled. "Guess I deserve a medal for that alone."

"They don't give people like us medals," Maverick replied. "They don't even admit they knew us when we get blown apart by KGB thugs or Soviet troops."

"Your point is well taken," Cassidy said.

By then, Logan had passed through the wreckage of the interior doors, while Maverick kept his AK-47 trained on the inside of the police station. None of the cops had moved. They weren't idiots. They'd give chase, sure, but they'd wait until the threat of instant death had passed.

Wolverine cracked the double oak exterior doors and saw nothing.

"Stash your weapons but keep 'em handy," he said quietly.

He cracked the door again, but this time, he closed it quickly.

"What?" Silver Fox asked, her face stricken.

Logan knew what she was thinking: that the op had gone sour, and it had done so because he'd insisted on coming after Cassidy. There was still that possibility, but he smiled to show her that she was wrong. In fact, her fears couldn't be further from the truth.

"You guys want to catch up to the Widow? Figure out where she's headed next, where she'll cross the border?" he whispered.

"Get to the point," Creed snarled.

"Don't kill the man coming up the steps," Wolverine explained. "We're taking him with us."

When the doorknob turned, they pulled the doors open, throwing the KGB's interrogator off balance so that he nearly stumbled into the foyer. He looked up, his face burning with righteous anger. Anger that disappeared the moment he saw the weapons aimed at him and the hardness of the faces of those who wielded them.

"Turn around," Wolverine said in Russian. "Down the stairs, to the right, and all the way down the side street to the next block. If you turn around, if you call out, if you try to run, you're a dead man."

"For once, things are going our way," Silver Fox said softly.

"Don't worry, squaw," Creed sneered. "It's bound to get down to bullets and blood any time now."

THEN

Natasha was exhausted.

If she'd simply flown back from East Berlin, none of this would have happened. She'd already be home in bed; alone and lonely but at least getting some rest. But that wasn't the way these missions worked. Public airlines were simply too conspicuous, and a private flight sometimes even more so. The KGB didn't want their most secret and covert operatives to be traceable by any other agency, ally or enemy.

But when she returned to Moscow, the Widow was going to have a little talk with her controller about the wisdom of such things. If she'd flown back, Cassidy would never have caught up with her. Mikhail would not be in the hospital on a respirator. And she wouldn't have had to commandeer a vehicle in Warsaw.

She knew what would happen. Comrade Turgenov would smile falsely, play with the band of his gold watch, and then speak to her in the soothing tones one reserved for children. But Natasha Romanova was not a child, and she was tired of being treated as one. She had married and suffered the horrible grief of her husband's death. She had lied and stolen and killed in the service of her country. She was the Black Widow, and at the very least, she would demand the respect that her suffering and her efforts had earned her.

The thought of the condescending smile on Turgenov's face was made all the worse by her current situation. Even after all she had been through, she might not be so frustrated, nor anywhere near as exhausted, if not for the fact that the car had screamed in grinding agony and belched its final breath nearly twenty miles from the Soviet border.

She'd been walking since then. Her feet were sore and the

ligaments in the backs of her legs strung tighter than a high wire. She had taken nothing from the car that wasn't completely necessary. A small zippered pouch at the belly of her jumpsuit held the disk that had been the cause of all her troubles. Over her black jumpsuit she wore a long peasant coat she had stolen in Warsaw. The old Walther P38 she had also acquired in Warsaw was in the right-hand pocket.

Natasha trudged along in darkness and silence. The road was deserted this late at night, but even during the day there was little traffic. Most people had nowhere to go. In truth, most of those individuals who lived behind the Iron Curtain simply learned to enjoy their homes, their villages and towns, because they would likely never travel far beyond them. It was a simple life that Natasha wanted badly to protect from the depredations of the West.

On the other hand, no nation was perfect. There wasn't a place in the world without crime. And so, as she walked, the Widow did her best to remain alert. She was a young and attractive woman alone on a remote stretch of road in the middle of the night—it was probably at least midnight by now, she realized. It was best to keep an eye out for trouble, whether from foreign agents or from the predators who stalked such lonely roads.

A light breeze stirred the tall trees on either side of the road. In the distance, a dog began to bark over and over again. A second joined it, and then a third from much farther off, as if they were communicating with one another. Natasha was momentarily fascinated by this observation, and appreciated the chance to think of something other than the soreness in her joints for a while.

Natasha almost didn't notice the way the trees atop the next rise were silhouetted against the night sky. Something drew her attention, though, and she thought perhaps it was that the trees themselves looked almost artificial, as if they'd been painted as a backdrop for a film. This eerie quality came from the unnatural light that shone on them from up ahead.

Then she crested the rise, and there it was: home. Or, at

least, the border guards' gate at which her papers would be demanded and she would undoubtedly be interrogated by soldiers annoyed that their quiet night had been disturbed.

Or that's what would have happened if her contact weren't there to greet her. But he would be, of that Natasha was certain. The KGB had proven to be less perfect than she had once imagined, but the importance of her mission had been stressed to her enough that she knew they would not delay in meeting her.

In fact, her contact had likely been waiting at the border crossing for hours. *He'd better not complain,* she thought briefly. After the day she'd had, the Widow was afraid she might have to hurt the man if he complained about how boring it was to sit and wait for her.

As she approached the guardhouse, with the gate that stretched across the road and spotlights on either side, Natasha had the momentary impression that the sound of dogs barking was coming from there, right up ahead. When she heard a male voice shouting at the dogs to be quiet, her suspicion was confirmed.

Had the dogs smelled her already? she wondered. Unlikely. But if they'd been spooked by someone, Natasha realized, she'd better be ready for anything. It didn't seem logical to think that Cassidy could have escaped, or that any of the other agencies' operatives would have been willing or able to come after her this far, but she grew cautious anyway.

Two dogs continued to bark—the one in the distance having gone quiet or its owner having taken it inside—and one of the guards continued to roar at them to be silent.

Hands out at her sides to show she was unarmed, the Black Widow walked into the light at the center of the road, moving directly toward the guardhouse. For a moment, she wondered if they were so incompetent that they would fail to notice her.

"Stop right there," a voice said in Russian, off to her left.

Slowly, the Widow turned to see where the voice had come from. A skinny man in Soviet uniform had a Kalishnikov pointed in her general direction. When the Widow turned back toward the guardhouse, the other guard—the one who'd been shouting at the dog—had emerged and also had her covered.

Natasha was both perturbed and relieved that they had been able to get the drop on her. A part of her had been expecting idiots who had drawn border patrol because they weren't fit for anything else.

"Identify yourself," the one at the guardhouse demanded.

The Widow raised her hands and slowly began to walk toward the guardhouse.

"Stop right there!" the one off in the trees ordered her.

"I believe you've been expecting me," she said loudly. "My name is Natalia Romanova."

The soldier at the guardhouse opened his mouth to respond, but something behind him caused him to turn his head. He nodded slightly, then returned his attention to the Widow, lowering his weapon.

"Come ahead, Comrade Romanova," he said. "I am sorry for the rude greeting. We expected you some time ago."

Natasha lowered her arms and strode gratefully forward, blissful at the thought of a cup of coffee and a long ride in the comfortably wide back seat of one of the dark sedans favored by the KGB. A moment later, the guard who'd snuck up on her from the tree line joined her, smiled an apology, and fell into step beside her.

"Long night?" the man asked amiably.

"Very," she admitted. "Thanks for asking. You have coffee, I hope?"

"Austrian," he confessed in a whisper. "I hope you won't report us?"

"Not if you share," she said, and felt a smile creep slowly across her face.

She was home. Not Moscow, not yet, but this was still home. She could breathe easier now, could forget all about the stress of the previous twenty-four hours and start dreaming of a night she had planned at the Bolshoi later in the week. There were perks to joining the KGB.

"Welcome, Oktober," a deep voice said from just ahead.

Natasha started. She blinked and peered into the shadows of the guardhouse, and could make out a tall, thin silhouette, but nothing more. Then the figure within stepped forward, past the soldier who stood there, and she recognized him right away.

"Ah, Piotr," she said, and her smile broadened. "Even better. Now I truly am home."

The Widow went to Piotr Bolishinko and nearly collapsed in the KGB man's arms. Piotr's cousin Oksana had been a friend of Natasha's for years, and she had been relieved to find a friend already inside the KGB when she joined.

"Thank you for coming out to get me," she said.

"Not at all, Natasha," Piotr said.

She stiffened slightly. Something about his voice wasn't quite right, but obviously Piotr wasn't prepared to tell her just yet what it was all about.

"Where is your car?" she asked.

Piotr only nodded in understanding. He thanked the guards for their company and the coffee they had shared. The men were pleasant enough, and the one from the trees, who had blue eyes that Natasha found herself gazing at a moment too long, gave her his own Thermos filled with the forbidden brew of a Western nation.

She thanked him, blushing a little at the way his eyes lingered on her face, and turned to follow Piotr to his car. Natasha was surprised at herself. As the Black Widow, she had learned to use her sexuality as a tool, to seduce the smallest or the largest things from the men with whom she came into contact. It was a skill.

But it was a skill she was too tired to use, and it had not yet become second nature to her. She wondered if it ever would.

Ahead of her, Piotr stopped, lifted his hands, then turned to walk past her.

"Where are you going?" she asked.

"I left my gloves in the guardhouse," he told her. "I'll just be a moment. Enjoy your coffee and wait at the car."

She watched him walk back up toward the guardhouse, then

shrugged and continued along the side of the road. She saw the dark sedan parked another fifty or so yards up, then heard a loud cough of laughter behind her. Then another, as Piotr joined in the guards' humor. She had the odd feeling that the joke was about her, but she brushed it aside. Piotr was not like that. He was a good man.

At the car, she tried the doors and found them locked. Natasha wasn't going to let that prevent her from tasting the Viennese coffee, so she walked to the back of the car and slid up to take a seat on the trunk. The rear tires seemed low, but she wasn't surprised. These KGB vehicles got a lot of use and probably needed—and didn't receive—constant attention.

"Vehicles and agents too," she mumbled to herself as she poured coffee into the cup/cover of the Thermos.

Its aroma was enough to send a shiver through her. She sipped from the cup as she watched Piotr walk back down the road toward her. When he arrived at the car, he smiled and pulled his keys from his pocket. They jangled in his hand as he unlocked the front door, then reached around to unlock the back door.

"I brought you a pillow," he said.

She could have hugged him then. But she didn't. Even through her exhaustion, she couldn't shake the feeling that there was something he was keeping from her.

"What's wrong?" she asked bluntly, unable to control herself.

His smile faltered. "You don't miss anything, do you?" he asked. "Get in, and I'll tell you all about it on the way to Moscow. You can fall asleep to my boring problems."

Natasha smiled and removed her coat, folded it in half and laid it on the floor inside the car. She ducked her head to climb into the sedan's back seat. The door began to close behind her.

She spun on the seat, lifted her leg, and kicked against the closing door with all her strength. The door slammed into Piotr, the window smashing against his hands and the gun that he had held aimed at her back. The glass shattered, the gun flew to the dirt, and Piotr fell back away from the car.

By the time the Widow was out of the car, Piotr was gone. In his place was a beautiful woman with blue skin and red hair. Her yellow eyes blazed with pain and anger as she cradled her bleeding hands to her chest and rose quickly to her feet.

"I don't know how you figured it out," the woman said in English, "but a bullet would have been much cleaner than what I'm going to do to you."

The Widow was exhausted, but fury urged her forward. She launched a kick at the woman's head, and was surprised at how fast her opponent was. Her mind reeled with the knowledge that the creature who stood before her wasn't completely human. It was like a legend come to life, a shapeshifter from mythology. But she knew that, more than likely, the woman—if woman she actually was—would turn out to be a member of the advanced race of humans called *homo sapiens superior:* a mutant.

"You're exhausted, Widow," the blue-skinned woman said. "You can't win. You're a better fighter than I am, but even you have your limits. I think we've reached them, don't you?"

She threw a punch that caught Natasha in the side of the face, threw her off balance, and forced her to stumble back against the car. But the glass shards in her hand made the Widow's attacker grunt loudly in pain, and took away the advantage of the blow.

"You should have killed me when you had the chance," the Widow said. "Killed the guards before I got here and caught me coming up the road. You used the codename Oktober, which is top secret. Piotr would never have done that. He never called me 'Natasha' either, but Natalia, which is my real name.

"I was almost too tired to notice such things," she admitted as the two women faced each other again, circling like wolves fighting to lead the pack. "But then you mentioned driving to Moscow. That's home for me, but it isn't where we are headed next. You should have killed me first, then you would have the disk now."

"I only just got here myself," the blue-skinned woman said. "But if the offer's still open, I'll be glad to take you up on it."

"Look at you," the Widow said, and lifted her arm to fire her widow's bite at her attacker. "You're in worse shape than I am. You—"

Then the woman started to change. It was over in a heartbeat, and the Widow found herself staring at her mirror image. Natasha Romanova smiled back at her as shards of glass fell to the road with a sound like a snatch of distant music stolen by the wind.

Then the assassin lifted her hands to show perfect, unbroken skin. No more blood, no more wounds.

And while Natasha was distracted, the woman kicked her in the face.

The Black Widow stumbled backward, slammed into the car again, and then the alarms screamed in her brain. *This is it,* she thought. The woman really meant to kill her.

Natasha flipped backward across the hood of the car just in time to avoid another attack. She was surprised the woman hadn't gone for the gun, and then realized that in the darkness, she had lost track of it herself. And her own gun was in the pocket of her coat inside the car.

Not that she needed it, of course. Hand to hand, she was more than a match for the shapeshifter. The woman had admitted as much.

She looked across the car, saw that the woman had changed back. Her flesh was blue again, and a light breeze stirred her long red hair. She was eerily beautiful, but savage as well. Natasha moved quickly, taking two steps to the right and firing her widow's bite. The shapeshifter ducked out of the way.

Fast, she thought. *Very fast.* The Widow couldn't be certain what kind of abuse it would take to defeat a shapeshifter. What kind of wounds would she be capable of simply shaking off? No, it was death or unconsciousness, whichever came first.

She prepared for the blue-skinned woman's next move, gauging her position though she was clearly hidden behind the car. She glanced down, just in case the shapeshifter might try to squeeze under the car.

A huge shape leapt in the darkness, and the Widow raised her arm and fired the widow's bite at the figure. There was a roar of pain and as the Widow leaped from his path, the man known as Sabretooth thundered past her, and fell onto the road. Already, "Sabretooth" was changing, the shapeshifter turning, preparing for another attack.

"In case you were wondering, your friend is in the trunk," the blue-skinned woman said.

Natasha lunged, screaming. Despite her exhaustion, she was as swift as she had ever been. Her widow's bite flashed out and bit into the pavement, and sparks flew to either side of the shapeshifter. The blue-skinned woman had a moment to decide which way to bolt, or if she should attack, but she hesitated for just a second.

The Widow backhanded her across the face and the assassin dropped to her knees. Natasha kicked her, hard, in the ribcage, and all the air went out of the shapeshifter.

The widow's bite kept her down and nearly stopped her heart. Natasha wasn't certain if she was happy to see that her attacker was still breathing—particularly after she had killed Piotr—but she wasn't about to kill her as she lay there on the road. She looked around until she found the woman's gun, dropped it on the front seat of the sedan, then took the keys from the unconscious woman and started the car.

As she turned the car toward Minsk, hoping she could make it without falling asleep at the wheel, she thought of the grisly contents of the vehicle's trunk. Her friend. *So much for the Bolshoi,* she thought. Instead, she would be at Piotr's funeral.

Warm tears slipped down her cheeks, making it difficult for her to see the road. But Natasha did not try to wipe them away. Tears were good.

Tears had made her what she was, had kept her alive time and again. Tears and grief and rage were the only life she knew and the only weapons she would ever need.

The KGB interrogator was named, of all things, Igor. Only Creed had been in a good enough mood to make a joke about it.

But that had been hours ago. The truck had made it all the way to the Russian border, not far from the town of Brest, but over the past fifty miles or so it had protested loudly. Still, each time they were certain it would die for good, the vehicle had simply kept chugging along with Igor at the wheel, and Logan sitting beside him ready to shoot him in the head if anything happened that wasn't part of the plan.

Igor had been eager to tell them whatever they wanted to know. That, in itself, had been grimly amusing. The man was an interrogator, skilled at getting answers from others, however painful that process might become. Logan would have thought a few years on that job would have taught him how to keep secrets to himself. Instead, it had apparently taught him that his own tolerance for pain was about nil.

But other than answering their specific questions about the Widow's destination, Igor was gravely silent. He gave directions when asked, and kept his eyes on the road, and, Logan imagined, thought about the tortures he wished he could inflict upon Team X.

For his part, Logan found it fascinating that Creed seemed more interested in killing Cassidy than a KGB agent. He didn't know what Sabretooth had against the Irishman. It might have been nothing more than the fact that Wolverine liked him. In any case, Creed's jibes and taunts had grown increasingly worse as the trip continued.

Then they passed the Widow's car.

She'd stripped it of anything that would have identified its owner, but she hadn't been gone long enough for her scent to disappear. Both Sabretooth and Wolverine caught it immediately. Fresh. They'd literally run back to the truck, and Logan had instructed Igor to force the vehicle faster than it had any right to go.

It wasn't long before the border came into sight, with barbed wire disappearing off into the forest and a huge gate that barred the road. The guardhouse was mounted with huge spotlights, and Igor hesitated as they crested the hill and they were bathed in the light.

"Go on," Logan barked in Russian. "They'll be suspicious. You'll talk us through or we'll kill the guards and then you."

Igor scowled but did not look at him. He kept on.

"Hope you know your place, Mick," Creed snarled in back. "Just stay out of my way and your buddy Logan will protect you."

"The name is Cassidy, boyo," the Interpol agent said, his injured throat issuing a growl of its own. "An' I plan to do me job, whether ye like it or not. The Widow's mine."

Logan's eyes narrowed. He stared at the guardhouse. No soldiers in sight. No guns. Nothing moved inside.

"You're welcome to her, pal," Creed growled. "But that disk goes home with us. You got a problem with that, we'll just bury you next to your girlfriend."

"Ye might be the one needs a grave, ye big ugly git!" Cassidy snapped.

Sabretooth roared, and Wolverine heard a scuffle. He turned, hissing at them to be quiet. Fox and Maverick were holding Creed back, and Cassidy was about to hit him.

They froze when they heard the noise, the soft, subtle sound of Logan's Ingram cocking. A tiny sound, really, yet it carried right into the chaos.

Silver Fox stared at him. They all did.

"I swear to God I'll kill the first one o' you who makes another move," he said.

Fox's jaw dropped, and Logan knew why.

He meant it.

"I said whoever gets in the way of this op would die," he went on. "That includes the team. Cassidy, you got issues with the Widow, that's fine by me. But let me tell you somethin', bub. That disk is goin' home with us. You have a problem with that, you can get out now or I'll just shoot you."

The truck slowed to a halt. Wolverine risked a glance out the windshield. The guardhouse was still quiet. Something was wrong.

"We got trouble outside," he said. "Somethin' ain't right. So when I say 'go,' we go. As a team. But don't forget what I said."

They all relaxed, started to breathe again. Fox and Cassidy were the only ones worried about a single bullet; it'd take a lot more than that to kill Maverick or Creed, for different reasons. But the threat extended further than a bullet, and they knew it.

Problem was, Creed was still smiling.

"Hey, Victor," Logan said.

Sabretooth's head snapped around, and he snarled at Logan through the small window. The smile was gone.

"You got no right to use that name, runt," Creed said. "You ain't my friend, you ain't my mother, and you ain't my priest."

"As if you had any of the above," Maverick grumbled.

Creed ignored him, eyes still on Logan.

"You're right, *Victor.* I ain't your friend," Logan said. "Just wanted to remind you o' that very thing. See, bub, you may not think I can kill you, but I guess you know if it came down to it, I'd die tryin'."

Creed just snarled in response.

And that was where it ended. Today wasn't the day that fight would take place, but its inevitability was more certain than ever before.

They'd never been friends, but they had been comrades, allies, teammates. They were still that, at least. Members of Team X. They'd keep one another alive for the good of the team, for the success of the op. But Wolverine knew with a sudden clarity that when Team X was nothing but a memory, there'd be nothing left to keep him and Creed from tearing each other apart. Probably literally.

A part of him he'd rather deny existed was truly looking forward to that day.

"Go," he said.

Team X hustled out of the truck, and Cassidy along with them. Wolverine kept his weapon aimed at Igor's back, and they all trekked up to the guardhouse together, alert for any sudden movement or sound.

Inside, they found the guards, dead.

"I don't get it," Maverick said. "Why would the Widow—?"

"Not the Widow," Sabretooth grumbled.

"You've got her scent, too?" Logan asked.

Silver Fox grunted. "Whose scent, as if I didn't know?"

There was movement outside the guardhouse, on the Soviet side. Their weapons came up instantly and in unison.

"She got away," Mystique said. "And when I catch up to her, she's going to die slow."

"Sounds good to me," Creed snarled.

But Logan didn't respond at first. He'd left Mystique behind, and yet she'd managed to not only bypass them, but catch up to the Widow without them. They'd have to either kill her, or take her with them. Obviously she was too clever to be left to herself. She might jeopardize the op just by being out there on her own.

But kill her?

They'd let Cassidy live, and with his vengeance kick, he wasn't much better than Mystique. The Widow's death was a given, unless she just decided to hand that disk over.

Wolverine had begun to think he might be growing a conscience. And if that were the case, he shouldn't have field command of Team X. If he were truthful with himself, he would have to wonder if there was any place for him at all on the team.

For now, Mystique got to stay alive. But he'd keep a close watch on her. Maybe he wasn't as cold-blooded as he'd once thought. Maybe he did need a reason to kill.

Even so, he hoped Mystique would give him one.

NOW

Langley. A nice, quiet town in Virginia, as far as most of America was concerned. But to politicians and diplomats and conspiracy nuts around the world, that place had another definition, that word another meaning entirely. It wasn't a town; it was a facility. Langley was the national headquarters of the Central Intelligence Agency.

No matter what anyone said, Logan thought, no matter how many times they denied it, CIA HQ in Langley was the place where every other American covert agency and operation and assassin got their orders. No matter who they thought they worked for, it all led back here eventually. But nobody could ever prove that. As far as the public at large knew, the CIA were Boy Scouts in comparison to some of the covert units the tabloids wrote about. They might not have been as whitewashed as S.H.I.E.L.D. or SAFE, but they wouldn't get their hands dirty with the nasty work.

Which was, of course, exactly what the public was supposed to think.

Any records still in existence that referred to Team X or the "Agency" that had employed them would be inside those walls. Getting in wasn't going to be easy. Mystique's talents might get her in, but it wasn't a one-person job, and Wraith and Wolverine couldn't exactly walk right past the front desk.

On the other hand, Wraith was a teleporter, and he had, in his possession, a blueprint of the entire Langley facility.

"We'll start in the APO file room," Wraith said.

Wolverine nodded, but didn't turn to look at him. He stared across open ground to the fence that surrounded CIA headquarters. Something stirred in his gut, a warning, probably. This whole thing didn't sit right with him, but he wasn't sure exactly what was bothering him about it.

"Wolverine," Mystique said.

"I'm payin' attention," he replied. "Just thinkin' is all. So we pay a visit to the Authorized Pinheads Only library, and then what?"

"Anything on Team X should be in there. That stuff was a long time ago, almost long enough that it'll be public record soon," Wraith said. "Or some of it will, at least."

"But if there's an active file, it won't be in there, right?" Wolverine prodded. "It'll be 'eyes only' computer access, from a room that's impossible to get into and even harder to get out of. You maybe can teleport in, but you'll still set off alarms."

Wraith smiled. "You've seen too many movies, Wolverine," he said. "Why do you think our national secrets aren't so secret? Too many people have 'eyes only' clearance as it is. We get into that computer system, we'll be all right."

Wolverine narrowed his eyes, cocked his head slightly to study Wraith. "John," he said, "you'd better not be leadin' us astray, bub. You already left me hangin' once, back in East Berlin. It ain't gonna happen again."

John Wraith's smile faltered. "Why, Logan," he said. "I'm getting the feeling that you don't trust me."

Then the skinny man with the sunglasses pulled an H&K semiautomatic nine millimeter from beneath his armpit and checked the clip. He was about to put it away when Wolverine reached out and snatched it from Wraith's grip. He ejected the clip and slowly popped the bullets out one by one. Off to his left, he heard Mystique allow herself a soft chuckle. When the clip was empty, he slid it back into place, and gave Wraith back his gun.

"I don't trust you," Wolverine told him. "An' I don't want any killin' on this op."

He turned to glare at Mystique. "That goes for you, too, Raven."

She raised her hands in surrender.

"No matter what you may think, either o' you, this ain't like old times. We're gonna find out who's behind all this, and when it comes down to it, if there needs to be lives taken to save Maverick and the Widow and the others, well, that's one thing. But this ain't the field. CIA man draws down on you in the middle o' Prague, that's different from him doin' it when you're poppin' uninvited into his livin' room. Back then, we were stealin' secrets and takin' lives. Now we're here to expose secrets and save some lives. We all clear on that?"

Wraith patted a hand against the empty gun in the holster under his arm and nodded, without smiling.

"Crystal," Wraith said.

"All right, then, Kestrel," Logan said, "take us in."

The APO file room was actually more like a library than Wolverine had imagined. Smaller, of course, but not by much. The "librarian" had been a lanky research assistant with round, frameless glasses and a goatee. Hardly the dark-suited, stone-faced man in black so frequently associated with the CIA.

The man looked so pitiful when they appeared in front of him that Logan had almost felt bad when Mystique took him down. But unconscious was better than dead.

Instantly, Mystique morphed and became a precise doppelgänger for the research assistant. She looked busy behind the desk where a trio of computer terminals held records of what was within the aisles and aisles of bound records inside the APO file room.

There were guards outside. They'd suspected that and found out the hard way. Mystique had gone to the door and opened it, only to be confronted by a man and woman, both armed, who were a bit hostile about this break in procedure.

"Hey," Mystique had said, holding up her/his hands in defense. "I just wanted to know if either of you guys have any Advil. I've got a splitting headache."

Wolverine smiled as he ducked behind a row of bound volumes. Mystique's idea of a joke. The research assistant would certainly need something for his head when he woke up.

Logan and Wraith would have to stay back in the aisles as much as possible while Mystique checked computer references and tried to access modern records cross-referenced to APO files.

There were no files on Team X.

On the other hand, it took less than half an hour to find the file numbers on each member of the team, logged by their individual codename, as well as the numbers for the files on Mystique and the Black Widow. Mystique wrote them down, and Wraith and Wolverine split the list, keeping away from the door as much as possible.

"Found the file for 'Codename: Wolverine,' " Wraith announced in a hushed voice. "But the 'Codename: Sabretooth' file isn't where it ought to be."

Logan frowned and scanned the bound volumes in front of him. The bound file on Silver Fox was numbered 2797.5. That one was right where it should be. He thought about it, but ended up leaving the thick volume where it was. Fox was dead. They'd come back to that file if they needed to. But she wasn't really in this at all, except as a painful part of his memory.

For a moment, he thought of the cabin in the valley where he'd laid her body to rest. Once a year, he returned to that place, just to tell her that he would always love her, no matter what. And to tell her that he was sorry for everything that had happened. Sorry that he wasn't there to stop Creed from taking her life.

He hung his head a moment, and wondered again why Sabretooth was still alive, why he hadn't killed the maniac years earlier. And he knew the answer. Because he could never truly be certain of what was in his head, and it was possible Creed hadn't killed Fox at all. But Sabretooth was more than happy to take the credit, even if it was just to drive Logan mad. There was nothing Creed would like more than to draw the primal beast that lay within Wolverine to the surface.

Logan took a deep breath, held it, moved on.

"The file for 'Codename: Maverick' is missing as well," Wolverine said in a low growl.

"No file for 'Romanova, Natasha,' " Wraith reported.

"I've got the file on 'Darkhölme, Raven,' " Logan whispered.

He held the volume under one arm and continued checking numbers on the shelves against those written on the scrap of paper in his hand. His current objective was 4223.1. He scanned for it, fully expecting to find it there, given the pattern of what was missing.

But he didn't.

Eyes narrowed, he stepped out of the aisle and walked back four rows to where Wraith crouched, flipping through the file on "Codename: Wolverine." Logan dropped the book on Mystique to the ground, only to get an alarmed hiss from the woman herself. She was right, too. It wouldn't do to alarm the guards.

The only sound was metal on bone as he popped his claws and knelt next to Wraith.

"Where's your file?" he asked.

Wraith frowned and looked at him. "What are you saying, Logan?"

"I'm sayin' the files on the folks who've already been abducted ain't here," Wolverine growled. "My file, Mystique's file, we got those. Where's yours?"

They stared at one another for a long time. Wraith wasn't scared, and Wolverine had to give him credit for that. He was either brave, or too stupid to realize the fact they'd once been on the same team wouldn't stop Logan from using his claws if Wraith was involved with all of this. The no-killing rule only went so far.

"I can't answer that," Wraith said finally. "Maybe since I'm still an employee, all my files are still active and are only accessible under 'eyes only' clearance."

Wolverine sensed Mystique behind him, caught her scent as well.

"Sounds plausible, Logan," she said.

Suddenly, he was overwhelmed by the irony of the entire situation. He and Mystique, whom he'd once wanted to kill and never trusted, trying to figure out what to do about a member of Team X, whom he knew they couldn't trust, in order to save former friends turned enemies and former enemies turned friends.

"Yeah," he muttered. "Whatever."

"I can't get 'eyes only' access in here. We need to be in either the director's office or the central computer file area, both of which have to be heavily guarded."

"So we hit the central computer area," he replied. "Wraith teleports us in, then we're gone."

Wraith chuckled. "Again, this isn't the movies, Wolverine. CCF has huge glass windows in the front. Unless you're invisible, you can't get in unless you're supposed to be there."

"So we try the director's office," Mystique said.

Wraith nodded.

"Get us in, John," Wolverine said, a warning in his voice.

"Sorry, but I can't," Wraith replied. "Teleportation is not an exact science. I've been in this room before. I've never been in the director's office. There may have been renovations the blueprints don't reflect. There could be desks, chairs, houseplants—you should know these things, Logan. Didn't you ever discuss teleporting with Nightcrawler while you were X-Men together?"

At the mention of her son, Mystique blinked and looked away. That was a relationship whose dysfunction hadn't even begun to be examined. Wolverine thought that both Mystique and Nightcrawler would prefer it that way.

"So what do we do?" Logan asked. "How do we get in there?"

Wraith smiled. "You're gonna love this," he said.

Wolverine felt the gut-wrenching twist of reality falling out from beneath him, felt the momentary loss of equilibrium that came with teleportation, and then the three of them were standing inside a women's bathroom.

"What the hell are you doing?" Mystique snapped, a hand to her head, trying to focus again now that teleporting had stolen her concentration and forced her back to her true appearance.

"What do you think I'm doing?" a female voice asked from the farthest stall.

Wolverine, Wraith, and Mystique stared at one another. Then the two men turned to look at Mystique. After a moment, she rolled her eyes, threw up her hands, and walked down to the other end of the bathroom. Wolverine went to the door and turned the lock.

A toilet flushed. Mystique shook her head, covered her eyes with her hands. Wraith laughed softly to himself, but Wolverine didn't think it was funny. Not at all. This wasn't a game, but Wraith sure seemed to think it was.

The bathroom door at the end opened and a thirtysomething blonde woman emerged. Her hair was cut in a bob and she wore glasses; her pantsuit was very professional and she smoothed the jacket, looking down at herself as she stepped out onto the tile floor.

Mystique grabbed her, spun her, threw her against the tile wall, and, before the blonde could scream, chopped down on her neck with an open hand, striking a pressure point and driving her to her knees.

The woman swayed, blinked, and began to focus again. Mystique went at the pressure point a second time and the woman went down hard on the tile.

"Sorry," Mystique mumbled.

"You're losing your touch," Wraith told her.

"Yeah, maybe," Mystique replied. "But what I want to know is, if you have to have been somewhere before to teleport there, how comes we're in the ladies' room?"

Wolverine looked at Wraith, raising his eyebrows. Wraith only shrugged.

"It's a long story," he said.

"So how do we get into the director's office from here?" Wolverine asked.

Wraith pointed up at the wall in one corner, where a large grating covered a wide air duct. Logan shook his head, smiled slightly, and walked over to the wall with the duct.

"And you say I've seen too many movies," Wolverine said.

They'd crawled through the duct, one by one. It was a straight shot to the office of the director of the CIA, and Wolverine was relieved to find it empty. His adamantium claws made short work of the duct on the other side, and once inside, they found themselves in luck.

The director had left his computer running.

Which was, actually, both good and bad. Good, of course, in that they didn't need to know his passwords. Bad, because it meant he was likely to return at any second. Not to mention that the locked ladies' room door was going to draw attention in the very near future.

Fortunately, it took Mystique less than two minutes to run the search they needed. When the computer dinged to signal the end of the search, Wolverine looked at her, waiting for the revelations they had come here to find. When she glanced up at him, he knew she hadn't found them.

"Nothing?" he asked, incredulous.

"Nothing on Team X. Not one of you. Nothing on me. Nothing on the Widow or Cassidy outside of what was probably already in their APO files."

"How can that be?" Wraith asked.

"No file on you, either, in case you missed it," Wolverine noted. "So I guess your tenure as their employee is pretty much over."

Wraith didn't have a response for that.

"Wait a minute," Mystique said suddenly.

"What?" Logan asked.

But Mystique was already typing. She keyed ENTER and sat

back in the chair. Several seconds passed. She scanned the results of her search, and her eyes widened.

"Wolverine, I think you should take a look at this," Mystique said grimly.

Logan stepped to her side and bent to stare at the screen. Mystique had run a search on Team Alpha. Instantly, service records and codenames had come up. Only the codenames, however. There were no real names to go with them, as if the members of Team Alpha had ceased to exist beyond their service to the Agency. And in a way, Wolverine thought, that was probably true.

He was about to ask Mystique what was so stunning about this revelation. The information might be helpful, but it was hardly what they were looking for.

Then he saw the last name on the list.

CODENAME: KESTREL.

A roar built deep in Wolverine's chest. His claws popped out and as he spun, they sliced through the edge of the computer terminal without even snagging on the plastic. He was prepared to pin Wraith to the wall with a trio of claws through his shoulder, so his former teammate couldn't teleport without him.

"Kestrel!" he thundered. "You son of a—"

But Wraith was gone.

Of course.

In the halls beyond the director's office, the CIA headquarters at Langley, Virginia, was filled, suddenly, with the wail of a full security alarm. Langley had intruders.

"We're dead," Mystique whispered.

Wolverine growled low in his chest and stared at the office door.

"Not yet we ain't," he snarled.

19

THEN

Team X was inside the Soviet Union. From Wolverine's perspective, the road east of the border didn't look that much different from the road to the west. But it felt different, just knowing where they were.

He'd been around a long time. Long enough to remember when the Soviet Union and the United States had been allies. But this was a new era, and if they were caught conducting spy operations inside the U.S.S.R., they'd most likely be killed.

Or, perhaps, tortured and then killed. And it wouldn't matter to the Soviets that Wolverine was Canadian and not American.

As the truck rumbled through the dark, headlights weakly illuminating the road ahead and yet somehow not truly lighting the way, Logan could feel the wrongness of their presence. They didn't belong here. And, as far as he was concerned, the sooner they could get back out, the better.

He wasn't afraid. There weren't a lot of things on the planet Earth that could frighten Logan. But for the sake of the mission, and the lives of his team—or at least, the lives of Fox and Maverick—he wanted to end it quick so they could get out.

Their hostage KGB man, Igor, was at the wheel again. Logan rode in the passenger seat, with Sabretooth, Maverick, Silver Fox, Cassidy, and Mystique in the back. Their little troupe was growing, and the bigger they grew, the harder it would be for everyone to find cover if things went sour. And it didn't help that, with every personality added to the mix, there was an even greater chance of internal conflict growing out of control.

Logan glanced back into the rear of the truck and narrowed

his eyes as he saw the small smile that seemed to be permanently attached to Creed's mouth. As he looked at Creed, Logan realized that he might not only be concerned about his team staying in control. Too many times in the past he had let the berserk fury that lurked inside of him free to wreak havoc. Nearly every time that happened, he tried to keep it back, and regretted later that he wasn't strong enough to do that.

But right then he didn't much care to hold it back. Sabretooth kept pushing and pushing, as though he wanted it to happen. *Scratch that,* Logan thought, *he does want it to happen.* Only Creed's interest in Team X and their mission kept him from just snapping completely and killing anyone in his path. A year ago, Logan might have said that as a joke. But now, he believed it too much for it to be funny.

The truck bounced along ruts in the road. Despite his enhanced senses, Wolverine had to focus his eyes on the darkness to make out the features of Mystique's face. Her blue skin was smooth and beautiful, in its way, but almost invisible in the shadows. Even her red hair was nearly black in the dark. Only her yellow eyes showed, glowing in the back of the truck.

Those yellow eyes met Logan's gaze, then turned away. Not intimidated, just uninterested—and that was much worse. She was a dangerous woman, as dangerous as the Black Widow herself. Perhaps even more so.

"You haven't changed, Raven," Logan heard Creed whisper.

"Neither have you, Victor," Mystique replied.

"You look good," Sabretooth said, and his eyes shone like soulless black marbles, reflecting all available light because there was no light inside. None at all.

He was flirting with her.

Wolverine couldn't speak for a moment. Obviously their relationship was one of intense feeling on both ends of the spectrum, but in the middle of the mission, Creed was flirting with a woman who had already tried to pull the op out from under them at least once.

"That'll do, Sabretooth," Logan growled.

Mystique looked up at Logan, surprised, and she smiled. Creed snapped his head around and bared his fangs, staring at Wolverine through the narrow window between the cab and the back of the truck.

"Mind your own business, runt," Creed snarled.

"This is my business. Everything that affects this op is my business. We're gonna have to stop for fuel and some kind of food before we reach Minsk, Creed. When we do, Mystique is gone." Wolverine narrowed his eyes. "I'm not gonna let you throw this op to the wolves just 'cause you got the scent o' some skirt's perfume."

But when Creed's response came, it wasn't in words.

With a roar, Sabretooth launched himself from the floor of the truck, and his fist shattered the glass and frame of the little window. Creed's claws grazed Logan's cheek as a powerful hand gripped his throat and began to squeeze.

As if he'd been waiting for just that moment—and if he'd been listening closely, perhaps he had—Igor slammed on the brakes and the truck slewed sideways across the road. It teetered, threatened to turn over but did not, and came to a halt.

Even as Logan's right hand grasped the hilt of one of the knives sheathed behind him, he saw the KGB interrogator leap out of the truck and race for the woods. His rage blazed even higher, at Creed, and at himself for pushing Creed unnecessarily.

"Bad . . . timing . . . " he croaked as Sabretooth choked him.

Creed was trying to get his other arm through the hole, to get a better grip. A growl had grown in Sabretooth's chest, and his eyes were wilder than ever. His claws punctured the flesh of Logan's neck.

"Back off!" Wolverine snarled, and slammed six inches of tempered steel through Sabretooth's forearm.

Creed let out a terrible bellow of pain and rage and withdrew his arm. Wolverine caught his breath, the punctures on his throat healing even as he hit the door latch and tumbled out of the truck. He heard the rear doors slam open, heard Maverick and Fox shouting at him. Logan leapt to his feet, blood burning in his veins, temples throbbing. His lips were curled back from his teeth, and he crouched low over the ground.

The beast had been released. The savage berserk within him smelled Creed's spilled blood, and would not be satisfied until he lay in a pile of his own viscera in the scruff grass on the side of the road.

Logan withdrew his other knife from its sheath just as Creed came around from behind the truck. He was not alone. All four of the other passengers were following him. Cassidy and Mystique stayed well back, but Fox and Maverick were moving on Creed.

"Not another step," Maverick shouted, his weapon trained on Sabretooth. "I mean it, Creed. Two in the head will stop even you."

"Don't count on it, boy," Creed snarled.

Fox went for Sabretooth then. She leaped on his back, but he reached around, grabbed her by the hair, and threw her hard to the ground. He glanced down at her.

"Next time, squaw, I'll gut you," Sabretooth grunted. "Don't forget."

At the sight of Silver Fox injured, something surged within Logan. The tiny bit of reason that remained, somewhere beneath the raging beast, could have disappeared entirely at that moment. Instead, it burst through the fury and came quickly to the fore.

"Enough!" Wolverine snapped.

"You got this comin', runt," Creed snarled. "Don't tell me you're gonna go yellow on me now."

Logan seethed, barely controlling his rage. And only for a moment. Only long enough to set his priorities.

"Don't worry, bub," he said with a growl. "You need a lesson, and I'm here to give it to you. But first things first."

Wolverine turned to the others. "Fox, Cassidy, you go after Igor. Track him down and stop him, but don't kill him. Understand? We need him if we're gonna find the Widow in Minsk."

His gaze flicked over to Maverick. "North," he said, "you cover Mystique. If she moves," Logan glanced at Mystique, who smiled at him, "kill her."

Maverick turned his weapon on Mystique.

"Now," Logan said to Creed, "you wanna go, we're gonna go."

Wolverine heard Cassidy arguing with Silver Fox about something, but he tuned it out. All he saw then was Creed. All he thought of was how badly he had wanted to teach the psychopath a lesson. The time had definitely come. If that meant he had to kill him, well there'd be one fewer to worry about getting out of Soviet territory when it was all over.

Creed howled like an animal as he rushed at Wolverine. Logan met him head on. He ducked, drew his knife across Creed's belly and opened him up. Claws bit into Logan's side, and blood spurted from the wound.

They had both struck well. The scent of blood in the air drove them wild, and Wolverine used his left hand to defend himself and to get a grip on Creed. He swiped at Sabretooth's eyes, slashed him across the clavicle, and felt metal strike bone. The grating sound gave him a perverse thrill, and he barely felt it when the knife slipped between his tenth and eleventh rib.

Wolverine and Sabretooth were locked in a killing embrace. Wound after wound was struck, and Creed's claws were almost as deadly as the knives. Logan suddenly found himself staring at Creed's throat, only inches from his mouth. The urge to tear the monster's carotid artery open with his teeth was almost too powerful to resist.

He was growing tired from loss of blood. And maybe Creed was slowing down a little as well.

That's when Cassidy screamed.

The force of his sonic attack picked Sabretooth and Wolverine up off their feet and threw them with bone-breaking force against the side of the truck. Wolverine felt a rib go. He fell to the ground, disoriented, and he knew it would be several seconds before he could rise. Several seconds that could cost him his life. He was about to curse Cassidy in silence until his eyes focused on Creed, who lay on the ground next to him, barely able to hold up his head.

"What in the name of the Lord is wrong with ye?" Cassidy shouted, and Logan winced at the raising of the man's voice, though this time, there was no wave of power.

"See . . . ya got your . . . power back," Wolverine muttered, and drew himself to his knees.

"Is this the way Yanks do things, then?" Cassidy shouted. "Am I workin' with a group of bloody morons? Ye have a mission to fulfill, and people to answer to! Now I've put me own interests first, and that'd be stoppin' the Widow before she ruins any other lives. But this . . . hell, this is just ridiculous!"

Cassidy wheeled on Maverick.

"And you? Sittin' there guardin' the blue girl! Did you ever think about tryin' to stop this madness?" the Irishman shouted.

Maverick's face was stone. "I had my orders," Maverick said simply. "Unlike you, I follow them."

"That's just too beautiful!" Cassidy snapped, then spun on Logan again.

Wolverine had just risen to his feet, and Sabretooth was in the process of doing the same.

"Just tell me this, ye pretty ladies," Cassidy snapped. "Are ye done? I know ye'll recover from these lovely wounds of yours, 'cause ye're both mutants like me, aye? But are ye done? 'Cause if not, I'll go on ahead. I plan to finish this job, one way or another. Sittin' here watchin' you two great warriors hack each other up ain't on me agenda. So, are ye done?"

Cassidy's chest was heaving with his anger and frustration. Behind him, Logan saw that Fox had brought Igor back to the truck. Wolverine brushed himself off, inspected a couple of his wounds. He was in rough shape, but Cassidy was right. He'd recover. Though he wouldn't be sitting in the front seat for a while. In fact, Cassidy was right about a lot of things.

Logan stepped toward Mystique, pointed a finger in her face.

"I don't trust you, lady, and I don't want you outta my sight," he said. "Back in the truck. Maverick, you get up front with Igor."

Wolverine turned to Creed. He didn't offer his hand.

"Sabretooth, get back in the truck. We'll finish this thing when this op is completed, back on home soil," he promised.

Sabretooth stared at him a moment, then started to shamble toward the truck.

"Just so long as you know it ain't over," Creed snarled.

Wolverine nodded slowly.

"No," he agreed. "It ain't over by a long shot."

THEN

he sedan hadn't been meant to go so fast, at least not over roads as neglected as these. But the Black Widow wasn't about to slow down. She ought to have been able to relax by now. This was her country, her own territory. Home.

But until she rendezvoused with her controller and his bodyguards in Minsk, and handed the disk over to him, she would not rest easy. Nor would she slow down. It had been a long and unexpectedly difficult journey. When it was over, she would need a few days to decompress. To forget about Sean Cassidy and the things he blamed her for. To forget about the blue-skinned woman who had attacked her.

Most important, to forget about the Zhevakovs, who had died for their treason. But what she wanted to forget most about the defectors was not their deaths, but their treason itself. The KGB had always treated Natasha well. She could only imagine that it had treated the Zhevakovs equally well. And yet, despite her controller's commentary when assigning her this mission, what she had learned about them did not seem to indicate that they were evil or stupid or simply greedy.

And, if none of those things were true, then she still had to ask that question: *Why?* It was a question she felt certain was going to get her in trouble someday. The thought disturbed Natasha, for she had much to lose. So, instead, she pushed the thought away, and allowed her mind to concern itself only with dreams of Mother Russia's majesty, and the quiet time she would spend over the next few days.

Why, when she finally reached home, her bath alone was going to take an entire day.

"There is a military base not far from here," Igor admitted. "If you go into the village, there are likely to be soldiers around."

Wolverine stared at the KGB interrogator. He wished he had some way to determine whether or not the man was telling the truth. Short of torture, he could not think of one. And torture wasn't in his bag of tricks.

Dawn was just a little way off, and the truck was stopped atop a small slope in the road. There were few lights in the village below, but the sky was beginning to lighten and they could see it well enough. It was a tiny place, really. Like something out of a storybook but gray and withered as though the magic of old legends had leaked away over centuries. Newer, ugly gray concrete buildings stood among small houses and shops that looked as though they'd been standing there forever.

It was the Russian equivalent of small-town America, Wolverine thought. But there was no Main Street movie theater, or church, or five-and-dime. There was, however, a building that looked to be either town hall, or school, or both. Around that were several others that probably held some kind of market. The place was distant enough from other towns that he supposed they had a garage of some kind, but they were just as likely to have a blacksmith, he thought. Someone had to shoe horses and repair carts.

Around the village, the landscape opened up to accommodate a number of farms, probably a traditional Soviet collective. It was possible that the village itself was merely an extension of the collective.

"I don't see any base," Logan said at length.

"It's not far," Igor insisted.

"Fine," Logan replied. "Then we all go."

Wolverine narrowed his eyes and focused on the village below. One of the larger, more recently constructed buildings was at the edge of town. He had no idea what it was. Probably a firehouse or grain storehouse or something else that would require a two-story structure. But it was large enough to hide the truck behind.

"Get back in the truck," he said. "Me an' Creed'll give it a push. We'll roll down and leave it behind that ugly icebox down there." He pointed at the building. "From there, we split up."

He turned to regard them then. Wolverine didn't like the idea of splitting the team, especially with so many unknowns along for the ride. But he had to rely on their dedication to the op—and they really didn't have much choice.

"Sabretooth," he said, and Creed glared at him, nostrils flaring. "You and Silver Fox take the Russkie here and find some gas. Steal it, siphon it . . . hell, buy it for all I care. But get it."

Silver Fox nodded, and Logan knew she understood that he had saddled her with two ticking bombs, and that she was prepared to deal with both.

"Maverick," he said, "you and Mystique find us some clothes. Local issue. And while you're at it, see if you can find a shortwave. With the trail we've left, the Agency should be monitoring on our favorite emergency frequency by now."

Logan frowned at Mystique. "You could try to blend in a little," he said.

"I'll see what I can do," she said, barely acknowledging him.

Wolverine couldn't blame her. It wasn't as though she was deaf or blind. She was there for his fight with Creed. She knew what he thought of her. It didn't make him feel at all guilty, though. Mystique was bad news, and a bad risk. He could sense it. But while he had her, he might as well make use of her particular talents.

He winced. Thoughts of his brawl with Sabretooth reminded Wolverine how long it was going to take him to fully mend. None of the wounds was serious—at least, not now that his healing factor had gone into action—but with so many of them, he wouldn't be completely up to snuff for hours yet.

"What're you gonna be doin' all this time?" Creed asked. "Babysittin' the Mick?"

Wolverine ignored him.

"By the time we all meet back here at the truck in, say, thirty minutes, me and Agent Cassidy will have rounded up some kind of breakfast, and then we'll be on our way.

"Let's do this quietly, okay?" Wolverine asked. "The last thing we need is the Soviet army on our tails while we're still goin' *into* their territory."

The market proved to be almost precisely what Wolverine suspected. The breads, meats, and produce all seemed fresh, apparently products of the farming collective. He felt a small spark of shame to be stealing from people who so obviously needed what they produced through their own sweat, but it couldn't be helped.

"This isn't right," Cassidy said as he slid several loaves of bread into a sack along with a large cured ham.

Wolverine had a wooden box in his arms loaded with fruits and vegetables. He looked over at Cassidy and their eyes met briefly. Without a nod or a spoken word, he acknowledged the other man's misgivings, then turned back to the work at hand: petty theft.

Light splashed the large windows at the front of the building, and Logan ducked his head. The headlights moved on, and the rumble of a truck's engines could be heard. For a moment, he thought that one of his team had gone completely insane and driven their truck right down into the middle of the village.

Then he realized that it wasn't their truck, and he knew it was worse than that. It was the military.

Brakes squealed, laboring to stop the heavy vehicle. Wolverine surveyed the soldiers in the open back of the truck and came up with a quick count of sixteen. Not counting the driver and the other man in the front seat, likely this squad's commanding officer. They looked exhausted, and Wolverine guessed that they were coming off duty somewhere and must be on their way back to base.

The officer opened his door and stepped out. He barked orders to the driver, and it took Wolverine a moment to mentally translate the Russian. The driver started the truck up again and continued down the street, leaving the officer behind.

Fuel. That was the key word in the officer's orders. There must be some kind of refueling station there in the village, Wolverine realized. One of the more recent, ugly gray buildings. Chances were good that Sabretooth and Fox would have found it already, given the fear with which Igor obviously regarded Creed. The KGB man would have known, or at least suspected, the existence of such a station, and led Creed there, if Sabretooth's nose didn't show them the way first.

Which would have worked out very nicely if not for the truckload of soldiers who had just passed by.

Wolverine stared at the officer. The man looked up and down the street, then knocked lightly on a door along a row of buildings across from the market and the village hall. The door opened, and Logan briefly glimpsed a woman, clad in a flimsy nightgown, inside. She smiled at the officer and then the door closed behind them.

A second ticked by. Another. A third. Then Wolverine was moving. Cassidy followed behind him without a sound, and Logan took a moment to recognize that the man he was working with was a true professional. He wished that Cassidy really was a part of the team. But then, other than his vendetta against the Widow, Logan thought Cassidy might have trouble with some of the missions for which Team X was responsible.

Fast as they were able, they hustled along the backs of buildings for two long blocks. At the truck, only Maverick was visible, dressed in the drab clothing of the Russian civilian. Not peasant clothes, not farming clothes. Wolverine was satisfied. If they could get out of here without any trouble, they ought to be able to pass, even in Minsk.

But that seemed like a big "if" at the moment.

Logan glanced a question at Maverick, and North had the answer immediately.

"In the back," he said.

Wolverine dumped his crate in the back of the truck, and

Cassidy followed with his sack of meat and bread. He was relieved to see that most of the team had already reassembled and were waiting for him in the truck. Mystique was there, helping to distribute clothing to the others. Igor sat glaring into nothingness as Silver Fox kept a pistol aimed at his chest. There was only one person missing.

"Where's—?" Wolverine began.

"Went back for more fuel," Fox said without expression. "We found a depot or whatever, but we only found two containers, and he figured we would need reserves."

Logan cursed. When he looked up, he already had everyone's attention.

"For once he was right," Logan admitted. "But Creed's timing couldn't be worse. We got company, and they're probably right on top of him."

"They won't find him if he doesn't want to be found," Maverick noted.

"Yeah," Logan agreed. "That's what worries me. After the last twenty-four hours, he'll be lookin' to blow off some steam."

"And get us all killed?" Mystique asked incredulously.

"Hey," Logan shrugged, "he's your sweetheart—you tell me."

She frowned. "He's not my sweetheart."

"Whatever," Maverick interjected. "Point is, how do we pull him out of there without drawing extra attention to ourselves?"

Wolverine was still staring at Mystique. He nodded to himself and pointed at her. "You come with me," he told her. "Maverick, Silver Fox, watch the truck and our KGB friend, but be ready. I want you out of sight in case we need backup."

Then he turned to Cassidy.

"Irish, go on ahead and keep an eye out for Creed and the Russkies. I'll be along in a bit. We may be able to get outta this without a scuffle yet, but it's real important that you try to keep him from killin' anybody."

"An' how exactly do ye think I ought to go about doing that?" Cassidy asked.

"With your natural charm and scintillatin' wit."
To his credit, Cassidy laughed.

Several minutes later, Sean wasn't laughing at all. He'd stuck to the corners and shadows, but the sun was on the horizon and he'd seen several civilians on the street. The nearby farms would have been working long since, and the village wasn't far behind. He'd followed Silver Fox's directions to the fueling station, and now he crouched behind a four-wheel cart across the street and watched the soldiers as they milled about their truck.

Nearly half of them were smoking, and those stood well off from the fuel pump. The others either sat on the edge of the truck or stretched and yawned and leaned against the truck or the wall of the gray cinderblock structure.

But there was no sign of Creed.

Then he was there. A short block away, Sabretooth crossed the street with two black plastic fuel containers in his huge hands. Right in plain sight. Six and a half feet and nearly three hundred pounds of killer with a shock of almost Nordic blond hair, Victor Creed strode from one corner and just kept walking.

Cassidy had to give him credit. He was more than halfway to the opposite corner, where he could have disappeared behind a row of buildings and gone right on to where their own truck was hidden, when the soldiers spotted him.

It was possible, though Creed would never be inconspicuous, that had he been wearing different clothes they never would have looked at him twice. They were obviously tired. Probably just wanted to get home. But Creed wore ragged German peasant clothes, covered with dried blood from his clash with Wolverine.

How could they not go after him?

One of the soldiers shouted at Sabretooth to stop. To drop the cans and raise his hands. Creed kept walking. A pair of Kalishnikovs shot into the air, ripping the sky with rapid-fire punctuation. Creed could have run then. Cassidy knew it. A few bullets wouldn't kill him, and he might get back to the truck in time for an escape.

But he'd come back for that gas, and Cassidy figured a psychopath like Creed wasn't about to leave without what he came for. That, and he probably also figured a bunch of dead soldiers wouldn't pursue spies nearly as vigorously as the living, breathing kind.

Four soldiers ran across the street, their boots rapping staccato rhythm on the pavement. Sabretooth put the cans down and turned to face them. Cassidy had seen the smile on Creed's face before. It was gleefully savage, and yet smug: the face of a deadly serpent that has just sighted its prey.

Even as Cassidy opened his mouth to scream a warning, Sabretooth struck. The first slash of his claws tore out the throat of the man nearest to him. *So much for Logan's plan,* Sean thought.

Then he was in the air, his sonic scream carrying him aloft, propelling him forward, and making him a target.

But, for better or worse, Sabretooth was an even better target.

Creed lashed out at a second soldier, striking at the man's head with such force that it canted much too far to the right and hung nauseatingly loose from a broken neck as the man tumbled to the pavement. By then, Creed had a Kalishnikov in his hands, and it barked and spat angry black hornets that tore the other two soldiers to ribbons.

Sabretooth seemed to have grown even larger in his killing fury. And Cassidy didn't know what he could do, what Wolverine had really intended for him to do here. The Soviets were the enemy, sure, but he wasn't about to go around slaughtering soldiers who were truly only doing their duty. And on their own home turf as well. Sean Cassidy was an officer of the law, not some cold-blooded homicidal lunatic like the gore-spattered blond monster lumbering around on the street below.

A vivid image of the Black Widow blossomed suddenly in

his mind. Cassidy was no killer, but he'd vowed to take her life, hadn't he?

His reverie was interrupted as one of the soldiers finally took an interest in him. He'd only been airborne a few seconds, but now he needed to take evasive action.

On the ground, Creed had started toward the remaining soldiers, who congregated around their truck in front of the refueling station. Too close by far, the way Cassidy looked at it. Sabretooth swept his weapon back and forth, keeping the Soviet soldiers pinned for the moment, though he stood out in the open. His savagery must have stunned them, at least at first.

Then they returned fire, and it was all over.

The first strafing pass of Soviet ammunition across Sabretooth's chest forced the killer back several steps. Instead of falling down, Creed leaned into the hail of bullets like they were nothing more than a powerful gale. Cassidy didn't know how much even Sabretooth could take, and he figured a bullet in the brain would take down anyone. For half a second, he was tempted to just let Creed die. The monster had been spoiling for a fight and now he'd found one. There were at least nine soldiers left, and Sean would take odds that they'd finish Creed before he got close enough to finish them.

But he couldn't just leave him there.

He turned in midair, nearly caught a bullet as he crossed the line of fire of the soldier who was still trying to knock him out of the air. His sonic scream kept him aloft, but now he refocused it, turned its force downward. Cassidy knew how hard to hit a human being with his sonics. But there was no room for caution here. Not with bullets flying all over the place.

Three soldiers were blown back against the cinderblock refueling station. They hit hard, and crumpled to the ground. If they were alive—which Sean dearly prayed—they'd be nearly deaf for hours. And their comrades would have ringing ears for a while just because they were nearby.

Cassidy dropped to the pavement and glanced over at Creed. Sabretooth smiled that smile again, and for a moment, Sean was certain the monster was going to turn the Kalishnikov on him. Instead, Creed sprayed bullets at the truck again, and Cassidy flinched. He figured it was a miracle the fuel tank still hadn't exploded.

The ground rumbled. Cassidy turned to see two large trucks carrying Soviet reinforcements trundling down the street toward them. There were no civilians on the street, but apparently someone had been able to get in touch with the base pretty fast. If Wolverine had a plan, Cassidy thought, now would be the time to put it into action.

A soldier popped out from behind the truck and aimed his weapon at Cassidy, squeezed off a few rounds. Sean screamed, and the force of his voice turned the bullets away to punch harmlessly through the roof of the refueling station. He glanced, still screaming, at the soldier who had fired, and the man was thrown off his feet to land painfully.

The trucks had stopped and new troops were pouring out. Cassidy found himself back to back with Creed in the middle of the street, with dawn a memory and morning fully arrived.

"Glad you could join the party, Irish," Creed growled. "You're not half bad in the trenches, for a Mick."

"If that's your way of saying thank you, Creed, don't bother," Cassidy snapped. "Saving your life is not goin' to be one of the proudest accomplishments of me life."

"From where I'm sittin', it looks like you got a ways to go before you can brag about savin' my life," Creed snarled.

But that smile was back on his face. He didn't even have to tell Cassidy that he didn't think he'd needed saving. Or that he didn't think he needed any help at all. It was all there in that smile and in the way he scowled when he spoke.

As cold as it was, Sean couldn't keep the thought from coming. He looked at Creed one last time and thought, *I'm going to die for him. For a man that like as not deserves to be put to death himself.*

Then a voice cut through the morning air, a harsh crack like thunder. Cassidy didn't speak Russian, but he recognized the language. Two men stepped into the street. One of them wore a Soviet officer's uniform. *A major,* Sean thought.

The other man was Logan.

The major began barking orders at the soldiers who had piled out of the newly arrived trucks. Several subordinate officers ran over to him, and didn't even glance wrong at Wolverine.

"What in the name of God could he be saying that's keeping these men from killing us where we stand?" Cassidy asked breathlessly. "Ye just killed their comrades, and they've stopped their attack."

Under his breath, Sabretooth gave a dry laugh.

"Accordin' to the major over there," Creed said, "we're KGB. All three of us, even though you've got the map o' Ireland tattooed on your face. This was a trainin' exercise, top secret, and they're all confined to base while the KGB examines our performance and investigates the actions that led to the deaths of the grunts I just killed."

"Don't sound so bleedin' proud of yourself," Cassidy snapped.

"I ain't proud," Sabretooth replied. "Just amused."

Cassidy wanted to shoot him, but Sabretooth wasn't his biggest concern. No, that would be how Wolverine ended up with a Soviet army officer who'd pass off the slaughter of more than half a dozen of his men with such a ridiculously contrived story.

"I don't understand," Cassidy began.

But the minute he spoke the words, he did understand. He stared at the major for several seconds, feeling like an idiot for not realizing the truth sooner.

"Mystique."

THEN

Ten minutes after the Soviet soldiers had dispersed, the truck rolled east again, toward Minsk. Igor was at the wheel, Logan riding shotgun. The others were in the back, with one exception. Though Wolverine had been reluctant to let her out of his sight, Mystique had argued convincingly that she had to stay behind with the Soviet troops, at least for a short time. They were to drive on for ten miles, and then pull over and wait for her.

But Mystique never showed.

Logan cursed after they had waited half an hour. "I should've known better."

"It's possible she was discovered, even captured," Silver Fox suggested.

"It's possible she just ain't caught up to us yet," Sabretooth added.

"Yeah," Wolverine snorted. "An' it's possible she played me for a fool, and is goin' for the gold all by herself." He turned to Igor. "Better get a move on, bub," he snarled. "You're our ace in the hole; even if that blue-skinned femme fatale's gone on ahead o' us, you're gonna help us get where we're goin' first, aren't you?"

The KGB interrogator started the truck, put it in gear, and pulled out onto the narrow, dusty road. He didn't even look at Wolverine as he spoke in Russian.

"You've killed me already, 'Wolverine,'" Igor said. "You simply haven't realized it yet. Or perhaps you have. Even if your friend 'Sabretooth' doesn't take my life, my KGB superiors will execute me for my failure."

Logan considered the man's words. After a moment, he smiled.

"You wanna defect?" Wolverine asked.

Igor took his eyes off the road long enough to glare at Logan for several seconds. "I would rather die," he said coldly.

"I don't believe you for a second," Wolverine replied. "If you'd rather die, you wouldn't still be alive."

Igor stared at him a moment. The truck began to drift, and the Soviet snapped his attention back to the road. The man looked stricken, Logan thought. Almost nauseous. Sometimes the truth could do that.

"If I take you to where I believe the Black Widow will meet with her controller, you will bring me back to America with you?" he asked, and his words, even in Russian, seemed filled with self-loathing.

"If you get us there before Mystique, you've got a deal," Wolverine replied.

Igor's eyes flickered down to his lap, and his face went slack.

"I am a coward," he muttered.

"No," Logan said. "You're a wise man."

It was late morning, but the Black Widow was not going to take any chances. She skirted the edges of the city of Minsk, hoping to avoid any further entanglements. The sedan was low on fuel, but there wasn't much further for her to go. Three miles east of Minsk, she diverged from the main road, steering the car down into a shallow valley dense with foliage. The road there was little more than a cart path, but soon the shimmering surface of a small lake came into view and, on the shore of the lake, a home.

Yet it had not served as anyone's home for many years. Instead, the gray stone manse at the water's edge had been transformed into a KGB way station. Natasha had only been here once before, yet she guided the sedan unerringly along the crude roadway.

Two hundred yards from the house, she killed the engine and let the car bump and crash into the forest to the right of the path. Those inside might have heard her approach, but it would not matter. Once she was on foot, with the cover of the forest, they would not see her before she wanted to be seen.

Sure enough, moments later a trio of KGB soldiers bearing AK-47s appeared on the road, combing the woods to either side. Natasha passed right by them without being noticed, and approached the stone face of the house soundlessly. She moved quickly along one side, saw that a second-story window was open slightly, and began to scale the stone wall.

With one fluid motion, she slid through the open window and into a large office whose walls were lined with leather-bound books. She strutted to the high-backed leather chair behind the wide mahogany desk and sat down, pleased to finally be able to rest a moment. She leaned back in the chair, put her hands behind her head, and closed her eyes.

When the door slammed open to admit a pair of brawny gunmen whose weapons were aimed at her head, Natasha didn't even flinch. Instead, she smiled while the men shouted at her, put her legs up on the desk, and stretched, catlike. One of the men shouted again, cocked his weapon and took several steps toward her, ready to fire.

"Put that down, you idiot," a female voice snapped from the hall. "Don't you have any idea who you're dealing with?"

This time, Natasha was surprised. She recognized the voice, but had not expected to hear it within these walls. The woman who walked into the room then was taller than Natasha by several inches, and broader as well. Olga Lokhtina had once been the Soviet Union's greatest Olympian, a gymnast without peer. But she had also been one of the KGB's greatest assets. Now the woman's hair was getting gray to match her unsmiling face and dull eyes.

"You were expected, Black Widow," Olga said. "But I don't see why you felt it necessary to put us all on alarm when you might have simply knocked on the door."

Natasha sat forward in the chair, cocked her head slightly to look at Olga.

"Where is my controller?" she said bluntly.

Olga stiffened, obviously offended by Natasha's brusqueness. She had been the lieutenant to the Widow's controller since Natasha had first been recruited by the KGB, but Natasha had never liked her. In addition, it had ever been clear to her that Olga despised her, though she never knew why. Her youth, perhaps, or her skills, for despite Olga's achievements in gymnastics, Natasha had always exceeded the older woman's abilities.

"Your controller is otherwise engaged," Olga replied warily, eyes narrowed and focused only on the Widow. "Why? Have you failed in your mission, Widow?"

"Failed?" Natasha snapped, climbed angrily to her feet, and leaned over the desk to glare at Olga. "No, I have not failed, comrade. I am here, am I not? Would I have returned without the disk in question? The Black Widow has never failed. No, I ask where my controller is because his absence seems odd to me. I was told that he would be here, along with his bodyguards, and that he would take possession of the disk, after which I would return to Moscow."

Olga smiled. Natasha didn't like that smile at all.

"Ah, Comrade Romanova," she said patronizingly, "you are still so naïve. Do you think you are the only agent the controller is responsible for? You overestimate your importance, girl. I have come in the controller's place, as his lieutenant. These men are here for my protection and for yours."

Natasha studied the faces of the two men: hard, cold, and vacant. They would do what they were told, no more and no less. Then she looked at Olga again, and her mind was made up.

"Then I will hold on to the disk, and they can escort both of us back to Moscow," the Widow said. "For your own protection, of course, Comrade Lokhtina. At every step of this mission, it has been compromised. Several other agencies were after the disk and the traitors who stole it. They have known a great many things they never ought to have been able to find out, which makes me think we have a double agent working closely with us. So, you see," she went on, with a smile and a tiny shrug, "I must only hand this disk over to the controller when we see him in Moscow."

Lokhtina was livid. "If you are implying . . . " she began in a rage.

"I imply nothing," the Widow replied angrily. "I only tell you what I must do in order to see this mission through to its completion. Now if you'll show me to a room where I might shower and have a change of clothes, I'll prepare for our departure."

Olga stared at her a moment, then nodded toward one of the two bodyguards. "Sergei," she said. The man in question holstered his weapon, nodded respectfully at the Widow, then led her from the room.

"I will see to it that your behavior is noted by your superiors," Olga said coldly as the Widow stepped into the hall.

"Yes," Natasha agreed. "I would appreciate that."

The truck had rolled into Minsk just after eleven o'clock in the morning. For the first time since the whole op had gone wrong back in East Berlin, Wolverine actually felt as though they were in control of things again. Now that Igor had realized he was going to have to defect or he'd end up dead, he was more than helpful. The safehouse they were headed for was several miles outside of Minsk. Igor had been there many times—slept there, even. He'd been KGB for more than a decade, but he'd done it for the power, not because he'd bought into the load of double-talk coming out of the Kremlin.

Strangely, Logan found that he had a bit in common with the man behind the wheel. Igor didn't trust his bosses either, but he went on doing the job just the same. It wasn't much, but it was enough for Wolverine to feel the tiniest trace of sympathy for him. Igor would be better off when this op was over. As long as they all got out.

Which was why the KGB interrogator was even more cooperative when it came to finding them a telephone in Minsk. Not just any telephone either, but one that was guaranteed to have long distance service that wasn't in a government office. They found what they were looking for in the offices of a small academic book publishing firm. Of course, they were completely in line with the communist regime in the Kremlin. They'd have to be. But they also needed to be able to call London or Vienna or Stockholm when business called for it.

London would do. Wolverine had a number that would bounce the call to a safe line in the States. A line the Agency would never use again after that one call came in. Which was fine with him. It was an emergency line, and Logan couldn't think of a greater emergency than having his whole team stranded in the middle of the Soviet Union.

They might have been able to make it out the same way they got in. But chances were, when they caught up with the Widow, they were going to have the entire KGB on their trail. And it was a long way back to friendly territory, especially traveling with a tall red-headed, fair-skinned man with a brogue.

Igor was still KGB, that was the key. When Logan and North entered the publishing house's offices with Igor in the lead, the receptionist looked askance at them thanks to their attire. That was until Igor produced his identification, glaring at the woman all the while. The ranking executive in the firm fell all over himself to bring them to an empty office where they might place their call to Prague.

Or, at least, Prague was what they told him.

Inside the office, which was sterile and utilitarian, Logan picked up the phone, got a dial tone, hung up, and began again to make certain nobody else was on the line. He dialed the London number, got a series of beeps, a pause, and then it began to ring. Not in London, but in Washington, D.C.

"Code?" a voice answered.

"Kestrel on the wing, 5571," Logan replied.

The phone clattered on the other end, and then John Wraith's voice came over the line.

"Where have you been?" Wraith snapped.

"Finishing the job, Kestrel," Wolverine answered. "Now just shut up and listen. There's a field six miles due west of Minsk. Big enough to land a chopper. Two hours before dawn, come and get us."

A pause. "You've got what you went after?"

"We will," Logan replied. "Just be there."

"Wouldn't miss it," Wraith replied.

Logan hung up the phone. Silently, he and North hustled Igor out of the publisher's office, realizing that the clock was ticking. Once the KGB figured out that such a call had been made, it would be only a matter of time before they started scouring the city for Team X. And if they'd been listening, well, Wolverine wasn't stupid enough to give an uncoded message over an unsecured line.

Land masses substituted for bodies of water. A "river" would be a road. In this case, a "field" was a lake. Distances were doubled, and opposite of one another. Six miles west became three miles east. "Big enough to land a chopper" was just nonsense. Wraith didn't need any transport other than himself. And two hours before dawn was actually two hours after dusk.

It was simple if you knew what you were listening for. Igor knew the extraction plan, and even he looked at Logan strangely, trying to interpret the side of the conversation he'd heard. Eventually, the man simply shook his head.

A short time later they were back in the truck, on their way from Minsk. In the back of the vehicle, the others sat in mournful silence. Cassidy and Creed had barely exchanged a glance, but Wolverine knew that violence was brewing between them. The Irishman didn't think Creed had been justified in killing the Soviet soldiers back in that village. Wolverine figured Cassidy was right about that, but there was nothing to be done for it now.

On the other hand, Creed's savagery had the advantage of leaving them with a few extra weapons. Team X had crossed the Soviet border with a pair of AK-47s, various knives, maybe a dozen concussion grenades, and four semiautomatic pistols. Now they had three more Kalishnikovs that they put aside as backup. If they were going to storm a KGB safe house, they were going to need all the firepower they could lay their hands on.

Natasha felt renewed. She was still exhausted, body and soul, but she had gone longer without sleep in the past year. The shower had invigorated her, and she wore fresh clothes that Olga had brought along at the controller's instructions. The Widow wanted to kiss the man, or she would have, if she was certain he wasn't the double agent. It was difficult for her to believe, but not impossible. Someone was informing other agencies about KGB operations, or at least they had in this case.

She believed it was Olga, of course. But that bothered her. It was too easy to suspect someone she already disliked.

Somewhere on the first floor, a tea kettle whistled, and Natasha smiled as she walked downstairs. A pair of black garbed men with chiseled features glanced up at her as she peeked into the kitchen. These were two of the gunmen who'd come outside to search for her after she'd stashed the sedan in the trees.

They didn't say hello.

In the central area of the first floor, a large room with an enormous conference table, three women conversed quietly. One of them was Olga. The others were obviously agents on some assignment or other. Olga's bodyguards stood in a far corner.

"Ah, Natasha," Olga said in Russian, standing to greet her. "Are you ready to go, then?"

"Yes, if you don't mind," the Black Widow replied.

Olga smiled, but that smile was a lie. Its falsehood was more than mere dislike for the Black Widow. Natasha knew, in that moment, that Olga was indeed a double agent. But how could she prove it?

"I'm ready now," Olga said, and motioned for her body-guards. "Sergei, go get the car, will you?"

Natasha watched Sergei carefully. She was paranoid now, and she knew it. But it was impossible for her to know if Olga was working on her own, or if there were other traitors in the house.

"There must be other agents here, other guards?" she said, making the question sound as innocent as she was able to.

"Oh, yes," Olga replied, and moved around the table to come toward Natasha. A pair of many-paned glass doors looked out on the lake behind her. A beautiful view, placid and comforting in some way.

"It's a large house," Olga said. "There are several other agents upstairs, I would guess. And four men guarding the grounds. It isn't as though there isn't internal security." She smiled again. "After all, we knew immediately when you entered the house."

Natasha returned the smile, trying her best to make it more genuine than Olga's. How to deal with the older woman's duplicity was a question that she knew would haunt her the entire ride back to Moscow.

The front door opened. Sergei stepped in. He didn't smile, of course. His type never did. But he opened his mouth to tell Olga the car was ready. There came the crack of a single gunshot, and a piece of Sergei's forehead exploded. The man stumbled forward and fell dead in the foyer, bleeding onto the carpet.

"Get down!" Natasha shouted.

A body crashed through the double doors, landing on the conference table in a shower of glass and setting off alarms that pealed ear-shatteringly loud throughout the house. Gunfire shattered windows and tore into the furnishings. Heavy foot-falls tromped across the floor above her head.

With the exception of her widow's bite, Natasha was weaponless. She was on her knees when she spotted Sergei's corpse and realized that he must be armed. The Black Widow scuttled forward, planning to grab the dead bodyguard's weapon. Windows and mirrors exploded, and plaster chunks flew from the walls as bullets punched holes in them.

Something bounced heavily on the foyer carpet and rolled up to land right next to Sergei's body. Natasha blinked.

It was a concussion grenade.

She ran for the stairs and was three steps up when the grenade exploded. It threw her up and flat against the stairs, hard, knocking the wind out of her. Suddenly the air was split with a wailing sound that drowned out the alarms, a sound of fury and agony. A human sound.

Cassidy.

Natasha got quickly to her feet. A pair of concussion grenades detonated elsewhere in the house, shaking its walls and raining plaster from the ceiling. Before starting upstairs again, she took a glance back and saw something that bothered her even more than hearing Cassidy's sonic scream.

Two figures had just come through the shattered glass rear doors. A dark-skinned woman with long, silky black hair, and a huge blond man whose grin marked him as a killer. They carried AK-47s in their hands, and the guns leapt at their command, cutting through the pair of female KGB agents who had been returning fire from behind the conference-room table.

Olga peeked out from inside the kitchen.

"It's about time you got here," she said in English as she rushed toward them, her hands up and weaponless. "I was told the Widow wouldn't even make it back to the border!"

Before Natasha could even form the urge for vengeance upon the woman, the one called Sabretooth brought the stock of his AK-47 across Olga's forehead. She crumbled to the ground with a small cry, and then the huge killer shot her in the face. Her end was so violent that, despite Olga's betrayal, the Widow felt for her.

But that didn't slow Natasha down. She was up the stairs in a flash.

"Widow!"

She spun and saw another member of Team X standing in the hall with his weapon pointed at her torso. Maverick, she thought he was called.

Outside, Cassidy's shriek grew even louder, and windows shattered along the hall.

Maverick flinched.

Natasha ran for the open window and dove.

Falling, she spun, landed hard on soft grass and rolled. When she came up, she was four feet from Wolverine. He turned, a nine-millimeter semiautomatic in each hand.

But Natasha already had momentum. She leapt at him, held her gloves against either side of his head, and gave him thirty thousand volts at each temple.

Wolverine went down hard.

Another surge of adrenaline rushed through the Black Widow as she realized that she had a chance to escape. She might actually make it.

Natasha turned to run, and stopped short as the ground at her feet began to churn, dirt flying as bullets punched the earth. She spun, bracelets at the ready. Silver Fox and Sabretooth were there, AK-47s slung low and aimed right at her.

"The disk," Silver Fox demanded.

"Go to hell," the Widow snapped, in English.

"Fine," Sabretooth said. "We'll get it after."

His finger tightened on the trigger. Above, Sean Cassidy's banshee wail grew louder, and Natasha's thought her eardrums would burst.

She closed her eyes and waited for death.

NOW

The alarms that resounded through the halls of CIA headquarters died suddenly. The echo lasted mere seconds, and was followed by complete silence. Wolverine crouched inside the office of the director of the CIA with his claws popped. Muscles rippled across his back and thighs as he stared at the office door and tensed to spring at whatever or whomever might walk through it.

His upper lip curled back in a nearly silent snarl that rumbled in his chest, building to a roar that he waited to unleash. Waited. And waited.

"I don't get it," Mystique whispered behind him.

Logan ignored her. The pause might have her thinking the alarms weren't all about them, but that was just empty hope. They'd gone off right after Wraith disappeared—and Wraith had disappeared right after they had discovered that he was part of the conspiracy, a member of the covert ops team sent to capture everyone involved with a mission that took place during the Cold War.

No, it was definitely a setup. But Mystique's instincts were right on. If it was a setup, why the delay? Why weren't the CIA agents swarming this building, breaking down the door to capture Mystique and Wolverine? Why—?

"We gotta get out of here," Wolverine said.

But even as he spoke the words, Logan heard a rapid-fire sound like a butcher chopping meat.

"What's happening?" Mystique asked anxiously.

Logan pointed to the duct they'd used to climb through into the director's office. It was covered, now, by a thick sheet of gleaming silvery metal.

"Adamantium," he growled. "Probably got the whole place sealed off that way."

Mystique was too much of a pro to ask why. She knew what the next step was. Small panels, no more than two inches square, opened on each of the four walls, and a pale green gas began to churn out.

"No!" Mystique snapped. "We can't let them take us this easily!"

"Don't worry, darlin'," Wolverine replied grimly. "They won't."

He went to the office door, and saw Mystique react in his peripheral vision. She opened her mouth, reached out as if to stop him.

"Logan, stop," she said. "You don't know what they might've wired up to the door. Could be a nasty little surprise for us."

"They don't want us dead," Wolverine replied, growing angrier by the moment. The animal within him didn't want to be caged. "You want to hide behind the desk over there, I ain't stoppin' you. But if Wraith and his government cronies want to chat with me, it'll be on my terms."

Gas still pumped into the room, and Logan took a deep breath, held it, and brought his claws down, slashing through the door, the knob, the entire locking mechanism, and the door frame. But beyond the door itself, he felt the claws meet resistance. That was something that almost never happened. Adamantium was virtually indestructible, and when you had half a dozen claws made out of the alloy, you expected them to cut through just about anything.

He reached into the splintered space between the door and its frame, the place where the lock had been only seconds earlier. When he pulled it open, he saw that same gleaming metal that had covered the air duct was across the door frame. Behind him, Mystique began to cough, hard, and choke on the gas fumes.

Wolverine scraped his claws across the tempered metal

sheeting, eliciting a screech far, far more grating than nails on a blackboard.

"Adamantium?" Mystique asked, and covered her mouth with her hands.

"Yep," Logan agreed, and stared at the metal. His claws were made of the same thing, of course. Probably the one thing they couldn't cut through.

He shook his head, then tried to block out the acrid odor of the gas, the sting in his eyes.

"Uh-uh," Logan said. "It ain't happenin' like this."

"What . . . what are you talking about?" Mystique said between coughs. "They've got us. Unless you can teleport us out of here."

"No," Wolverine said, still staring at the sheet of metal across the open door.

"You're in denial, Logan," she said, and coughed again. Mystique sat down on the carpeted floor of the office, where the gas hadn't yet settled. "I know you only half-trusted Wraith, but you trusted him enough to get us into this trap. I don't blame you—I walked into it, too. But be realistic about it."

Her voice had become a bit shaky, as though she'd been drinking, and Wolverine grew angrier with every word she spoke. Not at Mystique, but at Wraith. She was right about that much. He should have known better. Wraith was such a loyal soldier that if his superiors were trying to capture him, for whatever reason, he'd likely just sit and wait for them. But they didn't have to capture him. He'd been working for them all along.

"Least we'll get to find out what this is all about," Mystique said airily.

With a roar that had been growing in the burning pit of his belly since he'd first seen Wraith's name on that computer screen, Wolverine launched himself forward and began hacking and slashing with his claws. Wood and plaster and insulation and wiring split like paper as he carved a huge section of wall away from the adamantium sheet that had fallen down inside of it.

"Logan, why bother?" Mystique asked.

From the sound of her voice, he thought she might be on the verge of unconsciousness. He couldn't have that. Wolverine turned and took four steps to where Mystique lay on the ground, lolling idly as though she were bored. He reached down, hauled her up by the front of her white dress and slapped her, hard, across the face. Her skin flared deeper blue for a moment, and her yellow eyes focused.

"That hurt," she said, her teeth gritted.

"You wanna get outta here, you'll do it on your own two feet," he said. "I ain't carryin' you, Raven."

Even as she began to ask him again how he planned to escape, Logan turned his back to her again and stomped to the door. Where he'd ripped the wall away, the adamantium sheeting kept them trapped inside. It would be all through the floor and ceiling as well, he knew. But it couldn't possibly have been all one piece. And if the door had been open before, the plate had to have slid over it from one side or the other. Didn't matter, really, because that meant on either side there'd be seams.

"Stupid," he mumbled, and found it hard to get his mouth to form the word.

He lost focus a second, and then it came back quickly. His mutant healing factor would hold off the effects of the gas much longer than Mystique would be able to hold out. But if he didn't get her a breath of fresh air soon, he *would* end up having to carry her.

Eyes narrowed, he focused on the dark line that marked the seam between one sheet of adamantium and the next. Wolverine tilted his head, his whole body, lifted his arms, aimed, and slammed both fists forward as hard as he could.

His claws punched right through the seam, and Wolverine began to pull. The plate would not rip, but Logan was incredibly strong. Veins stood out on his forehead and his biceps as he pulled on the plate, and he heard the grating sound of metal against metal as the adamantium plate over the door began to tear loose of its moorings above and below.

"How 'bout a hand?" a familiar growl came from behind him.

Wolverine glanced back a moment, and was startled to see Sabretooth standing behind him, reaching for the inch-wide gap he'd made. Then he realized it was Mystique.

"Thought Forge put somethin' in your head to prevent you from takin' the shape o' anyone in the X-Men or X-Factor, or close to us?" he asked.

"I've been practicing," Mystique growled in Creed's voice, and reached Sabretooth's claws into the gap next to Wolverine's fingers. She was no stronger in this shape—Mystique could only change form, not function. But Sabretooth's clawed hands gave her a better grip than Raven Darkhölme's ordinary hands would have. "I can't hold it for very long."

With a massive effort, they tore the panel from its frame.

"Long enough," Wolverine muttered.

Then he froze, stunned. The reception area outside the director's office was completely empty—sterile and abandoned. He'd expected a greeting party similar to the one led by Nick Fury when he and Mystique had broken into the S.H.I.E.L.D. base, only with Wraith at the head of the wolf pack.

Behind him, Mystique went into a fit of coughing. When she collapsed against Wolverine's back, she had morphed back into her true form. Logan turned, pulled her arm over his shoulder, and dragged her into the reception area. A cup of coffee sat on top of the desk of the director's assistant. Lipstick stained its rim and steam still rose from the cup.

Trying not to think about what was going on, what Wraith and the Agency might have cooked up for them in the middle of CIA HQ, Logan let Mystique slump, half-unconscious, against the edge of the desk in the reception area. He lifted that steaming cup of coffee to her lips and tipped it back.

Yellow eyes fluttered open, unfocused, and she turned away

from the burning liquid at first. But the taste or the scent or a combination of the two brought her back to it, and Mystique's hands came up to grasp the cup. She drained it, though Logan would have thought it still too hot to drink. Mystique stood up, a hand on his shoulder for balance, and shook her whole body as though she'd caught a chill or someone had walked over her grave.

"Let's get the hell out of here," she said.

Without further comment, Logan turned toward the glass door that looked out on an equally empty, carpeted hallway. The place was a ghost ship, running on its own. Or, at least, that's how it looked. But he knew differently. Wraith wasn't about to leave this operation to run itself. He'd be watching them, somehow, even now.

Wolverine looked around the reception area for a surveillance camera, and found it immediately, out in the open. Why not? This was the Central Intelligence Agency—of course they'd have video surveillance. Probably hidden cameras as well as the overt ones.

"You ain't gettin' us, Wraith," Logan said aloud. "We're leavin' now, but we'll be back when you're not lookin'. We'll be back for the rest of the team, for the Widow and Cassidy— but mostly we'll be back for you."

It occurred to him once again, with Mystique at his side, that everyone involved in that op so many years ago had all changed.

All but John Wraith.

Wolverine grabbed the computer monitor off the director's assistant's desk, ripped it away from the computer, trailing cables and sparks, and hurled it with all his might at the glass door that led to the hallway. Glass shattered loudly and then fell softly to the carpeted floor of the corridor.

Nothing.

The hallway was clear. Not a movement. Not a sound.

"They're not going to kill us," Mystique said. "That's their weakness. Difference is, I don't care too much whether I kill them or not. Wraith, particularly. I think I'd like that."

She started for the shattered door, its shattered glass hanging down like jagged teeth. Wolverine didn't stop her. Instead, he walked close behind Mystique, and tapped her gently on the right elbow. They reached the door, some of the broken glass crunching beneath the soles of their boots.

"Go!" Logan roared.

Mystique was through the door, breaking right, and sprinting down the hall as fast as her unsteady feet would carry her. Wolverine was right behind her.

"Nowhere to run, Logan!" Wraith screamed behind him. "You're just making this harder on yourself. Give it up now! You know you got nowhere to go!"

Dozens of weapons cocked. Wolverine didn't even look back. The wall to his left split horizontally, and its top and bottom began to slide toward floor and ceiling. He could see the hips and abdomen of jumpsuited operatives in the opening, some with their weapons slung low across their waists. He didn't slow down.

There had been no movement, no sound in the hallway. But Wolverine had smelled them. Wraith should have known he'd be able to. Maybe he had known, and just not cared. After all, they were seven stories off the ground, and the only way down was most certainly behind them. They had to fight if they wanted to get away, and Wraith sounded confident that Wolverine and Mystique weren't going to. He'd be well prepared, Logan knew that much. He'd already proven it, in fact.

But Wraith was always guilty of overestimating his own intelligence, and his usefulness.

"Not another step, or they open fire!" Wraith shouted.

Mystique had slowed down, and now Logan caught up with her. He placed a hand on her back and propelled her along, her feet moving beneath her just to keep her from falling.

Team Alpha was behind them, by the elevator banks, and Wraith was with them, shouting at Logan to stop. Behind the wall, that must be Team Omega, Wolverine figured.

"What . . . what are we doing?" Mystique asked breathlessly. "There's no way out up here!"

"You blind?" Wolverine asked.

She looked down the hall ahead of them. Wolverine heard the intake of breath as she realized what he had in mind.

"Oh, God," she whispered. "Not again."

"Fire!" Wraith shrieked.

Bullets tore up the floor and walls around them, and Logan smirked as he realized that keeping them alive had suddenly become less of a priority. Which was fine with him. He wasn't sure they were going to survive the next minute or so anyway.

Mystique grunted as a bullet passed through her shoulder, spraying her blood onto the white of her dress. Wolverine felt a bullet enter his back and puncture a lung. He took another in the meat of his thigh.

Then they had reached the end of the corridor. No time to turn left or right, and nowhere to go if they did. The window that ran the length of the hall to either side was certain to be bulletproof, blastproof, and seven other proofs he hadn't considered.

Wolverine dove.

He held onto Mystique's wrist with his right hand. Claws popped out of his left. With all his momentum, he slammed his fist into the window, claws splitting the glass. When his body slammed into it, those little holes were enough. The window exploded outward under the weight of Wolverine and Mystique and bullets that were meant for them.

Something smacked Logan in the back of the head with such force that he tumbled forward, falling out of control. The sky was still blue, the breeze smelled sweet, but the parking lot below was rushing up too fast for him to appreciate the beauty of the day. The pain in the back of his head subsided, he shook off the disorientation.

Mystique was screaming.

Wolverine still had her by the wrist.

He twisted, got control of his fall, pulled her on top of him, and hit the narrow expanse of lawn that ran between building and parking lot, hard.

Logan was out for a second. He never would have noticed if it weren't for the fact that he came to with Mystique slapping his face.

"Wolverine!" she screamed in his face. "Get up! We've got to go!"

His eyes opened, but he was already in motion. Never mind the pain, the blood running from his bullet wounds, including the one from the slug that had bounced off his adamantium-reinforced skull. Never mind the fact that even with his healing factor, his back and legs would be deeply bruised for days. Without the healing factor, his flesh would have been pulped between adamantium bones and freshly cut green.

Mystique struggled to stand, hand clamped to her bleeding shoulder.

"You're insane!" she snapped at him.

"I got us out, didn't I?"

Then the shooting started again, from all around them. But this time, Wolverine was the only target.

The legs. The back. The stomach. He took thirteen bullets before he went down, and the last one, incredibly, went through his open mouth and punched out through the back of his neck.

The warmth of his own blood, and its intense scent, were the only things Wolverine was aware of at first. Sunlight pricked his eyes. Wraith stood above him, silhouetted against blue sky. Logan tried to speak, but his throat was damaged and all that came out was a low, ragged growl.

His healing factor was on overdrive, trying desperately to compensate for so many wounds at one time. If he didn't bleed to death first, it would be days before he was completely recovered. Hours before the bullet wounds would actually begin to close. If he didn't bleed to death first . . . but the bleeding should stop soon, he thought.

Real soon.

Snikt.

His claws slid out, almost unconsciously. He wanted to kill Wraith, then. But even the berserk rage deep in his soul would not be enough to get him to his feet. Not this time.

"Don't even think about it," Wraith said. "We did want you alive, which is why my operatives were only supposed to shoot at you, Logan. After all, you can take it, can't you?"

Wolverine grunted. Wraith had always known about his healing factor. But the adamantium? That had been added later. Wraith must have known, sure, but he'd never seen it in action. Never seen what it could really do. Now he had.

"You even try to escape, try to touch me, so much as even bleed on me, and I'll execute Mystique right now," Wraith said.

Then he knelt by Logan, so nobody else could hear, and he whispered. "I'm sorry, man. I truly am. But you shouldn't have run. Should've just come in when you figured it all out. You brought this on yourself. Just play along, and you might live through it."

The thing that made Wolverine want so desperately to lunge forward and tear Wraith's throat out with his teeth was not the betrayal, not the pain he was in, but the sincerity in his former teammate's voice.

But Logan couldn't even get up the energy to spit in John Wraith's face.

Unconsciousness tugged at him, and, realizing he could do nothing more, Wolverine did not struggle as the darkness took him.

The next time Logan came to, he sensed immediately that he was no longer outside. The bright lights against his still-closed eyelids were not the sun, but harsh fluorescents. The smells were antiseptic and human sweat. Before he was completely conscious, even before he was aware of the restraints that bolted him upright to the wall, of the metal choker around his neck, he knew who else was in that room with him.

When he heard the voice, then, it came as no surprise.

"Welcome back to the land of the livin', runt."

THEN

The Widow had seconds to live, seconds in which bullets would rip through her flesh and splash her blood on the hard, cold earth. Seconds in which she would not even have time to aim her widow's bite before Sabretooth and Silver Fox would cut her down where she stood.

If Cassidy didn't get to her first.

The Interpol agent had become one of the banes of her existence, had made her his top priority. Though the first time they clashed, she'd thought him no more than another international peacekeeper, during this op it had become clear that he planned to kill her.

Cassidy was a mutant, or whatever they called themselves. With a thought, his normal voice became an ear-splitting wail that could shatter walls as easily as eardrums, and could carry him aloft as though he were some kind of rocket. Natasha had seen the destructive capacity of that voice several times. She hesitated to think what it might do to a human body if Cassidy really wanted to kill.

Being shot to death seemed, in some ways, infinitely preferable.

She crouched with her eyes closed, waiting for the bullets. Waiting for the pile driver of force that scream would bring down upon her from above. Cassidy's wailing grew closer.

Sabretooth let out a roar that was half grunt, but the bullets didn't come. The Widow opened her eyes in surprise to see the two members of Team X being thrown back across the road and into the trees. Silver Fox fell at the tree line, but with incredible accuracy, Cassidy swooped low, still screaming, and used his sonic scream to slam Sabretooth deep into the woods and into the thick trunk of a tree.

Cassidy rose up through branches and leaves, turned, and dove back down toward her, and Natasha felt her fear return. She lifted her arms, fired her widow's bite with both wrists, but the Irishman's sonic scream turned her attack away harmlessly. His voice seemed to recede even as he approached her, no longer in danger of shattering her eardrums. Cassidy's eyes burned with hatred, and Natasha realized what had happened.

He wanted her for himself. He had actually attacked Team X to keep them from killing her, all so he could do it himself. So much hate, and all for something Natasha had no control over, a nasty twist of fate.

At the last possible moment, Natasha tried to dive out of his path. But she was too late. Cassidy slammed into her hard enough to knock the air from her lungs, and then she was borne aloft in his arms, trying desperately to draw a breath.

As she gasped for air, the Widow hung limply in Cassidy's arms and watched the lake flash by beneath her at dizzying speed. Her ears pounded with the mutant's scream, but it was as though the noise were beyond her now. Somehow he could control it enough to protect her, and himself, to use the sonic power of his voice for precisely what he needed.

She waited for him to drop her into the lake, and thought about drowning. Then they were past the lake, and she saw a narrow cart path below. The ground rushed up to meet them, and Cassidy slowed abruptly and set his feet down easily on the hard-packed earth of the path. Unceremoniously, he dropped Natasha to the ground. She choked, lungs greedily sucking in air, finally beginning to get her bearings.

"If I were you, lass, I'd get moving as soon as ye can manage it," Cassidy said, his kindly voice such a startling contrast to his scream.

He bent over her and began to run his hands over her body. She stiffened, but was still barely focused enough to voice a protest. Cassidy found what he wanted quickly, and unzipped the front of her bodysuit to remove the data disk that had already been the cause of so much death and confusion.

"Why?" she croaked, even as she began to get to her knees.

Cassidy had turned away, but not yet taken to the air. He stopped short, turned to face her. In that moment, he was vulnerable. She could have used her widow's bite on him, but she didn't. Mainly because she really wanted to know.

"Ye put me in hospital last we met," he said. "I wasn't at home when I ought to've been. I blamed ye for that, but I know now 'twas nobody's fault but this bloody job's. I wanted to kill ye myself, lass. But ye're just a wee slip of a girl, and there's been enough killing already, there has. No, I won't be party to murder if I can help it.

"Ye'd best get on, now. I'll tell 'em ye're dead, but I can't be certain they won't get after ye. Wolverine and that other, Sabretooth, they're likely to know just from smellin' me that ye're still alive."

Cassidy narrowed his eyes.

"They'll be another time, though," he said. "Mark me words. The only reason I'm not takin' you in is 'cause that group would kill you sure as pass the time playin' cards. And 'cause this disk should buy me the kind of security I need."

Then he opened his mouth and began to scream, and his feet left the ground. Sean Cassidy sailed up and over the lake, his voice diminishing as he sped away.

Natasha Romanova sat on the hard earth and watched him go. She had lost. That was a strange realization. In her short career with the KGB, this was the first time she had ever lost. The Widow was certain to face censure for her defeat, and for her failure to bring the disk back to Moscow as instructed—no matter that Olga had betrayed her and the KGB, not to mention the U.S.S.R.

Yet, somehow, she didn't feel as though she had failed.

Wolverine was drawn from unconsciousness by the piercing wail of Sean Cassidy's sonic scream. It speared into his brain, interrupting a flickering dream-memory—of his finding Igor, sitting behind the wheel of the truck with his throat ripped out. The KGB man had been as good as his word, kept his end of the bargain. But apparently Creed had been so incensed at the idea of bringing him back to the West with them, as Logan had promised, that he had somehow managed to double back and slaughter the man.

Cassidy's scream, despite the pain it caused his already aching head, was a welcome interruption to the fury and sorrow he felt in his dream. Wolverine's eyes flickered open, and he cringed at the pain in his head and ears and spine. Though he was awake, he was still disoriented and couldn't focus well enough even to sit up.

The wind had begun to howl, as if the maelstrom they had created here in the countryside beyond Minsk had kicked up a real storm. Logan blinked, moved his head slightly and was rewarded with a spike of pain that ran from his neck straight up into his brain.

"He's comin' back!" Creed growled, not far off.

But Logan didn't know if Sabretooth was talking about him, or about Cassidy, whose scream grew ever closer until it simply stopped. The Interpol agent dropped to the ground from a height of just under ten feet up.

Wolverine tilted his head slightly and saw them, then, all four of them standing there—Sabretooth, Silver Fox, Maverick, and Cassidy. He wanted to speak, but he could barely form thoughts. One thought that did make it to his brain was this: if it weren't for his healing factor, the Black Widow very likely would have killed him.

And from the sound of things, Cassidy had just saved her life.

"You're askin' to get your throat slashed, Irishman," Creed snarled. "What the hell did you do with the Widow? You've got about ten seconds to tell us where you took her. After that, I ain't responsible for what's gonna happen to you."

Cassidy didn't look at all bothered by Sabretooth's threats.

He stood off to one side, legs apart, ready to use his sonic scream the second one of them moved on him.

"I was going to tell all of ye that I killed her," Cassidy said, his brogue heavy and his words slow and deliberate. "But I can't even do that. I let the girl go. There's been enough death on this mission. I've seen enough death in me own life, and I come to realize it wasn't her fault."

"That's all well and good," Maverick said angrily, "but we need that disk. You've made our job a whole lot harder now."

"Worse than that," Fox added. "Our pickup'll be here in fifteen minutes. We'll never find her and get back in time. You've blown our op, Cassidy. I'm starting to agree with Sabretooth. Maybe somebody's got to die for all this, and maybe it should be you."

"Never thought I'd see you agree with Creed, lassie," Cassidy said. "But ye're all welcome to try your best. I wouldn't take any bets, though. I didn't want to kill a helpless girl, but that doesn't mean I won't do it to protect myself. Aye, I've done it an awful lot the past few days. Besides, I believe I've a better way to resolve things," Cassidy said. "I just told ye that I killed the Widow. That's what ye report. And as far as the disk, well, I think we can take care of that, don't you?"

With that, the Irishman pulled the data disk from inside his jacket. Immediately, Sabretooth took a step forward.

"Well, that's a start," Creed snarled. "Give it here, Irish, and maybe we'll let you go home after this op."

"Even give you a lift," Maverick said.

"What are you going to tell your superiors?" Silver Fox asked, eyes narrowed in doubt.

"Leave that to me, lass," Cassidy replied. "Interpol is getting a bit boring these days anyway. I'm thinking it might be time for me to make a move."

"The disk, Cassidy, now," Sabretooth growled, and took another step toward him.

"Stay where ye are, Creed," Cassidy snapped. "I'll give it over, but not to you."

Cassidy glanced over at Wolverine. Logan opened his mouth to speak, even began to sit up a little. He nodded. As far as Wolverine was concerned, the Widow still being alive was unfortunate, but he understood what Cassidy had done and it didn't bother him. Cold-blooded killing was not a pleasant job. In a fight, okay. But gunning down an unarmed enemy? There'd be other chances to get the Widow.

As Logan watched, Cassidy looked from Silver Fox to Maverick, and back to Fox. Then he stepped forward and held the disk out to Maverick, who smiled as he took it. Wolverine shook his head, which was finally beginning to clear. There was something off about Maverick. The smile on his face, for one.

Then Wolverine noticed that the wind had died down. The scents of his team swirled around, theirs, and two others. Cassidy's and . . . suddenly he realized that Maverick's scent was coming from behind him, rather than in front. Wolverine began, slowly, to rise, coming to his knees.

"Logan!" Maverick shouted from the steps of the KGB safehouse.

And in front of him, the hand holding the disk began to change. For it wasn't Maverick at all, of course. It was Mystique. And in her other hand, she held a nine-millimeter semi automatic pistol. The muscles in her hand tightened.

"No!" Wolverine roared, and leapt from a crouched position across the space separating him from Mystique.

Her pistol barked twice, and Cassidy went down in a spray of blood.

Then Wolverine was on her, and Mystique fell beneath his attack. He speared her gun hand with a blade. Mystique let out a squeal of pain and a grunt as she hit the ground. Logan snatched the disk from her hand, and leaned in close so he was eye to eye with her.

"I never trusted you, girl," he snarled. "If anyone on this op needed killin', it was definitely you. But I ain't gonna kill you now. Better you go back to your Mossad bosses and tell 'em you blew it."

Still shaking the cobwebs from his mind, Wolverine spat orders: "Fox, see to Cassidy. Creed, make sure Maverick's all right."

"I'm fine," Maverick said, sitting up. "I'd cleaned it all up inside when Mystique caught me up from behind."

Cassidy was sitting up as well. Only one of the bullets had tagged him, and the wound was in his shoulder: looked like it had gone through cleanly.

Wolverine stood up, disk in hand.

But Team X wasn't done with Mystique yet.

"Kill her," Silver Fox said grimly.

"My call, too," Maverick said. "It's well within our op parameters. We know she's a lying, deceitful witch. And with that morphing ability, she's too dangerous just to leave around. Not in this game. We let her live, we'll regret it later."

Logan looked at them. Maverick had always been the least vicious of the team, though it had never been a handicap in a fight. And Silver Fox had been getting more and more concerned with doing the right thing of late. They weren't bloodthirsty, not really. Not any more than you had to be to be in this line of work.

No. They were just being logical.

Wolverine glanced over at Cassidy, expecting to get an argument. But Cassidy had just been shot by Mystique, and he only stared back at Wolverine for a few seconds before looking away.

Before Logan could answer one way or another—though he'd already made up his mind—Creed stepped forward and grabbed Mystique's gun from Wolverine's hands.

"Give me that!" he snarled. "You want to off the duplicitous tart, all ya gotta do is say so. I'm a little tired o' her usin' the fact that we've worked together in the past to manipulate this op. If she'd gotten away with that disk, killed any of us, it woulda been my fault."

Wolverine frowned and stared at Creed. But Sabretooth

seemed serious, no matter how much he'd fought to keep Mystique alive previously. He'd wanted them to trust her. Maybe he did feel somehow responsible, as out of character as that seemed.

Up the road a short way, a large hole suddenly tore itself open in the fabric of reality. The air shimmered and John Wraith appeared as if from nowhere. Even in the dark, Logan could see the sunglasses the man never removed. Wraith lifted a hand and signaled to them.

"Creed," Logan said. "Time to go."

"Go 'head," Creed replied. "I got business."

With Maverick helping the wounded Cassidy, the team began to move toward John Wraith. Logan paused, turned to watch Sabretooth. Creed snarled something so low even Wolverine couldn't hear him, then cracked Mystique hard enough across the face with the nine-millimeter to shatter bone. She went down.

Sabretooth aimed the gun down at her chest and shot Mystique twice. Her body bounced slightly on the road and then lay still.

Creed tossed the gun into the trees and then started up the road toward where Team X waited with Wraith.

The op was finished. They were bringing home the mission objective. They were victorious. But somehow, Wolverine did not feel as though they'd truly won anything.

NOW

The Black Widow was exhausted. Though her restraints kept her clamped tightly to the wall, she could not relax enough to sleep for more than several minutes at a time. Her muscles ached from holding the same position for so long. There were blessed periods of numbness and near unconsciousness, but it wasn't enough.

She had never wanted sleep quite so badly.

Natasha's eyelids fluttered in the half-rest that was the best she could manage, but snapped awake when the door to their cell clicked open. Two armored guards stepped inside and covered her and the other captives. *Why bother?* she thought. With the genetic dampeners working against her mutant fellow prisoners, they must all be as exhausted as she was.

But the guards kept their weapons trained on the Widow, and on Banshee and Sabretooth and Maverick as well, as a new captive was dragged into the room.

Mystique. The Widow hadn't run into her more than a few times since that first incident so long ago, but it wasn't as if she would have forgotten that blue skin and red hair.

Then they brought Wolverine in. The front of his clothing was saturated with blood and peppered with black, crusted holes. Plenty of blood coming from Logan, leaving a snail trail of pungent gore as his feet dragged beneath him. With the adamantium that had been bonded to his skeleton, Wolverine was much heavier than an average man of his build. The guards struggled as they brought him in and clamped him to his restraints, on the wall right next to the Widow.

The Widow glanced around at the others in the room. All had remained silent as the two new inmates were brought in.

Sean Cassidy was grim-faced and alert, mind obviously spinning as he tried to figure a way out of this mess. Maverick was awake, but looked drawn and distant, a reminder of the virus that even now raged within him.

Then there was Sabretooth. He merely hung there, eyes heavy-lidded but not with exhaustion. No, Natasha thought he looked more like a jungle cat on the prowl, patiently waiting for his prey to make a move that would put it within reach of his slavering, snapping jaws.

When the Widow looked back at Wolverine, who stirred now, despite his wounds, the guards were snapping a genetic dampener around his throat.

"Now wait a minute there, lads," Banshee said unexpectedly.

The guards hadn't expected it, either. They actually paused a moment and glanced at Cassidy.

"Y'know as well as I do that the only thing keeping Wolverine alive right now is his mutant healing factor," Banshee said. "You put that thing on him, and you'll be killing him, no question. You've kept the rest of us alive this long, for some reason. D'ye really want to kill him now?"

The guards glanced at one another, then at the other two who had just finished putting a similar collar on Mystique. Then they turned and walked from the room. The featureless door to the chamber closed with a solid click and the sound of bolts ratcheting into place in the heavy door.

"Wait a minute!" the Widow shouted, straining against her bonds. "You can't just leave him to die like that!"

"Sure they can," Maverick said bitterly. "That's what they do."

"Who? You sound like you know who we're dealing with here, Maverick," Cassidy snapped. "If so, I'd appreciate you enlightening the rest of us."

Mystique had begun to stir, to moan a little and shift uncomfortably in her bonds. The Widow stared at Cassidy and Maverick.

"I have some guesses, but they won't save Logan. If he's as

bad off as he looks, and his healing powers don't kick in, they'll just let him die," Maverick explained.

"The runt ain't gonna die," Creed growled.

Natasha glared at him. "What makes you so sure?"

"Look, it ain't like it'd break my heart if he went—though o'course I'd rather do it myself," Sabretooth went on. "But he's already done most o' his healin'. Ain't that right, runt?"

The Widow turned again, felt the stiffness in her neck from such prolonged inactivity. Wolverine stirred slightly again. A ripple seemed to pass through his muscles, just beneath the skin, from head to toe, as though he were shivering with a chill.

Then his eyes opened.

"I don't know," Wolverine croaked thickly. " 'Most' might be overstatin' things a bit."

Logan's eyes flicked around the room, glancing at each of the captives in turn. The Widow noticed immediately that Wolverine didn't seem at all surprised by the company he found himself in. Finally, his gaze rested on Natasha.

"Widow," he said, by way of greeting, and might have nodded almost imperceptibly.

"Wolverine," she acknowledged. "Glad you're not dead."

"Nice o' you to say so," he said. "I kinda feel the same."

The Black Widow smiled. A lot of time had passed since the first time she'd met Logan. They'd managed to not try killing each other—well, pretty much—since that first time. With the passage of time, as always, had come great change. Both of them had left government work and gone into the private sector.

Wolverine had become a member of the X-Men. Though that band of mutants was alternately considered heroes or outlaws depending on the month and who one asked, Natasha had always thought of them as freedom fighters. The Widow herself had defected from the Soviet Union, become partner and lover with the costumed vigilante known as Daredevil, and later become one of the Avengers, perhaps the most respected team of extranormally gifted heroes the world had ever known.

She'd even been their leader for a time—and all that without any "super" powers at all.

A lot of time. A lot of old grudges and missions skittering away into the past like a cigarette butt flicked from the window of a speeding car.

She'd always liked Wolverine. Well, perhaps not when he'd wanted her dead, but that was business. No, she'd always liked him despite his apparent savagery, because she knew that at the core of that, there was a man of almost impossible goodness. A man with a code of honor many would have thought did not exist outside of John Wayne movies.

The others she had mixed feelings about. Sabretooth was a homicidal maniac. His death would be a mercy to the world at large. Mystique was a criminal, no question, but the Widow didn't know much more about her than that she'd once been a spy and later a terrorist.

Maverick was a cipher. They'd crossed paths once or twice after that first time she'd run into Team X, but she never knew any more about him. He was a hard man, that much was clear. And still in the game, as far as she could tell. But he was sick and dying. This was no place for a man upon whom disease had already staked its claim.

Then there was Cassidy. For a long time, things between them had been uncomfortable. She wasn't even sure how it stood now. Once upon a time, he'd blamed her for his not being there when his wife was killed. But that had been resolved ages ago. Otherwise Cassidy would never have saved her life. Still, a certain coldness existed between them. To her shame, some people still saw KGB when they looked at her, and Cassidy was one of them.

Still, she trusted him and Logan, at least. The Widow looked to Wolverine once more, and it was him she addressed.

"So, what now?" she asked. "I mean, we're all here, I take it?"

"Far as I know," he replied.

"All but Silver Fox and Wraith," Maverick added. "And Fox is dead."

"Wraith is in it," Wolverine said with a snarl, and the Widow noticed that he looked a bit better than he had earlier. The blood had stopped dripping to the floor.

"Figured as much," Sabretooth snorted.

"Then that's it," Maverick agreed. "The principal players in an operation more than a decade old. But why? It doesn't make any sense."

"What I want to know," Cassidy interrupted, staring across the room at Mystique, "is something I've been wondering for years. That's how you survived, Mystique."

Raven Darkhölme smiled. "My little secret."

"Yours and Creed's," Wolverine said. "Easy enough, Irish. Creed let her live. Sure, he shot her, but he didn't hit anything vital. I suspected it then, but I'd have known it for sure if I'd known just how many times Creed and Mystique had crossed paths before that op."

"More than crossed paths," Maverick added.

"Shut your mouth, North," Sabretooth growled. "That's territory that don't have nothin' to do with you. Any of you."

"Victor!" Mystique gasped with mock astonishment. "Ashamed of our little tryst? Oh, I'm crushed."

The Widow watched this whole exchange in confusion. Obviously Mystique and Creed had been involved once, but there was more to this than just love among killers.

"What am I missing?" she asked.

"Graydon Creed," Wolverine answered.

With those two words, it all began to make sense to Natasha. Graydon Creed had been a U.S. senator who stood a very good chance of taking the Oval Office before getting assassinated in the middle of a campaign crowd months earlier.

"Sabretooth'll kill just about anything, Widow, but even he didn't want to kill the mother of his only son," Logan said.

"But," the Widow said, "Graydon Creed was running on an antimutant campaign. He was . . . was . . ."

"Human?" Mystique asked, her face cold. "Yes. He was. And a psychopath like his father. He deserved what he got."

"We're getting a little off track, here," Maverick interrupted.

"Agreed," Cassidy said. "So, anybody have any idea why we're here?"

The Widow opened her mouth to speak, but she was brought up short by the sound of bolts ratcheting back.

Then the door opened.

Logan straightened up as best he could when Wraith walked in. He didn't want the traitorous weasel to know just how bad off he was. His healing factor had kept him alive, but with that collar on, eventually he'd die of infection or just bleed to death.

And he didn't plan on dying alone.

For a moment, he was surprised at the apparent regret on Wraith's face. The man actually seemed sorry.

"Hello, Kestrel," Maverick sneered, then began to cough so hard he couldn't speak any longer. A small rivulet of bloody spittle sat on his chin after he finished coughing.

"Just wanted you folks to know it was nothing personal," Wraith said. "Just doing my job. No hard feelings."

"Sure," Logan growled. "Long as you don't have any hard feelin's after I cut you open."

Wraith sighed, raised a hand, and glanced toward the door. Wolverine didn't know what to expect. Maybe an old enemy, maybe just a retired KGB man looking for some payback. What he didn't expect was the handsome, thirtysomething man in the suit escorted in by armored guards. The man stopped half a dozen feet into the room and stared around at them. His eyes rested on Wolverine.

"Well, well," Logan drawled. "If it ain't Graydon Creed's replacement in the mutant haters hall o' fame."

The man ignored him. Instead, he smoothed his tie and turned to Wraith. "Which one?" he asked.

"We don't know yet, Senator, but we'll find out," Wraith replied.

"Senator?" Sabretooth barked with amusement.

"I recognize you, Senator Zenak," the Widow said.

"Clue us in, Widow," Creed asked. "He ain't familiar to me."

"Peter Zenak," Natasha replied. "Washington's golden boy right now. One of the men who's stepped into the void left by the assassination of—"

"Of Graydon Creed, yes," Zenak agreed. "A little poetic justice, don't you think? Delicious irony."

"You had him killed, then?" Mystique asked, and though she'd claimed to be happy her son was dead, there was a razor edge to her question that Logan recognized.

"I only wish I had," Zenak said with a shrug.

"Senator?" the Widow said. "Do you have any idea what you've gotten yourself involved in? I'm an Avenger, sir. There will be serious repercussions from this incident."

The senator looked over at the Widow and frowned. "What makes you think anyone's ever going to know you were here, Natalia Romanova?"

The Widow twitched, and Wolverine had heard it, too. The trace of an accent in his voice when he pronounced Natasha's birth name.

"You're Russian?" Logan growled, not bothering to hide his surprise.

"No," the senator snapped. "I'm an American. But I was born in Moscow. Lived there until I was four years old, then came to America to live with my aunt and uncle. My parents were supposed to come later, when they could manage it."

"They don't need to know, Senator," Wraith broke in suddenly.

Wolverine narrowed his eyes. What was Wraith playing at?

"So unlike Graydon Creed, you can never be president," Cassidy pointed out. "I'm Irish-born, but I'm American enough to know you've got to be born here to be the President."

"No, I'll never be president," Zenak agreed. "But it isn't the president who wields the true power anyway."

Wolverine's mind was racing. Trying to fit the pieces together. Zenak was Russian. He was obviously the one behind their abductions, or the person for whom they'd been abducted, at least. But it didn't make sense. He'd probably barely begun college by the time they'd all met up in East Berlin on the op that brought them together. How could he be connected to that mission?

Then he had it. Once he knew, it all seemed so obvious.

"They were your parents, weren't they?" he drawled.

Zenak looked up as if Logan had spit on him. Wraith put a hand on the senator's bicep and tried to steer him out of the room.

"What?" the Widow asked quickly.

The others followed suit, trying to figure out what Logan was getting at.

"The Zhevakovs," Wolverine said quietly. "They were his parents."

"Who the hell are the Zhevakovs?" Creed snarled angrily, his lurking predator's patience finally beginning to wear thin.

But his words cut the senator deeply. Wolverine could see it in Zenak's eyes, just before the man exploded toward Sabretooth. Only Wraith and the guards' presence kept him from attacking Creed.

"You evil son of a—" the senator sputtered, fumbling for words. "You monster! All of you, monsters! You slaughter my parents in cold blood, and then you can't even remember their names? All they wanted was to escape, to defect, to live without the KGB peering over their shoulders. All they wanted was to be with me! With the son they'd already been apart from for nearly sixteen years! They betrayed their entire nation just so they'd have something to buy their passage with! And you killed them!"

There was silence in the room for several heartbeats. Finally, Maverick spoke up.

"I didn't kill them, Senator," he says. "And in all that confusion, I couldn't even begin to tell you who did. You want to blame someone, why not blame the men who gave the orders. My God, they're the same men who you've been—"

Then Maverick started to scream. His body jumped in his

restraints as some kind of electric charge pumped through his body.

"What's going on here?" Zenak demanded.

But Wraith was already hustling him out.

The door closed. Maverick slumped in his restraints, barely conscious.

"I can't believe the game they're playing with that man," the Widow said grimly.

"Don't lie to yourself, Widow," Cassidy said. "You believe it all too well. The very same men who sent Team X to East Berlin are using their own former operatives as cannon fodder, just to try and manipulate one American senator."

"I'd be real concerned about the morality o' all that if I weren't tryin' to figure out how to stay alive," Wolverine said.

Logan's mind raced. His memories of his time with Team X were all muddled at best. Somebody'd spent time messing around in his brain since then, and he'd lost a lot. He remembered the op well enough, but the details were sketchy. He'd been in a rage during the fight in which Zenak's parents were killed. They'd all been trying to escape the East German authorities.

The worst part was he couldn't even be completely certain he didn't kill them himself. He'd changed since then. Chained the beast within him. But that didn't excuse the sins of the past.

"Anybody—" Maverick grunted in pain, coughed twice. "Anybody actually see the Zhevakovs buy it?"

"I did," the Widow said.

"And I," Cassidy added.

Wolverine looked at their faces, but they weren't looking at him. They were looking at Sabretooth.

"Oh," Logan said drily, "what a shocker."

"What are you idiots lookin' at?" Creed said with a growl.

"Wait a second," Mystique snapped angrily, and they all turned to look at her. Her yellow eyes flashed, and her skin had grown a deeper shade of blue with her anger. "What's this all really about? Is it about who did what back then, or is it about what's being done to us right now?"

"A little o' both, I'd say," Logan drawled.

"That's because you just want to blame someone else for what happened," Mystique sneered contemptuously at him. "You don't want to own up to what you did back then any more than the rest of us. Why? Because you've changed, Logan. Time goes on. We've all changed in some ways. Some more than others, obviously. Except for Wraith, maybe, we've all changed. And maybe Creed has changed for the worse. In some ways, it looks like Maverick has, too."

"What?" Maverick said, eyes narrowed.

"You're not the idealist you once were, North. Don't try to deny it."

Maverick said nothing.

"That op changed us all a little," Mystique said. "It started me thinking in new ways. Maybe made you all start thinking a little differently. Team X didn't last too long after that, as I recall. Widow, Cassidy saved your life that night in Minsk. That's got to have affected you."

"It's one of the things that started me questioning the absolutes of the KGB," Natasha admitted.

"If Sabretooth killed those people as part of that op, well, hell, Logan, that's what you were there for," Mystique went on. "I heard your debates back then, remember? You wanted to kill me yourself. You can't let what Sabretooth's become make him any more responsible for what happened then than you are. Than we all are. This is about now. This is about getting out of here and getting some payback."

Wolverine was quiet.

"Raven, darlin'," Creed said, voice thick with irony, "I didn't know you still cared."

"Shut up, you psycho," Mystique snapped. "Nothing I've said changes the fact that you're no better than Ted Bundy or Jeffrey Dahmer."

Sabretooth actually laughed.

"Wrong, sweetheart," Creed snarled. "I'm way better than those guys. Together, they didn't even begin to reach my numbers. And for sheer ferocity, nobody holds a candle to me."

"The few, the proud, the serial killers," Maverick chuckled drily, then coughed again. "I don't know what difference any of this makes. I'm with Mystique. It was a long time ago. Let's just figure out how to get out of this."

"Y'know, I appreciate the support and all," Creed responded. "But I gotta tell you losers this much: I didn't do it."

"What?" Logan snapped.

"You deaf, runt?" Sabretooth growled. "I said I didn't kill those folks. You and me both got memory gaps, but I got a runnin' count o' my kills goin' all the time. I remember that op. I remember all of it. I didn't kill those people."

Wolverine frowned, thoughts racing.

"You can't actually believe him?" the Widow asked incredulously. "Logan, I *saw* Sabretooth kill those people. So did Cassidy."

Wolverine remained silent until Cassidy finally spoke up.

"Logan?" Banshee said.

"Got a little problem, Irish," Wolverine said. "See, me an' Creed go back a long way. I know him better than anybody, maybe. He ain't afraid o' anyone or anything. You heard him crowin' about his kills. If he did this thing, he'd want us to know it. He's got no reason to lie."

Before anyone could respond, the door opened noisily once more. Five guards came in, heavily armed, boots clacking on the floor. Sabretooth stiffened, growling as electricity shot suddenly through his body. The guards waited patiently until Creed slumped down again, then they released his restraints from the wall, their weapons trained on him at all times. He was escorted from the room, and Logan could see that he was in no shape to fight back.

Wraith stepped in.

"You heard?" Wolverine asked, though it wasn't really a question.

"We heard," Wraith replied.

"He didn't do it," Logan said. "You know him."

"Two eyewitnesses said he did. Reliable ones."

"So what now?" the Widow asked angrily. "What happens now that you know? Now that the senator gets to have his revenge?"

Wraith lowered his eyes a moment.

"Sabretooth will be tortured to death in punishment," he explained. "The rest of you aren't guilty of anything, really. So your deaths will be painless."

"Why that's mighty nice o' you, John," Wolverine sneered. "Thanks so much."

Wraith lifted his head, all trace of regret gone from his face.

"Don't mention it."

NOW

Well, that's it, then," the Black Widow said.

Logan looked up at her, frowning. "That's what?"

"Who knows how much time we have? An hour? Minutes?" she went on. "If we don't get out of this right now, we'll all be executed. Not to mention that we can't just let them murder Sabretooth, no matter what he's done."

"I gotta be honest with you," Wolverine said, glancing around the room. "The idea o' Sabretooth bein' tortured does have a certain appeal. An' I ain't gonna shed any tears if somebody wants to execute him for bein' a homicidal maniac. That's only a matter o' time, you want my opinion."

His gaze stopped on Mystique's yellow eyes.

"But nice as that all sounds, I don't feel right about lettin' him die for somethin' he didn't do," Logan said, eyes narrowing. "If he's gonna fry, Raven, it shouldn't be for *your* crimes."

"What?" Maverick snapped.

"Come on, kid, who else could it have been?" Wolverine drawled. "Irish and the Widow saw Creed do the killin' but Creed says he didn't do it."

"Aye," Banshee said, nodding. "I've been wonderin' why Mystique was so passionate in Sabretooth's defense. I figured that was the answer."

"I don't understand," the Widow said, turning her head to look at Mystique. "With all the death you've been responsible for, all the horrible things you've done, why hide this one crime? What difference would it make?"

Mystique hung next to Cassidy on the wall opposite where Logan and the Widow were restrained. The side wall between them, across from the door, was where Sabretooth had been held before his removal. Now, Maverick was the sole prisoner clamped to that wall. Wolverine worried about him, but when David North grew angry, a fire blazed in his eyes that Logan didn't think the Legacy Virus could ever snuff out.

"There's no love lost between me and Creed, lady," he said to Mystique, "but I'm with the Widow. Why bother pinning it on him? They're gonna kill us all anyway."

Mystique's frown gave way to a thin, cruel smile. She snickered softly, shaking her head as much as she was able, consideng her restraints.

"Not that it's anybody's business," she said, "but that was a long time ago. Can you blame me for wanting to put it behind me?"

"So you pick *now* to turn over a new leaf?" Maverick sneered. "You've done a lot of killing over the years, Mystique. I don't buy any of this."

Wolverine heard Maverick's words, but he wasn't listening. He was concentrating on Mystique's face, on her reactions. And he thought he understood.

"It was murder," Logan said. "That's right, ain't it, Raven? It was murder, and you don't like bein' a murderer, do you?"

"Of course it was murder, Logan!" Cassidy snapped. "Are ye daft?"

But Wolverine ignored him. Ignored them all. When Mystique looked up and met his gaze, he knew he was right.

"I've killed," she admitted. "Of course I have. But there was always a reason. I killed for a cause, or to protect myself, or the secrets entrusted to me when I worked for the Mossad and other agencies. I can live with that."

"What makes this any different?" the Widow asked. "You had your orders, and you carried them out."

"Maybe it's a fine line," Mystique replied. "But that was different from the others. I'm not a killer for hire or some homicidal lunatic. But that night I killed for nothing. Just because I'd been told to do it."

"That is a pretty fine line," Maverick said.

Logan stared at Mystique, then looked, one by one, at the others, his gaze finally coming to rest on Maverick.

"Don't tell me you believe that crap?" Maverick asked, scowling at Wolverine. "I don't know what her game is, but Mystique's always been hard core, Logan. Don't buy into this."

"What difference does it make?" Cassidy asked. "It isn't going to get us out of here any faster. We should be focusing on that."

Wolverine knew Cassidy was right, but he also knew that he had to give Maverick an answer. It seemed important, somehow. And no matter what Wolverine, or Maverick, thought of Mystique, he had spent the past few days getting to know her better than he'd ever wanted to.

"I don't know what to believe," he finally admitted, eyes flicking back and forth between Mystique and Maverick. "But I do know what we were sayin' before is true. We've all changed. Doesn't excuse the past, but maybe it makes it a little harder to judge what happened then. We all done things we ain't proud of. Instead o' worryin' about the old days, I'd say we oughta be concerned about the next few minutes."

The silence that followed was agreement enough.

"You've all been here longer than Mystique and me," Wolverine added after a moment. "I don't suppose anyone's figured a way outta here?"

Natasha had, in fact, been trying desperately to escape. She had been trained as a gymnast and a dancer from childhood, and between missions for S.H.I.E.L.D. and running around with the Avengers and the Champions, she had continued to hone those skills.

Since the moment she'd been shackled to the wall, the Widow had spent all but her few minutes' rest shifting her body, working her muscles, wrenching her bones, trying to slip out of her restraints. She was human, after all, and they wouldn't be nearly as worried about her as they would about the mutants. After all, they had every piece of information imaginable on the former members of Team X. Wraith and his employers knew the limits of the others, except perhaps for Cassidy.

And one other. For when they had abducted the Black Widow, they had no idea what they were getting themselves into.

Natasha struggled against her bonds once again.

"If I could only get a little slack . . ." she began, then paused in midsentence and glanced to her right, where Wolverine hung beside her. "They overheard us discussing Creed. We're being monitored even now, right?"

Wolverine gave a slight nod. "What if I could give you what you need?" he asked.

"Then I have a few ideas," she replied.

Logan smiled. Wraith and his pals had it all worked out, or at least they thought they did. Maverick's powers weren't too useful in trying to get out of this mess. Cassidy and Mystique couldn't use their genetic gifts. The Widow didn't have any special powers, and Wolverine, well, his enhanced senses and his healing factor wouldn't have gotten them out anyway.

But the claws? It wasn't as if the dampener locked around his neck could make them disappear. Instead, Wraith had made sure his hands were clamped at such an angle that he couldn't possibly slash into the wall to which his restraints were anchored, or into the restraints themselves.

He looked at them each in turn. Met their eyes, let them know that a plan was coalescing, and that they should be ready for action. Maverick nodded. Cassidy closed his eyes in acknowledgment. Mystique smiled. Then Wolverine looked at the Widow.

"Ready?" he whispered.

She looked at him curiously, then nodded.

Natasha didn't know what Wolverine had in mind, but she hoped it wasn't something completely insane. As if he had sensed the direction of her thoughts, Wolverine turned and smiled at her.

"Trust me?" he asked.

"Oh, completely," she lied, returning the smile.

"Smart lady," he replied.

Then his face began to change. The smile disappeared as his lips pulled back into a grimace, then a snarl. Muscles rippled in his neck and shoulders and his left arm—the one closest to her. She looked up as best she could, given how firmly she was restrained, and saw his fingers protruding from the open top of his restraints. But he could never get his hand out. There wasn't room. Not even enough room for him to push through so that his wrist was free.

Natasha glanced at the door. Any moment now, Wraith and the others would come through. They couldn't all be watching Creed be tortured. Wraith would have posted a guard, no question.

"Saints, Logan, what're ye—" Cassidy began, but Maverick hissed him into silence.

The Widow looked at Wolverine again, and her heart skipped a beat in her chest. Blood ran freely down Logan's left arm from inside his restraints. Sweat had popped out on his forehead, and his face had changed even more, not the way a shapeshifter like Mystique might change. No, this was completely natural. But his face now was more like an animal than a man, and his eyes were no longer focused on her. They burned with a rage she had no desire to look at for long.

Lubricated by his own blood, and with a final, massive thrust, Wolverine's left hand popped out of the top of his restraints to the wrist. He roared in pain, and blood poured down his arm and over the edges of the restraints. The Widow's eyes went wide as she stared at the ragged, torn flesh of his hand and wrist. She thought she could see the silvery gleam of the adamantium that was bonded to his bones.

"Holy mother o' God," Cassidy whispered.

Snikt!

Adamantium claws spattered with blood popped from their

sheaths in his left forearm. With a twitch of his wrist, Wolverine cut into the wall several inches to his left—and just above the Widow's right hand.

"Hurry," Mystique snapped suddenly at the Widow. "Without his healing factor, he'll bleed to death."

"Not to put any pressure on me," Natasha mumbled, though she knew that wasn't the only pressure. The guards would arrive in seconds.

She had been stretched taut against the wall before, unable to get enough leverage even to use the weight of her own body to help her work her hands free. Now she threw her weight to one side, taking advantage of the little bit of space inside her restraints to fold her hand in on itself. She didn't have time to be gentle. With a huge effort, she hurled herself away, throwing all her weight into pulling her hand free. Either she'd snap her wrist, or . . .

"Yes!" she hissed, ignoring the pain and her own blood on her chafed wrist.

But that trick wasn't going to work with her ankles. On the other hand, it might not have to. With all her strength, and fighting the screaming of muscles that had been held in one place for days, Natasha wrapped her left hand around the wrist of her right, the one that was still encased in its restraint. She swung it down like a hammer, but not right at the restraint on her left leg. Instead, she pounded against the spot where the restraint met the wall.

On the third strike, the wall cracked and the restraint on her left leg came loose from it. Seconds later, the right leg was free as well. She still wore restraints on three of her four limbs, but she could move. That's all she needed.

"Whatever you've got in mind . . ." Wolverine started to say.

But the Widow was already moving. She crossed the room in a heartbeat, just as she heard the ratcheting of bolts in the door behind her. She didn't have time to remove anyone else's restraints. Just enough time, maybe, to save their lives.

Natasha reached out and grabbed hold of the genetic dampener collar around Sean Cassidy's neck. With deft fingers, she worked the catch, and the collar popped open, falling to the ground. Before it landed, Banshee was screaming.

The guards had come in, and Wraith was close behind. But Cassidy's scream threw the first pair back through the door, and they fell with Wraith in a tangle on the floor of the hallway. It bought them seconds, but the Widow believed that seconds would be enough.

Cassidy turned his scream on Wolverine, and the X-Man's restraints shattered under the force of the sonic blast. Logan stumbled forward, cradling his bleeding wrist. The claws popped from his right hand, and he turned to start hacking into the restraints holding Mystique and Maverick, even as Banshee looked at the Widow with a smile on his face.

"That was quick thinking, lass," he said, and then screamed at her.

The pitch of his voice was slightly different than before, but her remaining restraints shattered without doing any damage to her body.

"A long time ago, you saved my life," she replied. "It was the least I could do."

"I guess that makes us even," he said.

"I guess it does."

And as simply as that, the past was gone. It was a new beginning for them. Then a blaster bolt slammed into the wall next to Banshee, and the Widow looked up in alarm to see that the guards were up again, and Wraith was shouting orders in back.

Face grim once more, the Widow leapt forward, wading into the well-armed men with no weapons but her own prowess. She heard Banshee screaming briefly, but it was such close quarters that soon he was beside her, fighting hand to hand, and doing rather well at it. Eight against two was poor odds for the opposition, and soon the chaos had calmed enough so that only Wraith remained.

Wolverine had succeeded in freeing Maverick and Mystique, and now the five of them stood united against John Wraith, the man who had set them all up from the beginning.

"You can't kill us all," Wolverine growled.

"No," Wraith agreed. "But I'll kill some of you, and the others will stop you before you can escape. Then you'll think Creed was lucky."

Which was when Maverick leapt—a heroic lunge that Natasha would never have thought his diseased body capable of making. Wraith managed to squeeze off two shots before Maverick pounced on him, knocking the weapon skittering across the floor.

When Maverick stood up, the two spent slugs fell from where they'd lodged in his clothing and clattered to the ground. Logan breathed a little easier. North's skin wasn't impenetrable, but the X-Factor in his genetic makeup gave him the ability to absorb kinetic energy, effectively stopping the bullets before they broke the skin. He could also rechannel that energy into bio-electric blasts from his hands—normally. But the Legacy Virus was taking a swift toll on his powers as well as the rest of him. Wolverine hadn't been certain if Maverick was up to taking a bullet.

But he'd taken two.

Now he was weaker than ever.

Wraith slammed an elbow into Maverick's cheek, and despite North's mutant abilities, Wolverine heard the clack of bone on bone. Maverick was shoved aside, and Wraith climbed to his knees in an instant.

"Back off, all of you," he snapped. "You'll never get out of here. There are guards everywhere."

Wolverine stared at him, focused on his eyes, found what he was looking for: fear.

"You're not sure about that, are you, John?" Logan snarled. "They're all havin' their fun watchin' Sabretooth fry, ain't that right?"

Wraith smiled, opened his mouth to answer. But he never got the chance: the Black Widow hit him, hard, her fist connecting with the thin man's cheek with enough force to spin him sideways and double him over. And the Widow wasn't done. With a ferocity that surprised Wolverine, Natasha grabbed Wraith's head and bent him over, slammed her knee up into his gut, then propelled him with both hands into the wall where she'd been shackled only minutes earlier.

The man who'd given the orders to abduct them all, who had betrayed his former teammates, went down hard and didn't move at all, save for the gentle rising of his chest that showed he was still alive.

The Black Widow knelt by Wraith's still form, and when she spoke, it was in a whisper. But Wolverine heard her clearly.

"I had tickets to the ballet last night," she said.

Then she stood and went to the still open door. She stared at Wolverine, indicating that it was time to go. The others were all still staring at her. Maverick climbed wearily to his feet.

"Much as I hate to say it, Logan . . ." Maverick began.

Wolverine waved him off. "I know," he said. "I don't know as there's anyone in the world I hate more, but I'm not just leavin' Sabretooth to die here. Not like this."

Cassidy laughed a little, and Wolverine frowned.

"What's so funny, Irish?"

"Oh, aye, it's a riot," Banshee replied. "It's just that I was thinking, here you can't leave Creed to die, but if we break him out, he's liable to kill us all for coming to the rescue."

"You tryin' to say you wanna leave him with these losers?" Wolverine drawled.

The smile disappeared from Cassidy's lips. "No," he answered. "He deserves whatever he gets. If not for this, then for a hundred other things. But not while we're standing right here. And not at the hands of treacherous cowards like these."

"Sic the Widow on them," Mystique suggested. "She's primed."

The Black Widow stared at Mystique. Wolverine knew the look. He'd seen it in the mirror often enough.

"I don't think Natasha's in the mood for jokes, Raven," Logan said.

He might have said more, but he caught a scent from the hallway. Wolverine looked up and saw the barrel of a weapon just barely poking through the open door half a yard from the Widow's head.

There was no time to warn her, no time to do any more than growl as he launched himself at the wall, claws extended. The adamantium cut through the wall as though it weren't there at all and through the weapon and the man wielding it as well. The Widow dodged, in case he were still able to discharge the gun, then she kicked it out of his hands as the guard went down on the tile floor of the corridor.

Wolverine stepped around the ravaged wall and looked down at the man. It was Cassidy who knelt by his side and took his pulse, ignoring the blood spilling from the slashes in the guard's arm and lower abdomen.

"He'll live, I think," Banshee said.

"Yeah," Wolverine said. "Great."

"Thanks," the Widow said.

"Let's just get it done," Wolverine grunted.

Together, they turned and started down the corridor, moving quickly but cautiously. Maverick and Mystique were armed with the weapons they'd taken from the guards who'd been with Wraith. Cassidy was his own weapon. Wolverine and the Widow didn't really need them.

At the end of the hall was a solid door. Logan ripped through a control panel that required a keycard. The door didn't open. But Wolverine's hearing had picked something up on the other side of the door, still deeper inside the complex.

"I can hear Creed," he told them. "Screaming."

The shock on their faces was obvious. Banshee's greenish eyes grew wide. Maverick frowned dangerously, adding to the damage the Legacy Virus had done to his boyish good looks. Mystique's face went slack, as if, for once, she had no ulterior motive.

"They know we're out, of course," Natasha said.

"Yeah," Wolverine growled. "I can smell 'em. On the other side of the door."

311

The Widow stretched, turned her head like she was working some stiffness out of her joints, and nodded at Wolverine.

"Irish?" Logan said, and stepped aside, indicating that the others should do the same.

Cassidy opened his mouth and shouted, and the walls around the door buckled. The door blew off its moorings, erupting back into the hallway and slamming into the cadre of armored federal agents who waited there. Four of them went down, and two were wounded as the door's edges slashed through their armor.

Wolverine roared and ran through the opening. He dove at the remaining guards, more than a dozen of them, and started clawing through their armor. He could hear more of them approaching from down the hall.

"Logan!" Mystique shouted.

He looked up at the new arrivals. In the midst of weapons fire and the shouts of wounded guards, he recognized the black jumpsuits on the men and women running down the hall toward them.

"Why, if it ain't Team Alpha?" he snarled, then turned to the others. "Wake up, kiddies," he barked. "Payback's a bitch."

"So am I," Mystique crowed.

She pulled the trigger and started firing. Wolverine went for Team Alpha, not even bothering to slow down as he caught several rounds from Mystique. His healing factor had aleady been working overtime to heal the dozens of bullet wounds he'd taken the night before, and the damage he'd done to his own arm while escaping. Another couple of bullets weren't going to slow him down any more.

"Hang it up, old man!" one of the black-suited feds shouted as Wolverine came at them. "You're over—get it through your head. The new breed is here, and you just don't measure up."

A bullet ricocheted off Wolverine's femur. He slashed through the plasma rifle the black suit brandished in his direction, then withdrew his claws and grabbed the soldier by the shirt front and hauled him up short.

"Boy," Wolverine growled, "you ain't fit to spit shine my boots."

The others had caught up, and it was close quarters fighting for all of thirty seconds.

Then Banshee opened his mouth again.

Victor Creed roared in agony, every muscle in his body taut with pain. They'd burned him, at first. Shot holes in him. Even taken some samples of his flesh. But all those things had done was annoy him even more. He'd growled and snarled and promised to do the most dreadful things to them when he was free.

Then they'd cranked up the electricity and started pumping the volts into him—higher and higher, until any three normal men would have been frying.

Sabretooth smelled smoke, and that was the worst part. His clothes were smoking. His flesh was being slowly cooked.

Then somebody gave the order to shut it down, and it was over.

And he was still alive.

A pair of techs came over to the table where he was still strapped down. There were two guards behind them with plasma rifles, and behind them, Senator Zenak—who'd been smiling at first but wasn't smiling anymore.

"That the best you can do?" Sabretooth croaked.

His clawed hands shot up, and he ripped out the technicians' throats, snapping the bonds that held him to the table. He tried to sit up, but failed, and rolled off the table onto the mercifully cold tile floor. Then he just lay there a few seconds, unable to move.

"Dear God, you're nothing more than a monster!" Zenak screamed. "Those men, my parents, how many more have you killed?"

"Monster?" Sabretooth gurgled, choking on his own blood. "Welcome to the club, Senator."

Then, with no preamble, the laboratory door blew in. Creed

couldn't rise, but he managed to look up. To turn and see the group standing in the doorway. They all looked ragged, clothing torn, blood dripping from multiple wounds, but they were there by choice, that much was certain, given the weapons they held in their hands.

"Well I'll be—" Creed growled low, and with genuine surprise.

A team of black-suited federal troops was inside the lab, and they started to fire on Wolverine and the others immediately. Banshee let loose with a scream that set Creed's fangs on edge, and Maverick and Mystique opened fire.

The few armored guards that were left started hustling Senator Zenak toward what appeared to be a rear exit. Maverick saw them first, and shouted to Wolverine. Logan looked up, grunted, and started after them.

"No way he's gettin' outta here without hearin' the truth," Logan drawled.

His claws were popped, and the armored guards had learned to keep back from him. When he lunged after the retreating Zenak, they knew enough to get out of the way. He was leaving his prey alive, but some of them would be a lot better off dead.

"Senator, stop!" he snarled. "There's a few things someone's gotta get through your head!"

A hand landed on Wolverine's shoulder.

"Not now. Not you."

Even as Logan recognized the voice as Wraith's, he felt his stomach churn with the nauseating sensation of teleportation once more. Then he was standing with Mystique and Maverick, with Cassidy just above and Sabretooth lying crumbled at their feet. The Black Widow was using one of the armored guards as a shield while she fired a plasma weapon at another. She brought him down without killing him, and Wolverine thought again of how they'd changed, all of them in different ways.

Hell, he'd just saved Victor Creed's life.

It wasn't anything he ever wanted to do again.

"Let's go," Wraith said.

That familiar stomach churning started up again. When it ended, they were on a sprawling plain of grass that looked like it might be in the suburbs somewhere. Tall trees waved in the breeze, and white clouds floated across a blue sky.

Only the scents told Wolverine where they were: Central Park, New York City.

He spun on Wraith, ready to attack him again, and saw the bloody bruises that the Widow had given him earlier. Wraith held up his hands.

"You win," the little man said. "It's over, Logan. What are you going to do, kill me?"

When Wraith smiled that too-white smile, Wolverine was sorely tempted to do just that. Instead, he retracted his claws. He thought about hitting Wraith, at least. But it wouldn't make him feel any better.

"Hell, you don't have the stones to kill him, I'll be happy to do it," Sabretooth said, and surged forward.

Banshee and the Widow stopped him. And given his recent trauma, Sabretooth was in no condition to put up a fight. Not with the two of them.

"You won," Wraith said again. "Just enjoy it."

"So now what?" the Widow snapped. "We're supposed to forget all about this? You don't want the senator knowing what really went down here? What's to keep us from telling him? From telling all of Washington, for that matter?"

Wraith smiled. "Now why would you want to do that?" he asked, and the smile disappeared. "Everyone loves you, Widow. You're an Avenger. Sure, they know you were a KGB spy a long time back, but you're a hero now, right?"

The little man sneered. A breeze blew the smell of car exhaust through the trees, and there was a burst of laughter and conversation from a nearby walkway where a couple jogged by.

"Most people don't realize what it means to be a spy," Wraith went on. "At least, what it means for those who do it professionally. Lying. Stealing. Seducing secrets from diplomats during, hmm, extracurricular activities. Killing. We've got a big file on you, Widow. And let's face it, you're the only threat to us. The rest of you are mutants, just like me. Nothin' America hates more than 'muties.' Nobody's gonna listen to them. And you ain't gonna say nothin'. Are you?"

The Black Widow felt as if she might vomit, but she kept quiet. They might have made her life difficult for a few days, even planned to kill her, but she wasn't dead. No real harm done. Not enough to turn her life upside down. It wasn't worth it. This time.

"So what're you gonna tell the senator?" Wolverine asked. "He ain't gonna just give up on us all like that, and you guys ain't eager to give up the control you'll have over his vote in Congress. He's a powerful man now."

"Easy," Wraith said with a chuckle. "The Widow and Cassidy named Creed just 'cause they hated him. But under torture, other members of Team X revealed that Silver Fox had killed Senator Zenak's parents."

"That's a lie," Wolverine said with a vicious snarl.

"Yeah, but Fox is dead, Logan," Wraith said. "That means we can't go after her. You people are off the hook, and we've done so much for Peter Zenak in good faith."

The smile on Wraith's face was terrible, and the Widow turned away. It was just this kind of disgusting manipulation and conniving that had made her leave the Soviet Union to begin with. She hated the idea that people like Wraith operated within the government to which she had now pledged herself. The only saving grace was that she knew he operated without the blessing of those who actually ruled the country. He was working beneath the system, rather than within it.

It was cold comfort.

Wolverine narrowed his eyes and stared at Wraith. There was one question he wanted to ask, but didn't bother because he knew he'd never get an honest answer. That question was "Why?" Why would Wraith bother to fabricate such a story, to spirit them away instead of continuing to try to capture them, to give Zenak his vengeance, the blood he'd wanted to see spilled?

All he would have had to do would be to name Wolverine or the Widow, or Maverick as the killer, and the search would have continued indefinitely. Yet he'd dragged them all through this shadow game and managed to fulfill his own mission while somehow preserving the lives of his old comrades.

It was difficult for Wolverine to ascribe any benevolent purpose to Wraith's actions, nor would the man ever admit to such motivations if he'd had them. But it was food for thought: maybe even Wraith had changed a little since those dark days when they all were a part of Team X together.

"You won't see me again," Wraith said, and slipped black sunglasses over his eyes.

"Good," Maverick grunted.

Sabretooth began to climb to his feet, eyes blazing, obviously intent on paying Wraith back.

"You keep sayin' that," Wolverine said, "but you keep poppin' up."

Wraith said nothing. The air behind him seemed to ripple, as if it were a pool into which a stone had been dropped. He turned and stepped through before Sabretooth could get near him.

Creed sank to the ground again, still too weak to do much more than that. Wolverine looked at him, then at Mystique.

"I guess I can trust you to get him back to X-Factor?" he asked.

Mystique nodded.

"Trust her?" Maverick said, then coughed into his hand. "Have you been asleep through this whole thing, Logan?"

Before Wolverine could respond, Mystique's yellow eyes blazed, and she raised an accusatory finger at Maverick.

"You listen to me, North," she snapped. "You think just because you're dying you stand on some kind of pedestal where you can look down on the rest of the world? What a hypocrite!"

Mystique glared at Maverick, then glanced around the circle

at each of them. When she spoke again, it was with a sneer and a tiny, wicked smile that said all Logan would ever need to know about what was in her heart.

"You're all hypocrites," Mystique told them. "All but Creed, if that isn't a laugh. I was on a mission. Maybe I don't like what I did, but you all played that game, same as I did."

Sean Cassidy stood taller, stared down at Mystique with contempt in his eyes.

"Not I, lass," he said. "That wasn't the world I walked in. I've done some misguided things in my time, but never anything like that. You can say what you like, Raven Darkhölme, but know this. You got away with it, this time, but one day . . . one day, you're going to pay for your crimes."

Wolverine grunted. Chuckled lightly. Looked around at them gathered there. Maverick. Mystique. Sabretooth. The Black Widow. Banshee. Yeah, he thought, even Banshee.

All of them had done questionable things in their lives.

"One day you're going to pay," Cassidy repeated.

"Yeah," Wolverine drawled. "Aren't we all?"

Christopher Golden is a novelist, journalist, and comic book writer. His novels include the vampire epics *Of Saints and Shadows, Angel Souls and Devil Hearts,* and *Of Masques and Martyrs;* the bestselling *X-Men: Mutant Empire* trilogy; *Daredevil: Predator's Smile*; a series of *Buffy the Vampire Slayer* novels (with Nancy Holder) and *Battlestar Galactica* novels (with Richard Hatch); and *Hellboy: The Lost Army.*

Golden's comic book work includes *Wolverine, The Crow, Spider-Man Unlimited, Shi, Gen13 Bootleg, X-Man, Blade: Crescent City Blues,* and *Vampirella.* Most recently, he and frequent collaborator Tom Sniegoski have resurrected *The Punisher* for Marvel.

The editor of the Bram Stoker Award–winning book of criticism *CUT!: Horror Writers on Horror Film,* he is also one of the authors of the recently released *Buffy the Vampire Slayer: The Watcher's Guide,* the official companion to the hit TV series.

Golden was born and raised in Massachusetts, where he still lives with his family. He graduated from Tufts University. He is currently at work on a new, original dark fantasy entitled, *Strangewood,* which was published in 1999 by Penguin Putnam Inc. He invites you to visit him on the World Wide Web at www.christophergolden.com.

Darick Robinson is the cocreator (with Warren Ellis) and artist for the acclaimed *Transmetropolitan* monthly series for DC's Vertigo imprint. Darick started working as a comics professional at the age of seventeen with his self-created and self-published comic, *Space Beaver.* Since 1990, he has worked on *New Warriors, X-Factor, Cable, The Incredible Hulk,* and numerous Spider-Man projects for Marvel and *Superman* and *Justice League: A Midsummer's Nightmare* for DC. His illustrations appear in Diane Duane's Spider-Man novels *The Lizard Sanction* and *The Octopus Agenda,* as well as in Ellis's forthcoming Daredevil novel.

CHRONOLOGY TO THE MARVEL NOVELS
AND ANTHOLOGIES

What follows is a guide to the order in which the Marvel novels and short stories published by BP Books, Inc., and Berkley Boulevard Books take place in relation to each other. Please note that this is not a hard and fast chronology, but a guideline that is subject to change at authorial or editorial whim. This list covers all the novels and anthologies published from October 1994–September 2000.

The short stories are each given an abbreviation to indicate which anthology the story appeared in. USM=*The Ultimate Spider-Man*, USS=*The Ultimate Silver Surfer*, USV=*The Ultimate Super-Villains*, UXM=*The Ultimate X-Men*, UTS=*Untold Tales of Spider-Man*, UH=*The Ultimate Hulk*, and XML=*X-Men Legends*.

X-Men & Spider-Man: Time's Arrow Book 1: The Past [portions]
by Tom DeFalco & Jason Henderson
Parts of this novel take place in prehistoric times, the sixth century, 1867, and 1944.

"The Silver Surfer" [flashback]
by Tom DeFalco & Stan Lee [USS]
The Silver Surfer's origin. The early parts of this flashback start several decades, possibly several centuries, ago, and continue to a point just prior to "To See Heaven in a Wild Flower."

"In the Line of Banner"
by Danny Fingeroth [UH]
This takes place over several years, ending approximately nine months before the birth of Robert Bruce Banner.

X-Men: Codename Wolverine ["then" portions]
by Christopher Golden

"Every Time a Bell Rings"
by Brian K. Vaughan [XML]
These take place while Team X was still in operation, while the Black Widow was still a Russian spy, while Banshee was still with Interpol, and a couple of years before the X-Men were formed.

"Spider-Man"
by Stan Lee & Peter David [USM]
A retelling of Spider-Man's origin.

"Transformations"
by Will Murray [UH]

CHRONOLOGY

"Side by Side with the Astonishing Ant-Man!"
by Will Murray [UTS]
"Assault on Avengers Mansion"
by Richard C. White & Steven A. Roman [UH]
"Suits"
by Tom De Haven & Dean Wesley Smith [USM]
"After the First Death . . ."
by Tom DeFalco [UTS]
"Celebrity"
by Christopher Golden & José R. Nieto [UTS]
"Pitfall"
by Pierce Askegren [UH]
"Better Looting Through Modern Chemistry"
by John Garcia & Pierce Askegren [UTS]
  These stories take place very early in the careers of Spider-Man and the Hulk.

"To the Victor"
by Richard Lee Byers [USV]
  Most of this story takes place in an alternate timeline, but the jumping-off point is here.

"To See Heaven in a Wild Flower"
by Ann Tonsor Zeddies [USS]
"Point of View"
by Len Wein [USS]
  These stories take place shortly after the end of the flash-back portion of "The Silver Surfer."

"Identity Crisis"
by Michael Jan Friedman [UTS]
"The Doctor's Dilemma"
by Danny Fingeroth [UTS]
"Moving Day"
by John S. Drew [UTS]
"Out of the Darkness"
by Glenn Greenberg [UH]
"The Liar"
by Ann Nocenti [UTS]
"Diary of a False Man"
by Keith R. A. DeCandido [XML]
"Deadly Force"
by Richard Lee Byers [UTS]
"Truck Stop"
by Jo Duffy [UH]
"Hiding"
by Nancy Holder & Christopher Golden [UH]
"Improper Procedure"
by Keith R.A. DeCandido [USS]

CHRONOLOGY

"The Ballad of Fancy Dan"
by Ken Grobe & Steven A. Roman [UTS]
"Welcome to the X-Men, Madrox. . ."
by Steve Lyons [XML]
These stories take place early in the careers of Spider-Man, the Silver Surfer, the Hulk, and the X-Men, after their origins and before the formation of the "new" X-Men.

"Here There Be Dragons"
by Sholly Fisch [UH]
"Peace Offering"
by Michael Stewart [XML]
"The Worst Prison of All"
by C. J. Henderson [XML]
"Poison in the Soul"
by Glenn Greenberg [UTS]
"Do You Dream in Silver?"
by James Dawson [USS]
"A Quiet, Normal Life"
by Thomas Deja [UH]
"Chasing Hairy"
by Glenn Hauman [XML]
"Livewires"
by Steve Lyons [UTS]
"Arms and the Man"
by Keith R.A. DeCandido [UTS]
"Incident on a Skyscraper"
by Dave Smeds [USS]
"One Night Only"
by Sholly Fisch [XML]
"A Green Snake in Paradise"
by Steve Lyons [UH]
These all take place after the formation of the "new" X-Men and before Spider-Man got married, the Silver Surfer ended his exile on Earth, and the reemergence of the gray Hulk.

"C."
by Lawrence Watt-Evans [USM]
"Blindspot"
by Ann Nocenti [USM]
"Tinker, Tailor, Soldier, Courier"
by Robert L. Washington III [USM]
"Thunder on the Mountain"
by Richard Lee Byers [USM]
"The Stalking of John Doe"
by Adam-Troy Castro [UTS]
"On the Beach"
by John J. Ordover [USS]

CHRONOLOGY

These all take place just prior to Peter Parker's marriage to Mary Jane Watson and the Silver Surfer's release from imprisonment on Earth.

Daredevil: Predator's Smile
by Christopher Golden
"Disturb Not Her Dream"
by Steve Rasnic Tem [USS]
"My Enemy, My Savior"
by Eric Fein [UTS]
"Kraven the Hunter Is Dead, Alas"
by Craig Shaw Gardner [USM]
"The Broken Land"
by Pierce Askegren [USS]
"Radically Both"
by Christopher Golden [USM]
"Godhood's End"
by Sharman DiVono [USS]
"Scoop!"
by David Michelinie [USM]
"The Beast with Nine Bands"
by James A. Wolf [UH]
"Sambatyon"
by David M. Honigsberg [USS]
"A Fine Line"
by Dan Koogler [XML]
"Cold Blood"
by Greg Cox [USM]
"The Tarnished Soul"
by Katherine Lawrence [USS]
"Leveling Las Vegas"
by Stan Timmons [UH]
"Steel Dogs and Englishmen"
by Thomas Deja [XML]
"If Wishes Were Horses"
by Tony Isabella & Bob Ingersoll [USV]
"The Stranger Inside"
by Jennifer Heddle [XML]
"The Silver Surfer" [framing sequence]
by Tom DeFalco & Stan Lee [USS]
"The Samson Journals"
by Ken Grobe [UH]

These all take place after Peter Parker's marriage to Mary Jane Watson, after the Silver Surfer attained freedom from imprisonment on Earth, before the Hulk's personalities were merged, and before the formation of the X-Men "blue" and "gold" teams.

CHRONOLOGY

"The Deviant Ones"
by Glenn Greenberg [USV]
"An Evening in the Bronx with Venom"
by John Gregory Betancourt & Keith R.A. DeCandido [USM]
 These two stories take place one after the other, and a few months prior to The Venom
Factor.

The Incredible Hulk: What Savage Beast
by Peter David
 *This novel takes place over a one-year period, starting here
and ending just prior to* Rampage.

"Once a Thief"
by Ashley McConnell [XML]
"On the Air"
by Glenn Hauman [UXM]
"Connect the Dots"
by Adam-Troy Castro [USV]
"Ice Prince"
by K. A. Kindya [XML]
"Summer Breeze"
by Jenn Saint-John & Tammy Lynne Dunn [UXM]
"Out of Place"
by Dave Smeds [UXM]
 These stories all take place prior to the Mutant Empire *trilogy.*

X-Men: Mutant Empire Book 1: **Siege**
by Christopher Golden
X-Men: Mutant Empire Book 2: **Sanctuary**
by Christopher Golden
X-Men: Mutant Empire Book 3: **Salvation**
by Christopher Golden
 These three novels take place within a three-day period.

Fantastic Four: To Free Atlantis
by Nancy A. Collins
"The Love of Death or the Death of Love"
by Craig Shaw Gardner [USS]
"Firetrap"
by Michael Jan Friedman [USV]
"What's Yer Poison?"
by Christopher Golden & José R. Nieto [USS]
"Sins of the Flesh"
by Steve Lyons [USV]
"Doom²"
by Joey Cavalieri [USV]
"Child's Play"
by Robert L. Washington III [USV]

CHRONOLOGY

"A Game of the Apocalypse"
by Dan Persons [USS]
"All Creatures Great and Skrull"
by Greg Cox [USV]
"Ripples"
by José R. Nieto [USV]
"Who Do You Want Me to Be?"
by Ann Nocenti [USV]
"One for the Road"
by James Dawson [USV]
    These are more or less simultaneous, with "Doom²" taking place after To Free Atlantis, *"Child's Play" taking place shortly after "What's Yer Poison?" and "A Game of the Apocalypse" taking place shortly after "The Love of Death or the Death of Love."*

"Five Minutes"
by Peter David [USM]
    This takes place on Peter Parker and Mary Jane Watson-Parker's first anniversary.

Spider-Man: The Venom Factor
by Diane Duane
Spider-Man: The Lizard Sanction
by Diane Duane
Spider-Man: The Octopus Agenda
by Diane Duane
    These three novels take place within a six-week period.

"The Night I Almost Saved Silver Sable"
by Tom DeFalco [USV]
"Traps"
by Ken Grobe [USV]
    These stories take place one right after the other.

Iron Man: The Armor Trap
by Greg Cox
Iron Man: Operation A.I.M.
by Greg Cox
"Private Exhibition"
by Pierce Askegren [USV]
Fantastic Four: Redemption of the Silver Surfer
by Michael Jan Friedman
Spider-Man & The Incredible Hulk: Rampage (Doom's Day Book 1)
by Danny Fingeroth & Eric Fein
Spider-Man & Iron Man: Sabotage (Doom's Day Book 2)
by Pierce Askegren & Danny Fingeroth
Spider-Man & Fantastic Four: Wreckage (Doom's Day Book 3)
by Eric Fein & Pierce Askegren

CHRONOLOGY

Operation A.I.M. *takes place about two weeks after* The Armor Trap. *The* "Doom's Day" *trilogy takes place within a three-month period. The events of* Operation A.I.M., *"Private Exhibition,"* Redemption of the Silver Surfer, *and* Rampage *happen more or less simultaneously.* Wreckage *is only a few months after* The Octopus Agenda.

"Such Stuff As Dreams Are Made Of"
by Robin Wayne Bailey [XML]
"It's a Wonderful Life"
by eluki bes shahar [UXM]
"Gift of the Silver Fox"
by Ashley McConnell [UXM]
"Stillborn in the Mist"
by Dean Wesley Smith [UXM]
"Order from Chaos"
by Evan Skolnick [UXM]
These stories take place more or less simultaneously, with "Such Stuff As Dreams Are Made Of" *taking place just prior to the others.*

"X-Presso"
by Ken Grobe [UXM]
"Life Is But a Dream"
by Stan Timmons [UXM]
"Four Angry Mutants"
by Andy Lane & Rebecca Levene [UXM]
"Hostages"
by J. Steven York [UXM]
These stories take place one right after the other.

Spider-Man: Carnage in New York
by David Michelinie & Dean Wesley Smith
Spider-Man: Goblin's Revenge
by Dean Wesley Smith
These novels take place one right after the other.

X-Men: Smoke and Mirrors
by eluki bes shahar
This novel takes place three-and-a-half months after "It's a Wonderful Life."

Generation X
by Scott Lobdell & Elliot S! Maggin
X-Men: The Jewels of Cyttorak
by Dean Wesley Smith
X-Men: Empire's End
by Diane Duane
X-Men: Law of the Jungle
by Dave Smeds

CHRONOLOGY

X-Men: Prisoner X
by Ann Nocenti
These novels take place one right after the other.

The Incredible Hulk: Abominations
by Jason Henderson
Fantastic Four: Countdown to Chaos
by Pierce Askegren
"Playing It SAFE"
by Keith R.A. DeCandido [UH]
These take place one right after the other, with Abominations *taking place a couple of weeks after* Wreckage.

"Mayhem Party"
by Robert Sheckley [USV]
This story takes place after Goblin's Revenge.

X-Men & Spider-Man: Time's Arrow Book 1: **The Past**
by Tom DeFalco & Jason Henderson
X-Men & Spider-Man: Time's Arrow Book 2: **The Present**
by Tom DeFalco & Adam-Troy Castro
X-Men & Spider-Man: Time's Arrow Book 3: **The Future**
by Tom DeFalco & eluki bes shahar
These novels take place within a twenty-four-hour period in the present, though it also involves traveling to four points in the past, to an alternate present, and to five different alternate futures.

X-Men: Soul Killer
by Richard Lee Byers
Spider-Man: Valley of the Lizard
by John Vornholt
Spider-Man: Venom's Wrath
by Keith R.A. DeCandido & José R. Nieto
Captain America: Liberty's Torch
by Tony Isabella & Bob Ingersoll
Daredevil: The Cutting Edge
by Madeleine E. Robins
Spider-Man: Wanted: Dead or Alive
by Craig Shaw Gardner
Spider-Man: Emerald Mystery
by Dean Wesley Smith
"Sidekick"
by Dennis Brabham [UH]
These take place one right after the other, with Soul Killer *taking place right after the* Time's Arrow *trilogy,* Venom's Wrath *taking place a month after* Valley of the Lizard, *and* Wanted Dead or Alive *a couple of months after* Venom's Wrath.

CHRONOLOGY

Spider-Man: The Gathering of the Sinister Six
by Adam-Troy Castro
Generation X: Crossroads
by J. Steven York
X-Men: Codename Wolverine ["now" portions]
by Christopher Golden
   These novels take place one right after the other, with the "now" portions of Codename
Wolverine *taking place less than a week after* Crossroads.

The Avengers & the Thunderbolts
by Pierce Askegren
Spider-Man: Goblin Moon
by Kurt Busiek & Nathan Archer
Nick Fury, Agent of S.H.I.E.L.D.: Empyre
by Will Murray
Generation X: Genogoths
by J. Steven York
   *These novels take place at approximately the same time and several months after "Play-
ing It SAFE."*

Spider-Man & the Silver Surfer: Skrull War
by Steven A. Ronan & Ken Grobe
X-Men & the Avengers: Gamma Quest Book 1: **Lost and
Found**
by Greg Cox
X-Men & the Avengers: Gamma Quest Book 2: **Search and
Rescue**
by Greg Cox
X-Men & the Avengers: Gamma Quest Book 3: **Friend or
Foe?**
by Greg Cox
   These books take place one right after the other.

X-Men & Spider-Man: Time's Arrow Book 3: **The Future [portions]**
by Tom DeFalco & eluki bes shahar
   *Parts of this novel take place in five different alternate futures in 2020, 2035, 2099,
3000, and the fortieth century.*

"The Last Titan"
by Peter David [UH]
   This takes place in a possible future.